Love in the Paint

L.M London

Paperback ISBN: 978-1-7642113-0-7
E-book ISBN: 978-1-7642113-1-4
Hardcover ISBN: 978-1-7642113-2-1

ABOUT THE AUTHOR

L.M London lives in Queensland, Australia and has always had a dream of writing. Keeping it from family and friends to pursue things that society calls 'unacceptable' work, she finally has the courage to release her stories to the world. She hopes that there will be someone out there that enjoys the books and stories she has written.

In her free time, she is either writing or playing video games with her boyfriend. She loves fishing and music and enjoys spending time with her friends and her family, when she can see them.

If you want to see more of her, head over to TikTok or Instagram where you can find her posting about her journey or about other books that she has enjoyed.

TRIGGER WARNINGS

Even though Love in the Paint is a college romance,
there are a few things mentioned or spoken about
throughout the book that may offend some or gross
others out. Please read responsible:

- Swearing
- Mental health (including panic attacks, anxiety,
depression, etc.)
- Gun use and knife use (not sexual)
- Attempted murder, assault, verbal, and emotional
abuse (Happens and spoken about throughout)
- Sexual and sensitive content

Please, if you have any questions on anything, do not
hesitate to contact me through my website at
lmlondonwriting.weebly.com or you can message me over
on TikTok or Instagram.

DEDICATIONS

To anyone who had to hide away who they wanted to be just because it wasn't 'socially acceptable.'

PROLOGUE

This is it, isn't it?

Walking through these halls, smelling the antibacterial soap and the bright, fluorescent lights beaming down on me, I know it may be the last time I come here. My heart races as I approach the familiar glass doors, remembering the day Davis brought us in to see her when she was first diagnosed.

"How are you doing today, Mum?" I whispered as I slid her door close and sat in the hospital chair next to her bed. Her previously gorgeous, porcelain skin is now pasty and almost translucent from being locked up in bed, at this point she's practically skin and bones. Mum smiles weakly at me and my eyes start to sting, seeing her like this feels like a knife's being pushed into my heart, she doesn't have a lot of time left and I don't know if I'm ready for her to go.

Mum and I have always been close. Besides my siblings, Logan and Melaine, she's all I have left. Logan's almost an adult now, he's self-employed doing game development and Melaine, she's still in school but she wants to drop out to go to art school. She is amazing at art, drawing and painting specifically. My siblings and I are all so busy, Logan and Mel try to make time for mum but with everything going on, it's been really hard. Then there's Davis, my stepdad and Logan and Mel's real dad. He's always away for work and when he's not away, he's at home, sleeping and doing nothing, or drinking and screaming about how his life isn't fair. He never comes and sees mum in the hospital.

"I feel okay today," she winced as she started coughing hard, covering her mouth with her hand as blood splattered onto her palm and her eyes started to water with pain. I race to grab her a cup of water and grab some tissues. I hand her the cup, watching to make sure it doesn't spill as she sips on it, and I wipe the blood off of her palm. She looks like she hasn't slept in days, dark purple bruises printed under her eyes, and I can see her bones move as she moves to get comfortable.

All of this is a lot of responsibility for a fresh adult who's about to start university, but Davis isn't around to help, as partying and drinking with girls close to my age is more fun and freeing then being with the women who had his kids, and looked after him for so many years. I haven't told Mum yet, about the partying, she used to adore Davis, after my dad left, she was so depressed. Davis flipped her life around and ever since they met in that cafe, she was different, a good different but still, different. He said he loved her, and he did, but recently it's like something flicked in him. He isn't the same man that told me that I would be a big sister, he almost seems like a monster with the way he acts. Once we knew what was happening to Mum, Davis wouldn't help, he'd find literally any excuse to go away somewhere, leaving my siblings and I to mourn on our own about mum's sad news. Logan and Mel became depressed, not leaving their rooms or not eating. I tried everything but I too had the thoughts, knowing mum would leave us is how I got diagnosed with anxiety and panic attacks.

"Did you hear if you got the scholarship for basketball?" She asked, as if she's trying to fill the awkward silence between us. I looked up into her weak green eyes, she knows she doesn't have long left. My chest starts to feel heavy, and I look down at the bed, not being able to look at her in the eyes.

"Yeah, I got it today before coming here but I haven't opened it. I was too nervous to open it." I have been holding onto the envelope all day, I wanted Mum to be a part of this. She's always been so supportive of my basketball dreams, when I wanted to play before I could walk, she supported me. Putting me in every basketball after-school sports that my school held, paid for every game and the equipment, even taking me to my first basketball game when I was four, even though we didn't have a lot of money.

"Well, do you want me to open it? You'll get in, I've a good feeling."

I pulled out the envelope from my bag and started to open it, but mum started having a coughing fit again, holding her bony hands to her throat as she coughed.

Shit, she can't breathe.

I pressed the call button, and helped her put on the oxygen mask as nurses and doctors swarmed in. I stepped to the side, out of the way, and I took myself outside the room, so the staff had space to help her. I looked down at the envelope, my shaky hands holding it in front of me as I prayed that she'd be okay. She has to be okay, I need her with me when I open this.

I waited for the doctor to come out, holding my breath, praying to God or Jesus or anyone who'll listen that she'll be okay. A tall and scrawny man walked out after everyone else, holding mum's file in his hands, his sharp face unreadable. God, I hate that doctors are trained to be so good at being unreadable.

"Please, please tell me she's okay!" I whimpered, looking the doctor in the face trying to hold back my tears.

"She's okay, for now. She's deteriorating, we may need to intubate her soon, we just need her consent first." He said, trying not to look me in the eyes for too long.

"She won't, you and I both know that doc. She only agreed to the feeding tubes because I hadn't finished high school yet, and she wants to see me go to Uni before she passes." I can't hold the tears back any more as water fell down my hot cheeks. It's too much, I can't let her go yet. "I'll talk to her and see what I can do but don't hold your breath." I say as I walk into mum's room, her eyes are red and puffy from straining herself too hard with the coughing fit. I try to take a deep breath and sniffle my tears back as I sit back down, "You gave me a bit of a scare there, Mum, you can't do that."

"I'd never leave you before you've at least opened that envelope. We both know that it's coming soon though, Wallaby." She cups the side of my face as she wipes my cheek with her cold thumb, "I love you, take a deep breath and let's open that piece of paper." She shifts in her bed and there's the slightest sparkle in her eyes as she looks down at the paper. I know that she tries not to cry in front of me; to be strong and keep a calm front for me, but it must be painful to hold it all in, I just wish that she didn't feel like she had to hide her feelings from me. I'm not a little kid anymore.

I took a deep breath in before ripping open the envelope and I froze. I stared down at the folded paper as my hands shook. I can't do it, if I open this then mum will leave. I know she'll be gone soon, but I want to stop time, I'm not ready to lose her yet and neither are my siblings. I love Logan and Mel with everything I have but mum and I have been through so much and I can't let her go, not yet.

Mum grabbed my hand, "Sweetheart, are you okay?"

I looked into her green eyes, trying so hard not to shake or cry as I barely managed to shake my head, not saying anything. I don't know how to tell her how I feel, about what the doctor said, or about whatever's written in the little piece of paper glued to my hands. "Do you want me to open it, honey? Want to hand it to me?" She said as she opened her hand out, her wobbly voice cutting through my thoughts. I gave her the paper slowly and then covered my eyes, as if I saw the paper open, the world will end, which it may.

I heard the paper open in her hands and then a gasp from her mouth filled the room, my hands flew off my eyes and I stared at her. She looks shocked, which doesn't help because she could be shocked that I got in or shocked that I didn't get in.

"What does it say, Mum, you can't gasp like that and not give me anything else!" I said, reaching for the paper.

Oh. My. God.

"Honey." Mum mumbled, waiting for me to say something.

"I got in," I whispered, my eyes rereading the paper, making sure I somehow didn't lose the ability to read. "Mum, I got it! I got the scholarship to Ryder's University!" I screamed, I'm so excited and when I looked up at Mum, she looked like she's cured. She looks so happy right now, her skin had a slight glow to it and her face was covered with a huge smile, it's the happiest I have seen her in years.

"I am so proud of you, honey. I knew you would get it! They're so lucky to have you on their team, baby!" Mum cried as she pulled me into a hug, her cold skin resting on mine as it sent shivers up my skin.

I haven't been this happy in so long, I can't believe I got the scholarship. I was worried they weren't going to give it to me, I knew five other girls who applied, and we all know that there's only one scholarship and I got it! This will set me up for the four years of university I need to play basketball and study.

While I'm trying to gather all my thoughts together, mum moved on the bed and grabbed my face in her hands again. Her fingers are cold and fragile on my skin, "You're the best thing that has happened to me. I love your brother and sister, but you and I have been through so much and you're so strong. I could not be prouder of you, Wallaby." She wept as she wiped my tears off of my cheeks. My heart started to race again, now that we know I'm set up for University, she can go. She can leave me and my siblings here, to live on without her, and I couldn't bring myself to let her go without trying.

"Mum, the doctor wants to get your consent to intubate you. He said it could give you more time, please let him." I begged her but I knew her answer, she smiled at me and tilted her head slightly.

"Sweetheart, we both know I don't have much time left. I have lived two more years than they've predicted. You got into university, and you got the scholarship to help your dreams. Your siblings will be okay, they have you and I know that's a big ask," she paused, trying to catch her breath. I tried to hand her the oxygen mask to help her breath, but she pushed it away from her face. "But I can trust you, I love Davis but he's so busy and I know he parties," she whispered. She knew. That son of a bitch, I'm going to rip Davis a new one when he gets home. "Yes baby, you didn't have to tell me, I knew. He called me from 'the office' and I knew what he was doing." The thought of Davis 'working' while mum called him, and him spilling lies to her made me want to rip his pathetic heart out of his chest with my bare hands. "I love you, but I need you to take care of them. Make sure they're set up and that Logan and Mel are okay, Davis will pay for everything, I know that much but he won't look after them. I don't want any more tubes and I can't put you and your siblings in any more pain." I stared into her eyes, my heart breaking as I didn't want to believe the words I was hearing. "Tell the doctor I won't do it. I love you and you're strong. I know it's not fair to you, but please understand, I'll always be here for you, Wallaby." She sniffled, trying to hold back tears. "Oh, I want you to have this as well," she took the necklace off her neck and handed it to me, our grandmother gave it to her before she passed away. "It was my mothers, and her mothers, I'll always be here for you and if not in your heart, I'll follow you with this necklace at all times, think of it as a mothers protection." A tear falls on her face as she smiles at me like nothing's happening.

I turn and give her another tissue, and help her put the mask on properly, letting her rest while I go find the doctor.

She's ready, she's been ready for a while, and I can't help but feel upset for her. I'm the reason why she hung on for so long, she loved my siblings, but we all knew it was for me. "Hey doc, she won't consent to it. She's done fighting, she wants to sign a DNR. Please, I want to make her comfortable and stay until she's gone." I look up and see the way he's looking at me, he also knows that she's ready. His eyes soften as they go glassy.

"Let me get the forms, and I'll get you whatever you need Scarlet. She will be made comfortable and of course, stay as long as you need. We are all here for you." He grabbed my shoulder, squeezing it as he walked away.

Later that night, she passed away. I held her hand the whole time and told her that it's okay as I sobbed. She could go freely and watch over us while being in no pain anymore and I knew at that moment that I would do everything and anything for my siblings and I.

She trusted me, and I won't break her trust.

CHAPTER 1 – SCARLET

It's almost been a full year since mum passed away, her hands going still and limp in mine and the last eleven months have been so hard. Logan just had his eighteenth birthday, and we went full out, like mum dreamt for him. Now that Logan's done with high school, he plans on developing more games and finding somewhere to do either a degree or an internship in a game development company.

Melaine's sixteen now, about to turn seventeen in a few months and she is a straight A student at school while doing her art on the side for some money, trying to get them in some galleries around town.

For myself, I have just completed my first year of university and I'm loving it. As for basketball, I'm killing it, well when I get the chance too! The team's great mostly but the captain, Eva, is a little rude. Other than her, the rest of the team's amazing and school's going great. My siblings and I are all doing so well, I know mum's proud of all of us, watching down on us every day.

Logan, Mel and I are in the kitchen making dinner together as we have done for the last ten years. Every Friday night we make dinner together and sit as a family and eat, talking about our week and what our weekend plans are just like we did with mum and Davis. Davis has been gone for about three weeks, doing 'business' overseas in America. He could actually be doing business there but knowing what he's like now, he probably isn't. We haven't heard from him either, which isn't unusual, he never calls or texts to check on us while he's away.

As I am plating the food up, Logan and Mel are setting the table and the front door swings open as Davis walks in on the phone talking to someone about finance. His face is serious with his eyebrows furrowed and his hand on his temple, he must be talking to a coworker about actual work. The three of us stood in shock, looking at each other with confusion. What the hell's Davis doing home, none of us knew that he was coming home today.

He hung up the phone and turned to look at us three with a big smile spreading across his face, "Hey kids, mind making me a plate." He asked as he dropped his bags down in the living room.

I watch Davis walk over to the table where Logan and Mel are trying to set the table, trying to understand what's happening. One he's supposed to be in America, two he never eats with us on Fridays. He says it reminds him of mum, which he hates thinking about now that she's gone.

I snap myself out of it, shaking my head slightly, plating him up some food and making my way over to the table. My eyes darted to Logan, then Melaine and then Davis. I sat the plates down in front of everyone, clearing my throat before speaking, "so, your home early Davis, I didn't know you were coming home. How was your trip?" I mutter while looking at my siblings with a confused look, sitting at the opposite end of the table from Davis, in mum's old spot.

"The trip was really productive, it's actually why I'm home early. I'm sorry for not messaging any of you that

I was coming home. I thought that the news I have would be better shared in person than over the phone." He says while looking each of us in the eye with a slight smile on his lips. He never comes home and tells us about his work or his trips. Mostly because they involve more booze and sex than actual work.

As I look at Logan and Mel, they're baffled, Logan's fists are clenched slightly, waiting for whatever he's about to say and Mel's staring at him also waiting to see what bullshit comes out of his mouth. He has news to share with us; it could literally be anything. Maybe he has a new girlfriend, surely not. Mum died almost a year ago, that's too soon, right? Maybe not for him, he was cheating on her for years after she was diagnosed and probably before that but maybe it isn't so serious. Maybe he's selling the house, nope still serious and I wouldn't be happy about it. It's the first house mum was able to afford on her own.

"I got a promotion, I'll be CEO of the company," he smiled, waiting for us to say something.

Melaine screeched and jumped out of her chair to hug Davis. Logan looked even more baffled as his knuckles go white and anger radiated off of him as he snapped his expression to me, his eyes piercing into mine.

"Congratulations Davis, that's amazing to hear. I'm really happy for you." I put a smile on my face and looked back at Logan, trying to tell him with my eyes to stop looking at me like that.

Logan's not a fan of Davis either but he knows what he's like too, so I'm not surprised that he's pissed off right now. "Congrats Dad, but you said the news was better to say in person than over the phone and flying back from America to just say that you got a promotion is a lot of time and money. Is there something else you're not telling us?!" Logan seethed as his words barely got past his teeth and he turned his expression to Davis. I get why he's angry with Davis, he was never around. He didn't see mum before she passed away and never helped us raise Mel, when he did help, he just showed up with gifts and bought her love. Logan has watched Davis boss me around like a slave and hearing him verbally abuse me for years over all sorts of things. The drinking never helped but Davis was always drunk if he was home, or close to it, even before mum was gone.

"There's more." He whispered, pausing to give a shy smile to Mel and gestured to her to sit down, then he looked up at Logan with an awkward smile and then landed his gaze on me. His eyes softened and he looked gentle and pleading but he's only ever looked at me like this once, the day mum got diagnosed.

It's the same look he gave me before telling me the earth-shattering news. This can't be good, at least not for me. "I got the CEO position of the company and it's an incredible opportunity, and it's why I was over in America." He's still looking at me with that look and I'm trying so hard to not cry or climb this table and slap him myself, although Logan may do it for me at this rate.

It's amazing though, CEO of the company, he's worked for this for as long as I've known him. Mum supported him through all the hard times before he got to his position now, giving him money and working overtime in the cafe to help pay for things we needed but why the fuck am I getting this look? He flew all the way back from America to tell us the promotion, what the fuck's actually happening.

As I stare into his eyes, I try to figure out what he's trying to tell me as a lightbulb lights up above my head,

Oh fuck, wait. No, no way! No. Fucking. Way.

He flew back from America, where he's been for three weeks now. Please, don't fucking say it.

My head is about to explode as my eyes begin to sting, please don't say it!

"The position isn't based here," he paused again, "it's based in New York, and we have to move within the next two weeks so I can start working in the office."

Holy shit! What the fuck did he just say!?

The words are bouncing through my skull as I sit and watch him take a deep breath of relief.

"I'm sorry, what the fuck did you say!?" Logan shouted, looking at him like he's actually going to jump the table. "We're moving halfway across the globe and you're only giving us two weeks fucking notice, how the hell's that fair!" He explodes, his fists slamming down on the table, shaking the plates and cutlery.

I can't believe this, "I can't go, I have school here and my scholarship. Will it be able to be transferred, it's a different country?" I whispered then my thoughts came to a halt, oh my god, holy shit. "What about mum! There's no way I'll leave her here. How could you even consider moving, I'm staying!" I protested, I cannot leave mum.

"No one's staying!" Davis shouted, smacking his hand down on the glass dining room table. He turned to me, his anger slowly vanishing from his face. "I'll call the university and see what institutions and colleges will accept your scholarship and have everything transferred before the move." Davis then looked at Logan, "It's all the notice I was given, I was told and then got on a plane to come home. If I had more time I would have given it to you but you're all coming, no one's staying. I cannot leave you in another country." He demands. How the hell does he have the nerve not to even mention mum.

Logan looks furious, without saying anything else he just gets up and goes to his bedroom, slamming the door behind him. Mel's sitting at the table looking at her plate, she looks so stunned. She's doing so well here, moving could fuck everything up and I can't leave, there's school yes but there's mum, she's buried her. It's not like I can get her buried overseas.

I stand up, not looking at Davis and go to Mel. Her eyes are wide and blank, she's about to have a mental breakdown. I take her by the shoulders and help her up, taking her to her room, leaving Davis at the table.

CHAPTER 2 – SCARLET

I close her door behind us and sit Mel down on her bed, her stuffed animals falling off the edge of the bed as she squirms herself into the mountain of them.

"Hey Mel, are you okay? I know that was a lot and I'm sorry for not letting you speak." I break the silence, kneeling down in front of her to try and be at her eye level.

"It's okay, I didn't even know what to say, you and Logan said everything I was thinking anyway." Mel takes a deep breath, trying to come back to reality as she looks up from her hands and her eyes are full of tears. "Do we really have to move? What about school and mum, I know I didn't see her much before." I pulled her straight into my chest, cutting her off as I hugged her tight.

"No, do not finish that sentence," I placed my hands on her face, "Mel, you saw her as much as you could and she loved you, she was and is still so proud of us all. We'll figure it out, I honestly don't think there's a choice with moving. I don't want to leave mum, but I'm going to go see her tomorrow and chat with her about this. Do you want to come with me and talk to her? I'm sure she will love that." I smiled at her, trying to make her feel better. I know how she feels but I don't know what to do.

Panic rises in my skin, and I can feel myself slowly break down as Mel stares at me with her teary eyes. She nodded as I pulled her back into me, closing my eyes and trying to calm myself down as well before I panic in front of her.

"Scar, I can't breathe,' Mel struggles to say. My eyes shot open, and I loosen my grip around her.

"Shit, sorry Mel." I sit up, trying to slow my breathing as it becomes shallow and my vision starts to blur.

"Hey, you need to breathe," Mel scoots closer to me and squeezes me into her, "Breathe with me," she whispers, her chest rising and lowering as she takes deep breaths in and out. As I try to copy her, my breathe shakes and I can feel my body go limp, fuck Scarlet calm down!

Since being diagnosed with severe anxiety and panic attacks I try to not panic in front of my siblings and do it in private, but I can't leave Mel yet, not that I can move. The thought of leaving mum here while we leave's slowly killing me.

"We need you Scar, please calm down." Mel squeezes me more and I can feel her warm breath on my skin.

The squeezing helps me calm down and I can slowly take some breathes, she's right, they need me now more than ever and Logan's so angry right now that he might just stay. I need to talk to him and try to get him to come, I need them too.

The panic feeling slowly vanishes and my body slowly becomes mine again as Mel kisses my cheek. "There, all better!" She smiles, sitting back on her bed, "now, go see Logan before he knocks Dad out." I chuckle as I step out of her room and walk out to the dining room, Davis is still sitting at the table, staring out the window.

"You know that was a lot of information for us to

process Davis. How did you expect us to react?" I said to him as I sat down next to him. Anger biting my skin as I try not to take my feelings out on him.

"I know, I'm sorry for the little time I gave you, but I want you all to come with me. I know I'm not around often and you don't like me much, but I do care about you, and I care about Logan and Mel. I love you all and I made your mum a promise to keep you all close. I can't break that promise to her, please come with me." He begged, grabbing my hand and squeezing it, "I can handle everything, your scholarship and school, Mel's school, she would be starting high school over there as they have middle school." He looked up at me from the table and I obviously looked pissed off as he looked back at the table before continuing, "I can handle everything, Logan's simple, he just needs the internet. Please Scar, talk to him. He obviously didn't like the idea." He joked and it falls flat, who does he fucking think he is!

"No, he didn't but I don't blame him, Davis you're never home and when you are home, you order me around like a slave and he knows. But then you come home, unannounced and then tell us we are leaving everything we know to move to a new country!" I screamed I am not impressed but I'm not surprised either. He does this all the time, not to this extent but very similar shit, coming home and saying something stupid that we have to do.

"I know and I am sorry for all of it, but it may be good for all of us, a fresh start. With Kelly, sorry mum gone." He flinches as I squeeze his hands tight. Did he just say her name! "Everyone could use a fresh start, including me with you. We won't forget her, never, she always lives with us." He points to his heart, "I loved her so much, and I know that you might not believe me, but I want to start fresh with each of you, especially you. The way I treat you isn't fair, and the abuse is too much and I'm so sorry Scar, please."

What do I do, what can I say? A promise to mum is like worshipping god to this family, as it should be, she was a saint. I just don't know what to do with Logan, he knows everything, and he won't take any of this easily, surely.

"Fine, let me talk to Logan." I paused, snapping my hands away. "But if he doesn't want to go I can't force him, he's eighteen now, I cannot force him." I stand up from the table, Logan is very set in his ways once they are set so this conversation is not going to be easy.

I go and knock on Logan's door "Hey Logan, it's me," I say as I stand thinking about what Davis said.

"Come in Scar," Logan shouted.

Walking into Logan's room, you can tell he is a gamer, LED lights set up around his room with a full gaming PC and two monitors. As well as a console and a big TV at the end of his bed.

I find him on his bed though, with heaps of notes in front of him, probably about his new game he is trying to develop.

"Are you okay?" I whispered knowing the answer already,

"Not really, it isn't fair, Scar. How can he come home and say we are moving! No choice, no nothing! How are you not angrier with this?!" He throws his hands up gesturing out to the table where we all were.

"I am upset, but I'm not angry because mum made me promise to take care of everyone and that includes him. She also made Davis promise to keep us all together, he sucks, yes, but he's your dad. He is my father figure, and even though he's an asshole, this is an amazing opportunity for him, Logan." I say as I sit on his gaming chair, which is so comfortable and probably more expensive than my actual bed. "I want what's best for everyone, that includes him. Mel would have amazing opportunities for her art and you for your developments, and well, basketball is massive there." My eyes burn as I start to tear up. I don't like crying in front of any of them, but if I want to cry in front of anyone, it's Logan. He's been there for me through thick and thin and I love him too much to see him this angry. "Plus, now that you're eighteen now, the opportunities for you to grow in the development industry would be pretty incredible over there. You could rise so high and do it quickly with the skills you have." I gesture to all of his stuff he has around his room from the games he developed.

"I could be, it would be a very smart move for me and Mel, it could be a clean slate. You know, she has been struggling since mum died, we all have." He leans back against the bed head, his head resting on the wall as he looks at the ceiling. "I think a fresh start may help us all, so long as we are all together. What about you, Scar, I know basketball is huge to you, and New York could be a great move for you but what about your school and basketball team here. You love it and you love them."

The team and the school are amazing, and I enjoyed everything about it. But I could also use a fresh start. Plus, I won't complain about leaving Eva behind with her massive ego.

"I do, almost everyone is great here but there's too much attached to mum here." Don't cry, do not cry right now! My eyes fill with tears as I try to push them back down. "I can use a fresh start too, and if you guys want to go I will come but it is your decision."

I can't look at Logan, he will know how I feel about it. I do not want to leave but I will follow my siblings anywhere.

"Hey, mum's death was hard on Mel and I, but you were there Scar, you held her hand and watched her go. That is harder than seeing her after she's gone or at the funeral. I love you but you can't hide your feelings from me." He said while getting up and moving next to me, "We all could use this, I just can't believe he thinks it's so simple, up and leaving everything behind."

"I think he knows it's hard, but he thought it would be

simpler to just say it and get it out so we could have our feelings and then deal with it. I don't want him to go on his own, we are all he has for family." I looked at Logan as a single tear fell out my eye, "I'm going to visit mum tomorrow with Mel, maybe you should come, say whatever you're feeling to her. She had a knack for feelings." I giggled and watched Logan as I wiped my tear away, waiting for an answer. He chuckled with me and nudged me,

"Of course, it's been a while since I spoke to mum. She will probably want us to go, she always liked it when we were all together." He got up, passed a controller and we played games for hours.

As I got up the next morning I threw some old workout clothes on and put my shoes on to go out and clear my head before Mel and Logan woke up. So much has happened in the past twenty four hours and I need to process it the only way I know how, going for a jog. As my thoughts cloud above my head, I can feel panic boiling in my stomach, trying to understand what to do and how this is all happening.

I'm running down my street, back towards our little cottage style house as I see Logan and Mel sitting on the stairs, "Hey Scar, are you ready to go see mum?" Mel shouted as she walked over to hand me water.

"Morning guys, yeah I'll just change and then we can go, okay?" I grabbed the water off of Mel and ran upstairs to change. We all got into Logan's car and drove to the cemetery.

As we got out of the car I can hear Mel already sniffling as she walks around the side of the car, her hand over her mouth. "You can go first Mel, we will wait here for you, go. Be with her." I reached for her and pulled her into my arms, pulling away from her as she walked over to mum's grave, letting her have a private moment with mum. We all need this, to say our goodbyes one last time.

After twenty minutes, Mel came back with tears rolling down her face and Logan went next, knowing that he will be quick and I can have a long moment with her. He came back about ten minutes later, and he took Mel from my arms and hugged her while I walked over to mum to say goodbye.

"Hey mum, how are you?" I asked, sitting down in front of her stone. "I have been better, school and basketball were going okay, I bet you heard about Davis and the move to New York." I shifted on the ground, trying to get comfortable for this awkward interaction. "Logan thinks it will be good for Mel and her art which it will be, she will have amazing opportunities to advance in that field and Logan's game development would grow so fast and he could advance so fast if he joins a company." I smiled, the thought of them succeeding makes me so happy. "I.." I stutter, "I don't know what to do mum." Tears leaving my eyes, "I want to be supportive, but I have a life here. The mistakes I have made, with school, boys, basketball. I have a future and a past here, how can I leave, how can I leave you mum." I sob as my hands fly to my face and my breathing quickens, this is so hard, I can't do it, I can't leave.

Right as I am thinking about everything and sobbing into my hands, I hear a rustle from behind mum's stone, and I shuffle back on my ass. "Hello?" I whisper, thinking someone might be behind the stone, spying on me while I was talking to mum. I crawled onto my hands and knees, peeking over mum's stone and saw a little kangaroo pop out from behind the stone.

Hang on, not a kangaroo, a wallaby!

"Hi there, little guy." I whispered, sniffling away my tears. "What are you doing here?" I asked, holding my hand out to let the small animal smell my hand. It's little nose nudge my hand and then it walks up to me slowly and carefully. The little creature's eyes staring into mine as I see a little sparkle in its green eyes. I fall back onto my ass as the creature tilts its head at me.

Holy Shit. Mum?!

The wallaby hops over to me, flicking my hand with her little nose, lifting it to its face. "Mum?!" I whimper, "Mum, is that you?" I touch the animal's head, it's eyes close and open as it stares into me again. She's here, I can feel it.

The wallaby hops into my lap and reaches up for something, my face maybe. I lean down a little so it can grab whatever it's trying to touch. "I miss you so much." I whimpered, a tear falling onto the wallaby's head. A small tug pulls on my neck as I look down and see that the tiny animal's hand is playing with the necklace as it shines in the morning sun. The necklace, the one mum gave me before she died.

"I still wear it, I even wear it to bed, it helps me sleep." I whisper, wiping the tears off of my face and clearing my throat as I put my hands on its back, "Now little one," I gently push the wallaby off my lap and put it on the ground, "go find your family, it's not safe being out here on your own." It hops away a little before turning back around, its eyes shining at me, "Thank you for letting me talk to my mum again." I wave the wallaby goodbye and kiss the stone, saying goodbye to mum as I walk back to the car.

"Was that?" Logan gasps as he too sees the tiny animal going back to the forest of trees that surround the cemetery.

"A wallaby, yeah it was, it sat in my lap and touched mum's necklace." I can feel the tears building up again as I take a deep breath, "She wants us to go, to start fresh, she will always be with us." I say as I turn to Mel, her face red and tears still falling as she watches the trees where the wallaby hopped away. "I know, I know. I miss her too." I pull her in again, letting her cry and breakdown before we get back into the car to go home.

Over the next few weeks, we slowly packed up and got ready to go, organising school and trying to get stuff sorted for Mel's art and Logan's development. All while Davis is nowhere to be found, probably tying off loose ends here in the office before the big change that we are all about to have. The thought of all this happening and Davis begging me to convince everyone to come only for him to not help us pack or sort anything out for the move makes me want to just stay and not worry about it. Logan and Mel both started to get excited about the move though, so we continued without him and then on our last day we headed to the airport.

CHAPTER 3 – MILES

"It was an away game for the championships, what did you want me to say to my team, no?" I asked, trying to get through security while on the phone with my girlfriend, Samantha. She and I have been dating since the start of high school off and on but have known each other since being in diapers. The last few times I broke it off was because, well I don't love her anymore, we grew apart and I need something different, someone different.

"Yes, I need you here! What about me or my team? We are suffering now!" She shouted through the phone, pretty sure the whole airport could hear her tantrum.

"I am literally coming home now, it's a long flight though so you will just have to wait until I get home. Also, thanks for asking but we came first." I said sarcastically, it's a big achievement, becoming champions but I know Sam wouldn't care. I did love her, but she always thinks her problems and achievements are higher than mine. Anything I say or do isn't good enough for her, yet she insists she loves me and wants me. I just don't know how much longer I can handle this. I am having enough issues of my own, let alone Sams.

"At least you got to go, we didn't even get to go because Annie broke her leg!" Sam scoffed, their vice-captain Annie broke her leg at qualifiers and Sam didn't want anyone to take her place, not that they would, considering Sam's massive attitude.

"Way to make it sound like it's her fault, I was there, it was an accident." I rolled my eyes. I finally made it through security and had to wait for my flight to be called. "My flight has been delayed so I won't be home until late now." I say, as a smile grows on my face, only because I have a little peace before coming home to chaos.

In my family, there is just me and my dad, he works as a top lawyer in the biggest firm in New York. I am in college, mainly for my basketball scholarship. I want to play pro but if I can't, I'm studying to be a lawyer to help my dad out. Mum passed away when I was 12 in a car accident, leaving Dad heartbroken as he was too late to say goodbye. I was at school when I got told the news and I swore to look after Dad from that day forth. Dad later told me that he never thought it was actually an accident, and someone tried to target him for putting them away.

"What do you mean your plane has been delayed, DID YOU CHANGE YOUR FLIGHT MILES!?" Sam shouted even louder through the phone, this woman is going to blow my eardrums. "Also, I know it wasn't Annie's fault for her leg, but that girl should have been suspended or removed from her team, she is playing this year, Miles. What if something else happens?" I can hear her start to cry, this may go one of two ways, either she is actually sad, or they are alligator tears.

"No, I didn't, why would I do that?" Jesus Christ, this woman needs to get a grip. "And she did get suspended, she missed her championship game because of that but look, I have to go, I'll message you when my flights leave." I hang up before she can get in another... *oof.*

"Oh my god, I am so sorry, are you okay?" A girl

asked as I got my thoughts back together.

"Yeah, are you," I pause, as I look up I see the most beautiful girl I have ever seen. She has the most elegant wavy, auburn red hair, the greenest of eyes and full pink lips. She is stunning, plus that Australian accent! Jesus Miles, get a fucking grip dude. "Yeah, yeah I'm okay, are you?" I asked as I quickly got to my feet, holding my hand out to help her up. She stares at me, her emerald eyes tattooing themselves on my skin as she looks me over for injuries or she's checking me out whichever works. Honestly, I'm doing the same, definitely checking for injuries and not checking her out, I think.

"I think so, I am so sorry, I should have been watching where I was going. I have to get going and find my family." She finally pulls her hand away from mine, god her skin is so soft.

By the time I looked up from my hand, she's gone. Fuck, I didn't even get her name. As I sweep my hair out of my eyes I notice there's a necklace on the ground, it's silver with a small red stone in it, and I knew it was that girl's necklace, it must have fallen off when she bumped into me. I bent down and picked it up, the chain dangling in my fingers. I looked up and tried to find her. You would think I would be able to find her in a crowd with hair as bright as hers but I couldn't see it, being six feet and five inches tall, so I was quite tall but she had to be like five, eleven, maybe in six feet tall herself but I still can't see her.

For Fuck Sake.

Good one Miles, you don't even know her name, I thought to myself as my flight got called over the speakers. My flight wasn't actually delayed, but a moment of peace from Sam's shouting is what I needed before getting on a plane. My love faded a long time ago but my patience for her is fading, with all the arguing and fighting, it's not worth it anymore. Our families want us married so we can merge our families businesses together and continue their lines but I'm a senior now, I want to explore before leaving college. She isn't the only girl I have been with, we had our break ups where I could actually be me and explore but the moment she wanted me back, my dad told me I had no choice and she wouldn't let me talk to any other girls.

As I go to board my flight I turn and look one more time, for that red haired girl in the crowd but I don't see her. I'll hold onto the necklace for now, at least that way if I somehow run into her again I will have it rather than leaving it at the airport where someone may not give it to her or the staff will keep it for themselves, who knows.

CHAPTER 4 – SCARLET

"I don't think I have ever missed the ground so much." Mel whispered, she has never been a fan of flying and she looks a little pale and green from the flight, her black hair making her lighter face look even more lighter.

"If you're going to be sick, the bathrooms are right there, I will go get you water and a snack, okay?" Logan pointed and I walked with her to the bathroom while Logan did what he said he was going to do.

"Do not miss, I will not clean vomit, I already did that with you two, I won't do it now." I joked, I would if I had to, but she could also just not miss, baby vomit is a little different to adult vomit.

"I didn't miss, I am okay now, god I wish we could have driven here." Mel steps out of the stall and washes her hands and face while I spray some perfume in here because it didn't smell good.

"Good, now are you okay? Water or food first?" I asked, cupping her face, making sure she looks okay enough to be removed from the toilet.

"Water, I don't think I will eat much at the moment," Mel gave me a weak smile, and we walked out of the bathroom and found Logan and Davis over by some seats.

"You're joking right?" Logan firmly said, "you cannot be serious, we just got here." Okay, maybe it's more of a shout now, but either way something is happening.

Mel and I hurry over to make sure he's okay, "What's wrong, we can hear you over by the bathrooms?" I loudly whispered, we do not need Logan punching Davis here.

"Davis has to go to the office and start sorting stuff out instead of taking us to our new home and helping us unpack stuff. You know, like a happy family that sacrifices everything." His fists are closed, and his knuckles are turning white.

"Hey, easy. It's fine, we can do it, the three of us." I turned to Davis, who had his face shoved in his phone. "Davis, how long will you be?" I asked, still looking at Logan.

"I won't be back until late by the sound of it, I'm sorry, I'm not supposed to start until next week but obviously things don't always go to plan." He is still looking at his phone and a call comes up on the screen, he looks up at me, silently begging me to let him go like he's my child.

"Go, we will be fine, just send me the details." I roll my eyes, why am I not surprised.

"Thank you Wallaby, there is a car here to pick you up and the moving trucks won't be long behind you," he said, running off through the crowded airport.

"Okay, let's go, we have a new house to see." I chirp, trying to lighten the mood. Logan grabs his stuff and takes Mel's hand as he walks with her. Talking to her always helps him, same with me but I think it's like an older brother thing. I grab my things, and we all get into the car to go to our new home.

We turned the corner into our street, and I spotted the house from the pictures, it's stunning. We live in a Cul de sac, with our house and one other one in the street. It is very modern, about three stories, with white and black exterior and inside is white with accents of gold throughout the house. Big grand stairs as you walk in with the kitchen on one side and the living room on the next and the second floor has four offices and a cinema room, and the third floor has the bedrooms with their own wardrobes and ensuite bathrooms. We got out of the car and swung the big double doors open, my mouth dropping to the floor. The pictures don't do this place justice!

"This is insane, it's beautiful." Mel whispered as she sat her stuff down inside the door.

"He is definitely trying to win us over isn't he?" Logan grumbled, looking at me.

"Probably, but if this is what he is planning on doing, I won't say no." I giggled and sat my stuff down next to Mel's.

The trucks finally showed up just after lunch time and we helped the company take the boxes off the truck by sitting them in the entryway and living room. As I get into a truck to grab another box, I hear running footsteps coming towards us,

"Oh my god, hi! I have been dying to meet you all." A girl shouts as she makes it up our driveway.

"Oh, hello, you must be our neighbours, Davis was telling me about you guys on the plane." I smiled and hugged the girl, "I'm Scarlet, and this is Logan and Melaine." I gestured to my siblings as they come over,

"Nice to meet you guys, I'm Lauren and this is Travis, my older brother." She pointed to a tall, light haired man coming up the driveway. He's cute.

"Nice to meet you guys too, I would offer a drink or something but as you can see." I pointed at the mess of boxes in the house. I love having guests over and being a host, but right now, well it's not really possible.

"No no that's okay, we are here to help you guys move in!" Lauren shrieks and starts grabbing boxes, the three of us look stunned. Lauren has long blonde hair that reaches her waist and blue eyes that look like the sky and her brother looks just like her but more built. I went to grab my necklace on my neck and there's nothing. I pat my neck, checking that it's actually missing. No, please no.

"Have you seen mum's necklace?" I turned to Logan and Mel, hoping it was on the ground here and that one of them found it.

"No, I haven't. You wear it all the time, oh no," Mel turns and notices it missing from my neck. Both of them put their boxes down quickly and start looking for it.

"Are you okay?" Travis asked, grabbing my shoulder as I looked under the truck.

"No, I was wearing a necklace and it's gone, it was my mothers." My eyes start to sting, I cannot believe I lost it and who knows where it fell.

"Where was the last place you noticed it?" He whispered, holding me still as I wobbled in his grip, I was about to pass out.

"At the airport, in Australia before we boarded." Fuck, please, please no. Did I really lose it at the airport, "I had it in my hand, around my neck and then I bumped into someone, and I haven't noticed it since." My voice is starting to shake, that dark haired, blue eyed man, I bumped him and heard a clang on the ground, but I thought that was from him, not me. "It came off and I thought it was him, but it must have been my necklace." I dropped to the ground out of Travis's grip as tears flooded my vision. How did this happen, it's gone.

"Hey, it's okay. It's okay, Scar, it was an accident," Logan grabs me as he falls beside me and pulls me into a hug. "Don't blame yourself, it was an accident. Mum will still be here no matter what." He whispered, trying to calm me, but I couldn't breathe. It's gone, that necklace means everything to me and I lost it.

"Scarlet, breath dude, breath." Logan shouts trying to bring me back to reality. The memory of mum handing it to me with a weak smile and then fast forwarding to watching her soul leave earth. Logan gently taps my face, trying to get through my panicked thoughts. I slowly start to breathe slowly, I must have stopped breathing for a sec or passed out in his hug because everyone is looking at me like I just died.

"I'm okay, I just can't believe it's gone, I can never get it back." I slowly got up and took a few deep breaths, everyone watched as I shoved down the tears and panic, grabbing a box, continuing to unpack. Everyone continued with the boxes and Travis came up to me and stood in front of me with a box in his hands.

"Are you sure you're okay, want to talk about it?" He asked, putting the box down beside us.

"Are you asking me to tell a total stranger about my past who just made me have a panic attack?" I teased, he seemed sweet and he's hot. His blonde hair moves in the wind, flicking his eyelashes.

"Maybe, but I am your neighbour, and we will get to know each other well because Lauren is on your basketball team." He smiled, god he is cute. Nope, nope don't do that, Scar, leave that out of your head.

"Really, well that's exciting, I can't wait to start here. It's been my dream to go pro." I hesitated, the smile on my face slowly vanished. "The necklace was my mums, and she gave it to me right before she died. I was with her the night she passed in the hospital; cancer took her." I can feel a tear leave my burning eyes as they make their way down my face.

"Wow, I'm so sorry. That had to be a lot, especially for one person." Travis looked down into my eyes, wiping the tears from my face. "If you need anything, let me know. I know what Davis is like too, Dad works with him. If you ever need me, I'm here." He smiled; Travis has the most beautiful blue eyes with the longest lashes I have ever seen. Any girl would be jealous of them. Travis stood there for a moment, staring at me, not in a bad way but like I was pretty, like he could see me. We stood there for a moment, staring into each other's eyes. I can feel my cheeks heat as he smirks at me. I looked away realising I was staring at him for a little too long and stepped back.

"It's okay and thank you. It's nice to have someone other than family to talk to about everything." I say as I grab a box, and we start helping the others. It took us all day to get the boxes inside and unpack most of our stuff.

"Thank you so much for all the help guys, please stay for pizza?" I asked as I walked out of the kitchen into the living room.

"That would be lovely, thank you." Lauren said as she sat with Mel and Logan.

"Are you doing okay now?" Travis asked from behind me, sending a shiver down my spine as his breath hits my skin.

"Umm, yeah I think so. I'm devastated about the necklace, but I know she will forgive me and that she is still around." I say as I turn to face Travis, "I really appreciate everything. Really, thank you." I start to fiddle with my thumbs and without saying anything, Travis holds his arms out in front of him. I stare for a moment and walk into his embrace. His solid arms wrapped around me as he rested his chin on my head. His cologne overcomes my senses. The minty smell makes me take a few deep breaths in to save the scent, god he smells so nice.

"Of course, Scarlet, I meant what I said, I'm always around, even just for a hug." I look up at him and he smiles down at me as a knock on the door startles me out of the hug. I grab the cash and open the door, grabbing the pizza and taking it into the living room. We all get settled and watch movies and play games, until it gets late and Lauren and Travis head home.

I can't believe I lost the necklace! As I lay down in

bed I went over the airport scene over and over again. Hoping that I knew the man, but I knew that there was slim to no chance of finding him or the necklace ever again.

CHAPTER 5 – SCARLET

Today is a massive day for me, I'm so nervous that I got no sleep last night, with the stress of no necklace and my basketball meet today, who could get any sleep. It's ten past five in the morning, I try to roll over and go back to sleep but it's no use. I get up, get dressed and go for a run, I really need to clear my mind again.

About thirty minutes later I make my way back home when I hear footsteps behind me, "Hey, Scar. What are you doing up so early?" It was Travis, I could tell his voice from anywhere.

"Hey Travis, I couldn't sleep, plus I'm nervous about today so hence the running." I huffed as I tried to catch my breath. "What are you doing awake so early? I know you don't play basketball, so." I teased.

"Ha, no I don't play anymore, I go for a morning walk or a run every day. Helps with the stress and anxiety." He smiled.

"Well, maybe I should join you for the runs, only if you don't mind. Also, you handle that well, the anxiety." I whispered, "Sorry, I don't want to offend you or anything, I know it's a touchy subject."

"No, please, it's okay. It's common knowledge, plus it should be talked about. At least if something happens you know." He grabbed my hand, "also, the running, you are more than welcome to join me, I insist actually." He lets my hand go, trying not to look at me as we start walking back to my house.

"I may take you up on that, want to come in? I'm going to make breakfast for Logan and Mel before I have to meet with Lauren." I walk up the front stairs and turn to look at Travis, "if Laurens up she can come around to, if you want to check?" I sit down to take my jogger's off.

"Yeah, I'll go check and come back over." He said, walking back to his place. I open the doors and step into the kitchen to gather everything I need to make a big breakfast for my siblings and my new friends and start cooking. As six rolls around, Logan comes down the stairs, rubbing his temples.

"Hey Logan, big night?" I asked, flipping bacon in the pan.

"Yeah, big night of game development and problem after problem. Is there coffee?" Logan paused as he noticed the extra coffee mugs, "Do we have other's coming for breakfast?"

"Yeah, Travis and maybe Lauren are coming around for breakfast, I ran into Travis on my run and invited him to breakfast, said to see if Lauren's up and bring her too." I said, putting the bacon on the plates.

"What, Lauren's coming?" Logan raises from his chair quickly and runs upstairs. What is wrong with him?

Logan comes back downstairs a minute later, all dressed, and hair done. He doesn't look so tired anymore.

"Damn Logan, who are you dressing up for?" I teased, his eyes snap to mine as his cheeks blush. "Aww, Logan, you like Lauren. Oh my god, that's so cute."

"I ship it" Mel says coming down the stairs in her PJs, rubbing her eyes.

"So, what, leave me alone, I'm still tired as shit." He grumbled, grabbing his coffee and sitting at the dining table. Mel grabs cutlery and the plates to set the table while I bring over all the breakfast foods I cooked. Pancakes, eggs, bacon, fruit, coffee, toppings, the whole platter and right as I sat the last plate down, the door opened up and Lauren and Travis came through, both dressed and ready for today.

"Morning guys, how are we feeling?" I asked as I grabbed some coffee and sat down.

"Good, got a good night's sleep and ready for the meet today, are you ready? Nervous?" Lauren asked, sitting down next to Logan.

"I'm ready. Nervous, fuck yes, but I'm excited. Hopefully everyone likes me. Can you tell me a little about the team, just so I'm prepared." I asked as I took a sip of coffee.

"Yeah, so there's our captain, Sam, she's strict and lately very moody but she has relationship problems," She said, rolling her eyes hard.

"Mostly her own problems, she's a bit crazy about him." Travis adds, taking bacon and pancakes and putting them on his plate.

"Well, yeah. Then there's Annie, she's sweet and Sam's best friend, very opposite to Sam, but she broke her leg in our championship qualifier game, and we didn't make it. So, they want a new vice-captain today, I don't want it but there's also May and Tegan. They are my friends and are lovely, crazy but lovely, just like me." We all giggle at the comment. "Then there's Jamie and Chloe, they fill in when we need it. They are busy with their studies, but they know how to play so they sit on the bench most of the time." She shrugged, drinking some coffee.

"They sound like a good team, besides Sam, I'm not excited about meeting her," I whispered, if she's crazy, she may be similar to Eva.

"If you need help with her, Annie is always around,

so am I and my girls." She sassed, "She is bossy though, so just don't get on her bad side." Hopefully that won't be too hard.

As we all finished breakfast, Mel and Logan offered to do the dishes as Lauren and I went to the meeting.

Lauren and I walked into the gym, I noticed the courts look a little worn as two women are there already, practicing. "Girls, Oh my god, hey!" Laruen put her bag down and ran over to them and they all hugged and jumped together, muttering things to each other. "Oh shit, girls this is Scarlet, Scar for short. Scar, this is Tegan and May." Tegan is slightly taller than me with brown hair cut into a rough bob and brown eyes. May is my height with blonde hair and hazel eyes.

"Hey, nice to meet you, we watched your training and game videos from Australia, and I have to say, amazing!" Tegan said, her face lighting up as they walked closer to me.

"Your three pointers are crazy, you have an arm on you," May shrieked as she pulled me into a hug.

"Thank you, I can't believe you guys watched the videos," I'm shocked! I didn't think people watched those games.

"Yeah, Sam and Annie wanted us to get a scope on your skills, and they were impressed, although Sam isn't easily impressed." Lauren mumbled, grabbing the ball from the sidelines.

About ten minutes later, Jamie and Chloe arrive and then Sam and Annie come through the door. Sam's tall with blonde hair and is slim and lanky, with deep brown eyes while Annie has black hair, hazel eyes and she's shorter than most of us, about five feet and ten inches tall. "Morning ladies, finish up and come over by the benches." Annie shouted, hobbling her way over to a chair with her crutches and cast on her right leg.

We all walk over as we grab our water and stand in a circle around Annie and Sam. "Okay, we've had over a month off, I hope you guys still trained because we will come out on top this year." Sam stated, putting her hand on Annie's shoulder. "After last year's accident," Sam and Annie looked down at her leg, "we need to prove that we are good enough to be on top, and that is what will happen."

Annie looked up at me, "We have a new addition to our team, to step into my place, please welcome, Scarlet Bowen."

Everyone looks in my direction and starts clapping and congratulating me. "Thank you, I am excited to start and help you all get to the top." I smiled and looked at Sam, her gaze sending shivers up my spine.

"Okay, let's cut to the chase," Sam shouted over the clapping. "Now that Annie is out, we have the vice-captain spot open, you all are qualified for it, so I want to put it out to you and ask if anyone wants to volunteer," She looks over the group and no one says anything. Everyone looked around at each other.

"I think that it should be given to Scarlet," Lauren says, putting her hand on my shoulder. "She is an amazing player, we all have seen her videos, and she has been filled in for vice captaincy in the past." She states pushing me forward, towards Sam and Annie.

"Oh, umm, I would be honoured but I have literally just joined the team. I do not want to step on toes." I stepped back, I cannot fuck this up already, I have been here all of five minutes and Sam does not look pleased with Laurens outburst.

"I think we can settle this basketball style, two versus two, what do you think Sam?" Annie looks up at Sam and she is staring at me, trying to figure out what to do.

"Fine, two versus two, Scarlet and Lauren versus Tegan and I. If you win, the spots yours if you lose, I give it to someone else." She snarled, rolling her eyes and crossing her arms over her chest.

God, what is Sam's problem, she has been staring daggers into me since she walked in. She is acting like

I have fucked up already, but I haven't done shit yet. We make our way over to the court and we get in our positions and Lauren, and I start with the ball as I bounce it to Sam, and she bounces it back to me and the game begins.

We go back and forth for twenty minutes as Annie finally calls last shot and it is thirty-eight to thirty-nine to Lauren and I. Basically either Sam or Tegan has to get a shot in, or they lose.

Right now, Sam has the ball while I'm defending her. Sam has two options, she can either risk the three-point shot, which I know that she isn't a strong three-point shooter or she can try and go around me and do a lay-up which she is amazing at.

These guys did their research, and I did mine. Sam has an amazing layup technique, meaning she can run in and jump the ball into the hoop as she's right under it.

She goes to take a step forward, but I block her off, Sam stares me down as she hesitates and steps back to take a three-point shot. Right as the ball leaves her hands, I jump up and grab it, taking it to the three-point line as I turn and shoot, getting it in making the score thirty-right to forty-two to us.

"Woohoo, yes, Scarlet!" Laruen runs at me and jumps in for a hug and then the rest of the girls come in and join in for a group hug as they cheer.

"Thank you, you did so good too." I laugh as everyone crashes into us.

"Okay, okay, break it up team. We now have a decision, congratulations Scarlet, the position is yours, if you want it." Annie shouts over the girls as she makes her way over, hobbling over with her crutches.

I look over at Sam and she isn't happy, she looks angry but also hurt and I have no idea why.

"Only if I'm not stepping on toes, I would be honoured." I smiled as everyone hugged me again and congratulations were running wild.

"Okay, enough." Sam shouts and everyone quiets down, "We are here for training. Now, Scarlet, go hang out with Annie for a bit and she will get you up to speed on the vice-captain job. The rest of you, we are training. Let's go." She gestures to the court, and everyone moves away from me with an awkward smile as they run to train.

Annie and I go over the vice-captain job, on the warmups and training schedule that everyone does.

"So, do you have any questions?" Annie asked, watching everyone train.

"Nope, I will go over everything when I get home and I will text you if I have any questions." I say as I stand up and go join the others in training.

The doors to the courts swing open and a man walks in. A tall, dark-haired man with the bluest of eyes walks over towards Annie. He smiles gently at her and turns to look at our team when our eyes meet. Holy shit, it's the man I bumped into at the airport.

CHAPTER 6 – MILES

Even with the championship title, we have to go back to regular college games that start on Saturday after having a month off. We now need to train even harder to be able to keep our spot at the top.

I was given the captain position last year and I led our team to victory and this year, we will fight for it again. I drove over to the courts to come up with a new training schedule for the team and as I parked, I noticed all the cars in the carpark. I know Sam and her team are practicing today but I need to fix our schedule. I haven't been able to stop thinking about the fight Sam and I had at the airport on the phone, I haven't spoken to her since then. I just needed a break, from all the fighting and arguing. The images of the girl I bumped into have been popping into my head so much over the past few weeks. She was so beautiful, and I have her necklace, but I have no way to get it back to her now, I can't believe I didn't even ask her name!

I grab my stuff out of the car and walk through the court doors, I see Sam and her team huddled over the other side of the court and she spots me immediately, smiling at me as she finishes her conversation and walks over. While she walks over, I notice bright red hair walking over to the team. The long wavy auburn red hair, the most beautiful green eyes and the full lips. It's her, the girl from the airport, she's here!

"Hey babe, how are you, I'm sorry about the fight that we had over the phone a few weeks ago." Sam starts talking as she tries to pull me in for a hug. "Hey, are you listening to me?" She asked and my gaze dropped down into her eyes.

"Hey Sam, yeah sorry. I'm okay, I just needed some time." I pulled her in tight, looking over at the woman, her mouth slightly open with shock. I can see her thoughts trying to understand what she is seeing as Lauren calls her over. She pulls her gaze away from mine and walks over to the group of girls. She plays basketball, she is at my school, she's in New York, my brain is bouncing around my skull as I look back down at Sam. "Hey, who is that, she wasn't in your team last year?" I asked, trying not to make it sound obvious that I am very much intrigued by her.

"Oh, that is our new member, Scarlet. She just got Annie's job as well, she's good I suppose." Sam turns and rolls her eyes, "She won a two v two against Tegan and I, but I hesitated and let her win," she snarled. Obviously Sam isn't a big fan of the new girl.

"Wow, she beat you, you must not be in a good mood then." I held back a laugh as Sam huffed at my comment. She is competitive and doesn't like new people. "She has to be good if she made it straight to the vice-captain spot."

"She's good enough, hopefully she can make us win and get us to the championship." She said, I know how heartbroken she was when Annie's leg broke and they couldn't go to Australia for the championships.

"Well, I have to fix my team's training schedule, plus you have training too. I will let you go, have a good day." I step back away from Sam.

"Yeah, I suppose I should go over there and join in. Will I see you later?" She whispered, looking at my lips.

"I will wait for you to finish training, we can talk after that." I say stepping back, I wasn't in the mood to kiss her, still not over that fight.

Sam's brows rose as she walked back over to her team, and they started their training. I sit down and take my notebook to take notes for our new schedule. I can't believe she is here and Christ, she's so beautiful. The way she moves while training, she's fast and agile but she is also strong and focused. I don't think I can do this any longer with Sam, she's always been a lot, but the last year has been so stressful with everything that has happened that we both need a fresh slate, we want different things now and I don't want her.

It's been about an hour since I got to the courts, and I am adding the final touches to my notes when Sam walks over after their training session.

"Hey babe, sorry we ran a little late, the new girl needed a little more of a push through training." She laughed, sitting down next to me and grabbing my hand. "I am so sorry about the argument we had, I crossed the line." She sighed, giving me her big puppy dog eyes.

"How is the new girl? Scarlet, wasn't it?" I asked, closing my notebook and sitting it in my bag.

"She's good," Sam hesitates. "Why do you care about her name Miles? Huh? Do you think she's cute?" She shouts, shooting up off the bench.

"Sam, please, you literally just apologised for the argument we had from weeks ago and now you instantly start another one, come on." I grumbled, I knew she would do this, but I didn't think it would happen after she just apologised for another fight literally five seconds ago.

"No, Miles. Why do you care, do you want her instead? She is amazing, okay, she is so good at basketball that she will go pro, and I am not even sure if I can make it this year and I only have this year left, she's only a sophomore!" Sam whimpered, tears falling off her face, "I can't compete with that."

"Sam, you are amazing at basketball, okay. If you want extra help you have your team. But for the love of god, why does everything have to be an argument with you." I put my hands on her shoulders, "I love you Sam, but I don't think it's enough. I will always be here for you, no matter what, but I think we should break this off." I pull her chin up so she looks me in my eyes, "Sam, understand that I will always be your friend, but I can't handle this anymore. It's our last year, we need to focus on school and explore ourselves. Please, understand." I wipe her tears off her cheeks as she pulls away from me.

"I know, I just can't believe you want this. You're done with us, you don't want to fight for us anymore?" She asked, cleaning her face off with her towel.

"All we do is fight and fight, but we aren't fighting for the right reasons, everything is an issue with us, and we need to start fresh."

"Whatever Miles, if you won't fight for us then I will." Sam grabbed her things and left out the doors in a huff.

I take a long breath in and out as I sit back down. I look over my notes and test them out one last time to clear my head and finally have a perfect training schedule for my boys.

I am finally free, I can do what I please and what I want without having to ask permission anymore.

I take the necklace out of my bag and look at it in my hand. Remembering her bumping into me at the airport, with her big green eyes staring up at me. I have been fantasising about her ever since, hoping I would see her again. Her wavy orange hair in my hands and her green eyes looking me in the eyes as she. Fuck Miles, I need to calm down. Getting a hard on right now is not the best idea, but what's crazy is that Sam or even thinking about Sam has never turned me on as much as this before, let alone this fast. I need to give this back to her, back to Scarlet when I see her next, I will not lose my chance next time.

CHAPTER 7 – SCARLET

He was there, that man, the one at the airport. He must play basketball, he had a Hudson jersey on. So that means we go to the same school, Holy shit!

I lost my train of thought as I stepped up the stairs and heard Davis and Logan screaming at each other in the kitchen. I run up the stairs and take my shoes off as I open the door quietly and lean against the pillar connecting the entryway and the kitchen to listen to what they are arguing about.

"What do you mean we need to date and marry for you, this isn't the fifties anymore, you can't choose who we date, Davis!" Logan slammed his hands on the kitchen bench.

"It's Dad to you, Logan and I can do whatever I want, I am your legal guardian and until you're twenty-one it doesn't matter what you want." Davis said, having an evil grin on his face, as he's holding a brandy glass full of a brown liquid. "You and Mel will date and marry these people so that way we can be in business with their companies, you and Melanie would be marrying into a lot of money, do you not want that?" Davis asked, stepping closer to Logan.

What the fuck is he saying, marrying off my siblings?

No, he can't do that. Logan is eighteen now and here in New York he is considered an adult plus he's an Australian citizen, so he is classified as an Australian adult. Mel, she isn't an adult, but I will not let him do this to them.

As I am trying to come up with a plan, Davis is in Logan's face, "I am your father Logan and you will do what I say, Mel will do it, she loves me and will help me with whatever I want." This manipulative shit.

"Davis, get out of his face." I shout, stepping out from behind the pillar, "He is an adult and in New York, eighteen is considered an adult so he can do whatever he wants. As for Mel, you will not manipulate her, mum made me sign papers to make me her legal guardian because she knew what you were like, so no she will not do that!" I step closer to the two men in the kitchen, "and if you have a problem with that, we can take it up with the police or court, but no one will be forced to marry anyone in this century." I snarled, what a dick! Who does he think he is, being absent for more than half their lives and then demanding they date people to benefit him.

"How dare you speak to me like that!" Davis marches his way over to me and now he is in my face, and I can smell the whiskey on his breath. "I will do whatever I want," He whispered, raising his hand up and as he went to swing Logan jumped in and punched Davis in the face.

"Do not touch her," He growled as he went to step closer to Davis, I pulled Logan back, stopping him from doing more damage,

"Logan?" Mel whimpered! She's over on the stairs and she definitely saw everything.

"Mel, how long have you been there?" I ran over to her when she dropped to the stairs and started sobbing, "Hey, hey it's okay." I grab her and pull her in for a hug. "Logan, take her upstairs, see what she saw and tell her what happened, she needs to know." Logan nodded as I gave her to Logan and they walked upstairs to Mel's bedroom as I got a message notification on my phone, Travis.

"Hey, are you okay, I heard screaming?"

I didn't think we were that loud, as I try to type back I hear a grunt, I quickly look up and Davis is on his feet, walking towards me. "How dare you, you think you're in control? You are nothing and your mother isn't here to save you anymore." He growled and he raised his hand again and I covered my face with my hands as I heard someone stand in front of me and crunch. All I hear is a thud on the ground and when I uncover my eyes I see Travis, well his back and his scent, mint overwhelms me.

"Do not touch her! The police are on their way, stay down and no one else has to get hurt." Travis demanded and he turned to me, "Are you okay, did he touch you?" He scanned me for injuries, making sure I didn't get hit.

"I'm okay, Travis, how did you get here? I was trying to respond to your text before he got up." I asked, I am so confused, he came out of nowhere.

"I was out for a walk when I heard Logan and Davis, so I messaged you and when you didn't text back I came up the stairs to knock on the door. I saw him screaming at you through the door and he raised his hand above his head, so I ran in to help." He catches his breath, the adrenaline calming down.

"I'm fine thanks to you and we are all safe, how's your hand?" I asked, looking at his bloody hand, "That doesn't look great."

"I'm okay, it's just the skin that broke open, I can wrap it." He rips part of his shirt and wraps it over his knuckles, leaving part of his torso visible, and damn. There is definitely a six pack under there and I slightly turn away so he doesn't notice me staring but I wouldn't mind seeing him shirtless. God, get your head out of your ass Scarlet, he is a friend that just saved your life.

I hear the sirens in the background and the lights show over the trees as they come up our driveway. "Well, I'll grab him if you want to go explain what happened?" Travis smiled at me and then walked over to Davis, who's still passed out on the ground.

"Yeah, just be careful." I whisper. Why do I find this so hot?

I went outside and spoke to the officer, explaining about the fight between Logan and Davis. Then how Davis tried to hit me, and Logan acted in self-defence for me and then when Travis did the same. They wrote every detail down as another officer put Davis in cuffs, putting him in the back of the police car. "Is there anything else you can remember?" The officer asked, checking me for injuries.

"No, that was everything, what will happen to him now?" I asked, partly already knowing the answer but I need to tell Mel what happened.

"He will be processed and then it will be up to you and your family if you want to press charges, but he will have a DV charge on him now. If you have any other questions or need anything, here's my card, don't hesitate to call." She said, handing me a card with all her details on it, I nod and walk back to let the police vehicle go.

Last night was insane! With all the stuff that happened with Davis, who is now staying in a hotel as he can't come near my siblings or me with the restraining order that the officers got last night. Mel was devastated, she has always seen Davis as a father figure, someone who could never do any wrong in her eyes, a role model and now all of that has come crashing down to a pit of a dumpster fire.

"How could he do this, to you? And you?" She cried, "Why didn't you tell me?"

The words bouncing in my head from last night, trying to answer them was hard to explain. She was young and he's never done anything to her, but he also has never laid a hand on Logan or me, just verbal abuse which is just as bad. It was all he did to me for so long and Logan saw one night when he was thirteen and then he started on Logan too.

I shook my head, trying to get the memories out and got dressed to go for a run. Travis wasn't out this morning, but I don't blame him, we all had a long night, and he has some explaining to do to his family about his hand. Once I got back to the house, I cooked breakfast for everyone. Today is both, Mel's and my first day at school, and Logan has interviews with big development companies today, so big day for everyone. Logan comes down first, straight to the coffee and sits down.

"Are you doing okay?" Logan asked, his hand red and angry from the punch he landed.

"Yeah, I will be, just hope Mel is okay. I can handle this and so can you, but I am not sure about her." I feel awful, maybe we should have told her ages ago, but she was too young, and she loved Davis so much and now everything has changed for the worse.

Mel makes her way down the stairs, all dressed, ready for her first day of school and she looks so pretty. Her long wavy black hair, courtesy of Davis, blue eyes and makeup that is simple yet elegant. "Good morning, and before you guys ask or tip toe around me, I am fine, I have come to terms with everything. It was just a bit heartbreaking to lose our only other parent." She whispered, sitting down next to Logan.

"Well, I am glad you're feeling better this morning. I made your favourite, just in case you weren't feeling good about today, but if you're better," I teased, pretending to throw her blueberry and Nutella pancakes out.

"No, no I would still like them, I can be sad if you want," She smiled, teasing back as she pouted her face, pretending to cry.

"Okay, okay," I bring over the big stack of pancakes and bacon and eggs with French toast and toppings. "Well, dig in, I just need to get dressed and I will be back." As I make my way to the stairs, a knock comes from the door, and I can see Lauren and Travis standing at the door.

"Oh, hey guys, I wasn't expecting you until later." I open the door, letting them in.

"Yeah, well Travis told me what happened, so we bought muffins and food that I made this morning." Lauren showed the basket and walked in, saying hi to Mel and Logan, sitting down for breakfast.

"How are you doing, are you okay?" Travis asked, checking me over one last time for injuries, his eyes looked heavy as they watched me.

"I am okay, we all are. Thank you for last night, I might not be okay if you didn't come in and save me. Please, come have breakfast, I am just going to get changed and then I will be down." Travis walks in and sits down with the others as I go upstairs and get changed. When I come down I grab some coffee and a muffin, and we all head out for school.

The first day of classes was long, second year into exercise and sports management isn't easy. It's quite boring but I want to go pro for basketball and then coach for pro's or run my own centre, so it's very much needed.

I make my way over to the courts as I hear crying through the doors. I walk through and see Sam and Annie over on the bench and Sam's crying in Annie's arms. I take my bag and sit it on the benches and walk over to the hoop where Lauren, May and Tegan are.

"Hey, is she okay?" I whisper, standing next to Tegan.

"No, her boyfriend broke up with her on the weekend after our meeting and she's super sad about it. I don't know why though, they only fight and argue now. They haven't been a real couple in years." Tegan said, shooting from the three-point line and missed. "Shit!" She mumbles.

"Wow, that's a lot." I say, grabbing the ball and handing it to Tegan.

"Okay team, bring it in." Annie shouts and we make our way over when the men's team walks in. "We will be doing drill training today, usually we coordinate with the men's team but today we will be sharing the court so we have half, Scarlet, stay here so we can chat about some extra things for you. Okay, off you go," Annie waves everyone off and hugs Sam as she also walks off with the team, still staring daggers into me through her blood shot eyes, fantastic.

"Hey, what's up?" I asked as I sat next to Annie.

"Sam isn't in a good headspace right now, so you will need to coordinate with the men's team about their training schedules and their times. We can be flexible, I just want her to be able to focus." Annie looked over at Sam, "She is my best friend, but those two weren't good together, she needs to focus on something else."

"I can do that, who is the captain?" I asked, scanning the men's team.

"His name's Miles, he is the dark-haired guy over by the bench." She pointed to him, holy shit!

He is the guy I saw the other day, the one from the airport. That was Sam's boyfriend, no wonder she is heartbroken. The man's drop dead gorgeous! His deep blue eyes peeking through his wavy short black hair before he runs his massive hands through it.

"Umm, okay, can I wait until after training?" I hesitate, I need to get my head out of my ass, they just broke up and I just moved here. I do not need problems already.

"Yeah, of course. I will let him know to wait for you until we are done, but wait until we all leave, especially Sam, she still isn't your biggest fan and even I don't know why." One of Annie's eyebrows raised while she thought about it, "Now, go train, I know you're good but we all can get better." She pushes me off the chair and I run over and join in.

We train for about an hour, doing every drill under the sun. Everyone talks for a bit before they all grab their stuff and walk out the door. Miles is still on the court, practicing his three-point shots, missing every once and a while.

"So, your name's Miles?" I shout, walking over to him.

"And yours is Scarlet, it's nice to finally meet you." He smirked, passing me the ball, "Now, I want to see how many three pointers you can get in before we talk, I hear you're an expert and more than half my team can't get them in consistently." He demands, those bright blue eyes staring into mine.

"Fine, it's been a while since I have tested myself, give me thirty seconds and we will see how many I miss." I declared, bouncing the ball once at the line and starting shooting. Over and over, getting the ball in and then Miles jumps in to defend trying to make it challenging, but my eyes never leave the ring. He's good, I'll give him that, but I get the ball past him every time.

"Holy shit, you didn't miss once." His eyes sparkling with excitement, "That's fucking impressive, how did you learn to shot like that?" He asked, stepping closer to me.

"I just practiced, I don't know, drills I guess," I shrug, there isn't a real technique to be the best at something except for practice.

"Mmm, I see. Well, I was watching you train, and I do have to say, you have some fire in you, Ember."

I smirk and an eyebrow raises as I cross my arms. "Ember, huh. What's this? First day and I already have a nickname?"

Miles turns, grabbing the ball and tries one last time to get it in from the line, "Shit!" He whispered under his breath.

"Here, watch me." I grabbed the ball and explained what I was doing as I shot the ball and got it in.

"That was amazing, you're amazing, Ember. I," He paused, "Sorry, Annie tells me you want to discuss schedules and times?" He dropped the ball, went over to his bag and pulled out a notebook.

"Yeah, with what happened with you and Sam, she wanted to see what time you guys are training so that way we don't cross paths too often." He looks up at me from his book.

"What, she can't be that heartbroken, she knew it was coming." His lips frown and his voice turns cold.

"Well, you did break up with her, should she not feel heartbroken?" I asked, walking over to him to see what is written in the notebook.

"Do you want the short or long version?" He whispered, looking as heartbroken as she did today.

"The whole version."

CHAPTER 8 – MILES

Scarlet and I sit for a while, talking about mine and Sam's relationship. It's so easy to talk to her, it's nice to have someone understand without being biassed.

"And that is when I broke up with her after the meeting, the fight that we had on the phone while at the airport was the last straw," I say quietly, hoping I didn't just overload her brain.

"Wow, that is a lot, why didn't you break up with her sooner, instead of breaking up and getting back together, leading her on?" She asks, tucking a beautiful red curl behind her ear.

"She would come back and apologise and beg to get back together. Our dads are best friends so my dad would lecture me about it and tell me to get back with her so she's happy. So that's what I did, I didn't want to hurt her, but I can't do that anymore." I whispered, it shouldn't hurt this bad, I will always be here for her, just not in a romantic way anymore.

"That's rough, I'm sorry that happened." Scarlet whispered back, putting a hand on my shoulder and I shiver. Electricity ran through my body as she rested there, her touch was soft and meaningful.

"Thanks, it's fine, I am trying to move on and so

should she. She could use a distraction," I say, grabbing her hand into mine, "Thank you for listening, I appreciate an outside perspective."

"Of course, if you need someone to talk to, I'm here." She squeezed my hand before letting go, "But we should really talk about the schedule, at least for Sam." She cleared her throat, grabbing out her notebook and we spent the next half an hour going over times and drills that she uses for her three-point shots because my team could really use the help. Once we went over everything we grabbed our bags and went out the doors

"Oh, did you want a ride home? Lauren said you live next to her, so I know where you live if you want a lift?" I asked, walking towards my car.

"Oh, you know where I live, that's a little creepy don't you think?" Scarlet teased, stepping closer to me.

"Maybe, I just have good sources, Ember." If she wants to tease, I will tease back.

"Mhmm, well I may need those." She was right in front of me now, she smells so good her perfume runs through me as caramel hits me.

"Well, I can give you them if you want a lift home," I lift my hand to touch the strand of her hair that is waving in her face and she flinches, covering her face as she falls to her knees and her breath quickens.

What. the. Fuck.

"Scarlet, hey, I'm sorry, I was just going to move the strand from your face. Are you okay?" I rushed over to her as she covered her face and started sobbing. "Hey, hey, it's okay. I am so sorry." I sat next to her and pulled her into my chest. We sat on the ground for about ten minutes before she stopped crying into my arms and tried to get herself back together, taking in deep breaths.

"I am sorry, I just," she hesitated, tears started balling in her eyes again.

"You don't need to explain anything if you're not comfortable." I whisper, grabbing her hand. "You're safe with me, Ember. I will never lay a hand on you." I grab her chin gently and pull her tearful face up to mine. "Who did this to you?" I asked, looking into her pretty green eyes and a tear fell out, rolling down her pale face. I rub my thumb over her cheek, taking the tear with my finger. "If you ever want to talk about it, I am here, Ember, always." I whisper, as I grab her hand to help her up she bumps into my chest, and I remember the airport. "Oh wait, you're the girl from the airport right?" I walk over to the car, bringing her with me, "I have something for you." I open the door and open the centre console, reaching for the ruby necklace. "Here, I believe this is yours," I whisper, handing it to her and more tears roll over her face.

"You have it! Thank you, thank you so much." She cried and looked at it for a moment, "Can you put it on for me please?" she sniffled and handed it back to me as she turns, lifting her hair out of the way,

"Of course," I put it over her head, and I grab the clasp, my fingers graze her neck and her body shivers at my touch. "All done," she turns, holding the stone in her hand.

"Thank you, it was my mums, she died a year ago from cancer and she handed it to me before she died. When I lost it, I thought I lost her too. I just can't believe that we are at the same school." She looked up at me, her eyes are red and puffy from crying.

"I know, it's crazy. I held onto it just in case I saw you again, but I didn't think it would be here." I whispered, it was like fate, and she was right in front of me. "Let's get you home, it's getting late." I go over and open her door for her,

"So, he's sweet and a gentleman." Scarlet mocks as she sits in the chair and we drive to her house, talking about basketball, of course. "Well, here we are." I say as I get out and go to open her door before I see a man come to her door before I can.

"Scarlet, are you okay? You didn't answer my text."

I knew him, the blonde hair and big build, Travis.

"Hey Travis, I am okay, Miles and I needed to talk about basketball stuff. Logan knew I would be home late." Scarlet looked over at me and smiled, I smirked back and snapped my eyes to Travis, but he didn't seem pleased.

"Here let me help," he grabbed her hand to help her out and she flinched again, pulling herself away.

"Do not touch her!" I demanded, pushing past Travis and looking at Scarlet, "Are you okay, Ember, here," I put out my hand, letting her take a second before she took it, getting out of the car.

"Scarlet, I'm sorry, I didn't mean." Travis tried to plead.

"No, not right now, go home Travis, I've got this." I snapped. His mouth opened slightly with shock, but his look changed as he went home. I walked her inside to the kitchen and made her tea. "Here, have some, it's good for panic attacks." I have herbal tea in my car from my mum.

"Thank you," she sipped the tea, and I heard footsteps coming down the stairs, it was another man.

"Hey, Scar, are you okay?" He said, walking over and I shot up out of my chair.

"Hey, it's okay, this is Logan, my brother." She put her hand on my chest and I melted, sitting back down. "Yeah I'm okay, just had a rough night, but look." She showed him her necklace and his face lit up at the sight of it.

"It's mum's necklace! How did you get it?" He says, walking over and sitting on the other side of the Scarlet.

"I had it, I bumped into her at the airport in Australia and I held onto it just in case I found the girl it belonged to and well, here we are." I held my hand out across the table, "I'm Miles, I go to Hudson, I am the men's basketball captain." I say, as Logan shakes my hand.

"Logan. Thank you for bringing her home and for having the necklace, it means a lot."

I look at my phone and realise the time.

"Of course. Well, I am going to go home. I'll see you at training tomorrow, Ember." I get up from the table and walk out the door. As I get back to my car I hear footsteps coming up to me.

"What was that?" Travis shouted as he walked over to my car.

"She had a rough night and you made it worse by going to grab her, she obviously had some issues in the past and you weren't thinking. I won't apologise for helping her, now I am going home. If you want to talk to her, do it tomorrow. She needs the night man." I get in my car and wait for him to step out of the way so I can leave. He's lucky I waited for him to move because I could really hit him with my car after the stunt he pulled.

I get home and see Dad in his study, working like always. "Hey Dad, wanted to check that you still wanted to go to the shooting range tomorrow night?" We go every Monday night, after mum passed away we wanted to protect ourselves. It was an accident but we didn't think it was and we realised that we didn't have much besides strength.

"Hey son, yeah, is eight still okay? I have a late meeting tomorrow."

"Sure, well I have to go to bed for school tomorrow. Night Dad."

"Night son, close the door please." I shut the doors and go for a shower and make my way to bed. Thinking of Scarlet's panic attack and then Travis scaring her makes my blood boil, well now I can't fucking sleep.

CHAPTER 9 – SCARLET

I can't believe that I found the man from the airport and he held onto my necklace, god this is insane. Once in a lifetime thing, right?

I was so exhausted this morning, with the long week for classes and training plus the fight with Logan and Davis, and last night with Miles and Travis.

I wanted to go for a run, but I was so tired so I opted to sit on the steps at the front of my house and just have some fresh air before my first ever game day in New York with my new team.

"Hey, Scar, how are you this morning? You were a bit upset last night?" Travis walked over with a smile on his face.

"On your morning walk, Travis?" I asked, raising an eyebrow,

"Ha, yeah I was, but I was waiting for you, wanted to check in after what happened last night." He said, taking a seat next to me on the stairs,

"I'm okay, Miles and I were talking about sensitive stuff and he was the man I ran into at the airport in Australia. He still had my necklace so I was a bit emotional." I grabbed the necklace and showed Travis, "It's the one mum gave me before she died." I whispered.

"I'm sorry for asking, I'm glad you got it back though." He said, bumping my shoulder. "I wanted to ask you about Miles, he seemed a bit protective of you last night, are you two together or what? You know he dates your captain right?" Travis's tone cut me like a knife, I could not believe this man right now!

"First of all, Sam and Miles aren't together anymore and by the sound of it, they aren't getting back together ever again. Second, I had a panic attack last night. I flinched and broke down when he went to reach for my hair to push it out of my face. It reminded me of Davis the other night, and the same when you shoved your hand in my face." I spat, what does he think he is doing? Who does he think he is, my boyfriend?

"I'm sorry, I just," He hesitates, "Miles is dark, okay. He had a dark past, did he tell you about his mum?" I shook my head, not looking at him. "He barely told Sam about it and they have been together since high school and friends since being in diapers. I just don't want you to get hurt." Travis says, grabbing my hand, "I care about you, Scar, I just want to make sure you stay safe."

Travis's my friend, him and Lauren are my closest friends right now, my best friends. Of course, he just wanted to keep me safe, "I'm sorry too, it wasn't fair to blow up at you like that." I whispered, "I am also really nervous about today." I squirm, thinking about what Travis said about Miles and his mum. What happened?

"Oh, yeah, your first game is today. Don't be nervous, you are amazing from what I hear from Lauren. You will be great." He got up and held his hand out gently as he helped me up from my spot.

"Thank you, yeah, I am sure we will be fine, just haven't played against anyone in a while. Want to come in for coffee while I cook everyone breakfast, text Lauren she can come too when she's ready." I open the door and we walk to the kitchen and I notice a note on the bench.

Scarlet,

I want to apologise for my actions and all the trauma I have caused you and your siblings. I love you all, but I will not come near you guys ever again. I know I have the restraining order that protects you all but I wanted to say that I won't come near you guys or interfere with your lives again. I will pay you guys weekly allowances so you can be comfortable but other than that, I will not contact you in any way. I am sorry and I love you all.

Davis

My blood runs cold and I stare at the letter, how did he get this in here? What does he mean that he won't contact us? The order was to keep distance unless we granted it but he isn't ever coming around again.

"Hey, what does it say?" Travis grabbed the paper from my hands as I sat down. I have to tell Logan and Mel that their dad will never come back and never wants to see them again. "Holy shit, can he do this?" Travis exclaimed, rereading the note to make sure he read it right.

"He can and he did, what am I going to tell the others, this day is already stressful enough but with this." I cover my face, trying to breath before I freak out.

"Hey, I can help you cook breakfast and we can tell them together if you want, I can help." Travis puts the paper down and goes to the fridge, grabbing breakfast ingredients out. I take my hands off my face and get up to help him, trying to breathe through the feelings.

"Good morning, Scar, coffee ready? Oh, hey, Travis," Logan looks around, "Is Lauren here?" He asked, his voice going quiet.

"No not yet," I giggled and Logan went back upstairs, Travis looked at me with a confused look, "Logan likes your sister, I think he is going to ask her out today." I say as I grab out the food and start cooking.

"Oh, I see it. That makes so much sense now." He laughed as we continued on with breakfast and Logan and Mel walked down together, both dressed for the day and Lauren came through the door.

"Morning everyone, are we ready for our first game today?" She came in, already dressed for the game today.

"Aren't you just energetic this morning?" I asked, grabbing her a coffee and a plate.

"Are you not excited for today?" she asked, looking confused as her eyebrows almost shot through the roof.

"No, of course I am excited, just really fucking nervous for today, and with Sam staring at me like she could kill me with just looking at me, it doesn't help." I take a sip of coffee, still don't understand why she is looking at me like that.

"Yeah well, I don't know what her problem is but for now, we will focus on the game and do a good job, now finish your coffee and go get dressed." Lauren demanded and I finished my coffee and went upstairs to change.

When we walked through the court doors, Sam and Annie were already at the bench and the other team we were playing against were over on the other side of the courts.

"Morning guys, these are my siblings, Logan and Melaine. Guys this is Sam, my captain and Annie the vice-captain, well was." I say and they all shake each other's hands. Sam has the fakest smile on her face as she crosses her arms over her chest.

"Nice to meet you guys," Annie says, looking at Sam and nudging her with her elbow,

"Mmm, nice to meet you," Sam seethed, barely getting the words out through her teeth.

We walk over to the bench and Logan and Lauren sit together for a moment and then I see a big smile on her face when I hear someone clear their throat from behind me.

"Hey, Ember, just wanted to check in from last night." I turn and see his gorgeous blue eyes beaming at me with a small smirk on his face.

"Hey Miles, yeah I am okay now, thank you for everything last night." I grab his arm and squeeze it, "It meant a lot." I stare into his eyes and his smirk turns into a cute smile,

"Of course, if you need anything, I am here, Ember, always." He whispers and looks up to see Travis, "Morning Travis. Logan nice to see you again man," Miles goes over to Logan and Logan introduces Mel to him and they all sit together and start chatting.

"You need to be careful with him, Scar, please just promise me you won't get close, he just broke up with Sam too." Travis begged and I looked over to where Sam is and she looked pissed, well that's one reason to be mad at me.

"I will be fine, Travis. Thanks for the concern." I smiled at him and walked over to the group. Tegan and May have both arrived while I was talking to everyone. "Morning are we ready for today," I ask all the girls.

"We are ready, now let's talk about strategy." Annie shouted and we huddled, going over the other team and the strengths and weaknesses of each member. "Now for our team, Lauren, you are fast and agile, you will be our runner, getting the ball from one end to the other. Tegan and May, we need you to defend, you guys are tall and have great defence. Sam and Scarlet, you will be our shooters, Scar can do our three pointers and Sam is our best player for layup and closer shots." She demands, pointing at each of us as she speaks to us. "If Lauren needs help, Scarlet can come up from the shooter's end and May can come up from the defender's end. If they catch on, rotate who goes up but communicate to each other. Got it?" We all agree and we make our way to the courts. As we position ourselves, I can feel Sam's gaze staring at the back of my head. For fuck's sake!

The game starts and our strategies are working, communications are great and at half time we are twenty-nine to nineteen to us.

"Okay, you are all doing so well, there are a few mistakes going, what are they?" Annie askes, looking at everyone.

"Our communication is good but there are some that we can work on, especially our shooters." May said, looking at Sam and I.

"Yeah I noticed too, what's the issue? Sam, you can't shoot three pointers and Scar, can you need to pass the ball to her or go for the layup? You do not have anything to prove, we have to win our games to get to the qualifiers so no messing around." Annie said looking at Sam, she scoffs and turns away.

"Okay, everyone else, you are doing great, keep an eye on them, the other team is getting a bit sloppy so be careful." She said, pushing us back onto the courts.

The game starts again and we are doing so well, getting shots after shots in. Sam and I are doing great work until a girl comes to defend me. I spot Sam open on the other side of the circle, I pass the ball to Sam and she looks like she's going to catch it but then she side steps it, pretending to miss the pass and the ball goes out.

"Time out!" Annie shouts and the whistle blows as we all come in. "Sam, what in the actual fuck are you doing, do I need to put Jamie in your place because I will do it?" Annie shouts as Jamie gets up and starts stretching.

"No, I am fine, I just missed the pass." Sam rolled her eyes and crossed her arms over her chest.

"This isn't funny Sam, they are catching up to us on the score now, thirty-two to twenty-eight, and that is cutting it too close for our first game." Annie yells, Sam rolls her eyes again and looks at me with daggers, once again. For fuck's sake man, I can't take it anymore!

"Do you have an issue with me, because I have none with you, plus I want to win this game and every other game so if we could get along that would be amazing."

I sassed as I too crossed my arms across my chest and she snapped her gaze to me and I saw Laurens mouth open, gasping at what I said.

"My issues with you, you want to know why I have issues with you." Sam gets in my face and panic rises so fast through me that I cover my face, dropping to the ground. I start sobbing and everyone steps back as everything goes into a blur.

"Scar, Scarlet are you okay? Hey, it's Logan, are you okay! Can you hear me?" He grabs my arm, the thoughts of Davis raising his hand to me bounce in my view. My heart rate spikes and all I can see is stars, "Scarlet, please calm down." He said giving me a hug and circles my back with his hand and my vision slowly returns.

I take a few deep breaths in rhythm with his hand on my back and look up. Everyone's staring at me in shock and confusion. "I'm okay," I whisper and Logan helps me up as I take a deep breath. "I am good." I stand up and stare at Sam, who doesn't even look sorry. "Next time Sam, chill out!" I demand as I wipe my face from the tears.

"Are you okay, Scarlet, I can put Jamie in if you can't go on?" Annie asked, grabbing my hand.

"No, I'm good, a little panic attack isn't going to take me off the court." I say, walking back over to the court and the game starts again. I take shot after shot, even with Sam staring at me like she is plotting my death right now, the score becomes forty-three to forty-four to the other team and now we have 10 seconds on the clock and Lauren passes me the ball,

nine seconds… I grab the ball,

eight seconds… I dribble it to the line,

seven seconds… I take my place on the line,

six seconds… a girl comes to defend me,

five seconds… I take a breath,

four seconds… I concentrate on the hoop,

three seconds… I fake a jump and the defender jumps

up,

two seconds... as she comes down from the jump, I jump and the ball leaves my hands,

one second... the ball hits the rim and then the backboard,

The buzzer starts for the end of the game and the ball falls in the hoop making the score forty-six to forty-four.

"Yes," Annie shouts from the sidelines and everyone starts clapping and running over to me hugging and jumping around me. I did it, we won! We split and we shook hands with the other team, Sam just walked off, not something a captain should do but whatever. I went to grab my water and I noticed Miles holding it as he walked over to me.

"Congratulations, Ember, I believe you got the winning shot." Miles says handing me my water, I take the top off and take a sip.

"Yeah I guess I did." I smile and hand the bottle back to him, "So, I see you over by my family, what are you all talking about?" I ask, a smirk stretches over my lips.

"Oh, nothing much really, just you, Ember," he teases, with that big grin, and a mischievous look in his eyes.

"Oh really, hopefully all good things, but I need to go over and celebrate with my team, so I will be back." I whisper and walk back over to my team and everyone claps at me as I walk up to Annie.

"Well done, you got the winning shot, Scarlet. You should be very proud of yourself, you also scored the most points on the team tonight." She clapped and everyone else followed her lead.

"Thank you, we all played so well today and I am glad to be on such an amazing team." I say as Lauren pulls me into a hug and everyone starts cheering.

About fifteen minutes later, we are all packing up and getting ready to leave when I see Miles standing by the chairs, looking at me.

"Hey you, I just wanted to thank you again for last night and for this back." I grabbed the necklace on my neck.

"It's all good, but are you okay, Ember. Was it because of Sam?" He asked, stepping closer.

"It was, she got in my face and it set off a trigger I guess, she wasn't the reason for it, just the way she walked up to me is all." I whisper, god I wish I could curl up into a ball and die right now.

"I'm going to talk to her, I notice the way she looks at you and it isn't okay. She is your captain, whatever the issue is she needs to get over it and grow up." He stated, reaching me and looking down at me, "I will let you know what is happening but I am talking to her no matter what you say, Ember." He whispered, running his knuckles over my cheek and my cheeks instantly went red.

"Scar, are you coming?" Travis shouts and I hear his hurried steps come over to me, "Miles," Travis states. "Are you okay, Scar?" He asks, standing close to my side.

"Yeah I am okay, let's go," I turn back to look at Miles, "Thank you, you have my number," I smile and walk off with Travis. God, I hope she tells him what the issue is because I am over her shit.

CHAPTER 10 – MILES

I waited around, practicing my three pointers with the tips that Scarlet gave me and watched her leave with her family. I waved her goodbye and she smiled as she walked out with everyone. I would've gone with her, but I need to talk to Sam, first about that pass and then the way she was in Scarlet's face. If it were anyone else I wouldn't care, but she did it to her!

"Hey babe, you wanted to talk to me?" Sam walked over placing her bag on the ground, coming in for a hug.

"First, don't call me babe, it's been over a week now since we broke up. Second, what was that?"

"I apologised to you, now you're supposed to forgive me and we hug and make up, also what was what?" She crossed her arms across her chest, I know what this means, she is going to play pretend and ask for me back. Not happening.

"You apologised and I forgave you, but I told you we were done, we have been since before I did it. We haven't loved each other romantically for ages now." I seethed, Christ this is going to be so hard. "And I'm talking about the game, the pass that you "missed" or the way you got in Scarlet's face, you don't do that to anyone else, so what was that?" I demanded, slamming the basketball down, the ball bouncing away from us.

"I still love and want you, you may not love me, but you're still mine." She whispered, her face going red.

"Is this what that was all about, because I spoke to Scarlet. I am spending time with other girls and you are mad that it's not you, Christ Sam." I drop my hands and start to walk away,

"You like her don't you! That's why you broke up with me to 'explore' with her right? She is the reason you broke up with me!" She shouted, stomping over to me and grabbing my arm, "You are mine and once I tell my dad, we both know your dad will tell you to get back with me. Our wedding has already been planned out and our futures, you can't think you control your future," she seethed, yanking my arm back towards her.

"I broke up with you because you're crazy Sam!" I shouted, pulling my arm back. "We have spent some time together and she's cute, but I didn't break up with you to be with her, you're the issue, not her. Also, I am a grown ass man, I control my own future, my father has no control over me now. He only wants me to be happy and you don't make me happy!" I demanded, grabbing my jacket and I walked over to the door, "Also, while we are on the topic of Scarlet, do not touch her! If I find out that you have hurt her or said anything that makes her upset, I will release your dirty secret. Don't think I won't." I go to push the door open as Sam starts sobbing.

"Don't shout at me, I don't know what you're talking about, you have nothing on me." She shouted as she stomped towards me.

"Oh, I think I do. I know about what you did at the end of last season. When you and your family went away right after Annie's leg broke. I know what you did, plus I'm sure Annie won't like to hear that your family was the reason why her leg broke during qualifiers last year." I said as I walked towards her, "I will say this once and once only, touch her and I will destroy everything you love." I whisper as I walk away from her and I see Scarlet and her family outside the gym. I take a breath, "Hey, Scar, you guys okay?" I ask as I walk over to her.

"Hey Miles, no not really. Logan's car won't start, so we have no way home. Travis and Lauren are already gone and they aren't answering their phones." She said looking at her phone.

"I can give you all a lift if you want?" I say looking over Logan's car. "It looks like you might have an oil leak, I can call a tow car and get it to my mechanic, they will fix it by the end of the day, free of charge." I grab the hood and close it.

"Really, are you sure I don't want to cause any issues, I can pay," Logan hesitates.

"No really, it's okay. So, would you like a lift? I have a game later so I will be here when they pick it up."

"Yes please, thank you." Scarlet smiles and I lead them to my car and take them home. "Hey, do you think I could come back with you and watch your game? I can pay for the extra fuel, I just want to change so I don't smell." Scarlet askes, her cheeks going pink. She doesn't smell, not to me anyway, her caramel scent is strong on my nose.

"Of course, you can shower if you want, not that I think you stink but my game isn't until two and it's only eleven thirty right now." I say as I turn the car off, stepping out and grabbing her door.

"Really, thank you, please come in and I will get Logan to make you something to drink or eat if you want." She grabs my hand and leads me inside. Her hand's small in mine but her touch is so soft, god I can imagine her touch on my skin, on my abs and down my, oh for fuck's sake now I'm hard and I'm about to be in front of her brother.

"I just need to grab my phone out of the car, I have to make a call to the mechanic and then I will come in." I say, trying to cover the fact that I am so bricked up right now that you can see it through my basketball shorts.

"Okay, I will tell Logan you're coming in. I will be in the shower but I won't be long." She goes inside and I sit in the car for a minute and make the call, that works to bring that excitement down then I head inside to the kitchen where Logan is having coffee. "Sup Logan, can I have a cup?"

"Hey bro, yeah of course, help yourself." He gestures to the cups and coffee jug. "I need to chat with you about something." Logan said, his voice lowering, sounding serious.

"Of course, what's up man?" I take a seat at the kitchen bar bench and take a sip of my coffee, fuck that's good.

"Do you like my sister?" He says, raising one of his dark eyebrows up, staring me down.

I almost spit my coffee out across the kitchen as I stare at Logan. "Ah, well, I guess so, why do you ask?" I cough down the coffee.

"Scarlet has had a rough life, I don't want her to have more issues then she has had already. She has seen a lot for a twenty-year-old and she needs a break." He said, his protective look not fading from his eyes at all. "She has had Travis around since we moved here and I believe he likes her too, she doesn't need two men fighting over her. If she wants you, it's up to her, but I like you. Travis, he is very, what's the word, possessive, assertive, overprotective. But he has helped us out through some of our drama, so he knows things you don't." Logan stares at me with determination, trying to figure out who I am. "What do you think of Travis, because what I have heard of you isn't too crash hot, Miles." He demanded, sitting down next to me, not losing eye contact.

"Well, Travis is a protective person of things he thinks are his. So, no surprise that it's happening with Scarlet, if he has helped her through some things then he will automatically think he is her knight in shiny armour, but he is obsessive, be careful. Other than that, though he is a nice guy, a good friend but with girls, that's a whole other story." I say, sipping on more coffee.

"Okay, well from what I hear Miles, you're quite the character. Besides that, you and Scar's captain have been dating for years, I hear you broke up with her last week, why?" Logan asks, still staring at me, damn this kid is good, he's really trying.

"She and I have known each other for years, dated for some but she is obsessive too, but not in a good way. I noticed the pass she 'missed' from Scarlet today. She's mad that I broke up with her and I was talking to your sister, and the way she got in her face, I am sorry about that, it's my fault it happened." I do feel really bad that she has to put up with Sam's shit because of me.

"Sam is a grown woman, not your fault man. But you said Travis's obsessive, he says the same about you. How are you different from the crazy obsessive type like you think he is?"

"Travis makes promises and threats he can't keep, if I make them I follow through." I am not about to lie to him, I know who his dad is and I know that Logan is great with computers, if he wants something he will find it.

"Hmm, straight to the point, I respect that. So, you won't hurt her?" He nodded upstairs, probably where Scarlet is.

"No, I won't, and if someone does, they won't have a chance to even try in the first place, but if they do, I will handle it." I seethe, not towards Logan but the thought of someone hurting her breaks something inside me that I didn't know I had.

"Well then, you passed the test, but I would get in before Travis does. I'm dating Lauren now and she said that Travis is planning on asking her out." He said with a grin on his face.

"Well, congrats on that, but I have Sam to deal with first, if he asks her out before I can then he can have a go, but it won't last. If he does anything to her, I'll know." I put the cup on the sink as I hear Scarlet coming down the stairs.

"Okay, I am ready. Are you two okay?" She asked, a confused look across her face.

"Yeah, just talking about how Lauren and I are dating now." Logan says, trying not to be obvious about our topics.

"Oh my god, congratulations bro, I am so happy for you, it's about time. You have been after her since we moved." She hugged Logan and pinched his cheek, "Okay, well are you ready to go?" She turns her gaze to me, letting go of his cheek.

"Yeah, let's go," I laugh and we walk out of the house and drive back to the courts. "So, why do you want to watch my game?" I am curious about what she says, hopefully it's to watch me and not anyone else.

"I want to see if your team has used my hints for the three pointers and see what you and your team need improvement on." She grabs out her notebook and goes over what she told me,

"Ahh, you want to scope us out, Ember, I get it, a bunch of hot guys, sweating it out on the court, who could resist," I tease as I get out of the car, going to get her door and help her out.

"Umm, no. I could go without the smell of sweaty men running in a gym, thanks. But scoping you all out, yeah maybe that's it." She giggled, her face going red as she slightly hid her face.

We make our way to the courts and I see Sam over with my vice-captain, Callum. "Hey, give me a sec?" I asked as I sat my bag next to her, she nodded and I walked over to them, "Hey Cal, what's happening, you ready for today?" I grab his hand and bring him in.

"Hey bro, yep boys are warmed up ready to go, Sam was just telling me about their game and how the new girl missed a pass and how she dropped to the floor after Sam just walked up to her, sounds like she isn't as good as Annie thought." He said, looking at Sam and I am about to explode, I look over at Sam and she looks guilty as hell.

"Mmm, from what I saw, Sam missed the pass and then got in her face, making her panic and she dropped to the floor. Did she also mention that the new girl got almost double the amount of points Sam did and got the winning point to get them first place." I seethed, I cannot believe she is going this low, but then again, it's Sam.

"I, ah, was getting to that part." Sam whispered and excused herself as she walked out of the courts.

"What was that?" Cal asked, "I thought she was your girlfriend dude?"

"We broke up over a week ago and now she is targeting their new member because I spoke to her. If you know anyone who would want to date Sam, please send them to her because for the love of god, she needs to move on asap." I say, walking onto the court to warm up with the group. After we are warmed up we have a few minutes to grab a drink before we start,

"Hey, was that Sam here before talking to your VC?" Scarlet asked, handing me my water,

"Yeah it was, she was talking about your game to him," I say, "Don't worry, I shut it down." I take a sip and hand it back to her, "Hey, let me make you a bet, if we win the game, I can take you on a date, if I lose you can pick whatever my punishment is?" I ask, giving her a charming grin,

"Mmm we will see, oh Travis is calling me. Good luck and I will be back in once I am done talking to him." She kissed my cheek and ran out to answer the call. My face goes bright red, her lips are so soft and her perfume instantly has turned me on, fuck, man.

"Miles, come on, we are huddling then the game is starting," Cal calls over and I sit down, trying to cover my boner.

"Uhh yeah, huddle without me for a sec I'll be there in a few." I wave him off and hide my boner before getting up and walking over to the group. I wonder what Travis wanted, but I need to focus otherwise I will think of her soft lips and, well for fuck's sake, how is this possible. I need to chill out, because this is so fucking wrong, now I'm too late.

I make it to the court without a boner this time and the game starts. I have shot three, three-point shots and got them all in as well as a few other guys testing the new skills out and getting the ball in. Wow, she's something else, these guys haven't been able to get constant three pointers in and now we are on fucking fire. I notice Scarlet walk back in all flushed and I immediately get pissed, Travis, that fucker got in before me and I knew he fucking would.

Half time hits and we are twenty-nine to nineteen to us and I go over to grab my water. "Hey, Ember, was Travis okay?" I ask, taking my water and having a few mouthfuls.

"Yeah, he ahh, asked me on a date, I told him I wasn't sure and I will let him know. By the look of it my answer is probably going to be no with how the score is looking." She smiles shyly pointing at the score, and her cheeks blush.

"Mmm yeah I guess so, well I have to say, your advice has worked well, Ember. The boys have never shot so many threes in their careers and their accuracy is insane." I am so impressed with my team but with her too.

"Thanks, but you still have another half yet, we will see how they go, their arms might be fucking sore right about now, I know mine usually are." She laughs and looks at her phone, her face slightly dropped.

"You okay?" I notice her face drop a little and then she smiles again, as she looks at me.

"Yeah, Travis just replied but it's okay, looks like

your team wants you." She pointed over to the group and Cal is calling me over with his hand,

"If he is threatening you," I pause, I cannot believe him, I will kill him, I swear.

"No, no not like that, go I will explain later," she hurried me off and I run over to Cal and the team huddle, going over our second half strategies and she was right everyone's fucking sore, but we can push through it. We got back on the court and pushed hard to the end. By the end of the game, we were fifty-nine to thirty-seven, we won. We all cheer and shake the other team's hand before huddling up and talking about what was wrong and right. I excuse myself and go over to Scarlet.

"I believe you are the reason we won that game, come let me introduce you to the team, plus they can thank you for the tips and not act like barbarians." I say grabbing her hand as she giggles and we walk over to the team, "Okay, guys, this is Scarlet the new vice-captain of the women's team. She is also the reason why you idiots can shoot three pointers now, so make sure you thank her too for the win, she is the reason." All the boys cheer and gather around her and she is so happy, talking to everyone and giving them tips if they ask. God, she is so beautiful in her element, her gorgeous red hair pinned up in a high ponytail with strands around her beautiful face. I notice one of the boys, Brenndon getting a little close for comfort, a goofy smile spreads across his face.

"Brenndon, come here!" I demanded and he looked like a sad puppy as he made his way over to me, "What are you doing? Do you know what personal space is?" I asked, he knew I would rain all of hell on him if he fucked up.

"I do, but she smells so good, I got carried away, sorry Miles." He pleaded, he isn't wrong. Her perfume has to be magical.

"Just keep your distance dude, it's creepy," he nods

and goes back with the rest of the team.

After about twenty minutes we all pack up and we wait for Logan's car to be picked up. "So, what happened with Travis? Did you want to go out with him?" I asked, hoping she wouldn't.

"I told him that I would let him know by the end of the day, you won your game but with Sam, I don't know if I can go there with you yet. She is my captain, she can get rid of me so fast." She looked down at the grass,

"She won't do that, if she did she's an idiot. You score the most points on any team you're on and the skills you have, you're a natural. Plus, I love Sam, not like a girlfriend but as a friend and have for a while." I see her face gleam with happiness. "But, if you aren't ready for me yet, I can wait and I will talk to Sam, she doesn't control me. I am always here though even if you do date Travis, always, Ember." I say as I grab her hand and kiss the back of it.

"Why do you say that, always?" She asks, she is a curious little thing isn't she.

"I don't know, after I first met you I just started saying it, I never had anyone to really lean on and you're the first person I feel like I can be myself with, so I want to remind you that I will always be around no matter what and after you left at the airport, I said to myself that I would always remember you, even if I didn't see you again." I admit, she is good at breaking my iron walls down but I won't hide anything from her.

"Mmm I like that, well I'm here for you too." She smiles up at me, "I think I will go on a date with Travis, only to see what he's like, but if Sam won't go psycho I would like to see what you're about too." She gets up and grabs my hand,

"That sounds like a plan, like I said I will wait for you."

"Always," Scarlet whispered.

CHAPTER 11 – SCARLET

I swear, why is it so hard for girls to get ready for dates? Guys just have to chuck on a shirt, wear some cologne and walk out the door and nine times out of ten, they look amazing. Oh, but girls have to do the whole thing. I have showered, scrubbed, shaved, scrubbed again and then washed my hair. After a shower, I put lotion and oil on my skin, then did my skin care, blow dried my hair and applied my makeup. Then I have to decide what the hell I'm wearing because we are going to a fancy restaurant in town and I am not a big going out person. I have my entire wardrobe on the floor, covered with dresses and jeans, trying to figure out what fancy but casual is, that's what Travis said the restaurant dress code is. I decided on a deep red maxi dress with half sheer sleeves, black boots and a red and black handbag. I put on my necklace and some nice earrings as I hear a knock on the door. Logan answers it and I hear them mumbling to each other as I come down the stairs.

"Wow," Travis whispered, his mouth hitting the floor and Logan gave me a big smile and a nod as he walked to the living room where Lauren is waiting for their movie date. "Scar, you look," Travis paused, he looked a bit lost for words.

"I look, what?" I whisper as I make it down the stairs, trying not to roll an ankle in these boots.

"You look beautiful, amazing, stunning, gorgeous, there isn't any word that can fully describe how pretty you look right now." Travis grabbed my hand and kissed the back, "You ready to go?" He asked as he grabbed my hand to lead me down to the car and opened my door.

"Yeah, let's go, I'm excited." I say, stepping into the car as he closes my door and walks around to his side and drives us to the restaurant.

The restaurant was in the middle of New York, it was very busy as well which has me on edge already.

"Hey, are you okay?" Travis asked as he squeezed my hand, reassuring me that he was here.

"Yeah, just very crowded." I give Travis a nervous smile and we walk over to our table. "This place is beautiful though." The lights are a dim yellow colour, making the atmosphere calming and romantic, the tables have red tablecloths over them with roses and candles on the tables, again romantic.

"Yeah, it was hard getting a table here on short notice, but my dad got it for us." Travis pulled my chair out and pushed me in and then sat across from me. "The food here is great too, small but it's still delicious." Travis seems very happy, not nervous at all, unlike me who is extremely nervous.

"So, you're a senior at Hudson and your sister plays basketball, but you seem to know Miles well, did you play basketball?" I have been curious on how Miles and Travis seem to hate each other so much, not that it's really noticeable but with what they have said about each other, something happened.

"In freshman year we both tried out for the team and got in, we became close friends by the end of the season but at the start of sophomore year the spot for vice-captain came up and we both wanted it. Miles and I had to compete over the spot and he cheated, told me if I didn't let him win that he would pull dirt up on my dad and destroy me." Travis closed his fists and his knuckles started going white. "So, I let him win and left the team, I didn't want to put my family in danger or myself so I left all that behind and changed classes so I didn't have to be near him. Then Lauren started on the women's team and I tried to warn her but basketball's her dream so I have gone to her games just to make sure she's safe." Travis's hands start to relax and he reaches for my hand, "I know that you have to talk to him a bit because of the vice-captain spot but you need to be careful with him. He lost his mum in an accident but they always suspected that it wasn't actually an accident. He has been trying to find out if it was for years, he has so much control over things with the connections he has and still hasn't found the reason. I just don't want you to get hurt." He gives me a weak smile and pulls his hand away,

"Hey," I reach for his hand, "Thank you, I appreciate the warning, I asked so it's not your fault, but I'm a grown woman, I can handle myself," I say, winking at him.

"Oh, I bet you can," he sipped on the wine and we ordered our food. We talked about all different things from his family to what he wants to do in the future. As we are talking about what he wants in five years, I realise that Travis talks a lot about himself and wants a girl who will stay home with kids, very old fashioned and traditional. "You're quiet, are you okay?" He asks, raising his eyebrows in confusion.

"Yeah, I'm okay. Just very crowded in here is all," I say as I hear yelling from next to us, a man is arguing with the woman that sits at his table. My heart starts to race at the sound of screaming and arguing as Travis goes to get up, "hey, no, do not get involved, please," I begged Travis to sit back down but he gets up and walks to the table.

"Hey ma'am, is everything okay?" Travis asked the young lady at the table, she doesn't say anything but looks at the man she is with.

"She's fine, this is none of your business, man." The man stands up and steps closer to Travis, "Leave us alone."

"You shouldn't be yelling at her, it's not very gentleman like," Travis says, not moving when the man is in his face.

"Yeah, well I never said I was a gentleman." The man shouts as he raises his hand to hit Travis. My body reacts instantly as I get up to help but I stand as Travis throws him by his arm and the man lands on me. I fall onto the table and then on the ground with glass everywhere, the fully grown man landing on top of me. All the wind knocked out of me as he rolled off and ran out of the restaurant.

"Scar, holy shit! Scarlet, are you okay?" Travis runs to me and grabs my head. I don't answer him, I can't move, my body's frozen as I start panicking more, waves of panic rush through my body and I can't breathe. Flashbacks of Davis run through my head when he hurts mum, Logan or I. I can hear Travis trying to say something but I can't make out what he is saying through the memories that are playing through.

Half an hour later, I am in a hospital bed and I have a cut on my arm from the glass that shattered when the man landed on me. Travis has been apologising since before we got to the hospital and I have told him that it was fine but he didn't believe me, Jesus I didn't believe me either.

"Oh my god, Scar are you okay?" Logan rushed over and grabbed my hand seeing the bandage on my arm, "Did he do this to you, I swear I will." His face went red with rage.

"No, it was an accident. A man was yelling at a woman and Travis stepped in and the man went to hit Travis when he acted on reflexes and threw the man but he threw him in my direction. The man landed on me. I just have a few bruises and this small cut, that's it." I say, trying to calm him down before he rips Travis's throat out. Mel comes around the corner and a wave of relief hits her as I give her a smile.

"You're okay?" She whispered.

"Yeah Mel, I'm okay, just a small cut and a panic attack." I gestured to her to come to me and the three of us hugged for a while before we let go. "They said I can leave once the doctor comes and signs off on the wound care." They both nod as we sit and wait for the doctor.

Logan drives us home where Travis and Lauren are both sitting on our steps.

"I can tell him to leave if you want?" Logan seethes as he parks in our driveway.

"No, it's okay." We get out of the car and Lauren walks over and hugs me tightly.

"I am so glad you're okay, I am sorry for Travis, he sometimes doesn't think before he does shit and he does feel really bad if that helps?" She says, pulling me in for another hug and walks off with Logan and Mel before Travis comes up to me.

"Before you speak I need to say something," I say, putting my hand out in front of me so he can't step any closer. He steps back and drops his head. "What happened isn't entirely your fault, but you didn't need to get involved with them. If you had just sat there and not worried about them or even called the police if you wanted too." Tears of anger flowed down my face, "that would have been fine, I understand why you did it but I got hurt on your watch." I wipe my face as a tear falls from my eye, "that's not okay, I have had enough complicated shit happen in my lifetime and I don't need more. Tonight, I realised that all night you talked about you and what you wanted and never asked me about my life and what I wanted. So, for now I just want to be friends, we are close and I love having you around and love having you as a friend to turn to but I don't think romantically we would work out and I can't lose our friendship." My voice broke and the tears fell freely onto my cheeks.

"Hey, don't cry," Travis steps closer and wipes my face with his thumbs, cupping my face in his hands. "I'm so sorry for tonight and I will beg for your forgiveness forever if I have to, but I understand about not wanting to date, I wish you felt the same way as I do but I understand. I will be the best of best friends ever, okay?" He wiped the final of my tears and kissed my forehead. "If you ever need anything I am here for you."

A few weeks go by and I have already had two exams and my arm's all cleared for my basketball game today even though I had to sit out for most of the training while it healed, but I can boss people around still and it turns out I am really good at that. I haven't seen or heard from Miles since the accident. I sent him a text to ask if he was busy and he looked at it but never replied.

Logan, Mel and I drive over to the courts for the game today and when we walk in to the courts most of my team is already warming up but the other team isn't here yet but the game doesn't start for an hour so they have plenty of time yet. "Morning girls, how are we doing today, ready for the game?" I ask as I walk over, Sam isn't here yet either, which is a little weird.

"Hey, Scar, we are good, how are you? How is your arm today?" Annie asks as she sits down in a chair next to the sidelines.

"It's good, all clear for today which is good. Where is Sam, she's never late?" I walk over to Annie and sit my bag down next to her while I change my shoes.

"Her and Miles are chatting outside, they were in here but Sam started screaming so they went outside, she wants to get back together but he won't budge." Annie rolled her eyes and rubbed the bridge of her nose.

"Why is she still trying if he won't budge? Can he not date anyone else?" I asked, obviously I am curious but I don't want to get on Sam's bad side, she needs to relax a bit before I can even think about making a move on Miles. But after what happened with Travis, I want to talk to Miles. I'm sure he knows what happened because it seems Sam loves to bring me up in her arguments.

I lose my train of thought as I hear the doors slam open and I can hear Sam shouting in the distance, I look up at the sound and I see Miles, and he looks pissed.

"Scarlet, we need to talk! You, Sam and I, right now." He comes over to me and waits for me to get up and I follow them outside, Logan gets up out of his chair and I nod to him to sit down as we go outside.

"What the fuck Miles, why do you need her out here," Sam shouted, pointing at me.

"Because I am sick of you and all this drama, Sam. Look we broke up and if I want to date Scarlet, I will, if she wants but it's not up to you anymore. Scarlet, I wanted you here to witness me saying this because it's going overboard." Miles looks over at me and then looks back at Sam, "We are done, go inside, I spoke to Annie she knows everything, she will be there for you like always, but you need help." Miles turns away from Sam and she starts sobbing and turns to run back into the courts.

"Sam told me what happened with Travis that weekend. I'm so sorry I didn't answer your message. Sam stole my phone and deleted your messages from my phone. I would have been there right away otherwise." He steps closer to me and takes my hand in his and drops to his knees. "Please forgive me, Ember."

This man is on his knees, begging for my forgiveness? What the fuck, is Miles begging me, literally on his knees begging for my forgiveness.

"Ah Miles, please get up," I grab his hands and help

him up, "I forgive you, it's not your fault, it's her fault. Not that I think she will be begging for forgiveness." I tease, "and yes I would like to date you, but until stuff blows over with Sam, I can't, and the stuff that happened with Travis, I am fine, just some bruises and a small cut, which has been cleared for today. I can explain more over lunch, before your game maybe?" I say, pulling Miles in closer to me but far enough that our lips aren't touching.

"Oh, I would love to talk over lunch. Come on, your opponent team is here now. You need to get warmed up." He leans in, close to my ear. I can feel his breath on my neck and I shiver, "I will be watching you today though, if anything happens, I will be there, Ember," he whispers, brushing his lip over my ear lobe and my cheeks go as bright red as my hair is.

"O-Okay, let's go." I stutter and walk over to the door. As we walk in I can see Sam death staring at us and Annie is trying to comfort her but it doesn't seem to be helping at all.

"Don't worry. I am here, always, Ember," Miles winks at me and walks over to Logan and Mel as I walk over to the team and start warming up.

"Okay team, huddle up." Annie shouts and we come in, huddling around Annie. "Scarlet, you run huddle today," she gestures to the team and hobbles over to Sam, who looks like she is about to explode.

"Ah, okay, well let's talk about strategy for today. We can't use last week's strat because this team is different from them, we'll all need to run, defend, and shoot if we have the opportunity. But the main point will be watching their feet and hands, they're dirty, they will do anything to get the ball. So please be careful." I say as Annie and Sam walk back over. Sam seems calmer, which is great, "Alright team, let's do this." Sam says as we walk on the court and the match begins.

Our team's doing good today, our defence has been alright, they have got some really good shots in and our offense is good, I have got most of my shots in but Sam has missed all of her shots, she obviously isn't in the game headspace today.

As an opponent came up to shoot from the three-point line, she jumped for the shot but fell forward straight on top of me and the whistle blew to stop. I can't breathe, the girl rolls off of me and she instantly turns to apologise and check on me. My head is pounding and as she grabs my arms to help me up, pain rushes through my body and I scream. The sound echoing through the gym as I start bawling my eyes out.

"Are you okay, what is it, where does it hurt?" The referee asks, trying to find the source of my pain.

"Everyone backs up, give her some space, teams go to your coaches and wait." A male voice in the distance demands and then I can smell vanilla and wood cologne. "Hey, where does it hurt, Ember?" Miles whispers, looking over me for obvious injuries.

"My arm, ouch, fuck," I seethed as the ref grabs my right arm to look it over, and Miles grabs the ref's arm and stares at him like he is about to rip his arm off.

"Let her go!" Miles seethed and the ref let my arm down slowly and I heard Logan in the background calling an ambulance. "You're going to be okay, I am going to grab a sling and put your arm in it okay, Ember?" Miles asked and I nod, gritting my teeth together. Miles comes back and puts his arm up, "I am going to cover your mouth with my hand while I do this so you don't blow everyone's eardrums okay?" He whispers and I nod again as he puts his hand gently over my mouth, god he smells so good right now. I tried to focus on his smell while Miles grabbed my arm gently but fast and I screamed, trying to release the pain. "It's okay, it's okay, Ember, I'm done, the ambulance will be here any second. Can you stand?" I shake my head, no fucking way am I going to stand with this much pain running through my body. Miles looks at me, checking for any more injuries and looks back at me, his eyes filled with rage and what looks like worry. I haven't looked at the damage but I know it isn't pretty.

CHAPTER 12 – MILES

I cannot believe Sam did that, that she would scope so low to get payback on Scarlet. The girl that landed on her was like six foot and was definitely big enough to do damage and now Scarlet's arm's either out of place or broken. I am hoping for the first option, if it's broken, she will be out for the season.

Scarlet starts to cry as they lift her onto the bed to take her to the ambulance, "Hey, it will be okay, I will bring Logan and Mel to the hospital soon, I just have to sort something first. They'll follow you out, Ember," I whisper to her as they take her out, "Logan, Mel, follow her out and wait by my car, I'll take you guys to the hospital." Logan nods as he grabs Mel, who's sobbing and takes her out, following the bed Scarlet's in. I snapped around to see Annie with Sam, trying to get answers out of her and Sam didn't look sad or sorry, but happy, a small smirk on her lips.

"What the fuck did you do?" I march over to Sam and Annie and Travis comes out of nowhere and stands in between the girls and me. "Get out of the way Travis, this has nothing to do with you." I seethed, the words clashing against my teeth, if she did this on purpose!

"No, you need to back away from her," he demands,

stepping closer to me with his arms crossed over his chest. He's just taller than me but I know that I'm stronger than him, and faster.

"You need to step back and let me talk to Sam, this has nothing to do with you." I try to walk past him but he stands in the way again and I close my fist. "Move Travis or did you forget what I said to you in sophomore year." I whisper to him, seeing if he remembers that I can destroy him and his family with one phone call.

"That won't be necessary, Travis, it's okay." Sam says, walking up to Travis and kissing his cheek. "What do you want?" She demands.

"How could you do that to her, she's your best player and she's done nothing to you? What the fuck's your problem?" I stepped closer to her and Travis steps another step to me, Sam throws her hand up at Travis and he steps back, grabbing her hand, "and what the fuck is going on between you two, don't say your dating?" I step back, she was literally shouting at me before the game about liking Scarlet and now she is with the guy who she friend zoned years ago and he wanted Scarlet, they literally just went out!

"No, we aren't but it may be a possibility down the line, we are just talking right now, but that with Scarlet, I tripped and bumped the girl while she was jumping it was a simple accident." She said, walking up to me with a devilish grin on her face, "She got what she deserved, she took you from me and she's taking my place on the team, scoring the most points, running games and training smoothly." She whispers in my ear, "I'm the best, and you'll come back to me, one way or another." She goes to kiss my cheek but I step back and she falls on her hands and knees, I slowly bend down, pretending to help her up,

"If you lay a finger on her again, I'll come after you." I help her up and turn to leave the gym. Logan, Mel and I all go to the hospital and find Scarlet's room. When we walk in the doctor is in there giving an update,

"Are you family?" He turns and Logan nods, grabbing Mel in close and I walk over to Scarlet's bed. "Okay, well it looks like a mild sprained shoulder, a few week of no physical activity should heal it up, so long as you rest and don't use that arm for anything, your family will help you I'm sure?" He turns to look at all of us and we nod.

"I am so happy you're okay, how are you feeling?" Mel steps over and grabs Scarlet for a hug.

"I am okay, I feel okay now that it's wrapped, just need to be careful this week, it means I'll miss a few games," she whispers, her eyes starting to go glassy.

"Hey, one game will not hurt even if they lose without you, your scores will leave your team at the top for qualifiers." Logan says as he sits on the bed, "We'll help you, whatever you need." Scarlet nods and a tear falls from her bright green eye, wiping it away she turns to me with a weak smile,

"Can Miles and I have a sec please?" Scarlet looks to Logan and Mel, "I could really use some real food, the food here looks inedible," she points over to the tray of who knows what and Logan and Mel let out a laugh.

"Here, take my car," I throw my keys to Logan and he nods as they both walk out together. "Are you sure you're okay, Ember?" I ask Scarlet after I know they are far enough away.

"Yeah, I'm just really upset that I can't play for the next few weekends. What happened? I remember jumping to defend and the girl fell straight onto me." She looks at her arm that's slinged and wrapped to secure her shoulder, "Was it Sam?" She whispered, I grabbed her other hand and kissed it.

"As you and the girl jumped, Sam 'tripped' and landed on her, making her fall straight onto you. She's claiming it was an accident, but I know it wasn't. You need to be careful with her from now on, I am so sorry, it is my fault." Scarlet cups the side of my face and I look into her emerald eyes,

"It's okay, it's not your fault she's psycho," she puts her hand over my chest, "obviously, she isn't changing about wanting you back so I need to know, do you still love her?" She asked and her eyes fill with tears again.

"She was my first love, but at the moment. No, I don't love her. I won't go back to her and I told her that. The attitude she has isn't something I want to be around." I grab her hand on my chest and hook her fingers through mine, while my other hand reaches for her face and I wipe her tears, dragging my thumb down her bottom lip, "I like you, Ember, she won't change that, but with what happened you aren't safe with me, I can't put you in danger," she follows my gaze as I look away and I see Travis at the door, trying to peek through the little glass panel. "What does he want?" I growled and she squeezed my hand.

"It's okay, let him in." She waves him in and lets go of my hand. "Hey Travis," she grins and I can tell that her smile is fake. The way her eyes strain and the way she looks at him is different.

"Hey, Scar, are you okay? Sam feels awful about what happened, is anything broken?" He scans her over for injuries and sits on the other side of her.

"Just a sprained shoulder, the doc has given me a week off of sports and any sort of movement with my arm so Logan and Mel will be my servants for the week." She giggled and he smiled at her, his eyes going soft as she looked at him.

"I am glad you're okay, god I can't believe it happened, Sam wanted to come and apologise but she knew you were here." Travis snapped his eyes at me quickly before slowly looking back at Scarlet. "She thought flowers would be a nice apology gift, asked me to bring them," he pulls a bouquet of flowers out and sits them on her bedside bench.

"Wow, thank you. They're beautiful, I'll thank her when I see her on Monday, just because I can't train doesn't mean I can't run the sessions." She said as she leant over to smell them and Travis looked over at me with the same devilish smile that Sam had at the courts and winked at me. I wanted to jump on this bed and strangle him but I just stared back. I will fuck him up if he hurts her again.

"Well, I should go but I am right next door. If you need anything just send me a text, okay?" He stands up and Scarlet nods as he walks out of the room and turns to me.

"Sam is really sorry about all of this, maybe you should talk to her?"

"I have nothing to say to her," I don't pull my gaze from Scarlet as he turns and walks out of the room. "When did the doc say you can leave?"

"He is waiting for the final scan to come back to make sure there wasn't any extra damage and then we can go." She grabs my hand again, "Can I ask you a favour?" she whispers and I come closer to her, sitting on the edge of the bed and lean in so my face is barely touching the skin on her neck,

"Of course, Ember, anything." I whisper into her ear, putting my mouth close to her neck so my breath hits it when I speak.

"Can you come stay at my house, help Logan and Mel out with me, plus you can come to my training sessions with me, look out for Sam for me?" She shivers and tries not to lean her neck into my face.

"Of course, I'll stay with you for as long as you want, Ember, always." I drag my lips over her neck and she stutters, her breathing shakes and as she goes to say something Logan and Mel come back with food and I pull my face away from her sweet skin.

"What do we have here?" Logan says, trying not to laugh, Mel on the other hand giggles her way into the room and puts the food on the table.

"Nothing, please tell me you have a burger there for me," Scarlet's face is as red as her hair and she gets up from the bed,

"No, I will grab it for you, remember no physical movement, sit," I demand and she turns to look at me, sitting back in bed and huffing at me as I grabbed her food and handed it to her.

We get back to their place and Logan and Mel start on dinner as I take Scarlet up to her room, this house has so many stairs, for fuck's sake, lucky it wasn't her leg that was hurt. Not that I wouldn't mind carrying her up the stairs.

"I am going to change and come downstairs for dinner, you can drop your bags in my room. We haven't cleaned Davis's room out, Mel doesn't want to touch it yet," I nod, opening her door for her and dropping my bags inside the door then closing it behind her. Scarlet had got Logan to set a mattress on the ground in her room so I had somewhere to sleep.

I wait for her to come out and I hear a crash, I open the door and I find Scarlet on the bed, crying with her shirt half on. "Are you okay?" I walk over to her and she starts flipping out, trying to pull her shirt down with one arm.

"I can't even get a shirt on, I feel useless!" She cries, her shirt covers her bra but I can see red lace on the bottom.

"I can help, Ember, here," I help her up and grab the shirt, "do you have any button up shirts, they are easier to put on with arm injuries?" I ask and she nods, looking over at the dresser.

"The second drawer, right hand side, I have PJ button up shirts in there." She wipes her tears and I grab one out and help her put it on,

"You're not useless, just need a little help is all," I kneel down to button the shirt and my fingers graze her stomach and her core tightens and her breath is shaky again. I can smell her perfume and I can feel my dick harden in my jeans, pushing against the zip. "You okay, did I hurt you?" I ask and she shakes her head as I finish the buttons and I immediately stand behind her, trying to hide the bulge in my pants, "After you then, Ember," I gesture to the door and we walk down the stairs and we all sit for dinner.

After dinner I help Scarlet to the living room and Mel brings in popcorn as she helps Scarlet pick a movie and I notice Logan waiting in the kitchen and he nods to me.

I walk over to him and he nods to the chair, "I need to talk to you, now!" He demands and I sit in the chair at the table,

"Sure, what's wrong?" I ask as I get comfortable, I'm pretty sure I know what this is about.

"What happened today wasn't okay and I have a feeling it has to do with you," he walks over to the table next to me, "I can't let your drama affect her future, Miles, I like you, more than I like Travis. He has always had something off with him but I still can't put my finger on it, so I need to know, will my sister be okay with you around?" He sits down, staring at me.

"I will always protect her, today was because of me, but I will sort this out no matter what, but Travis and his family have a history, but his sister has nothing to do with that, she's sweet and caring so don't let her go because she's perfect for you." Lauren has never had anything to do with Travis and his family's shady background from what my intel tells me, Logan should keep her around if he wants.

"Good, because I do like Lauren, she wants to move in together soon and I want to do that but I didn't know if Scarlet would be safe. If I wanted to move out with Lauren, Mel would come with me because Lauren wants to move to Manhattan, it's closer to Mel's school and her gallery job." He says looking down at the table, "I don't want to leave Scar on her own with everything that's happened. Has she told you about our dad or the reason for her panic attacks yet?" He asks, looking at me full of worry.

"No, she hasn't, but I'm sure she will when the time's right, I like her a lot and I don't want to push anything unless she's ready." I stand from the table and push the chair in, "So, does this mean I have your blessing to date your sister when she is ready?" I ask Logan, putting out my hand to shake his.

"Yeah bro, you have had my blessing for a while, I didn't think Travis was the one for her." He gets up and shakes my hand, "Now, we need more snacks because if Mel and Scar are picking the movie, we will need something to make the time go by," he laughs and we grab more snacks and make our way to the living room.

CHAPTER 13 – SCARLET

The next few weeks are all similar, I would wake up seeing Miles on my floor, wishing he was in bed with me instead, go to school with Miles, have a full day of classes, go to training, run the training while Sam and Annie sat on the sidelines talking, while Miles and his team were at the other end training. I could see him looking over at me, checking in to make sure I was okay and then we would go home together.

"You know I'm okay right, you don't have to take me to and from school or be there at training or stay over if it bothers you." I say as I look out the window, Miles has done so much for me these past few weeks and I don't know how to pay him back for all his help.

"It's fine, you need the extra help, we go to the same school and train at the same time so it would make sense. Plus, you can't drive until you see the doctor on Monday so it saves time for Logan and you." He says, taking his gaze from the road and looks at me, grabbing my chin with his fingers, "You're not a burden to me, Ember, and if I can help, I will."

"Thank you, you have been doing a lot so I was worried that I may be using you," I sigh and he drops his hand to my leg and grazes his fingers on my thighs.

Holy shit.

Miles glides his fingers up and down the inner part of my thigh and my core clenched, my breath starts to shake and I grip the door until my knuckles go white.

"You okay, Ember?" Miles asks as he stops the motion of his fingers, I snap my gaze to his face and he's looking at the road while having an enticing smirk.

"Yep, fine," I snap my gaze away and turn to look out the window and his hand doesn't move again.

"I need to talk to you about something before we get to your house. Logan's planning on moving out with Lauren but he's worried about leaving you. He said that they are looking in Manhattan and that if they do move there that Mel would go with them being closer to her job and school. He wants to make sure you're okay on your own." I lower my eyes to the door, it's the next move for them, they're so cute together and they deserve their space plus it would be amazing for Melaine, being so close to school and work. I want to feel happy for them but then I'm alone, all my life I've looked after others and had people that love me around but for the first time ever, I would be alone.

"I'll talk to him when we are home, he deserves to be happy and it would be great for Mel." My voice stutters a little and my eyes start to sting.

"Ember," Miles' hand raises to the side of my neck and I turn to look at him, "What is it?"

I hesitate, "I'd be alone, for the first time ever. I have always been the one to look after everyone else and I am always surrounded by my family but if they leave I'd be on my own. I know that's so selfish," tears fall from my eyes and Miles pulls over the car and unclips our seatbelts and pulls me into him.

"It isn't selfish, you can have these feelings. It's new to you and from what I can gather you have had it rough, Ember," he tightens his grip and lets me go, staring into my eyes, "if you want, I can come stay with you. Then you won't be alone, plus I can hang out with you more often." He gives me a kind grin and kisses my forehead,

"Okay," I sniffle, "Let me talk to him first, see what's happening and then we can figure it out."

"Let's all sit down and talk about it, okay, Ember? That way everyone's there and we can all talk about what's happening." He lets me go and puts my seat belt back on for me and we start driving again.

When we get home, Logan is outside with Lauren, they wave and smile as I get out of the car, "It's okay, I know what's happening so let's get Melaine and all have dinner and talk about this, Miles came up with a plan." I look over to him as he grabs our training bags and then helps me get up the stairs into the kitchen. I sit down while he goes up the stairs to drop our bags off.

"So, Miles spoke to you then," Logan asks as he sits with Lauren and Mel grabs our plates and sits them in front of each place.

"Yeah he did, I hope he didn't overstep."

"Nope, I asked him to. I was worried how you would react, so what do you think about us moving?" Logan says as he grabs Laurens hand and squeezes it.

"I think it's a fantastic idea, you two deserve the world and it would be perfect for Mel with school and work being so close. I did get upset at first I have to admit," I hesitate and then Miles comes into the kitchen and sits beside me. I take a deep breath to calm myself.

"I got upset because for the first time ever, I'll be alone. I've always had to look after you two or Davis, even mum when she got sick, but now I'll be alone and I don't know how to do that." A tear falls from my eye and the words vanish into thin air. I feel Miles' hand on my leg under the table and his finger moving up and down with my breathing, I turn to look at him and he gives me a worried look and I shake my head.

"I suggested that I permanently move in, with

everything that has happened and with Travis next door
I proposed to stay here with her. Just as a friend, with
the spare rooms we can sleep in separate rooms and I
can have an actual bed but we go to the same school
and we train at the same time so it would be easy to
move into a routine." He looks at me as I take some
deep breaths and his fingers still match my breathing. I
concentrate on his movements rather than the thoughts
in my head.

"Well, I think that's a great idea, at least I won't have
to worry about you then. We would visit every Friday
night for family dinner and stay over to come watch
your games like always, nothing changes there okay?"
Logan grabs my hand and I nod, thank god.

"Sounds like a plan, now let's eat because this smells
so good and I'm sure Mel put in a ton of effort." Mel
smiles and we chat while eating dinner. They have
already found their dream apartment but wanted me to
be okay with everything first before they put in their
offer.

"Oh, Miles, what did you mean with Travis next
door? What's wrong with Travis, I thought you two
were friends?" Laruen questions, looking over to me,
confused.

"We are, I think, but we have a suspension that he
now likes Sam and well we know what Sam is like." I
roll my eyes and Miles nods,

"Well, let's hope nothing bad happens then, I was
hoping that if you two dated that he would calm down
but if he's in with Sam. I'm just glad you're living here
now Miles," Lauren says and Miles gives her a small
smile.

Today's the final game I had to sit out of. I get up at
five thirty in the morning like every day and slowly get
dressed to go for a walk. As I walk out of my bedroom,
buttoning up my shirt when I run into a wall. Nope,
walls don't smell like vanilla, Miles.

"Good morning, Ember, where are you off to this early in the morning?" He tilts his head and the ends of his lips flick up.

"Usually, I go for a run in the mornings but my arm has been too painful to do that and this morning there's no pain, so I'm going for a walk instead." I struggle with the top buttons and Miles' hands touch mine as he finishes the buttons off for me, "I can do it, you know." I sigh and roll my eyes.

"I know. I'll come with you for this walk, Lauren said Travis usually is up at this time too and you two run into each other all the time." His face changes from being happy and a little tired to angry and alert.

"I want to talk to him, alone. You can sit on the steps, I'll only go to the end of the street and come back okay?" I step back and we walk down the stairs together,

"Okay, Ember but if he does anything I'll hurt him," his hands are in fists and I can feel the anger radiating off of him.

"I wouldn't expect anything less, you know, it feels like you're my bodyguard more than my friend."

"Well, I would rather be your bodyguard than your friend," he teases. I sit down on the stairs while he grabs my shoes and helps me put them on.

"Mmm I'm sure you would," I whisper, he opens the door for me and sits on the stairs while I make my way down the street. As I'm coming back, low and behold, Travis is standing out the front of his house, watching me.

"Morning Travis, about to go for a run?" I ask, looking over at Miles who is no longer sitting but standing, waiting for Travis to do something stupid.

"No, I was waiting for you actually. How are you feeling? I know you had to miss out on games, are you still going in today?" He asks, coming to my side and looking down at me.

"Yeah I am, I'm doing really good today, no pain so

101

I'm hoping on Monday that the sling can come off and I can play next weekend, we're getting close to the qualifiers and I need to play." I stop in my tracks as I notice something in Travis's hand, "What's that?" I ask, trying to see what's in his hand.

"It's a note, Sam asked me to give it to," He says as he hands me the note, his face looks curious almost. Doesn't he know what's in the letter?

"She knows I will be seeing her today, right?" I open the note and my mouth drops to the floor as I read the note.

Take my boyfriend and I will take your best friend away.

Did she just threaten me in a note? What is this bitch's problem, god!

"She asked me out yesterday and I said yes, I hope neither of you two mind," Travis says and I can hear Miles's footsteps coming closer,

"Nope, she's all yours man. Please take her out, she needs it," Miles says with a friendly yet evil grin and looks down at me, "You okay, Ember?" He asks, looking at the paper. I hand him the note with raised eyebrows and he scoffs, handing me back the paper.

"It's fine, if you like her you should go out with her, I want you to be happy Travis. If she can do that for you then I'm happy for you." I smile and Travis smiles back at me, walking towards my house,

"I heard Lauren and Logan are moving out, is Mel staying?" Travis questions as he lifts an eyebrow at me,

"Yeah she is going with them, it's closer to work and school for her so it's a smart choice." I sigh, knowing they are leaving in a week still makes me sad but they'll visit for our family nights and my games so nothing really changes.

"That's good, so you will be home alone now?" Travis says, I notice a weird undertone to his voice but I don't pay much attention to it.

"No, I am moving in with her next week, it's closer to

school and the courts so it was another smart choice." Miles says, his tone drops and Travis trips a little before gaining his feet again.

"Well, I'm going home, if you need anything text me okay?" I smile at Travis and he turns back to his house, Miles and I walk home.

"Did you notice the undertone in his voice when he asked if I would be home alone?" I ask Miles, seeing if I was going crazy or just nervous being on my own, well almost.

"Yeah I noticed it too. He is definitely up to something and that note was weird, I don't know how she can take him away from you, if I could take him away from you, I would have done it." Miles's voice is dark, he really hates Travis.

"Sam is seeing me today so I don't understand. If they are going on a date, that means that Sam isn't your problem anymore right?" I look up at Miles and he turns to me with a grin on his face, realising what I'm hinting at.

"I guess not, Ember. Is this you asking me on a date?" He teases, grabbing my hands in his and pulling me closer.

"No, if you want to go on a date, you can ask me. I am your Ember after all," I whisper as I roll my eyes playfully, letting his hands go. I start walking back to the house and Miles is a bit stunned, he stands in his spot for a few seconds before I turn around, "You coming, bodyguard?" I shout, getting his attention. He smiles and jogs his way back to my side and we go inside the house to cook breakfast for everyone before we have to go to the courts.

When we get to the gym, I pause at the doors. All thoughts of the last game comes back to me and I can't move. I hear Miles tell Logan and Mel to go inside and put himself in front of me.

"Hey, Ember, are you okay?" Miles tilts his head and I look him in the eyes and shake my head. I can't say anything, I can feel the panic raising through my body.

"Hey, it's okay. Nothing will happen to you. Want me to come sit next to you and Annie today?" He cups my cheek with one of his hands and the other grabs my hand and squeezes it, I nod at him, not able to say anything.

"Okay, but first you need to breathe, Ember. Come on, breathe in." He pauses and takes a deep breath in, "And breathe out," he pauses again and lets out the breath. We do that for a little bit until I can move,

"Thank you, I didn't think I would freak out today." We walk in the doors and see the opponent team already warming up and my team is huddled together, "You're coming with me right?" I stop and turn to Miles.

"Yes, Ember, anything you need." He kisses the back of my hand and leads me over to the team.

"Scar, how are you feeling?" Annie gets up and pulls me in for a hug.

"Hey, I'm good, no pain today so I'm hoping to be back in training on Tuesday after I see the doctor Monday afternoon. Oh, I won't be here to run training Monday either."

"That's okay, Sam can do it," she smiles at me and turns back to the team, "okay team, because Scarlet can't play today, Jamie will be in today. Scar, want to coach today? Be good practice." Annie asks and gives me a sweet smile. She knew what I was studying and some experience would be amazing!

"Oh my god, yes, thank you," I smile at her and turn to the team, "okay, are we warmed up?" I shout, everyone nods back, "Good, the team today's really good, last year you guys lost to them but we are stronger this year. Now what's the plan for the day today?" We all chatted for fifteen minutes about the plan and what the team is like and set up the strategy for today's game. The buzzer goes off and the teams walk onto the court and the ball's released.

At half time the score is fifteen to twenty-two to the opponent team. "Okay, bring it in." I shout and Miles and Annie grab the bottles for the team to have some water, "What's going on out there, you guys aren't communicating. You guys are split, what's the issue?" I ask, looking over at everyone, seeing if anyone will actually come clean about what's going on.

"I'm sorry, Scar, we're trying," Lauren says, trying to catch her breath, "but it's hard to play with someone who hurts their own team member." Everyone turns to Sam and her face goes red. Christ, who would think that the team would split after that?

"It was an accident, she apologised to me. You guys need to get over it. This is the last game I'm out for and if I can forgive her so can you, now cut it out." Sam's eyes widen and there are a lot of rolling eyes and sighs going around. "Now, you know the plan, follow it. We aren't far from the qualifiers, we can't lose now. Back to the court." I wave them off, they drop their bottles and run back to the court.

The second half isn't much better then the first, there are fouls all the time, missed shots and our defence is off. The ending buzzer goes off and the score is twenty-three to thirty to the opponent team. We lost. I can see it in everyone's eyes how devastated they are. We have had such a good season so far and after today's game, it brings us down from the first spot to the third.

As I look over at Sam, she has a grin on her face and when she walks back over she covers it with the same look everyone else has.

"Okay team, bring it in." I say as they grab their water, "Today wasn't a good day, this is what happens when you don't act like a team," I stand up, looking over everyone,

"It's what happens when we don't have you playing, Scar, if you were playing today we would have won. Broken team or not." May says as she takes a sip of water and everyone starts mumbling and agreeing,

Sam's face drops, she knows that she is outnumbered right now.

"Look, even if I was playing today, we're broken. It wouldn't have changed the game that much. We need to build the team back up again. Annie has some ideas for team building for Monday and Tuesday training days. If we want to go to championships this year, we need to be a team." I turn to look at Annie and she nods, "I won't be here Monday, but come Tuesday hopefully I'll be back in business, figure out your shit by then. What happened was an accident, let it go." I know it wasn't and so does everyone else, but we have to put it behind us for this to work. "Alright, let's go home." Everyone claps and goes to grab their bags and walk out,

"Good speech. Can I talk to you?" Sam walks over to me and I look over at Annie and Miles and they nod.

"Ah, sure." We walk over to the side, away from earshot.

"I want to apologise for last week, it wasn't an accident and I think you know that." Sam pauses, taking a step closer to me "but Miles is mine, always will be. So, I'll say this once, leave him alone otherwise I'll ruin you and everything you have," she whispers, as she steps back I can see her famous devilish grin on her face, she thinks she won, we will see about that.

"Well, thank you for the apology for last week, you've been forgiven for it. But Miles is his own person," I pause and put on a devilish smirk of my own, "if he wants to date me, I won't say no. You can try and ruin me, but I won't have to do anything, Miles will." I step back and turn to walk away,

"He won't stay for you, I was his first love. That never fades." She shouts back at me and I see Annie's and Miles's heads whip to our direction.

"We'll see about that." I continue to walk away and I go up to Annie and Miles

"Do I need to go talk to her or does he?" Annie asks,

grabbing her crutches.

"Probably you, if Miles goes over there it won't be pretty." Annie nods and makes her way over to Sam.

"So, she threatened you again, twice in one day. That's a new record for her." Miles laughs and takes my hand.

"Yeah she did, but I have my bodyguard now so she'll have to get through him first before she can get to me." I laughed and he smiled back at me, his eyes a little wary and unsure as he took my hands gently.

"You know. I was going to wait a while longer hoping all this will blow over but I don't think I can." He murmurs, taking in a breath. He tucks the loose strands of my auburn hair behind my ear, his warm hands leaving an imprint on my skin. "Scarlet Bowen," He steps in closer until our faces are inches apart, his breath warms my face and I can feel my cheeks heating. "Do you want to go on a date with me?" he whispers looking at my lips, his bottom lip is pulled in under his teeth and his eyes are staring deep into mine, seeing if he can search for any answer.

"Miles Grove, are you nervous?" I tease and I take a small step closer, we are so closer that if one of us sways our lips will touch.

"Of course not, Ember, but an answer would be nice," he whimpers and he moves his hand slowly to the back of neck,

"Yes Miles." Before I can say another word Miles leans in slowly and our lips are touching, soft and uncertain at first like he wants to make sure it's okay. I lean into the kiss, making it deeper, my hands search for his chest and the world goes blank like it's only us two in the whole world, folded up into the quiet sensation of all the feelings finally being able to surface.

"Erhm," Logan clears his throat and we pull away from each other, Miles's cheeks are flushed and he turns slowly to face Logan.

"Mhmm, well. I think we should get home," Miles smiles at me and takes my hand.

As we walk out I turn to see if Sam saw us, I don't need her planning my murder just because we kissed, but she was gone, thank god.

Once we are home Logan and Mel go up to their rooms, obviously to give us some space and we go to the living room.

"So, about the kiss," Miles mumbles, sitting down with popcorn and a blanket.

My heart begins to break, "Was it not good?" I whisper, not being able to look at him.

"No, NO! Ember, nothing like that." He brings me in for a hug and brushes my hair with his hand, "I just wanted to make sure that you wanted it. I loved it by the way, if that helps." He laughed and I sit up to look at him.

"Miles, I've been waiting for you to kiss me for a while now," I admitted and I hear a knock on the door.

"I will get it and once I come back we will be discussing what you just said, in great detail," Miles teases as he gets up and opens the door, "oh hey Lauren," Miles pauses and I feel the air go cold, "and Travis," I rush up out of the chair and race to the front door.

"Travis, what are you doing here?" I ask, "oh, Lauren come in, Logan's upstairs in his room packing if you want to help?" She nods and pushes past Miles and I while Travis stays at the door.

"I wanted to come over and let you know that Sam had to reschedule our date. She's upset because she said she saw you two kiss, is it true?" Travis questions, he snaps his eyes to mine and I can feel the anger in his eyes.

"Yes, it is. Not that it's any of your business, you and Sam are going on a date at some point so you two are moving on, the same as we are." Miles states, moving his body in front of mine. "Now, if you will excuse us, we are watching a movie." Miles steps forward to the door and Travis just stands there in silence. I can tell he is angry about what's happening, that he can't have me to himself, just like Miles had said.

"After everything I've done for you this is how you repay me! Whatever!" Travis storms off in the dark, Miles closes the door behind him and turns to me.

"Are you okay, Ember?" He breathes, checking my face for signs of panic.

"Yeah I'm fine, but umm," I pause, fuck I am going to have to tell him about Davis now. "We need to talk about some things first," I grab Miles' hand and lead him into the living room to sit down. "I need to tell you about my stepdad, Davis and the reason why I have panic attacks." I whisper, my hands have gone clammy and I can feel the rush of panic raising through my veins.

"Hey, only if you're ready, I'm here for you, Ember, always," he puts his hand on my thigh and I can feel his teasing fingers going up and down my leg again.

"Always," my breath shakes and he stops, he knows when his hand becomes too much, but it helps to concentrate on something else. "Okay, so the panic attacks started when my mum got diagnosed with cancer, long story short, I had to look after everyone because Davis, my stepdad, was away for work all the time and it was a lot of stress with mum's cancer, Logan and Mel being kids and then school." I can feel Miles's sad glare at me as he tries to keep a calm front. "It's okay, it gets worse." I chuffed and Miles raises his cyebrows in surprise.

"It can get worse?" He says, surprised.

"Yeah, so obviously by the accent, we lived in Australia and Davis got a CEO position here so we moved in two weeks, I bumped into you at the airport and then we moved here. After being here for about a week, Davis and Logan get into a fight about who he wanted Mel and him to date and marry to benefit Davis and Travis saved me from being hit by him," Miles straightens and his knuckles go white. "It's okay, Davis's gone. He left a note on the kitchen bench saying he won't ever be in touch again, he will pay for everything still because he promised my mum but other than that we are on our own. That's what Travis was talking about, he's been here for me since we moved here so I guess he's hurt by that." I take a deep breath and shift in my seat. The air has gotten a little awkward, Miles is trying to figure out what to say and I can't look back at him. "I've been through so much more than that and I don't know what else I can handle before I break, that's why I wanted the Sam issue sorted before we date," Miles grabs my hand and shifts closer to me.

"I want you, I know we technically haven't even gone on a date yet, but I am here for you, and no matter what I won't leave you, I promise, Ember." He gently kisses the back of my hand and I look up at him.

"Thank you, now I would count this as our first date, movie date. I don't like going out, not after what happened on the date I went on with Travis," I giggle and Miles stares at me, his eyes slightly filling with rage.

"That wasn't funny, Ember but I'm glad you can joke about it. Now what movie are we watching?" He asked and he pulled the blanket over both of us as we went through to find a movie.

CHAPTER 14 – MILES

Scarlet and I landed on a horror movie because they're her favourite. I can handle horror movies but I wasn't paying attention to the movie as so many things are running through my head. Davis left her to look after everyone, moved them here and then got a restraining order on him, and then said he won't return. Sam threatened Scarlet twice and Travis is being all petty about her being with me. I'll need to do some digging on Travis and Sam, even though I have enough to destroy their families, I don't have much on them on their own. My train of thought was interrupted as Scarlet jumped from her chair because of a pretty good jump scare.

"Holy shit," she whispered, her heart is about to pump out of her chest.

"You okay, Ember," I giggled, trying to hold back my laugh, "We can watch something else."

"No, I am good, it was just a good jump scare," she laughed and paused the movie, "I'm grabbing a drink, want one?" I nod and she walks off to the kitchen and I pull out my phone. I sent a message to my private investigator to do some digging into Travis and Sam. If they want to threaten Scarlet and try to take her from me, I won't stand back and let that happen.

"Here you go," she hands me a glass of water and gets comfortable on the couch, snuggling into my side and unpausing the movie. I can smell her shampoo and conditioner on her hair as I brush the top of her hair with my hand, taking in the smell and I can instantly feel a nudge on my pants under the blanket. I grab a pillow and put it on my lap to try and hide it from her. I can't do this on the first date, that is way too fast and I am letting her set the pace of what she wants.

"You okay?" Scarlet whispers over the movie.

"Yep, just getting comfortable, you okay, Ember?" I tried to avoid the elephant in the room and hope to god that she didn't see it before I covered it.

"Yep," she giggled, fuck! She definitely saw it.

"What's so funny, you know we are watching a horror movie right? People will think you're a little nuts laughing at a horror movie, Ember," she gets up on her arm and sits up, shifting her ass closer to me so she is on my side.

"Oh nothing, I just saw something is all," she turns to look at me, her eyes hungry and seduced. She leans in so her lips graze my earlobe, "You sure you're okay Miles?" She whispers, my body stutters and my cock pulses with the sensation of her lips on my ear.

"Mhmm yep, perfect," I lie as I shift in my spot, trying to realise the tension that's in my pants.

"Mmm see," she drags her hand down my chest and holds it just above my stomach, "I think you're lying," she breathes and I let out a breath, she is playing with me and god she is good at it.

"Do you now?" I tease back, seeing where this goes.

"Yeah I do," her hand continues down my stomach and I can feel her hand lift my shirt as her hand drags under my shirt over my abs, "Want to tell me the truth, Miles," she moans. Oh, she is one hundred percent teasing now, but I don't want to push over the limit,

"What happens if I do," I ask and her lips drag down

my ear and kisses my neck.

"Well," she kisses again while nipping at sensitive spot behind my ear, "you have two options right now, you can either tell me you're okay again," her hand makes its way slowly down stomach, "and I will leave you here like this," her soft touch reaches the buckle of my pants and teases along the waistband, "or you can tell me the truth," her other hand softly grazes my jawline and turns my face to hers and she's inches from me, "So what will the answer be? What are you thinking about Miles?" I hesitate, my breath shakes and her thumb runs over my lips and her gaze is stuck on mine.

"You, Ember," I say softly, "I was thinking about you." Scarlet's breath hitches and the air gets thicker with anticipation. "I don't want to ruin this before it even has a chance to start."

"You won't," she whispers, "unless you stop right now Miles."

I lean in and kiss her gently, testing to make sure she wasn't just teasing, but she wasn't. She grabs my shoulders, deepening our kiss. Her soft lips are in time with mine, working perfectly. She moves herself closer to me and I can feel her lift the blanket, her leg rubs across my lap, stroking my dick, a groan slips past my lips. I can feel a smile on hers as she straddles herself on my lap and gently sits on top for me, crossing her arms behind my head, all without breaking our kiss. I sweep my tongue across her lips, asking for permission as she opens and all I can think about is the way her mouth tastes, salty and sweet. I shift in my chair, trying to get a little more comfortable and a small moan slips past her lips onto mine, making my cock flinches. Scarlet lips break from mine, moving her head back and I shove my head into her neck. Dragging my tongue up her neck until I find the sensitive spot, leaving kisses and nibbles. Her hands find their way back down to my waistband, and she is playing with the buttons on my pants.

"Maybe we should go upstairs?" She whimpers, I nibble her ear and breath down her neck, sending shivers down her spine.

"You know," I mutter in her ear, "You have a full house right? We won't be able to do much with them all here." I continue my way back to her mouth and bite her bottom lip, "For that part, we will have to wait. But I can do plenty while you watch your movie, Ember." I lean forward and crash my lips to hers and open my mouth with hers and glide my tongue through every inch of her mouth. She moans again and I go down to put my hand under her shirt, reaching around her back to wear her bra sits and snap the buckle with a flick of my finger.

"Did you just do that with one hand?" She shouts, her cheeks flushed and her mouth slightly open in shock.

"Yeah, it's not hard," I tease and my hands raise up her stomach and massage her breasts as I lean forward, "now, you better get back to your movie, Ember, you're missing out, this is supposed to be good." I breathe as I pick her off of me and sit her on the couch.

"I don't think I will be watching much of the movie," she mutters as she reaches for the bottom of the blanket and puts it over us as I kneel in front of her, not breaking eye contact once.

"Well, at least if someone comes down they won't suspect anything." I lift her shirt, putting my head underneath as I shove my face in her breasts, taking my warm tongue over the peak of her nipples, nipping and sucking them as I go.

"Miles!" Scarlet moans and I smile.

"You have to be quiet, Ember, they will hear you." I pinch her nipple with my fingers and her head goes flying back, gasping for air. I caress her breast in one hand while I drag my mouth down her stomach and I can feel her shaky breathing as I lower myself, before I touch her pants, she grabs my face.

"I can't be quiet, I am so sorry," I take my head out of her shirt and I can see how sad she is in her eyes.

"Hey, it's okay. We can wait, no need to be sad, Ember." I pull her in and kiss her long and deep, "next time. But for now, we have two options, we can watch movies or we can go upstairs and make out. Up to you," I tease as I move her hair out of her face.

"I feel so bad. Miles, I am sorry," She cries, tears start to fill her eyes.

"Hey, don't worry about it, I'm not leaving just because you can't keep quiet." I cup her face, wiping her tears away, "Not being able to be quiet is hot, don't cry over it, Ember," I can feel my face drop and her eyes grow sadder, "Why are you so sad, did someone do something to you?" I ask, gently taking her hand into mine.

"Just an ex-boyfriend, he wanted me to be quiet and when you said I had to be quiet it just reminded me of it. I'm so sorry, you're nothing like him." She pulls her hands away and pulls her legs up to her chest, burying her head in her knees and starts crying.

"Ember, hey. I didn't know, I am so so sorry, please forgive me." I move closer, pulling her into me and pat the top of her hair.

"I know," she sniffled, "Can we just cuddle and watch like a romance or comedy movie please," her sad little eyes look up at me, begging to change the topic.

"Of course, why don't you go wash your face, maybe have a shower if you want and I will make some more popcorn and grab some snacks, we can watch whatever you want," I whisper, giving her a small smile. She nods and gets up from the couch.

Holy fuck, this poor women has gone through so much already and only being twenty, I wouldn't wish that one anyone.

After about ten minutes, Scarlet comes downstairs in a onesie that looks like a bear with something in her arms. "So, I know I may have scared you a little there and I'm sorry but I have a gift for you," she whispers, kicking her feet on the ground.

"Hey, don't apologise. Your body may have been ready but your mind wasn't, I get it and what's the present," I raise my eyebrows as she hands me a blanket, no, a onesie.

"It's a tiger onesie, it matches mine. I got it yesterday, hoping we would have a movie date at home one day soon. Do you like it?" She shyly asks, her cheeks start to turn pink while she fiddles with her thumbs,

"Are you kidding," I pause and look at her with the biggest smile, "I love it, let me go change, pick a movie and we will have the best movie date ever!" I pull her in gently for a kiss and get up to go change. I hear her giggling as I leave to go get change. She knew my size, it doesn't surprise me because Logan's a pretty similar build and height to me so she would have used him.

"Hello Miles, what the fuck are you wearing!" Logan laughs as we both walk out of our room at the same time,

"Your sister bought it for me for our movie date, how's the packing going?" I lean against the door, acting all cool and tough. I know I look fucking good in this onesie and he will not shit on my parade.

"It's going good, so the date is going good?" He wipes his tears from laughing so hard from his face,

"It is, well it was. Did you know about a shithead boyfriend who had sex with your sister. I know it's a lot of TMI for your sister but you all seem to share everything so I thought I'd ask." I would love to know that dickheads name, even if he is overseas I can fuck his life up so hard for fucking with hers.

"Yeah I do, Dylan Flyer. He was the first guy she had sex with and he was a dick and extremely rude. Also, why are you asking, do not tell me you had sex on our couch." He rolls his eyes and rubs the bridge of his nose in disgust.

"No, we almost did," I laughed, "but she said that she

couldn't be quiet and freaked out, the poor thing's traumatised so I wanted to know who did so I can ruin him as badly as he did with her."

"Well, it would have been him. Also, she isn't ruined, just some twat hurt her. I hope you can hurt him good because I promised her I wouldn't." Logan closes the door behind him and we walk down the hallway together.

"I know she isn't ruined, your sister is perfect to me, but he fucked her up mentally and she has already gone through so much. I just want to help and be there for her." I whisper, already messaging my PI about this cockhead.

"Well then, tiger, you better get to your date before you have to wear that all night long," Logan laughed making his way to the kitchen.

"Hey, I look fucking fabulous right now, I would wear this to school if she asked," I shouted at Logan and turned to the living room where I can hear Scarlet pissing herself laughing. "What, I think I look fucking great, what do you think," I ask her, doing a twirl for her.

"You look amazing, I love it," she pulls herself together and pats the seat next to her. I sit down and we snuggle for hours watching movies.

"Ember? Hey, Scar?" I try to wake her but she won't budge. I know she's breathing so she isn't dead which is great but fuck me she's a heavy sleeper. "Well, guess I'm carrying you to your bed," I whisper as I pick her up and take her upstairs to her bedroom. I put her down gently on her bed and tuck her in and as I bend down for a kiss, she grabs around my neck and pulls me in like I am a teddy she wants to cuddle, "Hey, Ember, I have my own bed on the floor to sleep in." I whisper, climbing over her so she doesn't break my neck. God she has some strength to her. "I will stay here if you want me too," I try to wake her up again but she only groans and rolls over. I guess I'm staying here. I put my arm under her neck and I scoot into her back, putting the other hand on her waist and I fell asleep.

CHAPTER 15 – SCARLET

My head's pounding as I slowly wake up confused, I'm in my bedroom. Last I remember I was on the couch with Miles in our ridiculous onesies and we fell asleep together, but I'm now in my bedroom. Did Miles bring me up here or did he wake me? I open my eyes, looking around to see if I noticed anything and I can feel something warm behind me, hot breath softly touching my neck and I realise there is a hand just under my shirt. Holy shit, Miles is in my bed! His right arm is under my neck and his other is relaxed just under my shirt, his fingers grazing the skin of my stomach and his head is buried in the side of my neck. My thighs tighten and my body shakes as I try to take deep breaths, how did he end up in my bed? I try to move without waking him, gently trying to lift his big hand as he groans and shifts his body closer to mine and holy mother of gods, I can feel his dick on my ass! What should I do? I slowly move again, trying to move myself off of him and his breathing changes and he pulls me in tighter.

"Good morning, Ember, are you feeling okay?" Miles whispers in my ear, his lip brushing my skin.

"Morning, I'm fine, how did we get here?" my voice cracks, why am I so nervous right now?

"You fell asleep on me last night and I tried to wake you but you are a heavy sleeper, Ember. So, I carried you to bed and when I placed you down, you reached for my neck and rolled me into your bed. You basically forced me into your bed, Ember," he paused, pulling himself away from my back slightly, relieving the feeling in the bottom of my stomach, "I can get up if you want, I don't want to make you uncomfortable." He goes to pull his arm out from under me, but I grab it and roll myself over to face him, god he is beautiful in the mornings. His bronzed skin shining in the morning sun, his dark curls messy and his sculpted muscles, how did he become mine?

"No, please. Stay?" I whimpered, trying not to sound nervous. He gave me a sleepy smile and adjusted his arm and pulled me in.

"Of course, Ember, always." He wrapped his muscular arms around me and squeezed, he smells so good even in the mornings, his classic vanilla and wood scent fills my senses and I lift my head to trace the smell to his neck and lick the delicious smelling area.

"Careful, Ember," he moaned, "if you start this I'll finish it," he warned, I pulled my face out of his neck and looked at his eyes, hunger and desire is all I see.

"Mmm, I'm sure you would," I moaned back, teasing the area on his neck with my breath. I roll over and slowly get up, I am wearing a singlet with short bike shorts, definitely not leaving much to the imagination, I turn back to face him and his eyes are tracing every inch of my skin, the hungry look in his eyes never leaving. "You know, we could skip breakfast," I whisper as I crawl back onto the bed.

"No, Ember," Miles smiles and rolls to get up, he is wearing nothing but his boxers and it definitely leaves nothing to my imagination, his massive body on top of mine, his cock poking out the middle of his boxers, "I am starving, plus," he stalks around to the end of the bed and puts both hands at the end of the bed frame, leaning into me, "you'll need your strength for later," he growls, his eyes trace down to my lips and then slowly down to my breasts, they stay there for a moment and then they make their way back to my lips.

"For later, what if I have enough strength right," I pause as I crawl over to him on my hands and knees, his mouth opens slightly, his breath staggers, "Now?" Miles's mouth closes and a devilish smirk takes over his lips.

"Now, Ember, I have warned you once already," his face inches closer to mine, "do I have to warn you again?" his lips touch mine and his teeth draw in my bottom lip and he pulls at it as he moves backwards. A moan slips off my lip and he stands up and puts his shirt on, "Come on, let's go down for breakfast, it's the last one we will have with everyone for a while, I know you don't want to miss it for me, Ember." He puts out his hand, I slide mine into his and he helps me off the bed, "Now go get ready, we'll wait for you." He whispers, kissing me deeply and then leaves me to shower and get ready for today.

I can hear Logan and Miles laughing as I come downstairs while Lauren and Mel are talking to each other at the dining table, "Morning everyone," I say and everyone says it back as I walk up to Logan and Miles.

"Coffee, Ember?" Miles asks, handing me a mug. Logan and Miles cooked this morning which is unusual as Mel or I usually cooks for everyone, not that I'll complain, it gives us a break. We chat about the move and what's in their area.

"So how was your onesie date last night," Logan snarks and I choke on my coffee, did he see us on the couch last night?

"It was good, someone fell asleep during the movie and I had to carry her to bed, who knew she was such a heavy sleeper," Miles laughs and the others follow.

"Hey, I have always been a heavy sleeper, it's why I have multiple alarms. Also how did you know about the onesies?" I look over at Logan with one of my eyebrows raised,

"Oh, I saw Miles coming out of his room in it, had a good laugh about it," Logan tries to hold back his snicker and Miles rolls his eyes at Logan.

"I looked good in that onesie, no one could pull it off better," Miles poses and Mel and Lauren start laughing, Logan shakes his head and I just sit and smile. I have wanted us to be this happy for so long and we are finally here, one big happy family.

"Well, I thought I would let you all know now that my appointment has been moved to this morning for my arm. I told them there wasn't any pain and they wanted me to come in to confirm that I'm all in the clear." I state as I take another sip of coffee,

"That's fantastic, Scar, means that you can go to training strong tomorrow, after their efforts last week, they really need you back," Logan said, everyone mumbles in agreement. I knew this already but the team is broken, with Sam and her issues, it'll be hard for everyone to get on the same page.

"Yeah, it's going to be a lot of work to get everyone in sync again, we have a plan though."

Once we're done with breakfast, Miles takes me over to the doctor's office and they examine my shoulder,

"Well, Scarlet, I would say you're one lucky woman. Your shoulder is all healed and your mobility should be back to normal. I'm clearing you to go back to your physical activities, I know you'll be training until Saturday right?" The doctor asks, I nod in response, "until then, just focus on trying to strengthen it, if it hurts pull back the amount of physical strain and come see us." He hands me all the paperwork and sends us on our way.

"You healed so fast, I wish I could heal that fast." Miles puts his seatbelt on and looks over at me, "How are you feeling?"

"I'm good, Annie and I are planning on team building

today and tomorrow but until Sam gets over herself I don't think we'll ever be the same," I look down at my hands and my panic begins to rise again,

"Hey, what she does and says isn't your fault. If she does anything you let me know, Ember, okay?" Miles grabs my hands and I look up at him, the worry look on his face makes me feel so bad for all the things that are happening, why did I have to fall for him so fast?

"It is my fault, if I didn't fall for you so fast, she may have had a chance, or even just a chance to let everything blow over and move on." My voice shakes and my eyes start to sting, "I don't know what to do anymore," tears hit the back of Miles's hands.

"It's not just your fault, it's mine for not making sure everything was handled properly, but she isn't helping by doing everything she can to threaten and hurt you, Ember." He pulls my face closer to him, "Ember, I know we haven't been dating long. But ever since I ran into you at the airport I knew that you were it for me." his voice hums in my head as his thumb caresses my lip, "I love you, Ember, and she can't change that."

Did he just... did he just confess his love for me?

"What.." I pause, the words still bouncing around in my head, "What did you just say?" I whisper, trying to understand what he just said to me.

"I love you, Ember, only you, always," the words fill my head, my heart begins to ache.

"Miles, I-." I can't speak, the words won't leave my lips.

"You don't have to say it back if you're not ready, but I know what I feel. It takes time for some and I will be here no matter what, I won't leave just because you aren't ready to say the words yet." He pulls me in and gently kisses my forehead, "Are you okay with that?" The worried look begins to grow in his eyes, I nod at him as I pull him into me, I pour all my feelings out into the kiss so he knows that I do love him but I just can't say the words back yet.

"Alright, let's go home, Ember."

Every day this week has been more painful than the last, classes are kicking my ass. Training though, the team building exercises didn't work, the training schedule was all over the place and the girls weren't in sync at all. Every day, Sam tried to say something rude to me but Annie would tell her off and she would go straight back to the court. I think even Annie's over her shit, which doesn't surprise me because she has been there for her for so long and this little game she's playing is getting really old and repetitive.

When I got up this morning it's still dark outside and I didn't want to go for a run or a walk knowing that Travis could be out there waiting for me again. He has also been on my case about Miles which is really starting to piss me off. The house has become empty with Logan and Mel all moved into Manhattan. There's Miles but it's quiet around the big house that we live in. I walk downstairs in nothing but a t-shirt and my panties. Right now, I just need coffee.

As I turn into the kitchen I see a figure in the dark room and I scream. The figure runs at me with swift speed and I turn and run back up the stairs. I can hear the heavy footsteps behind me and I run as fast as I can to my door and slam it behind me, locking it quickly.

"Ember, what the hell is happening. Are you okay?" Miles was already out of bed and right behind me, I turned to him and the tears seared my face as I wrapped my arms around his body.

"There's someone in the house, they were in the kitchen and chased me up the stairs," I could barely finish my sentence before Miles kissed my forehead and moved me to the side.

"Stay here, I will go and check it out. Lock the door behind me and don't come out until I say so." He grabs a gun out of his drawers and I step back, "Ember, please. Did you hear what I said?" His face is straight determination, but his eyes are filled with panic. I give him a nod and kiss him quickly as he unlocks the door and peaks out with his flashlight and gun. When he leaves the room I gently close the door behind him and lock it. Panic rushes through my body and I drop to the floor, pulling my knees to my chest, trying to make myself as small as possible and let the panic ride itself out. Thoughts of Miles being hurt or someone getting to me filled my head and it feels like Miles has been gone forever. There's no sound coming around the door but I do see the lights that Miles turned on under the door as he went through the hallway. It gives me a little hope that he is fine and that the person in the house is gone. I hear a knock on the door and Miles begins to speak.

"You can unlock the door, Ember," I crawled onto my feet and unlocked the door, swinging it open fast. I scan Miles for injuries and his face is filled with fear. I pull him in for a hug and wrap myself around him,

"I was so worried, did you find them? Are you okay, did they hurt you?" The questions came flying out before he even got a chance to say anything.

"I am okay, Ember, I'm fine, just breathe." He pulls me in tight and takes some deep breaths with me to help me calm down. "Now, I need you to come downstairs with me but you cannot panic, okay?" He puts his gun down and cups my face, "I've called the police and the person is tied up in the kitchen. I need you to not panic when you go down there, they aren't hurt but you know them so you need to breathe, show no fear okay, Ember?" He grips my arms gently and wraps them around his stomach, I hug him and breathe in deeply. I let him go and he took my hand as we walked down the stairs.

What. The. Fuck.

I can feel the panic rise in my stomach, how did he get in? Why is he here, in the house? Miles squeezes my hand and I know he can tell I am starting to panic,

I breath in slowly and walk towards him.

"What the fuck are you doing here?" I demand as I walk closer to the chair, I rip the tape off his mouth and he works his jaw, he's covered in bruises, obviously he put up a fight, not a good one considering Miles doesn't so much as have a scratch on him,

"I wanted you, Scarlet. You have been the solution to all my problems, so I came to get you." He snarled, his eyes looking into my soul and the wicked smile across his face made me confused.

"What for, stop playing fucking games," I shout, taking a step closer to him, "What the fuck do you want?"

"I needed you to vanish, Scarlet, my accounts are frozen and because your useless sibling wouldn't marry who I picked, my only option was to go off the grid until the perfect moment."

"Vanish? You mean." I stagger on my feet, he came to kill me. "You want to kill me but you knew that they moved out, how?" I gain my feet and rage runs through my veins, "How, Davis!" I shout again, I lift my hand and slap him across his cheek, leaving a massive red handprint on his skin. He spits out blood from his mouth and begins to laugh.

"And why, oh dear, Scarlet, would I tell you that? I needed you dead so I could get your money your mum left for you when you turn twenty-one, and because today is the day, you have access to it." He growls.

She- she... She left me money, she knew what he was like. "H-how do you have no money, you're the CEO?" My voice shakes and my head feels heavy,

"I was, but they caught me embezzling money and I knew I was going to prison sooner or later, so I went away for a while and now you're twenty-one. That money was going to be mine." He tries to pull himself out of the chair and I trip backwards, Miles runs and catches me before I land on the floor and helps me to my feet, "You! You are the reason why I couldn't get here." He snarled and Miles didn't respond as he checked me over for any injuries and helped me sit down on a chair. "I didn't know you had a roommate, when did this happen?" Davis asks, the wicked smile still across his face.

"That isn't any of your business," Miles growls, standing in front of me to block Davis's view of me, "Police are on their way, you will be going away for a long time."

The police took Davis and said he'll be going to jail for a long time for breaking and entering, attempted murder and embezzlement. I couldn't believe what just happened, my stepdad just tried to kill me after everything we went through. This is what it was all for, the money mum left me.

"Scarlet!" I heard someone shout in the crowd of people around my house. Mel ran out of the crowd and jumped in my arms, "Oh my god, are you okay? Did he hurt you?" She pulled me out of her arms and spun me to check for any injuries that he may have done.

"No, he didn't get to me, Miles saved me." I whispered, Logan and Lauren come out of the crowd and join in the hug,

"What happened?" Logan cries.

"Mum left me money for when I turn twenty-one and because that's today he wanted it for himself," I mutter under my breath, she knew something would happen and I didn't see it coming.

"He tried to kill you!?" Logan said in shock, looking around the crowd.

"Yeah, the police took him and he's going away for a long time," I take a deep breath and see Miles over by an officer who's taking his statement when I see Travis walking over, worry and stress fills his face,

"Scar, what happened?" Travis asks as he makes his way over to me, reaching for a hug and I step back out of his reach.

"Davis broke in and tried to hurt me," I stated, trying

to figure everything out. He said that he didn't know I had a roommate but knew that Logan and Mel were gone, someone told him?

"He what! Are you okay?" Before he could get any closer, Miles came up beside me and pulled me behind him.

"She's fine, you need to go!" Miles demanded, his tone dropping, sounding deep and assertive. Travis stumbles back in shock and his face filled with sadness.

"She is my friend, I can ask if she's okay," he states as he takes a step forward.

"If you take another step closer, I will hurt you." Miles steps closer to Travis and Travis's face is filled with confusion.

"In front of the police, really?" Travis playful says, his mouth rises with the same wicked smile Davis had on his face a few moments ago.

"Miles, come on. Let's go." I grab his hand before anything happens, "Go home Travis, I'm fine." We walk away and Travis stands in his spot for a few moments before turning around and going home.

"Well, what an eventful twenty-first you're having, huh, Scar." Logan says as we walk into the house. I stare at the wall in the kitchen while Mel and Logan cook breakfast for us all. "You okay, Ember?" Miles kneels down beside me, taking my hand in his.

"Can I have some coffee please," I whisper to him, he nods, kissing my hand and goes to get coffee.

"So, let's try to put all that behind us, happy birthday, Scar!" Mel pulls out a present from behind her back and I look up at her with a smile, "just because he tried to ruin it doesn't mean it has to be bad, right?" She returns the smile and I pull her in for a hug, my eyes well with tears.

"You're right, let's make the most of today." I say, the box is huge and I start to pull the wrapping apart, oh my god, "Mel, this is," I pause as I pull open the box and inside was a photo album of all my years from birth to now. "This is so thoughtful, thank you," I whimper as I pull Mel in for another hug, the tears seep out of my eyes.

"All good, Scar, plus this isn't it. It's your twenty first birthday, collectively Logan and I got you twenty-one gifts. So, eat up, you have a big day. Well, it's already been massive but if we ignore that, the rest of today will be amazing!" She gleamed with excitement as we all sat and everyone handed over presents one by one. I got jewellery, new shoes, a new basketball, tickets for the NBA and more, I felt so spoiled.

"Alright well, we have five minutes before we have to get going to your game, get dressed and we will meet you at the courts." Logan came up to me and pulled me in for a hug. As they left, I went upstairs to get ready and I noticed a box on my bed with a note.

Happy birthday, Ember,

I know you're not ready for 'I love you' yet but please accept my gift. I will always be yours, no matter what.

Love Miles.

I smile at the note as I put it down and open the box. Wow, it's gorgeous.

I was stunned, it was a ring but I knew what it meant. It was a promise ring and I know a lot of people think it's stupid but it means so much to me especially now, after everything that happened today. It's silver with a red stone in the middle, wrapped around with smaller clear stones about ten of them. I placed the ring on my ring finger and I can feel the tears falling down my cheeks. I haven't had anyone love me like this before, like yeah I had mum and my siblings love me so much and I know that, but this type of love is different, I haven't had anyone love me like this, not even previous boyfriends who said they did.

I pulled myself together and got dressed and grabbed my bag. As I turn to leave out the door I see Miles leaning in the doorway. "Did you see the present I left you, Ember?" his body is relaxed, he must have come up and changed too but I got distracted so he beat me.

"I did," a smile spreads across my face, Miles smirks.

"And?" He pushes himself off the door and walks over to me, I show him my hand and the smirk becomes a massive, goofy smile that spreads from one of Miles's ears to the other.

"Do you like it? The big stone matches the one in your mums necklace," He pulls me in and touches the necklace that wraps around my neck.

"It does, and I love it. Thank you, it's beautiful." I reach on my tippy toes and kiss him, pulling him down to my lips.

"I'm glad you love it, now I have been sent to collect you because otherwise we will be late." He sweeps me off my feet and I squeal, laughing as he takes me down the stairs and sits me down, "Shoes on, I'll meet you in the car." He kisses my forehead and opens the door, leaving towards the car. I put my shows on quickly and we leave for the courts.

We walk in and we are the first of my team here, so Lauren and I go over to the hoop and practice our shots, just to check how my shoulder will go.

"Good morning ladies. Happy birthday, Scarlet!" Annie shouted, making her way over.

"Annie! No crutches anymore?" Lauren and I run over to her, she reaches in to hug me.

"Nope, doc cleared the crutches so I just have to wear this moon boot for a few weeks and then I will be out of it." Her smile gleams brightly with happiness. "Scar, can I talk to you please," Annie looks at me and I turn around to Lauren, as she walks over to the hoop to continue practicing.

"It's about Sam, she is talking about leaving the team. She says she can't handle seeing you and Miles together. I know how it sounds and believe me I am getting really over it too, her playing the victim all the time, but I need to know if she does leave, will you be okay taking over as captain?" Her voice lowers more than a whisper, she knows about Sam's game. At least she is looking out for the team.

"Of course, but as I have said before I don't want to stand on anyone's toes, so if she wants out she will need to stay out." I quietly demand, Annie nods and pulls me in for another hug.

"She isn't planning on doing anything bad today, I have told her to pull her finger out so hopefully the game will go smoothly."

Annie and I walk over to Lauren and Sam, Jamie and Chloe all walk in as we get to the bench. We all huddle around each other,

"Happy birthday, Scar," everyone shouted at the same time and handed me a wrapped present,

"Aww guys, you didn't have to!" Sam hands me the present and she nods at me, I nod and give her a smile as I open the gift. It's my favourite basketball team's jersey with my name on the back, "Oh my god, thank you! I love it!" I grab everyone in for a group hug and even Sam joins in for the hug.

"I'm glad you like it, now we need to get to work, warm up time ladies." Annie shouts and we all run onto the court and warm up.

After we warmed up and talked about strategies, the buzzer went off. I was back in action, defending, shooting, the works. By halftime the score was thirty-eight to seventeen to us,

"Well done guys, you're all doing so well today. Okay, what do you think we need to work on and keep doing?" Annie says as we all run into a huddle.

"I think we are all back in sync which is fucking fantastic," Lauren says as she takes a sip of water,

"I think so too, which it's about time," Annie glares over in Sam's direction and back at me, "Now, there's something I have noticed this game that we can work on, you guys have used so much energy for the first half, playing your hearts out, but now you all look fucked." She sits in her chair, "you guys need to conserve your energy, run, jump, shoot and defend where needed. Now back to the court, we have a game to win," she waved us off back to the court and I heard Logan, Mel and Miles cheering me on. They're holding up a sign that they made, I smile back and Miles blows a kiss at me. For the last half of the game the team is reserved, still strong but only playing when they need to. The final buzzer goes off and we win, fifty-two to twenty-nine, and our team is back on top for the qualifier championship. We all celebrated and Annie invited us all over for a barbeque party at hers tonight.

"So, want to come with me to Annie's party tonight?" I ask Miles as we walk back to the car,

"Yeah, I would love to go," he turns and pulls me in, kissing me and the pit of my stomach heats.

"Mmm if you do that more often it will become dangerous," I whisper to Miles, his lips curve.

"So maybe I should do it more often then," He brushed the hair on my neck out of the way and gently placed his lips on my neck, I let out a moan and he pulled me in closer. I open my eyes and see Sam and Travis together around the side of the gym.

"Hey, is that Sam and Travis?" I whisper, pulling away from Miles,

"Ember, when you say their names it ruins the mood. Oh, yeah that is."

We move behind his car to watch what they are doing, they seem to just be talking and then Travis pulls Sam in and they start to make out,

"Umm, what am I looking at? I didn't think they were ready?" I grimace, this is not what I want to be looking at.

"I guess they have decided to move on," Miles grabs my arm and opens my car door. We get home and I place my jersey with all my other presents and get ready for Annie's party.

CHAPTER 16 – MILES

I can't get over the panicked look in Scarlet's eyes from this morning. I knew her stepdad was a dick and I knew he was wanted for embezzlement but I never thought he'd come after her to kill her and for money. While she is upstairs getting ready, I decided I should do some more digging on him, see who told him that Logan and Melaine moved out and that she will be on her own. My PI did some digging for me today so I thought now's a good time to read through what they found. There are reports on all the accounts that Davis embezzled from and reports of his frozen accounts. Jesus he was loaded, well it wasn't really his but I get why he said that he would pay for all their stuff. I finally found some message chains he had on a burner phone to another burner, all conversations were about Scarlet and her siblings, about how the person would get part of her inheritance money if they helped him, but no name was mentioned on who the other person was. Fuck.

My guy did some digging on who worked with Davis on these accounts and I noticed Travis's dad's name on the report. I asked my PI to look into Travis's dad for me as I heard Scarlet come downstairs.

"Hey, are you ready to go?" She asks, stepping closer to me. I get up and turn,

Holy. Shit.

She's wearing a red and white sundress that stops at her ankles and wearing white striped sandals, her red stone necklace and ring matching the dress and her gorgeous hair's up in a messy bun.

"Wow," is all that comes out of my mouth before I take a step back and fall back into my chair,

"Look that good, do I?" she teased, doing a little spin as well.

"I.. Um.. you look-..." every word I try to say disappears on my tongue and I just sit and take in the beautiful view, "You look gorgeous, Ember, do we have to go?" My cock rubs against the seam of my pants, fuck she looks so good.

"Yes, we still have to go, plus it'll be good, we can finally go together, you know as a couple." She walks up to me and I can see that she's nervous about going, especially as a couple.

"Okay, Ember, we go but when we get home, I'll be tearing that dress off of you, if you'll allow me too of course," I pull her in and hug her stomach, I can hear her heart racing.

"We'll see. Now, we're going to be late. Let's go," she kisses my forehead and I take her hand and walk her to the car.

"In you go, Ember," I swing the door open and hold my hand out. She smiles and takes my hand as I help her into the car and close her door. I take a deep breath, trying to chill out before we are in front of a bunch of people and go around to the driver's side and drive us to Annie's house.

I help Scarlet out of the car and I loop her arm in mine as we walk around the back to where the party is, people are drinking and dancing, some come up to us and congratulate us on being together and wish Scarlet a happy birthday and she's glowing, she looks so happy to be surrounded by her team. Then I see Sam and Travis walk in together, wrapped around by the arm.

"Heads up, Ember." I nod towards them and Scarlet follows my trail, spotting them together.

"So, they are dating?" She questions, she sounds just as confused as I am.

"Guess so, I'm going to go get a drink. Do you want anything?" I kiss the back of her hand and she nods as I walk away to the kitchen.

"Hey Miles," Sam says behind me, her hand reaching for mine,

"Hey Sam, what do you think you're doing," I step back and give her a stern look,

"Sorry, reaching for a drink," She giggles and grab a drink,

"Congratulations by the way, on you and Travis, I saw you walk in together," I'm still not convinced, just because they kissed and walked in together doesn't mean they are dating.

"Thank you, I am finally happy again so I appreciate it," she takes a sip of her drink and a smile appears on her face. "I heard about Scarlet's stepdad this morning, how is she doing?"

"She is fine, how do you know about that?" I think my eyebrows hit the fucking roof,

"Travis told me, he went over to see her and you got all defensive over her. It's cute, you think you can protect her," her smile turns wicked.

"What-What did you say?" I step closer to her, I swear I would never hit a woman but right now, it could be debatable.

"You, protecting her. She has such a dark past and if you think only Davis is after that money, you're wrong." She whispered and slid her hand in mine, "I have a way to help, if you want to protect her." Her hand makes its way up to the side of my face, I step back.

"Do not touch me, what are you on about?"

Scarlet. I push past her and go outside to find Scarlet, usually she isn't hard to spot with her hair but with all the lights, it's not easy. I see Annie and I race up to her.

"Have you seen Scarlet?" I panic, my composure has completely gone out the window.

"Yeah she is over with Logan and Lauren, over there." She points over to where Logan and Lauren are and I see her hair peeking over everyone. I push past everyone and once I get to her I pull her into me.

"Hey, what's wrong, are you okay?" She grabs my face and she must see my panicked look, I pull her in for a deep kiss, my heart pounding over the thought of losing her.

"Yeah, I'm okay, just have something going on." I wipe my face with my hand and push my hair back,

"Where are our drinks?" She looks at my hands and giggles, "Did you forget?" She teases.

"Yeah, I forgot, sorry. Let me go back and get them, just stay with them please, Ember," I begged her, she smiled and nodded at me as I walked back to the kitchen where both Sam and Travis are making out. I roll my eyes and grab two drinks,

"Oh, sorry man, didn't see you there," Travis says, wiping his mouth.

"All good, just getting some drinks, continue," I go to walk out when I feel a hand on my arm and Travis pulls me towards him. I turn and lift my arm up and punch him in the side.

"I just warned your girlfriend not to touch me, that includes you," I straighten myself up.

"Miles, what the fuck, he was just wanting to talk to you, you didn't need to punch him." Sam shouts, bending down to help Travis back up.

"Sorry man, I didn't mean to fright you or anything," he groans, standing up with the help of Sam,

"Whatever, I have nothing to say to you two, I also don't want to hear what you have to say so you can piss off and leave Scarlet and me alone." I walk out, ignoring Sam's plea to stay and chat and I make my way back to Scarlet.

"Here, Ember," I hand her a drink and we hang around for about an hour and my phone rings, it's my PI. "Hey, do you mind if I take this?" I ask Scarlet and she shakes her head.

"No, it's okay, go, I'll stay here with these two." She nods to Lauren and Logan, I pull her in for a kiss and go answer the phone.

"You couldn't text me?" I demanded, he never calls unless it's super important,

"Sorry boss, I thought you might want to hear this over the phone and not text," He pauses and I take a breath.

"Is it about Travis's dad?" I whisper, walking out to the driveway, looking to make sure no one's listening.

"Yeah it is, he was in on the embezzling with Davis and he was taken to jail a week ago, they took him at his job. I saw some text messages between him and Travis," he pauses, the silence is thick as I wait for him to continue.

"Okay? What did he say, was it about Scarlet?" The frantic tone in my voice must have translated to 'get to the fucking point'.

"Yes, he told him that she had a lot of money and would get access to it today. He told Travis to get close to her and gain access to her account," he stopped, I hear his keyboard ticking in the background.

"Well, I can stop that. It's been easy so far." I take another deep breath, we should be in the clear now.

"No boss, Travis's family is in bankruptcy now that he was taken. Travis needs that money, if he can't get close, he'll also try to kill her, just like Davis."

No, this can't be happening, "Anything else?"

"Yes, Davis wired Travis hundred thousand to get the money and from what I've gathered if he gets the money, he won't be sharing with Davis. So, he is planning to fuck over Davis as well."

I hang up the phone and race to the party, is that what Sam warned me about, or tried to earlier. I find Scarlet near Lauren and Logan.

"We need to go, Ember, now." I grab her arm and she quickly says bye to Logan and Lauren as we make it to the car.

"What the fuck is going on Miles," she shouts, her eyes filled with worry and confusion.

"Okay, don't get mad at me," I pause, praying she won't be mad at me for using a private investigator on her and her family. "Well, I did some digging on Davis after this morning and he wired one hundred thousand to Travis to get close to you for the money. His dad was arrested a week ago for helping Davis embezzle so his family's going into bankruptcy. Davis told Travis this morning after he was arrested that if he can't get close he needs to kill you himself," I stare at her eyes and the panic comes racing out, her eyes flying close.

"Wh-what, why do they want my mo-money so badly," She stutters, her hands starting shaking.

I pull her in for a hug and place my hand on her inner thigh and move my fingers up and down with long and gentle strokes, it's supposed to help distract from the panic feeling.

"Shh, it's okay, Ember. You have me here now, I'll burn them before they can touch you," the strokes grow longer and higher and her breathing hitches.

"You can't burn everyone that wants my money," she breathes, her breathing calms slightly.

"Ember, I would burn the world for you." I gently turn her face to mine and I plant my lips on hers, my tongue sweeping her mouth and the strokes of my hand go higher and higher and I can feel her heat on my hand, she lets out a little moan and arches her hips into my hand.

"Should we go home?" She whispers and a sinful smile arches across her flushed face,

"Sure, let's go. Just so you know, I'm installing a top

of the range security system in the house, they're coming tomorrow morning, so you're stuck with me all night long." I start the car and we start driving home, I place my hand back on her thigh and I put my hand under her dress so my hand is touching her soft skin. I hear her shaky breath as I glide my hand gently over her skin.

"You know, Ember," I growled, moving my hand higher. "I told you I'd rip that dress off when we get home but you haven't said that I can yet," my hand starts doing circles higher and higher up her thigh and I can feel her thighs tighten the closer I get to the apex in between her legs,

"Miles," she quietly moans, her head flies back and her back arches slightly.

"Yes, Ember?" I tease, my fingers stroke the side of her lace panties, she's already wet.

"Please, Miles," her moan grows louder as I flick the side of her underwear.

"Please what," I follow the seam of her underwear and her breath quickens, we stop at a stop light. I lean over into her ear, "Come on, Ember, do you want me to touch you?" I whisper, my lip grazing her ear.

"Yes, please," she begs and I move my hand down and rub the fabric of her underwear over her apex. Her underwear's already soaked and I can hear her breathing stagger as I move my hand down slowly and tease her entrance through the fabric. "Miles," she moaned and I teased her all the way back home.

"Now, Ember, that was just a taste." I reach over to take her seatbelt off and I kiss her neck, sinking my teeth into the side of her neck. "If you want more, tell me now." I demanded and her breath slows down.

"Alright, but I got a taste so now it's your turn, right? If you want a taste, you will take me out of this car and kiss me all the way up the stairs." She obviously underestimates me. I open my door and swing hers open, I scope her up and slam the door closed. I plant my lips to hers and I walk us up the stairs, open the front door and close it, walk all the way up the stairs and walk into her bedroom without having to break our kiss once. I throw her on the bed and shut the door, locking it behind me.

"You know no one else lives here right?" She whispers, her dress has hiked up just below her hips and I can just see her soaked red lace underwear.

"You never know, Ember plus, once we start," I crawl onto the bed, "I won't stop until I shatter you," I growled and she got a devilish grin on her face.

I crawl on top of her and my lips drop to hers. Her hands pull my shoulders in to deepen our kiss. I sweep my tongue across her lips and when she opens her mouth, I explore every inch of her mouth. I flip her on top of me and she straddles herself, placing herself in the right spot for her pleasure, moving her hips slowly and my cock twitches with the sensation. She lets out a moan and moves her mouth to my neck, kissing the sensitive spot, slowly moving down kissing my collarbone and sending a line of kisses down my stomach, she undoes my jeans and pulls my cock out. Her small hands wrap around it and start slowly moving her hands in up and down motions, a growl slips past my lips and I look down to see her bright green eyes staring into my soul. She stops right above my cock and sits up.

"Move to the end of the bed?" She asks gently, I get up and move to the edge of the bed as she gets on her knees and sits, the dress covers every inch of her.

"Ember, take the dress off." I demand and her eyes beam, she slowly undoes the corset in the back and pulls the straps down, releasing her breasts as the dress falls. "Now, come stroke it." She crawls closer and sits down, putting one hand on my inner leg and the other over the edge of my cock, staring at the bead of pre cum on the tip. Her pace quickens and I swing my head back as another moan explodes from my chest. I've been waiting for a long time to feel her hands, her mouth, her wet pussy around my cock and now I don't have to imagine it anymore. Before I can even say anything, Scarlet licks the tip of my head, takes the bead with her tongue and I look down in her eyes. "Eyes on me, Ember, if you look away, I will stop you, understand?" She nods, "if it's too much, tap my leg," she nods again and I fist her wavy locks through my fingers, the hot heat of her mouth covers the head of my cock. She pushes my cock to the back of her throat and moans, I think I have found what heaven feels like.

"Fuck." I growl, looking into her eyes and I can see the starved look in hers as I push her down the length of my cock. I keep my hand in her hair but I let her pick the pace. She goes deeper and deeper, faster and faster and her moans grow hungrier each time.

I lift Scarlet's mouth off my cock and sweep her up, throwing her back on the bed and removing the dress from the rest of her body. I put her knee over my shoulders and set my mouth on her. I swirl my tongue around her clit and she arches her back releasing a moan.

"Miles," her hand slithers its way through my hair and holds my head there, her hips grind against my face and I set my tongue to the rhythm of her, matching her movements. I suck and nip at her clit while I slide two fingers into her and she thrashes against the pillow. This isn't my first rodeo, but I haven't felt like this with anyone else, she tastes so sweet and I could be down here all day. The moans become louder and louder as I move my fingers with her rhythm, using my tongue on her clit at the same time and I can feel her tightening around my fingers. I growl against her as she releases in my hand and on my face, I clean it all with my tongue and snake my way back up her body.

"Are you done, Ember or can you handle more?" I find the tender spot in her neck and lick it up her ear, nibbling on her ear lobe. Her body shakes as a quiet moan creeps from her lips. She nods and I reach for her wrists and put them above her head. "If it's too much just say so." I whisper in her ear and she nods in response. I move my face in front of hers and settle my mouth to hers, I take my fingers and tease her entrance ·again.

"I have an IUD," she whispers and places my head at her entrance, gliding it around her. Her eyes roll to the back of her head and I plant myself on her neck, gliding my lips across her skin. Thrusting my head into her entrance and her hands come flying to my shoulders.

"Did that hurt," I pause, checking her out, making sure she's okay.

"A little, it's been a while." She whispers, her flushed face turns shy.

"It's okay, I'll go slow then. Hey, eyes up here, Ember," I whisper, gently moving her face towards mine. Her eyes stare into mine as I gently thrust forward and pull out slowly. Scarlet bites the bottom of her lip and a whimper passes her lips and her eyes vanish. She takes me in, inch by inch, the pressure of her pussy around my cock is phenomenal. The stretch is flawless, it's like she was made to fit me perfectly. Her legs wrap around my back as I pull out slowly and drive one long thrust into her, her back arches and she lets out a cry as I pull out slowly again, I can feel her legs wrap tighter around me, I thrust hard again and then pick up the pace. Thrill drives through my veins as she tightens around my cock.

"God, Ember, you feel so beautiful." I growl and I can feel her release around my cock, her hands gripping the sheets as she moans and I shatter. I pull her in and our mouths go wild while the pleasure passes. I roll to her side and scoop her up into my heaving chest.

"That was," She huffed, trying to come back down to earth.

"Amazing, Ember, you are so beautiful." I kissed her and we lay there for a while. "I'm going to get some water, want some?" She nods and I go downstairs to get water and when I come back upstairs she is still naked. "Ember, if you don't get dressed soon, we'll be going again." I rumble, putting the water on the bed side table.

"Well, I thought we could go for a shower together?" She pushes the blanket off of her naked body and slowly walks over to the bathroom, "You coming?" She turns to look at me with that smile and walks into the bathroom.

"Don't have to ask me twice," I jump out of bed and strip down as we get into the shower.

The water on her skin makes it radiate and my hunger doesn't seem to be satisfied yet. I stand behind her and pull her into me, my hard cock against her ass. My face dives for her neck and her hitched breaths make my cock twitch against her ass.

"Miles," she whispers.

"Mhmm."

"I love you," she moans and I stop, all my thoughts fly out the window,

"What did you say, Ember," I whisper into her neck.

"I love you Miles, always."

She said it, she finally said it back! I take one of my hands and pull her hair back, giving me full access to her wet neck, sinking my teeth in. The other hand goes down to her clit, rubbing circles as I put more pressure on the point.

"I love you too, Ember." I put my hard cock down through her legs and pushed her against the wall, arching her back. I drive my cock into her and she lets out a loud moan, pushing herself against me. Her soaked hair trapped in my hand, I pulled her head back and leant forward to taste her on my lips. Her tongue runs over mine and her cries are muffled into my mouth. Colours fly past my eyes as her pussy tightens around me again and I burst. Filling her with my cum, dripping down her legs. Her body shakes and I help her stand up,

"You okay, Ember?" I whisper, holding her steady in the water.

"Yeah, just tired. I might need help cleaning myself up," she mumbles and I stay to help wash her body, cleaning off my cum from her legs and wrapping her in a towel and placing her on the bed.

"What clothes do you want to wear, Ember?" I ask, going to her drawers.

"Just underwear please, I don't usually sleep with any other clothes on." She grins, my imagination goes wild and she knows it. I grab a pair of dark blue panties and put them on for her, kissing her inner thighs as I go up. Her staggered breath sets me off again, my cock trying to escape my boxers.

"Sorry, Ember, you're just too beautiful, I can't help myself." I chuckle as I make my way off the bed, tucking her in.

"Are you not staying with me," she whines, her eyes filled with tears.

"Well, I have my own bed and room now, unless you want me to stay. Do you want me to sleep here, Ember?" She nods and I climb in next to her and pull her into my chest, "Good night, Ember."

"Good night Miles, Love you," she whispers.

"Love you too, Ember," I kiss her forehead and we fall asleep.

CHAPTER 17 – SCARLET

Yesterday was both scary and amazing! I was still shaken up by Davis breaking in and then with Miles' news on Travis helping him. To think that Travis was with me since day one of moving here, no wonder he knew my stepdad. Other than all that terrible shit, the game we played put us back at the top for qualifiers, the morning was filled with presents and family. Then we went to Annie's party and I had an amazing time, but all I could think of was the night I had afterwards. Being on my knees in front of that man, watching him shatter right before my eyes, the feeling of him inside me and him helping me in the shower, gliding his hands over my wet skin. Just thinking about it puts me back in the mood.

I roll over and see Miles, still sleeping. His short dark curly hair messily hanging on his forehead, his muscular arms wrapped around the pillow, his skin glistening in the morning sun. I gently push his hair back from his eyes and he flips me around and pulls me closer.

"Morning, Ember," he mumbles in my ear, his hot breath caressing my ear.

"Morning, my love, did you sleep well?" I pushed

closer to him and I could feel his long morning wood against my back.

"My love? That's new, Ember," he places his lips on the back of my neck, gently kissing the area.

"Well, I wasn't ready to say the three words and now that I am I thought it was a perfect pet name considering you have called me Ember since we met at the courts." I shiver, his sleepy kisses sending waves of heat through my skin.

"I love it, Ember," he moves his hips into my back and he groans in my ear, "here's two options for you, Ember, we have half an hour before the security people are here," his hand glides onto my breast and circles my hard nipple. "One, we can get up, get dressed and make breakfast before they come," his other hand makes its way down my stomach, tracing a line up and down the seam of my underwear. "Or two, we can have sex again, then get dressed and make breakfast," his hand stops at the middle of my seam and my breath hitches.

"Option two," I moan, I can feel his face turn into a smirk against me as his kisses become more dominant on my skin and his hand moves under my underwear, circling my clit with his fingers.

"I will make it quick okay, Ember, you're going to need breakfast after last night and this morning." Miles rolls on top of me and his lips crash onto mine, our tongues playing with each other. His fingers move down me and find my entrance, my breath quickens as he inserts his very talented fingers in me.

"Miles," I moan into his mouth, arching my back. My hands glide through his hair and down to his shoulders. He bites my bottom lip and drags it through his teeth.

"I know, Ember," he stares into my eyes as he places his head at my entrance and thrust himself in with one long stroke. The pleasure runs wild through my body as he picks up the pace, my hands find their way to his shoulders and I pull him back in, his head buries itself into my neck, leaving his marks on my neck as I moan into his ear. The stretch of him every time he thrusts in makes me see stars and I can feel myself right on the edge, my core tightens but I fight against the urge. I'm not ready for this moment to end. For everything to go back to the way it was, I want to stay here.

"Don't fight it, Ember, let go," his hand reaches down to my clit and applies the best amount of pressure to it. "Let go for me, Ember," he growls in my ear, his steaming breath hitting my ear, followed by his teeth and I shatter to pieces. The world goes blank and all I see is stars, I can feel Miles finish at the same time as I do but he continues thrusting into me until it's over.

"Now, Ember," he huffs, leaning into my face, "You should shower, I'll go downstairs and start breakfast, they'll be here soon." His knuckles run down the side of my cheek and he kisses my swollen lips. He smirks as he gets up, putting his shirt on and goes out the door.

I lay there for a moment, recollecting my thoughts.

That was amazing, I can't believe I held out for so long.

I got up out of bed and went for a shower, putting on a cropped shirt and short denim jean shorts, then went downstairs to the kitchen. As I walk through the doorway, I see Miles wearing my bright pink apron with music blasting and he's.. dancing?!

I lean against the doorway and watch him hum and dance to the beat of the music until he turns around, stopping in his tracks as his cheeks go bright red, "Hey, Ember. How long have you been there?" His voice cracks as he places the frying pan down on the stove.

"Only a little while. Nice apron, my love." I cover my mouth, trying to hold back a laugh.

He looks so cute, he's the total opposite to the hottie that was just in my bed.

"Thanks, uhh.. Have a seat, it's almost down," he finishes up the bacon and brings both plates over to the table.

Holy shit, that looks amazing.

"Wow, I didn't know you could cook so well, my love," I whisper.

"Yeah, my mum taught me, please enjoy, Ember," he takes the apron off and turns the music down, sitting down next to me he waits to see how I react. The food explodes in my mouth, it may just be bacon, eggs, toast and sausages but it is amazing.

"Wow, my love, that's incredible." I smile at him and his face lights up.

"I'm glad you like it, Ember, now eat up. You used a lot of energy the past twelve hours." He smirks and hooks into his food.

Just as we were finishing there was a knock on the door, Miles got up and checked who it was and let the man in, it was the guy from the security company. It looks like Miles knows him which helps settle the nervous feeling of, 'what if they knew Davis and wanted me to vanish too'. Miles took my empty plate and washed them up, then he turned and took me to the living room.

"What do you want to do today, Ember? I have a spot booked for tonight, for your twenty-first birthday party, the team will be there and with no doubt Travis will come but I'll be by your side all night, I promise." He takes my hand and squeezes it with reassurance, "so, I want to take you shopping, the theme is masquerade. I'll have guards out the front, checking everyone under the mask before letting them in

He wants to take me shopping. What man wants to take his girlfriend shopping!?

"What do you say, Ember? We can also go get you some red lipstick for tonight because I know you don't have any, I checked."

Holy shit, this man knows everything!

"Really, yes. Holy shit yes please, thank you, my love. I will go get my wallet." I go to get up from the couch and Miles gasps.

"Ember," he puts his hand over his heart, "You think

you're paying? I'm heartbroken!" He dramatically falls back onto the fall, pretending to pass out.

"Sorry, my love, I just assumed. Please get up, I'll give you a kiss," I teased and he quickly opened his eyes and shot up, leaning forward for a kiss. I giggle and kiss him quickly.

"Thank you, I feel so much better. First, we have to wait for him to finish his work, it won't take long, so if you want to watch your show, I'll go grab coffee." He kisses my cheek and goes towards the kitchen, I grab my blanket and get comfortable on the couch. We sat and watched two episodes of my show before the security man was done and wanted to run us through the system. Basically, we'd have to enter a code to turn it off and on, it has a ten second timer before turning on to give us time to get outside and we can install an app on our phones that notify us if anything happens, doors opening or a window being open. Miles thanks the guy and turns on the system as we walk over to his car, opening the door for me as always. "Thank you, my love." I kiss his cheek as I get into the car. I can see his goofy smirk as he walks around the car and gets in. "You do really like the name don't you?" I tease, leaning into him.

'I do, and if you call me Miles again I will be offended." He states, I giggle at his response and he takes us to the mall that's down from the house.

We walk through the mall and Miles takes me into a fancy boutique.

"Good morning, Mr Grove, how can we help," a well-dressed, beautiful lady asked. She looked a little older than Miles but her eyes are all googly around him,

"Morning, Jess, my girlfriend Scarlet needs a dress for her masquerade party tonight, I assume you will help her?" He firmly asks, pulling me into his side.

"Of course, sir. Ma'am, would you come with me and we can have a look at what you want," I nod and turn to Miles.

"Thank you, my love." I reach to kiss his cheek and I can see his lips trying really hard to not flick up into a smirk.

"Of course, Ember, I'm going to go next door and grab our masks for tonight, find something either red or black. It'll match the mask, then I'll go get the lipstick, okay?" He whispers, looking into my eyes, seeing if I am worried or scared. I give him a big smile as he finally smirks back and gives me a peck before he walks out of the shop.

I follow the lady into the back where the dresses are and spot Sam shopping for a dress, my stomach drops as she turns to me.

"Hey, Scarlet, shopping for tonight?" She asks, nodding to the salesperson as they pull dresses out and take to the dressing room.

"Yeah, Miles brought me here, he's paying so he left me here with Jess while he went to grab our masks." I don't show her any feeling, none in my face or tone, I can't deal with her and any bullshit she's about to throw at me.

"Well, while your here I should tell you," she steps closer to me, "Miles will come back to me, and he won't have a choice and it will be all your fault," she pulls her face back and the smile on her face is anything but sweet and nice, she turns and waves bye at me.

I can't move, what does she mean it will be all my fault? He won't go back, will he?

"Miss, are you alright?" Jess asks, gently touching my arm,

"Y-yeah sorry, umm, I want a black dress, I want it quite fitting up the top to my waist and then it flows down from there." I state, showing her some inspo pictures I found in the car. She nods and pulls about three or four dresses before we go to the dressing room. As I try on the dresses, Sam's words bounce through my head,

He will come back to me, it will be all your fault,

Panic rises in my stomach and I turn to look at the dress and my jaw drops to the floor. It has beautiful lacy details at the top of the dress, covers my breast with shiny fabric and it fits at my waist, making me look snatched. I finally let out my breath that I've been holding for a while too long and admire myself in the mirror, this with red lipstick and my jewellery, it'll be beautiful. I take the dress off and let Jess know that this is the one. She smiles, taking the dress from my arms and wrapping it up, putting it in a bag and walks to the front desk. Miles is already there waiting with a few bags already in his hands, he smiles at Jess as she goes to the counter and turns to look at me and his eyes shine bright, his goofy smile returns,

"Hi, my love, how did you go?" I smile and hug his side.

"Good, I got everything we need, just have to pay for your dress and then we can go home."

"Okay, so your total will be fifteen hundred for today," my jaw drops to the floor for the second time today, Miles pulls out his card and pays for it.

"Receipts in the bag, have a good day, Mr Grove, Scarlet." She smiles and I return the smile as we walk out the shop.

"Miles that's too much," I state, stopping in my tracks.

Miles swivels around and his mouth is wide open, "Did you just call me Miles?" The sad tone breaks my heart a little.

"Sorry my love but that is too much on a dress for me, I can't let you spend that kind of money on me." I grab his hand and pull him down for a kiss, my stomach starts churning as I think about what Sam said.

"I forgive you, Ember, and I can spoil you. You have worked so hard to look after everyone else in your life, it's time someone else looks after you, now let's go home." He puts out his hand and I slide mine in his, getting into the car I can feel the panic shooting through me, Sam's words have really left an imprint on me. As Miles gets in the car, he turns to me and must've noticed the panicked look on my face as he places his hand on my thigh, circling his fingertips gently around the sensitive area of my leg.

"Hey, what's wrong?" He whispers, tears hurt my eyes as I break down. Miles leans over and pulls me in for a hug and holds tight, not letting me go. I can feel him taking in deep breaths to the same rhythm of his fingertips on my thigh and I slowly breathe with him, calming myself down.

"Sam was in the dress shop," I sniffled, wiping the tears from my cheeks.

"What? I am so sorry, I didn't think she would go in there." Miles grabs my hand tightly kissing the back of it.

"It's okay, but she said something to me that has obviously left me a little panicked."

"What did she say?" Miles' voice drops to a demanding tone, his knuckles on the steering wheel go white with how hard he is gripping it.

"She said," I pause, trying to go back to the moment in the dress shop, "Miles will come back to me, and he won't have a choice and it will be all your fault," my voice shakes and I can feel my hands go sweaty. "I can't lose you Miles," I whimper, she can't take him from me, he promised.

"I am all yours, Ember. I can uninvite her from tonight if you want," he grabs my hand and pulls me back in for a hug.

"No, it's okay. She is part of the team, no matter how crazy she might be." I breathe in and out deeply a few times, clearing my head.

"Okay, but say the word and she is gone, Ember." Miles starts the car and we make our way home.

Once we are home, Miles takes me up to my room and drops me gently on my bed.

"We aren't having sex right now, I just thought you

might like a cuddle before we have to get ready, so no getting any ideas, Ember." He smiles and he lays down next to me, pulling me in tightly.

"Of course not, my love, I would never." I tried to sound offended but he only laughed and kissed my forehead, moving the loose strains of my hair out of my face.

We laid there for a while before he gave me one final kiss and hauled himself up.

"I see you got a black dress, Ember, I am glad you did, it matches my suit for tonight." He turns and puts the bags up from the floor onto the bed, "Go for a shower, Ember, if you need my help with the dress just give me a shout." He walks out and closes my door, I go through the bags, he got me some updated makeup too, not just the lipstick and my mask. It's beautiful, black with little red roses around the edges. I get up and hop in the shower, scrubbing, shaving, and washing my hair before getting out and applying lotion to my body, and blow drying my hair. I style my hair, half up and half down with the up half being in a messy, pinned back bun. I curled the pieces that were down and did my makeup. I did light face makeup and did a little eyeshadow with a semi dramatic black wing, I applied small eyelashes to the outside of my eyes and applied my deep red lipstick that Miles picked out.

As I step out of my bathroom I hear Miles knock on my door,

"How are you going, Ember, almost ready?" He shouts through the door.

"Yep, just putting on the dress now, give me a sec." I shout back as I grab the dress and put my feet in it. I pull it up over my ass and put the spaghetti straps over my shoulders, "Okay you can come in."

I see the door open through my full-length mirror and Miles pops his head in through the door and his jaw falls to the floor, just like mine did when I saw myself in the dress. "What do you think, my love?" I ask, turning to face him, holding the front up so it doesn't fall down.

"Ember," he whispers and falls to his knees. "You look," he stutters, trying to get the words out of his mouth and then he places his hands on the floor, his forehead too. "You look like a queen." He whispers, lifting his head as he stares at me, checking over every curve. "You're lucky we have to leave soon because I would take you to that bed so fast you wouldn't ever realise." He growls, getting back to his feet, he sweeps his hair back out of his face with both hands and lets out a deep breath, "Fuck, Ember, this suits tight. You're making it uncomfortable to wear these pants." He adjusts his waistband, trying to relieve the pressure that I can see through the tight suit pants, "Now, do you need help with the back?" He walks over and I nod, turning around so he can do up the corset back for me, I can feel his warm breath on my neck and shivers run down my spine, "You look so fucking good in this dress," he laces the last of the corset up, "when we get home I will be bring you up here and destroy you along with this dress, understand, Ember?" He groans in my ear and I nod in response, not being able to say anything and his assertive grin grows over his face. "Good, now let's add the final touches," he turns to grab the mask and ties it on my face for me and takes a step back, he spins me to face the mirror and I couldn't believe what I was seeing.

"I look," I pause, now I am lost for words.

"You look phenomenal, Ember. Now we're going to be late, our car's waiting for us, let's go." Miles grabs his mask and opens my door, I grab my shoes and turn to look in the mirror one last time before closing the door behind me as Miles picks me up in his arms and carries me down the stairs.

"You shouldn't have to walk down the stairs looking like that, Ember. Here I will put your heels on for you," he takes the shoes out of my hands and sits me on the edge of the stairs, slowly lacing them up my leg and scooping me back up again. He set the alarm and we walked down to the car.

"Ready, Ember?" He puts me down and takes my hand, helping me into the car. I sit down and pull my dress in so it doesn't get caught on the door as he closes it and walks around the other side. The car's huge, he got us a limo, there's champagne and chocolates in the cup holders of the car and the glittery lights are beautiful.

"We've got to go get Lauren, your brother and sister, that's why we have such a big car." He whispers in my ear, handing me a glass of champagne and we clink the glasses and sip it slowly.

We make it to Logan and Mel's home where the three of them are waiting outside for the car.

"Woohoo, party time," Lauren shouts as she gets in the car, Logan and Mel follow. All of them are dressed in dark blue with white and blue masks.

"You guys look amazing," Mel says, smiling over at me.

"Thank you, I picked the dress but everything else was Miles's doing." I squeeze his hand and lean my head against his shoulder, he kisses my forehead and we continue the car ride with the champagne and chocolate, talking about my childhood, mostly the good things though and chatting about how lucky we are to be here now.

When we get to the venue, Miles helps Mel and I out of the car while Logan helps Lauren out and the place is so pretty. The decor's simple but elegant and the colours are mainly black, white and gold. When we walk in there are quite a few people here already, mostly just other basketball teams that we have met over the past months and my team are all already here. They come over and wish me a happy twenty first again and tell Miles how pretty the party is.

After a round of flattery, Miles takes me over to the

food table, thank god because I am starving. That's when a guard comes over and whispers into Miles's ear.

"Sam and Travis are here now, Ember. Just stay by me and you'll be okay." I nod and give him a weary smile, my limbs start to go wobbly with panic.

"It's okay, my love, they won't try anything in front of everyone, please enjoy the party." I beg, gripping his hand in mine to help me stand up.

"Of course I will, you're here with me, Ember." He kisses me and Travis and Sam come up to us, both smiling like crazy people.

"Wonderful party, Miles, well done and happy birthday for yesterday, Scarlet, sorry I wasn't around much yesterday." Travis says, looking around, seeing where everyone is.

"Thank you and it's fine, we had a rough morning anyway," I look up at Miles, who's acting very calm and collective even though he knows that there's more to Travis than what meets the eye.

"Well, I'm going to grab a drink, want to come babe?" Travis asked Sam and she shook her head.

"Nope, I'm going to ask the birthday girl to dance, you don't mind, do you Miles?" Sam smiled up at him and there is a hint of angry in her words.

"Of course, if you need me I'll be right here." He kisses my hand and I smile at him as Sam and I go to the dance floor where the rest of the team are.

We dance and laugh for a while and Lauren and I end up dancing with each other most of the night. I noticed that Sam wasn't around anymore, probably went to go get a drink or go to the bathroom but I also noticed that Miles wasn't where he said he would be, and now that scares me. I stop dancing and walk over to where Miles said he would be and I looked around but I couldn't see him anywhere,

"Hey, Scar, are you okay?" Logan walks over to me and he looks a little worried,

"Hey, yeah, just looking for Miles, have you seen him?" I ask him, trying to not sound nervous that he is missing,

"No, I haven't, I can go check the bathroom for you if you want?" I nod and he goes towards the bathroom when someone taps my shoulder,

"Hey, Scar, can we talk?" It's Travis, he grabbed me by the arm and dragged me out, "if you make a sound, I'll hurt you." He growled and took me outside, shoving me into a car and driving off.

CHAPTER 18 – MILES

Seeing Scarlet so happy with her friends and family, after everything that has happened just since she moved across the country, makes me beam with joy, she deserves to be happy. I stand and watch her dance under the lights, making her hair shine bright, her smile beaming across the room.

"Hey pretty boy, or is it my love now?" A hand slides down my arm and I can tell just by the sarcastic tone in her voice that it's Sam.

"What do you want Sam," I pull my arm out of her grip, "I already warned you once about touching me, I won't repeat myself," I growl, turning around to face her.

"Oh please, you used to love when I touched you," she whispers, trying to get close. I take a step back out of her reach as she sighs and rolls her eyes at me, a vile grin spreads across her mouth, "You need to come with me Miles, if you don't want your precious Ember to be hurt, you will come." She turns and walks through the crowd, into the back where the kitchen is. I turn to see Scarlet still with her friends, dancing away. I sigh and I follow Sam into the kitchen, the door closing behind me. She's with people, with so many around, she should be fine.

"Good boy, now there's a few things we have to discuss, one being the fact that Travis is taking Scarlet to his car right now and is waiting for me to call him." She waves her phone in front of her, toying with me. I rush over to her to snatch the phone out of her hand when she puts it behind her back, "Tsk tsk tsk, always so impatient. Now, step back, right now." She demanded as I take a step back, the panic began to boil in my skin and the rage and anger was running rampant through my head.

"Let her go, if you want money I can give you money, please Sam, I beg you not hurt her," I plead, trying to convince her to let her go.

"Mmm, okay I will call Travis to let her go on one condition." She pauses, stepping closer to me, our faces inches away from each other. "You'll break it off with that little red head of yours and confess your love for me by proposing to me. We'll get married after we finish college this year and you will forget about her, leaving her to whoever else wants her." She whispers, dragging her knuckles down the side of my cheek, the rage in my head explodes and I know I can't do anything, if I touch Sam, she won't call Travis and who knows what he will do to Scarlet.

The memories of us at the airport fly through my head, the visions of us meeting on the courts, her beautiful hair and glistening skin from the sweat of practice. Our first date, with the onesies and her falling asleep on me, carrying her up to her bedroom and her dragging me in with her. Our naked bodies intertwined with each other, her gorgeous green eyes staring up at me while her hot mouth moved across my cock. I'll never have that again; I need to do what she says. I could try and take the phone from her, but I don't know if she has a password and if I take it, I can't call Travis to tell him to let her go without the thought of him hurting her. God, I'll rip him apart bit by bit if he lays a finger on her.

"You don't have a lot of time here, Miles, Travis can easily just take her away and what did Davis say yesterday, make her vanish?" She starts playing with the phone and her grin never leaves her face.

"If I agree to this, what will happen to Scarlet? Will he let her go, not hurt her ever. I need to know!" I shout, taking a step closer to her, my fists are so tight that I can't feel my knuckles anymore.

"If you agree, Travis will drop Scarlet back off to her house and he'll promise not to hurt her ever because he came into a lot of money himself, he doesn't need her anymore but he'll tell her that she can never say anything otherwise he will come after her," she paces around me, prying me with her eyes, "So, if you want her to be safe, forever, you will be mine," she takes my hand and I don't pull away. Tears well in my eyes, God I have no control in this situation, it's either she gets hurt or she's safe but heartbroken.

"Fine," I grit my teeth, my heart shattering into a million pieces, "first, you need to call Travis and tell him to take her home, she better not have so much as a scratch or a bruise on her or I swear to god." The words barely passed my teeth. My heart shatters to a million pieces knowing Scarlet will be all alone.

Sam's grin grows wider and she takes out the phone and calls Travis, "You can take her home, I'll send you the money later tonight," she hung up the phone and she stalks up to me, "now, I need you to take me home, while she's at school tomorrow, you'll go get your stuff and never speak to her again." Sam reaches up and kisses my cheek, sliding her hands into mine.

What have I done? Scarlet will be heartbroken, torn into a million pieces. "Fine, I'll announce that the party is over, I'll tell everyone that Scarlet had to go home and then I'll take you home. Just know," I bend down, close to her ear, "I'll never love you again." I turn and walk out of the kitchen, leaving Sam giggling in the kitchen. She's fucking crazy, those two were made for each other, both evil. One just wanted money and the other wanted love, which she will never get from me.

I walk over and announce that Scarlet had to go home, and I see Logan, Lauren and Mel leave immediately, no doubt going around to Scarlet's to check in on her. God I can imagine how she is right now, tears down her cheeks, her knees up to her chest, panicking. The one good thing that she had, gone. Everyone slowly makes their way out of the venue, and I take Sam home.

"Thank you for a lovely evening, babe, want to come inside?" Sam reaches for my hand, basically dragging me out of the car.

"Fine, I guess I don't have a choice." I follow her up to the door and she opens the door, taking off her shoes and walks us straight to her bedroom. I fucking knew that she was going to do this, she knows she has me now, but there's one final breaking point to completely shatter my heart, sex.

"Come on, you know we're good together," she nips at my ear, slowly taking her dress off, "Now, why don't you take me to my bed and demand me around like I'm your little whore," she whispers as she walks back, standing with just her bra and panties on, waiting for me to take her to bed. Bile rising through my throat, no fucking way this is happening.

"I won't fuck you like the whore you are! I will never have sex with you. You took the one thing I wanted, no. Not wanted, needed. You took the one thing I needed away from me, and I will watch you and Travis burn."

"Fine, I'll just give you some time, but if I so much as catch a whisper of you contacting Scarlet, I will make her vanish." She closes her door behind me, and I walk back to my car, sitting in her driveway,

"Fuck!" I shout, hitting my steering wheel over and over again, red fills my vision and then water takes over. The tears falling down my face, what can I do?

Logan's name flashes across phone screen, I open the

text,

What the fuck did you do!?

Well, that didn't take long, Sam said I can't contact Scarlet but not her family. I call Logan, "Pick up, please pick up," I beg, fidgeting my fingers on the steering wheel.

"What the fuck did you do, Miles! I trusted you with my sister's life. I just spent the past thirty minutes calming her down, she was damn near inconsolable." He shouts through the phone, I can feel his rage through his voice,

"I'm sorry, I know. I had to let her go; I have no choice. Please I did it to keep her safe, please understand that." My voice cracks and more tears fill my eyes, "I love your sister, but I can't be with her. Sam threatened me with her life, I had to break it off with her and propose to Sam, please, Logan. You have to understand that I did it to protect her," I beg him, my breath shaky and I can hear the cogs in his head working, trying to understand the words that just came out of my mouth,

"Scarlet said Travis threatened her and that he got a phone call, he told her that you were done with her and to never contact you again, dropping her home and driving away. Is that what's happening, did they want money?" Logan's voice is full of confusion, trying to figure out what is happening.

"Yes, yes and Sam wanted me for herself, so I had to get back with her to protect Scarlet. At training tomorrow, Sam said I have to break it off harshly with Scarlet in front of everyone, so she gets the picture. I'm so sorry Logan, I love your sister, please she will need you. I'll come up with a plan and get her back. I just have to play along, and I need time, please don't tell her anything, I can't risk anything." I can't think right now, so many feelings, not being in control. I can't figure this out right now.

"I know, I'll be here for her no matter what, but you

need to hurry up with whatever plan you are planning because she needs you. It'll take time for her to trust you again, Miles but you need to hurry the fuck up," Logan hangs the phone up.

"Fuck!" I throw my phone at the passenger seat and drive away, taking in deep breaths. God, taking in deep breaths only reminds me of Scarlet, panicking in that seat next to me and my hand gliding along her silky skin, listening to her breath hitch and her eyes fill with lust. What have I done?

I go back to my house and pour myself a drink, sitting down in front of my fireplace with my laptop open. Going through reports and documents my PI sent me about Travis, Sam and his dad, trying to find a way out from this hell before tomorrow. I have plenty of shit on Travis's and Sam's parents but nothing on them, so I have to try and find something. I can't believe I have to humiliate her in front of her whole team. She won't be able to do anything, she'll drop to the ground and panic the moment I walk away, I know it and I have to just walk away. I spent my whole night looking over the documents and drinking, falling asleep in the chair.

I woke up and had a massive headache, fucking alcohol. I got up and had some pain killers and water, trying to numb my pain always has some sort of fucking consequences. I pulled out my phone to order some greasy food to help with the hangover and a message shows up on my screen,

Morning babe, can't wait to see you at practice today, love you xx

God, I think I am going to throw up, I run to the bathroom, putting my head in the bowl of the toilet, no way am I going to be able to eat food. I sit on the cold floor of my bathroom, thinking of ways to get back at them, trying to find a loophole that gets me back to Scarlet. I wonder how she's doing today. I have to think of her, I have to hold onto the little thread of hope I have left that I may get her back and focus on getting her back or literally anything else besides throwing up right now.

I lift myself slowly off the floor when Cal messaged me,

Hey bro, we all just got an email about the qualifiers. This weekend is the last round before they select who goes to the qualifiers in Los Angeles, then the teams that top two in the US College League go to France to compete in the championships. I have told the team that we need to meet today, when do you want to do it?

Holy shit, I forgot about qualifiers and the championships. LA and France, that's amazing! I need to focus on my team too, I can't let them down, this is my final year, most of our final year and we need to go out with a bang. I sent him a message back saying that we can't meet today as there is something I have to handle and for him to organise a time at the courts tomorrow to discuss. I couldn't handle shattering Scarlet and then meeting with the team, I'll need the whole day to heal and drink myself into despair before I clear my head. I have my PI searching for all information on Davis, Travis's dad, Travis and Sam to try and charge them all with whatever I can to get them out of mine and Scarlets fucking life, having a dad for a lawyer's helpful, he'll take anything I give him and he will always protect me if needed. I'm usually good with cleaning up my messes but this, it's too precious for me to deal with without blowing everyone into pieces.

I grab some electrolytes out of the fridge and grab my jacket and leave to go to school. Today's going to be rough.

I spent most of the day sleeping through classes, I'm usually a top student but today I was sloppy, and I can't slip again, I can't show weakness. The pit in my stomach grew as I got to my car at the end of the day, I knew what I had to do, I even rehearsed what I would say but I know I won't be able to hold myself back if she drops at my feet. Logan knew what was happening and I hope he told Lauren, at least that way she knew what was coming and could help her through this. If something happens to her after this, I will burn everything down, tear through all of them piece by fucking piece. On the drive there I rehearsed what I was planning on saying over and over again. Go in, say what I need to say to make Sam satisfied and just leave. I can't look at Sam, I will drop her right there if I do. I need to look Scarlet in the eye, so she knows I am serious, not answer her questions and just leave.

I got to the courts early but I parked around the back so no one saw me come in, I don't want to see her walk in and be all happy and gleaming just so I can crush her. Logan and Lauren will help her move on, for the time being anyway. After all this bullshit is over, I'll fight to get her back, I'll destroy anyone in my path from getting her back, she's mine now and no one can say otherwise.

I check my phone and its time. My heart's pounding at a million beats per minute, anyone would think I was having a fucking heart attack. My heart's telling me not to do it, to stay in the car and drive away, drive to her house and wait for her. To explain everything to her and beg her to forgive me on my hands and knees. I knew better though, if I don't make Sam happy, she will take all the things I love and cherish and take them away from me, it's what happened with my mum. My head's telling me that I need to man the fuck up, to go in there and make her satisfied so I can fuck her up later and then get on my hands and knees and beg Scarlet for forgiveness. Either way, I will be on my hands and knees only for her. I turn my car off and take some deep breaths. I need to be a fucking asshole otherwise Sam won't be satisfied. I get out of the car and walk to the front door and pause, what am I doing? I need to do this, she'll die otherwise, or be hurt or…

No, fucking stop dumbass.

I open the door and walk through to the basketball courts, I can hear shoes squeaking, basketballs bouncing around, laughter and grunts. As I open the doors to the courts the first thing I see is her beautiful auburn hair and I want to fall to my knees. I never told her but if she took her hair out at any point, I would drop in front of her if I could.

Cut. It. Out.

I shook my head and turned to look at Sam, she must have noticed the doors swing open because her grin already tells me she knows what I'm about to do and how much it's about to not only hurt me but hurt Scarlet and her team. For the first time since moving here she's finally happy, and I'm about to rip her own heart out with my bare hands.

I hear shoes come to a halt and the balls stop bouncing as I see Scarlet looking over at me, her smiling face staring at me, what am I doing?

I keep a serious and unreadable face on as I walk over to her, every step becomes heavier and heavier, my heart beats faster and faster, I can't do this. I look back at Sam, and she sits beside Annie and is whispering something to her but I see Annies face fall and turn pale. She just told her what was happening, Annie gets up and tries to race over to me before I get to Scarlet but that moon boot slows her down too much.

"Hey, Miles, I left you messages last night, you really scared me you know." Scarlet whimpered, the sadness in her eyes was there but there was really fear in there. After last night with Travis threatening her and the panic attacks she would have had, she knew something was coming if I didn't come home and check in on her.

"It's over," I quietly demanded, my voice threatening to crack but I cleared my voice. Speak up you fucking idiot, Sam will want to hear every word your about to cut Scarlet with. "We are over, Scarlet, you were nothing to me. Sam's the only one I love, you were just a fun fuck for me while we were on a break. Do not call me or text me, my stuff is already out of your house." My voice is deep enough that it should strike fear into anyone, and it's written all over Scarlet's face,

"Wh-What," her eyes start going glassy and her bottom lip quakes, "you- you said you loved me, that I was yours and that you only wanted me," her voice cracks, I can already feel her panic building up just by seeing her beautiful green eyes.

"What can I say, I guess I'm a good liar. Sam's my fiancée, I proposed last night and we're getting married at the end of the year. I don't need you, I used you and now you're nothing to me." I turn and look at Sam and her atrocious smile tells me that she is happy. I walk away and I hear Scarlet drop to the ground and I stop to turn.

NO, keep walking.

I sighed and continued walking out of the court, my heart shattered into a million pieces and my will to live has vanished. There's no coming back from this, I have fucked up everything.

I get back into the car and my steering wheel turns back into a punching bag as I let out my frustration on it. I haven't cried since my mum's funeral but this, this is just as bad. Water flows down my face, what have I done? As I go to turn my car on a knock on my window scares the fuck out of me, making me jump out of my skin, 'don't let them see you bleed', my dad always said and he never meant physical blood but crying was definitely on the top of that list.

"Aww poor baby, did I scare you," Sam's feral smile appears in the window.

"Fuck off, Sam, I am not in the mood for your shit right now." I go to roll the window back up when I see a flash of red go across my window,

"Oh, but I have a gift to give you," she holds out a ring, the ring that I gave Scarlet for her birthday,

"Why do you have that!" I growl, I unlocked my car

and jumped out of the car, ready to fuck her up,

"Gentle babe, your pretty little side piece threw it at the door as you left, she's now crying on the floor, unresponsive. Well done." Her smile makes me want to throw up again, I never knew the devil himself could come to earth but I think I'm fucking looking at him.

"She," guilt settles in the pit of my stomach and I can feel the ache of tears wishing to come out. I snapped my eyes to Sam's, "she threw it, well I guess you can wear it as your fucking engagement ring, if you want to hurt her and me some more," I growled as I get back into the car, turning it on and speeding off.

CHAPTER 19 – SCARLET

We are done,
You're nothing to me.
The words bouncing around in my head and I feel the cold basketball court floor on my cheek, tears filling my vision as I hear blurred voices around me.

He just...

He's gone and he went back to Sam.

Was it all a play? Was any of it ever actually real? Did he ever want me or was I a toy in his little game?

I spent twenty minutes on the floor, constantly crying and shaking as the paramedics came on the floor with me and transferred me to their stretcher. I'm still curled in a ball, sealed to the position not even the male parametric couldn't pry me open. My bones have locked in place and the shaking didn't stop even with a warm blanket.

Someone came in the ambulance with me, but my eyes are so blurry from the tears and being so sore that I can't see anything. I can't believe he did that, today was going so great especially after the night I had.

Travis threatened to hurt me if I didn't get in his car and he got a phone call.

The phone call? Holy fuck, it was Sam.

The thoughts of Miles' words still bounce through my skull and my body remains locked. He took me home and told me never to speak of this otherwise he would make me vanish. The same words that Davis used on me the day before on my birthday. Then I didn't hear from Miles at all, and he never came home. I had a massive panic attack last night, even Logan could barely console me, and he took me to bed and him, Lauren and Mel all stayed the night.

Once we got to the hospital everything went by so fast yet so slow. The nurses and doctors hooked me to machines and tried to talk to me, but I was unresponsive. I heard them talking to someone else about what they were doing and then I heard a male voice.

Miles?

My breathing steadied and my eyes calmed down for a second but when I saw the man my heart broke more. It was Logan and he looked like he saw a ghost and he brought Mel with him, who was crying at his side. Lauren was there with them, she must have come with me from the courts, explaining what happened to the doctor and Logan, who looked so pissed. My panic rose again, watching them look so worried didn't help but Laruen repeated the words that Miles said,

'You were nothing to me,' trying to explain to Logan.

The panic paralyses me again and the tears fill my vision. I just want to vanish, be taken away and never come back to reality ever again. I couldn't stop thinking about all the good memories we had, the first time we met at the courts, when he gave me back my mum's necklace, when he finally asked me out, our movie date, our first time, the present. All of them have been burnt in my brain, playing on repeat as I feel my heart about to explode and then everything goes dark.

When I wake up its dark outside, my head's pounding

and I'm fucking starving. I sit up and look around, I see Logan, Lauren and Mel all sitting in chairs in my room and I groan, fuck my head.

"Oh my god, Scar. Are you okay?" Mel jumped from her chair and jumped on the bed, hugging my side and tears falling on my shoulder.

"Hey, I'm fine. Just a bad panic attack." I rasp; my throat is so dry.

"Just a panic attack! You almost had a heart attack, Scar!" Logan cries, coming to my side and grabbing my hand. 'He almost broke you physically, Scar." I haven't seen Logan cry before, he didn't cry with us at mum's funeral because he knew he had to be the man in the house, but I knew he cried a lot since mum got sick, his red eyes were a dead giveaway.

"Miles, right," I whimper, the tears burn my eyes as they fill in them. "He was serious, wasn't he?" I looked Logan in the eye and the expression he pulled gave me the answer. "Knew it."

"It's okay, we're moving back in. You have had two panic attacks in the past two days and now that he's gone, you'll need family and friends who do really love you around." Mel whimpered, trying to smile through her sadness, almost making her smile look more like a grimace.

"What? What about your apartment?" I can't let them sell the apartment; it was perfect for them.

"I care more about you than an apartment, Scarlet, you do not have a choice here. We are coming home." Logan demanded and the tears fall out of my eyes.

"Thank you," I pull Logan and Mel in for a hug and see Lauren at the end of the bed, trying not to cry.

"Lauren, you were there. What happened." I adjusted myself in the bed and snapped my eyes back to her,

"No, I can't. If you go back into a panic attack like that because of me. I'll never forgive myself." She sniffled, trying to keep the tears in her eyes.

"I need you to tell me so I can process, I promise I

will not panic, if I feel the panic rising, I will squeeze your hand and you will stop so I can breathe through everything, okay?" I held out my hand and she stared at it, then looked over at Logan. He nods at her and walks over to me, sitting on the bed and sliding her hand in mine.

"Okay," She took in a deep breath and slowly went through everything that happened, even adding in Sam's reactions that I never saw. That bitch!

"So, you think she planned all this?!" I shouted, trying to get out of bed fast. Logan grabbed my shoulders and slammed me back to the bed,

"Woah, Scarlet calm down. You just had a massive panic attack that your heart couldn't handle and now you want to go into a fit of rage. Take a breath, please." He did some deep breathes with me to help me calm down and then he gave Lauren a look,

"What, what is it?!" I screamed, testing if I really could get out of bed or if Logan would shove me straight back in. His eyes lined up to mine and stared me down, okay guess not.

"Nothing, but you need to calm down please. He's gone and even if she did plan all this you can't do anything, please just let him go," Logan pleaded, his body whimpering down next to me on the bed, begging me to calm down.

"Okay, I'll try to let him go. You know, I loved him though. It won't be easy to let him go, even if none of it was really real." The scene on the courts flashed through my eyes again and I can feel the panic come back.

"I got a message about the qualifiers today," Lauren jumped in, changing the topic.

"Really, what did it say?" I took more deep breaths and focussed on basketball, if there was one thing that I would never lose love for it was basketball. It was my first love and will always have a special place in my heart.

"The qualifiers are in LA and if we get selected for one of the teams for the College USA team, we go to France to compete in the championships." Her face lit back up, her smile slightly healing a piece of my now shattered heart.

"Really! LA and then France!" They both are beautiful places and both big for basketball. We get to meet pro teams and other teams overseas at the championships. Teams all over the country for qualifiers come and watch, scouting out new talent for their teams and then at the championships, scouts from across the world come and watch to pick their talent. Some people get multiple offers and have to pick, some get one offer and can choose to take it or try out somewhere else without an offer or some get none and have to choose if basketball is their future or if they give up.

"Yeah, our last game is in a few weeks and then qualifiers are about a month later. Then we wait to hear about the championships and then they fly us to France, and we compete over the two days we're there." Lauren sits back down beside me, holding my hand and her face drops a little.

"What is it?" I squeeze her hand, bringing her back to reality for a moment before she looks at me with a weary smile.

"Well, because of what Miles did and said, Annie blew up at Sam. Sam said she couldn't believe her best friend and walked out, quitting the team. She already has offers for teams next year, so she didn't care about the championships, at least that's what she shouted in Annie's face." Her smile faded and her eyes changed, almost begging.

"Sam walked, because of Miles and I, why?" What the fuck, she's gone. We may have a chance at qualifiers if she's gone.

"She told Annie something and Annie looked like she was going to pass out right before Miles blew up at you.

Then once he left, Annie blew up at Sam, she's gone. Her locker's cleared, and I promise she isn't coming back." Lauren looks conflicted, happy that Sam's gone and isn't going to cause more issues than she already had, but worried too.

"Why do you look worried?" What could be worrying about Sam leaving the team.

"We need a captain, Scarlet," Lauren paused, the begging eyes really have come into play now.

"Okay... Wait, You-you don't think I," She isn't serious right?

"The team voted once we left, in the heat of the moment I couldn't give them an update, so they discussed next steps since she's gone. They voted to promote you." Her eyes glowed with joy and excitement.

They want me to be captain! They voted and I was vice captain so it would make sense, but I can't. What if Sam comes back? She will be more aggressive if she thinks I am taking her spot.

"I- I don't know, Lauren," my voice trembles, this is such a big decision and she is asking me in the fucking hospital. I know it's an urgent matter to sign up for qualifiers because we need a captain and Annie won't be ready to play for qualifiers. Fuck.

"Scarlet, you are the most talented play I have seen in so long. Your leadership skills are incredible and your game skills, communication, your understanding of the game. You would do so good, plus it would look good for teams when scouts come out." She nudges my shoulder, and a small smile crosses her face.

If the team really wants me then maybe I should do it, plus we have a few games left before we make it to the qualifiers. It's a short run but it will look good, nevertheless.

"Are you sure she is gone?"

It's the one thing holding me back. I can't take anything else from her, she has destroyed me too many times now and basketball is my baby, if she touches it, that's it.

"She's gone, and we won't let her come back." Lauren promises, pulling me in for a hug, "If you aren't ready, it's fine." As she pulls away her small smile looks sad. The sparkle in her eye isn't hope, its tears.

"Okay, but if she comes back, I get to yell at her," Lauren's smile grew, and a laugh passed her lips. Logan and Mel join in and then I do too. As we come down from our congratulations and laughing fit, someone knocks on the door and a head pocks in. It's Annie.

"Did she say yes?" She whispered, looking straight at Lauren,

"Yes, she did!" Lauren cheers and the door flies open, and everyone walks in cheering and celebrating.

"Oh my god guys, what are you all doing here?" I'm shocked! They all came to see me, to see if I would take responsibility for all of them.

"We wanted to check if you were okay. Lauren texted Annie saying you were awake and responsive, so we all drove over and waited for her to ask you about the captain spot." Tegan says, walking over to the bed, grabbing my hand, "I am glad to have you as our new captain." Everyone starts cheering again.

"Aww guys, you didn't have to." Joy runs through my body and tears fall down my face with laughter falling out of my mouth at the same time.

"Hey, teams stick together, no matter what." Annie reached over and gave me a smile.

"Thank you," I whimper, wiping the tears off my cheeks.

"Now," Annie cleared her throat, "We need a new vice-captain, it's your choice, Scarlet." Everyone looks at me with questioning eyes, trying to see who I will pick, "I already know who it will be, but you have to say it out loud," Annie poked my arm, teasing me.

"Ha, our new vice-captain will be... Lauren." The

cheering picked back up and Lauren's face lit right back up,

"Thank you, Scar, you don't know how much this means to me." She pulls me in for a hug and we laugh and cheer for a while.

"Okay, we have celebrated long enough, did Lauren update you on qualifiers, Scar?" Annie cleared her throat,

"Yeah, I know. So, I have come up with a game plan, but uhh, I don't think a hospital's the best place to be doing this. I'm sure we are all about to be kicked out." I pointed over by the door and the nurse and doctor are standing there, giving the team a look that basically says fuck off. They all hurry out, saying congratulations and byes.

"Okay, Scarlet, I have prescribed you stronger anxiety meds for your panic attacks, just take it easy okay. Not so stressful environments, maybe no boys for the foreseeable future if they cause so many issues."

"Don't worry doc, only basketball and competition for a while and then pro after that. No time for boys."

The doctor and nurses help me out of the hospital and Logan and the girls take me home.

When we get out, I see all their stuff inside the door, lots of boxes.

"You really didn't need to move back. Did Miles tell you about the security system?" I turned to Logan, lifting one eyebrow in confusion.

"Yeah, when you first got it. How do you think I got to you last night?" He grabs the last of his bag out of the car and I turn to look down at Travis's house, it looks... empty.

"Hey Lauren, is your family still there?" I pointed over to her family where Travis supposedly lives.

"They moved yesterday, which is good because Travis's psycho. He needs help but my dad's in jail and mum has been unwell lately so they don't have time or money to help him." She helps Logan bring the bags into the house.

Mel cooks dinner and we all sit in the lounge room and watch movies. I'm wearing my onesie that matches the one I bought Miles. It makes me remember him, I'm heartbroken and I'll never fucking forgive him, but a piece of me still loves him and hopes there's a chance for us.

The next day I get up and go for a run, going past Travis and Lauren's old house. It really does look empty.

Once I get back to the house, I take my shoes off and take one deep breath of the early morning breeze and go back inside, turning the security system on behind me. Don't need anyone breaking in while I am cooking breakfast. As I start cooking and Logan is down first,

"Coffees on Logan," I giggle and crack eggs into the pan.

"Good," he sits at the table rubbing his temples. He hasn't slept well since mum passed but I noticed it's been worse since Davis moved us here.

I pour him a mug and pass it to him with a plate of hot food, he nods in thanks and almost downs the whole cup of coffee as Mel comes down next and Lauren follows shortly,

"So, are you ready for training today? Not far until our last normal game." Lauren takes a sip of her coffee and looks me up and down.

"Yep, came up with our plan for training last night and strategies for all our games. We need to see how we go without Sam. She was a really good shooter so to lose her hurts us a little." I wince, fucking Sam. Of course she's hurting the one thing I have left, at least she can't sabotage me anymore by tripping me or someone else to fall on me and try to break my bones.

"Wow captain, you were busy then." She smiles through the cup of coffee and digs into her food.

"What can I say, I am excited about the new

position."

We all eat together, chatting about things that have happened lately. Mel got promoted at the gallery and a few of her pieces have sold to high value customers. Logan has joined a massive game development company making six figures straight out the gate, starting quite high up and Lauren and I talk about basketball.

I walked out of class and today I was refreshed, I was energised and ready to tackle the day until... oh no

I see Miles down the hall of students and his eyes snap to me. His eyes soften as he stares at me with those gorgeous blue eyes. I can't do this right now, I need to get away, but I can't move. I star into his eyes as he does mine, his expression of hurt can be shoved up his... oh for fuck's sake.

Sam's right there next to him, trying to get his attention. She follows his line of sight, and she spots me over the hundreds of students in the hallway. My face goes bright red; I can feel the heat coming off of it and the panic tries to explode to the surface. Sam's devilish grin can be spotted anywhere, and I didn't want her wrath on me right now. I took a deep breath, and I could feel my legs again and I bolted out the door.

Fuck. Fuck. FUCK.

I knew I would see him this afternoon at training and possibly Sam, just to rub it in that he's now her property, but I had time to prepare for that. I didn't have time to prepare for that fucking shit right then though. I ran and ran into the open space outside and went under a tree, dropping to my knees. Tears fall onto the grass and my heart begins to race; I can't do this.

"Scar, Scarlet!" I hear a female shout and footsteps get closer; I take a deep breath and turn slightly.

"Oh hey, Annie, are you okay?" I quickly wipe my tears and anxiety out of my face and give her a smile, trying to hide what just happened.

"I'm fine, you're not though, don't hide it. We are

family now. You can't hide things from your family. What's wrong?" She sits down next to me and takes my hand in hers, taking deep breaths and I follow.

"I saw Miles and Sam, in the hallway," I cry, "I knew I would probably see them both at training this afternoon, seeming as Miles has training and Sam will probably follow to rub it in my face and to see how good I am at the whole captain thing. I had time to prepare for this afternoon though, but I didn't have time just then." I whimper; my voice cracks and tears fill my eyes up again.

"Hey, if she wants to rub it in, let her. Basketball is your baby, don't let her take that from you too. Your too good for her to fuck it up for you and in my opinion," a smile crosses her face, "Your way better than her at everything, plus I hear your already doing well at being captain, already have a plan and you signed us up for qualifiers already." She giggled as she helped me up and the panic feeling slowly eases as I think about her words.

"You're right, I got this. We will win without her." I squeeze Annies's hand and we walk to our next class.

The rest of the day I went on with my classes and I aced my exams. I need to let him go, it'll be hard, and it'll hurt, especially if Sam rubs it in. But I can do this, I need to focus on basketball, on my team, they need me now more than ever.

CHAPTER 20 – MILES

Fucking Sam's ruining everything, Scarlet was in hospital because of me. I almost made her heart give out and it was all her fault.

Fuck.

I need a distraction, I need to focus so hard on something, so I don't have time for Scarlet in my head and for Sam to fuck with it. Basketball, qualifiers and then the championships, I need to focus on that. Even though Sam left her team, doesn't mean I need to let mine down because of her, she can't take that from me. Seeing Scarlet in the hallway gave me some hope, she's okay. She didn't die because of me, just a massive fucking panic attack. She's at school and as far as I know she will be training later. Her team will be working hard now that qualifiers are almost here, and it didn't help that Sam and Annie got into a massive fight and then Sam walked out, leaving them with no captain. I hope Scarlet took the position; it was made for her.

I got to the courts after classes. Today was rough. Sam was breathing down my neck about what she wanted but the deal was I broke Scarlet's heart, and she would be happy, done. She wanted me to propose, done. I'm just about at my wits fucking end with her and her demands.

I opened the doors and noticed Scarlet right away, her hair was out while she was training. Holy fuck, it's gorgeous. My body begins to shake with desperation and my legs are going to give out.

Do not drop, do NOT DROP!

I can feel Sam behind me, and I adjusted my pants so she can't see how much I was admiring Scarlet's hair.

"Hey babe, ready for your training session?" She asked, reaching for my arm and I pulled away.

"I am, I can't be distracted right now. Sit down on the bench, I need to warm up before the other guys get here." I placed my bag down next to where Sam sat and walked on the court. I could feel Scarlet's eyes burning into me, hoping I would go over there and sweep her up and apologise, but I can't.

She calls her team over and talks about their new training schedule and what they are doing to prepare for the qualifiers and about ten minutes later Lauren walks over to discuss what their plan is.

"Ahh hello, vice-captain, how are you?" I smiled and handed her the ball, pretending we were warming up and talking about strategies but I just wanted to know about Scarlet, but it was hard with Sam stares burning into me.

"I'm good, thank you for noticing, Scarlet took the captain spot and is killing it," Lauren shouts, turning slightly to see if Sam heard and of course she did, Sam went straight over to Annie, pulling her aside. No doubt to start another fight on why the fuck Scarlet's captain.

"Nice distraction, is she okay?" I threw the ball, landing it in the hoop.

"She is for now, Annie said she broke down after seeing you and Sam in the hallway today, but she is focussed on the team and the qualifiers as she should be, plus a good distraction." She went after the ball and dribbled it back over to us, "Have you found anything on them yet?" She shot the ball, and it hit the backboard and landed in the hoop, two for two.

"No, not yet. My PI's working overtime trying to find something plausible enough for my dad to take them to court and fuck their lives up, but until then you and Logan have to keep quiet." I grabbed the ball and threw it, missing the hoop slightly.

"You know, she almost figured it out on her own. You need to hurry up because she isn't stupid. If she thinks about it, she will put two and two together and then she is fucked. Your security system can only do so much, Miles." She passed me the ball, "now here's our schedule and the training Scarlet has us on now, go over it and adjust yours as needed, hope you do good on your games. Hate to not see you guys in LA." She runs back over to her team, and I went over her notes for the training and holy shit. Scarlet's a genius, Sam always forced everyone to their strengths but if they had to do the things they weren't good at, they would still suck because she never trained them to build the skills up. Scarlet has everyone on the same thing and wrote who is weaker and stronger at what and arranged it so they can work on their strengths but also work out their weakness, so they aren't fucked over the next few weeks. God, I love how her brain works.

My team comes in about five minutes later and I talk them through the schedule Scarlet worked on. The team agreed that we need to focus on their strengths but also their weaknesses. My weakness isn't on the court though.

We spent two hours practicing the new drills and training. I combined my new ideas with Scarlet's to help the team out a little more. There were a few kinks in her plan, but she planned it for her team. So, I spent the first half of training analysing everyone and figuring out what really needs work and what we need to finesse, the second half we actually trained and did fake scenarios and drills. Throughout the second half of our training the women's team finished up and I saw Scarlet walk out last with Lauren, her eyes staring at me. Sam must have noticed because she got up and walked over to me, kissing me on the cheek, taking my attention away from Scarlet and when I looked back at where she was, she was gone.

We packed up afterwards and walked out together, everyone excited about the qualifiers coming up. We have to win at least one game to get the top spot as we were fighting back and forth with another team for the top place, but we verse each other the last weekend before qualifiers, to see who gets the number one spot.

Sam waited for me over by my car as I said goodbye to the team and my face went from happy and relaxed to tense and serious.

"Come on, no need to be so cold, babe. You did good today," Sam smirked and waited for me to open the door for her. I was raised to be a gentleman but with Sam, there's no fucking way I'm going to be kind to her. "I think you're forgetting something Miles," Sam seethed, looking me in the eye and then looking at the door. I rolled my eyes and went over to open the door for her, once she was in, I slammed the door closed and went around to the driver's side and got in. "That wasn't necessary, you can't seriously still be this upset with me." I couldn't look at her let alone open my mouth because the words that would come out would be out of my control. "Come on," she snickered, "She's cute but surely you didn't fall for her that quickly, you're meant to be with me, everyone knows it. Your family surely would be happy to hear the news that we are engaged now." Her left hand shot up and she waved the red stoned ring in my face.

"My father knows, he knows I'm not happy at all, not like before. Now do you want a lift home or are you just trying to press my buttons? I'm busy, you know." I turned my car on and glared at Sam and her mouth was slightly opened with shock. I haven't spoken to her like this before, but she would have to know that it would happen.

"Mmm, see I love when you're aggressive. It's a real turn on." She bit her bottom lip, and her hand gently grazed over my leg. My head snapped in her direction, and I firmly grabbed her hand, removing it off my leg,

"Do not touch me. I'll not be yours ever." I growled, "Do you want a lift or not?"

Her eyes filled with anger and shock, she knew I was pissed and that I would never touch her again the way she wants me too. She always loved having rough sex but that is reserved for one girl and one girl only and that wasn't her.

"Fine, yes please." She slammed back into her chair, putting her seatbelt on, huffing and crossing her arms over her chest, throwing a silent tantrum like a child.

I leave the gym and drive her home, the whole drive home she didn't move. She was probably hoping for an apology, but I wasn't giving that to her, I'm tired of her games.

"We're here, get out." I demanded, not looking at her, pulling out my phone to check if I had got any message from my PI or Scarlet, nothing from either of them.

"Thanks, I guess, do you want to come in?" She whispered, slowly taking her seatbelt of her body,

"No, I'm playing along with your petty ass game but there are boundaries and rules that I have set for myself with you and I will only go so far, so no I won't come inside with you. No, we won't fuck ever again and no, I'll never be happy with you, happy now?" I shouted, still not looking at her. I could feel her anger spreading through the car like fire and some might find it scary but as long as I play along she won't hurt Scarlet, she knows I'll hunt her and Travis or anyone else involved down and kill them myself.

"Fine, if that's how you want to play, sure. Night Miles." She stepped out of the car, slamming the door hard behind her and I zoomed off, leaving a dust cloud for her to navigate through.

After weeks of training like crazy and many sleepless nights, thinking about Scarlet and the special night we shared, Saturday was here. Our last chance to secure the number one spot for qualifiers. Qualifiers is a three-day tournament where the top twenty-five teams across America play against each other for the top spot to compete at championships, because we play all the New York colleges and institutions we need to place first to represent our state, so today is a big day.

I got up at five and went on a run, trying to clear my head from the memories of that night and then when I got home I had a long cold shower to try and calm down the hard boner I had since twelve. No matter how many times I jerked myself off, it didn't help.

I went downstairs, cooked breakfast and had some coffee while looking over some stuff I had found doing my own research on Travis and Sam. They were pretending to date, obviously but the messages between Travis, his dad and Davis were bouncing in my brain. They had to have been trying to do this long before Davis and his family moved to New York.

Holy shit, that's it!

I pulled my phone out and it started ringing,

Pick up, pick up the *fucking* phone!

"Fucking hell, Miles, its six in the morning. I was up three hours ago, what do you want?" My PI spent late nights working on this for me and I knew that but I pay him good fucking money so he can work whenever the fuck I need him to.

"I know, I'm sorry but I just realised something. The text messages between the three dickheads, they had to be communicating before Davis moved to New York, right?" The other side of the call was quiet, nothing. Then I heard a groan and movement of sheets being pushed away,

"Ahh, I guess so why do you think that?" He groaned loudly, obviously frustrated about being awake.

"Because they had to know about Scarlet's account long before Davis moved. Her mum died over a year ago and he was her guardian. Why the rush to move here if it wasn't for work?" Which we had discovered that he did get the promotion, but he threatened the previous CEO with money he stole from him, getting the position.

"That would be true, but her mum could have done it without telling him." He questioned, I could hear his clicking of his mouse and keyboard on the phone, trying to find where I pulled this theory from.

"She could have, but she was only a waitress. She would never have made enough money to put a sum like that into Scarlet's account, she would've got it from Davis at some point and their prenup said she needed permission to use his money. He would have known if she took a sum like that out and put it somewhere else." I was pacing my kitchen, trying to slow down my shaky hands and take deep breaths.

"Mmm yeah, I see that. I will do some digging for you but for fuck's sake let me sleep. You also have a big game today right, focus on that and winning Scarlet back. Leave investigating to me." He hung up the phone and I could stop moving, what if that was all true. We could take that to Dad; he would be able to fuck all of them up. Sam would be in there with text message chains with Travis at least so he can get her too, but my PI is right, I need to focus on two things, basketball and how the fuck I can get Scarlet back after all of this shit is over.

I go for another run before I grab all my shit and head out the door to the car. I get in and blast music, trying to get into a good mood for today.

By the time I get to the court, I am energised and ready to go. I see my team walk in the doors to the gym when I see a flash of red pass my vision. Scarlet.

I stay in the car, watching her go into the gym with Lauren, Logan and Mel and thinking about what I need to do. Fuck, no, I need to just focus on my game right now. She's my number one priority but at this very moment my team needs a captain that's in the zone, ready to take us to the qualifiers.

I take a deep breath in and get out of the car, grabbing my bag and heading for the doors.

The women's team is playing first and then once their game's done, we go on. I wanted my team here to watch the women's team, to encourage them. Today's a big day for both teams. They're at the number one spot by a mile thanks to Scarlet's shooting skills and now without Sam trying to kill her on the court, she should be focused.

They're playing so well, the training has sent them from being amazing to being the best team I have seen in a while and I can see Sam's face next to me, burning up with rage, knowing that they don't need her to succeed must be eating her alive. Each time they shoot and score, my team jumps up out of their seats and cheers like crazy, boosting their confidence hopefully through the roof, not that they need it. They are all in sync and are like one person on the court.

By half time their score is thirty-eight to twenty-nine to our team and the smiles on all their faces show that they're not only kicking ass but they're all happy that they are there together as a team. I can hear Sam's heart about to explode out of her chest when she looks at me and I am gleaming with happiness, not just staring at their team but at how happy Scarlet is. I know it's only a mask from what Lauren tells me, but she knows the importance of her team and how much this means to all of them.

I turn to look at Sam and her face is so red and steamy from anger and rage that it might just pop off.

"What are you smiling at huh?" She snarled, if looks could kill, I would be dead right now.

"Do you really want to know?" I teased, knowing that I would piss her off more. She shook her head and sighed, "Maybe you should go for a walk outside for a minute, cool off because you look like a tomato right now." I whispered in her ear, and she turned to me and gasped so loudly that my whole team turned and looked at her.

Correction, now she looks like a tomato.

She quickly gets up and walks out, trying to cover her face from embarrassing herself and look back over to the team and shrug, "women." They all mumble to themselves, nodding in agreement and turning back to the women's team as they walk back onto the court.

Sam walks back in five minutes into the second half and gently glides her hand into mine, "I'm sorry for overreacting like that," she smiles, and my eyebrows shoot up to the ceiling, she just apologised? What's happening?

"Ahh, it's okay I guess." I turn to look back at the game and cheer them on every chance I get. Today's a good day and nothing will ruin that for me, not even Sam.

As the second half comes to an end, I see a male in my peripheral vision and my head snaps to him. What the fuck is he doing here?

I turn to look at Sam and red fills my eyes, "Did you call him? Is that why you were happy coming back in?" Our faces were inches apart and I could rip her black heart out right now with my bare hands.

"Maybe I did. I think you needed a reminder that I understand your rules and boundaries with me, but you also have to understand that there are rules and boundaries I have for you too. Giving google eyes over at Scarlet crosses a major line, and embarrassing me like that in front of everyone is not cool, so he's going to stay here for one minute and watch Scarlet to freak her out a little and then he'll leave." Her voice sounds almost evil as the words come out of her mouth.

"How could you do this, it's not right?!" I went to get up and go to Scarlet to warn her, but Sam grabbed my arm and dragged me back down to my seat,

"If you go over there, she's dead." Sam whispers and my face goes white, my body frigid. I watched Travis sit at the end of the bench closest to her and counted down the minute in my head and then I watched him walk out, leaving his imprint on my brain. "Good, now get up, you have a game to win babe." She pats my shoulder and kisses my frozen cold face as I get up.

"Yo, bro, are you okay?" Cal came up to me and put his hands on my shoulders, "Are you feeling okay?" I shook my head, bringing me back to reality again,

"Yeah bro, sorry, I'm fine. Let's get warmed up, we have a game to win!" I shouted and the team cheered as we ran onto the court and started warming up.

The women's team must have had the same idea I had because they are all sitting on their benches, cheering us on every time we score, encouraging us if we fumble. I looked over at Scarlet to see her cheering and clapping at us and then at Sam, and she looked like she was going to explode.

We played hard and strong in the first half, trying to tire the other team out, leaving us with a score of forty-twenty at half time.

"Okay boys huddle up," I shout, the team comes running over with towels and bottles in their hands. "We played a good first half and I know you're all tired okay, but now we just have to play safe. Defence is what we need to do now, focus on that. If we get the ball try to hold on to it for as long as you can and shoot if you need to, but we are high up with our score, so long as our defence is strong, we'll win this!" I shout and they all bounce and cheer as we finish up the rest and run back on to the court.

We spent a lot of time on defence, trying to block their paths, grabbing the ball where we could and shooting only if we needed to. The other team was strong but because of the first half, they were tired. I knew that they were great shooters, but their defence lacked majorly over their last few games and that was their downfall with us. They obviously trained more shooting drills and exercises, not finessing their weaknesses like we did.

Everyone played so hard that when the final buzzer went off we all dropped to our knees and cheered. The crowd jumped up and cheered like crazy for us, but holy fuck were we tired. The ending score being fifty to thirty-nine, beating them by a landslide, putting us in the top place while they were second. We caught our breath and got up to shake the other team's hand and thank them for an amazing game. We all went back to the bench and sat down on the chairs or laid on the floor, begging for more air to get in our lungs.

"Well done team, you all played fucking well!" I shouted, and everyone agreed but grumbling something that I couldn't understand. I smiled over my team, they worked so hard for this, and we are now going to qualifiers again and we have a big target on our back after winning the championships last year.

CHAPTER 21 – SCARLET

We did it, we're going to the qualifiers in LA next week! After the men's game, I had to get ready as I was holding a celebratory party at my house for the team. After all, we had worked so hard and now with Sam gone, we're more in sync than ever.

I stayed to watch Miles, and his team play, to see if they would be coming to LA with us and they won. They used my training plan. I noticed the way they played today with going hard in the beginning and then easing off and playing defence in the second half. I'm so proud of their team, they played so well last year. I watched their qualifiers video and championship video from last year to see how well they played last year, and they have a lot to live up to if they played like that last year.

When I got home, I quickly went for a shower and started planning out the party. Cooking food, tidying around the house, preparing drinks for everyone when Logan and Mel came downstairs,

"God you work fast women, let us help," Logan took the plate of food off me and took it outside to the undercover area where we're all going to be. I giggled as he walked away, and Mel came up to me and wrapped her arms around me.

"You played so well today, Scar. Mum would be really proud of you." She smiled and squeezed my hands. Mum loved watching me play, she was so supportive and wanted the best for me when it came to my love of basketball.

"I know, thank you, Mel." I kissed her cheek and wiped the lone tear that was falling down the side of her face, "she would be proud of all of us, not just me." She gave me a watery smile and helped me with the drinks. Logan came back inside, and he was fumbling with his thumbs and was looking down at the ground like a nervous child.

"You okay, Logan?" Mel questioned and I looked at him and raised one eyebrow,

"Why do you look like you saw a ghost?" I went around the counter and grabbed his hand, "Hey, what is it?" I whispered, Mel coming up beside me.

"I uhh have something to ask you two." His voice breaks and he sits down at the table, we both follow, wondering what the hell's going on. "As you both know Lauren and I are going really well right now and she is halfway through college same as you, Scar but I think she's the one," he mutters, still looking at the ground. Mel's face lights up and I couldn't help the growing smile that was spreading from one ear to the other,

"Oh my god, Logan!" Mel squeaked, running around the table and pulling him in for a hug, jumping up and down with excitement,

"Are you planning on proposing to her, Logan?" I asked, grabbing his hand as he let out a deep breath after Mel let him go.

"Yes, she's the one for me and I've got mum's ring that she gave me before she passed, I want to give it to her." He looks up from the ground with a weary smile.

"I think that's a fantastic idea Logan, I love Lauren. When do you want to do it?" I couldn't be happier for him; I have always wanted him to find love and he has found such a nice girl to fall for.

"Tonight, during the party while her whole team is here. You guys are like her family and well, because you're the captain, I wanted to ask your permission because you're like their mum you know," he shrugs, and his voice begins to break. I smile at him and get up out of my chair, taking his hands in mine.

"Logan, I'd be honoured if you did it tonight. She's amazing and you deserve to be happy. Mum would want it too and she would be so proud of you."

His face finally changes from the weary smile to a smirk, his eyes beam with excitement, he really is lucky and so is she.

"Well then, I'm glad that's covered. Now let's finish getting sorted so we can get ready ourselves." He takes the last plate of food, kissing mine and Mel's cheek and walks outside. Mel turns to me with excitement about to burst out of her face. We both jump and cheer quietly to each other and then hug each other for a while, knowing that everything's going to be okay.

I go upstairs to get ready and as I walk to my room, I remember that Miles used to live with me. I open the door slowly and the scent of Miles whoofs my senses, tears falling down my heated cheeks. I step in and look around, nothing of his is here anymore. I drop on the bed and his scent is strong on my bed, on his old pillow. I remember our night on my birthday, him on top of me, in me. His lips planted on mine, our bodies entertained, him inside of me and the way his groans came through my ears, making a shiver run through my veins.

"Miss him too?" Mel whispered and I shot up from the bed, quickly wiping my tears off my face, trying to hide them.

"No, of course not. He left without saying goodbye, I don't miss him at all!" It's only a partial lie, I did miss him around, he made me feel safe and loved but after he left me and completely shattered my heart on the courts, I've hated him every second since then. He broke me and I waited until this was sorted but obviously it wasn't, he was only using me for a good time.

"Mhmm okay, well Logan sent me up to check on you. Guests will be arriving soon and you're not ready. Do you need help picking something to wear?" She whispered, sitting down next to me. I shake my head, I had my outfit picked out already when I got home, I was just too worried about getting the rest of the party sorted. "Okay, well they will be here in ten minutes so why don't you go wash your face and get ready, if you're not down when they get here, Logan and I can take them out back and start." She clutched my hand in hers and I nod my head, the words turn to ash on my tongue, being here with his overwhelming cologne is obviously tipping me over the edge.

Mel helped me off the bed and closed my door behind her as she went downstairs. I went into my bathroom and washed my face with cold water. I applied some makeup to hide the fact that I was both blushing and crying at the same time and got dressed. I heard the door open, and voices come from downstairs as I finished getting ready and saw everyone at the door.

Happiness flooded my senses as everyone came in and hugged me, thanking me for helping them win today and for the party as they all walked outside. Everyone drank and danced for hours, and the food was a hit.

"Did you really cook all of this on your own?" Annie was shocked, every bite of my food made her mouth drop.

"Yeah, all were my mum's recipes so I hope you all like them."

"They are fucking amazing, thank you for hosting tonight," Lauren hugged me, I squeezed her back and saw Logan standing behind her as everyone forms a circle around him. Shocked faces and silent awes all around us as I smiled at Logan and he slowly dropped onto one knee. I pulled Lauren away from me and gave her the biggest smile I could, her confused face gave me joy, knowing she had zero clue what was about to happen made me gleam with excitement. I turned her around slowly as she looked over everyone and then she saw Logan down on one knee and instantly started crying.

"Lauren Green, you have made me the happiest man alive. You helped my family and I through so much and I want to make you my wife, so Lauren," he paused, pulling out the ring box from his pocket and opening it. Mum's beautiful sapphire ring shimmered in the light, leaving everyone starstruck as Lauren sobbed and giggled, "will you marry me?" His voice threatened to crack but he held his own, pushing through the nervous feeling and he gave her the biggest smile I had ever seen.

"Yes, yes I will!" She shouted and Logan laughed and jumped up, kissing her long and hard. Everyone cheered and partied over the announcement and Logan put mum's ring on her finger, it fit perfectly.

"Welcome to the family, sis!" Mel shouted, jumping in for a group hug. Lauren laughed out loud and turned to me,

"I'm happy to welcome you in, I'm so excited to have you as my sister-in-law, Lauren," I reached for her and squeezed her tight as she did the same. We've been friends for a while now and she helped us through too much. She has been a part of our family since we moved but now it's official.

"Thank you, did you know about this?" She wiped away her happy tears and took my hands in hers.

"Yeah, he told me this afternoon, asked for my blessing, you know, because I'm your captain so I'm like the mum of the group he said," we giggled and Logan's face goes red,

"Hey, no need to out me like that," he laughed as we all partied away and everyone had a look at her ring, congratulating the happy couple.

It was close to two in the morning when people finally started to crash, everyone was staying over at our place so they couldn't drink themself sick and not worry about having to find a way home. We had heaps of room anyway but most of them didn't make it up the stairs, they either crashed outside on the ground or in the living room.

I woke up at five thirty like always and quietly made my way around everyone, trying not to either stand on them or wake them up as I went for my morning run. I don't normally drink but when I do it's not a lot so I feel fine, but the rest of the team probably can't say the same.

The fresh cool morning air flowing across my cheeks feels like heaven, sucking in a deep breath to help set a pace for my lungs. I ran around the block and when I got back I slowly opened the door and all I could hear was groans of pain.

"Morning, Scar, by chance is there any coffee ready?" May got up from her chair and her hands immediately planted over her mouth.

"Please if you're going to vomit go outside or use the containers I left lying around. I'll go make coffee for everyone now, won't be long." I giggled as I walked over to the kitchen where Logan's already up and started on breakfast, "It's unusual seeing you cook, Logan, plus what are you doing up so early?" I asked as I went to take a cup of coffee for myself before all the hungover zombies hoarded my kitchen.

"Ha, yeah I thought I would get a head start on the poor hungover girls we have laying all over our house. I'm up early because Lauren's one of those drunk girls and has been heaving for hours, so some food would at least put something in her stomach to help her throw up." He puts out all the plates on the bench and walks out, "How are you feeling?" He turned, giving me sad puppy eyes,

"About last night? Good, I'm really happy for you," I smiled back and took a piece of bacon off the plate,

"No, I meant about you know, Miles? Mel said she found you in your room last night, laying on the bed and smelling his pillow before everyone got here." He stopped and properly turned to face me and the sad look in his eyes grew bigger,

"Oh, umm I guess I'm okay, still heartbroken, I am more confused than anything else, I shouldn't have fallen so quickly." I huffed as some of the girls started making their way into the kitchen.

"Glad you're good then, we can talk more later but first, probably should help your zombie friends out," he laughed and went up the stairs, leaving the hangover group with me. I rolled my eyes and gave everyone a plate and coffee and they slowly started eating.

It was probably around lunch time when everyone started looking more alive. We gave them food, coffee, electrolytes and painkillers to help with their hangovers and Logan started taking them home. Because it's Sunday, we have a break day today so everyone can spend the rest of today trying to make themselves feel better for tomorrow.

I went upstairs and started to study. We had exams all this week and now that we're a week from qualifiers and need to be in LA by Friday, our teachers squeeze all of our exams into a week for us, not leaving us much time for anything else besides study and practice.

This week has been so slow, exams after exams, I thought my brain might explode. I had eight exams this week and now I'm finally finished for the semester so I can focus on basketball and what we need to do when we get to LA. I booked our flights on the weekend once we heard that we are going from the basketball board and everyone was to meet at the courts today for our flight at six tonight.

I walk over to the courts when I hear footsteps coming from behind me. "Hey, Scar, are you ready for LA?!" Lauren wrapped her arm around my neck and bumped into me, she's the most excited. Her first year as vice-captain and even though it was a short stint, she will probably get it next year if I'm still captain.

"I am, I have everything ready for us when we get there and for training as well, I had to book the training courts in advance, so we had good times." I pulled up my phone to see if maybe Miles might wish me good luck. I sent him a text this morning, but I hadn't heard anything back, guess he was serious then.

"That's great to hear, last year we had to either train at five in the morning or at eight in the evening and it was fucking awful," Lauren's eye roll could be heard from a mile away and I laughed, it's nice having good people around. The team has gotten much closer since Sam left.

We make it to the courts, and everyone has their stuff packed, ready to go to the airport. Logan and Mel are coming too, they had to book their own flights but with my inheritance from mum, I could afford a lot of things.

"Alright team, we will go in groups to the airport. When you get there go straight in and sort out everything you need, then we'll meet up before we get on the plane." I walk around and hand everyone their tickets. "We're in business class. I thought it might help you all relax a bit if you were more comfortable so please enjoy the flight." Everyone's faces turned to shock and thanked me loudly for the upgrade. The flight was almost seven hours as we didn't have to make any stops and the hotel we are staying at is beautiful from what I saw in the pictures.

We gathered our things and group by group everyone got to the airport and checked in, waiting in the lounge for our flight to be called. I get there after them with

Logan and Mel and we check in together. I go first in the line of the three of us and hand my ticket over to the desk lady.

"Sorry miss it looks like you have the wrong ticket, let me print off your new one." The lady behind the flight desk said and I turned to look at Logan and Mel and they were just as confused.

"Uhh no that should be right, I booked the flights myself." I was in shock when she handed me my new ticket, first class. "I-uhh didn't book this," I'm at a loss for words, who did this.

"Well, it looks like your seat was upgraded along with Logan Taylor, Melaine Taylor and Lauren Green." She nodded and all of our mouths dropped to the floor.

"Does it say who did it?" I asked, trying to lean over the counter to see if there was a name on the screen,

"No, just the tickets, now if you will excuse me I have other people to board onto the flight." I moved over so Logan, Mel and Lauren could check in and I checked my phone, I had a message from an anonymous number.

'Enjoy the upgrade, Ember, have a safe flight.'

Did Miles upgrade my flight? He makes me fall for him and then shatters my heart, doesn't talk to me for weeks and then he upgrades my flight, what the fuck's going on with this man!?

I went over to the girls, and they must have noticed the confused and pissed off look I had on my face,

"What's wrong, Scar, is there something wrong with the flight?" May asked, stepping closer to me,

"No nothing like that just ahh, someone upgraded my seat to first class along with my siblings and Lauren, sorry guys I didn't know." I let out a big sigh and looked at the team, hoping they wouldn't be upset with me.

"Don't apologise, Scar, you guys deserve to relax before the qualifiers. You've all gone through so much plus you upgraded us so it's nice someone did it for you," Tegan started giving me a big smile and pulling me in for a hug.

We all sat and chatted about the plan once we got to LA. When our flight gets called, the four of us are called for first class seating and then the team board afterwards. I sat down next to Mel and we both chatted about what she's been doing at the gallery and how her art has been thriving. I couldn't be prouder of her, she wanted this for so long and now we all get to live our dreams, I just wished I had someone to share it with.

We landed at about ten at night and got cabs to our hotel, it was beautiful. Gold decorations and dull lighting to make the hotel look relaxing and glamorous. We each got our room keys and went up to our rooms, we all said goodnight to each other and immediately crashed, after a big few days we all needed some rest.

I wake up at five thirty like always and instead of going for a run, I walk downstairs to the gym, getting my warmup in as we are on the fifteenth floor of the hotel with lots of stairs. I go in to start working out and slowly one by one my team must have the same idea, coming in and working out before we go for breakfast and go train. I booked the courts from nine until twelve, giving us plenty of time to train and sort out our placements.

We all work out for about forty-five minutes before we go into the shower room that the hotel has at the gym and clean up before going back to our rooms. We yapped the whole way up the elevator because there wasn't a chance I was walking all those stairs again after working out so hard, we all got ready and met downstairs at the entrance to go get coffee and breakfast. The hotel had a complimentary breakfast but we wanted to enjoy our time in LA and explore a little while we were here.

We walked up the street to a cute breakfast spot that Lauren found on the internet and we all sat outside looking over the city. We ordered a lot of food, being athletes we kind of need to eat and coffee. We had a variety of different pancakes and waffles, fruit and cream, bacon, eggs, hashbrowns and everyone had their own type of coffee they enjoyed. We ate and spoke about our strategy for the next three days. Today was Thursday, meaning today would be our only time really to train and figure out what our plan is before the three-day tournament, it went from Friday to Sunday and then we would fly home Monday morning.

We finished up and got a cab for the group to go to the courts and they were massive. The gym had six courts in it instead of one like our college had but this was the basketball gym here not just for college students but the pro teams that live in LA train here too. I could feel the excitement radiating off of the team and we were ready to go. We stretched and started on drills that would help us get into the mindset. The team did defence and shooting drills while I sat down after a while to come up with a plan. We knew who we were playing over the next three days and every team was different. I already watched videos of most of the teams to learn what they played like to figure out what we needed to do against them.

"Okay girls, come in." I shouted, they shot the balls into the hoop and ran over, grabbing their water. "So, we only have today to sort out anything you're worried about so let it now or forever hold your peace." I shouted, and the girls looked around seeing who would say something first. "Okay, I will go first, I think we need to work on everyone's shooting. Yes, I'm pretty good and so are most of you but some aren't strong in that area. Same goes for defending, I definitely could work on it." I huffed and the girls all nodded in agreement.

"I think we need to focus on head space too, some of us are getting distracted on the court. I know we've all had our downs this season but we need to be focused." Lauren stated and the girls all started listing off some ideas and things we need to work on.

After three hours of training, we got back to the hotel and we spotted the men's team going into the same hotel we're staying in and I froze in my tracks. Seeing Miles over the rest of the team made my body freeze, why the fuck do they need to stay at the same place.

"Hey, Scar you okay?" Mel grabbed my hand and I snapped my head to her eyes.

"Miles, his-his team's staying at the same hotel," I whispered and my blood began to boil, fuck this.

"Just breathe okay, he made himself clear where he stands. You need to focus on the game." She cupped my face and stared at me until I calmed down. I nod my head and we walk to the hotel, going straight to the elevator. I can't do this right now, he may think paying for my flights to be upgraded will win me back but he can shove his flights where the sun doesn't shine.

The girls wanted to sit down and hang out for a while but I declined, I needed to do more research on the teams and get Miles out of my fucking head. So, I went into my room and pulled my laptop out, combing through footage of teams past games.

It took me hours of researching before I realised it was ten and I hadn't had dinner yet. I luckily packed snacks just in case I got hungry and had some before passing out, thinking of the games and of Miles. His hand reached up my leg, tickling the sensitive spot of my thigh and his fingers reaching my soaked panties.

I jerked awake, my alarm going off to wake me up. I was drenched in sweat and my face was flushed. For fuck sake come on, Scarlet, its game day, get your fucking head on straight. I got up quickly and immediately went for a cold shower, no way was Miles going to ruin this for me too. After I had my shower, I went to the elevator to go down to the gym and when I opened the door I ran into a massive wall of a person.

"Fucking hell, sorry," I covered my forehead and looked up, deep blue eyes stare back at me, soaking in every detail.

"Morning, Ember." Miles muttered, beads of sweat dripping down his gorgeous face.

Umm I think the fuck not.

"It's Scarlet to you now thanks, and I need to start working out. We have a game soon." I pushed past him, his scent floods my senses and I stop, turning slightly to face him.

"Ember, I mean fuck, Scarlet, I'm sorry for what I did. I didn't have a choice!" His voice went down to a whisper.

"I don't care, you broke me Miles, you fucked everything up. I should have never agreed to your date. You played me like a fool and then shattered me on the court and didn't say anything to me again. Oh, but then the cherry on fucking top, you upgraded my flights, are you kidding me!" I shout and step closer to him, pointing my finger at him, "You had a choice, and you broke me. How can I forgive you for that." I whimper, tears fill my eyes and I know I'm being way too loud.

"I know I'm sorry, sorry for everything. I will win you back, I just have something I need to do first, please believe me when I say that I did love you, I still do. You're mine, always." He goes to grab my hand but I step back and pull myself away out of his reach.

"Whatever," I turned and walked away, leaving him at the door. I can't believe him, who does he think he is? I worked out a little too hard and then got the elevator up to my room. I went for another cold shower, to cool off the rage building in my stomach and got ready to head to the courts.

CHAPTER 22 – MILES

What the fuck is wrong with me! Sam was in her room so I could speak to Scarlet freely but of course she hates me, I did fuck her up, turned her world upside down and threw it in the bin.

Once I got up to my room I went for a shower, trying to breathe. My PI had everything ready for me and I sent it all to Dad yesterday before my flight. He was shocked when he realised that Sam was behind most of the scheming which didn't surprise me one bit. I was just waiting for the call from Dad to tell Sam that it's over and the police already knew what was happening so they're on standby for when I'd tell her but I want to do it in front of everyone. I know, a little petty yes, but it's what she deserved. She wanted me to break Scarlet in front of everyone so I'll fuck her up in front of everyone, to prove what I did wasn't my choice. I did it to save Scarlet, now I want to save our relationship.

I got ready and grabbed everything when I heard a knock on my door,

"Morning babe, how did you sleep?" Sam opened the door and walked herself in.

"Help yourself I guess," I sighed and continued to pack my gym bag, ignoring her attempts to get my attention.

"So grumpy this morning, I know what will make you feel better," she tried to grab my face to kiss me when I pulled away from her, pushing her back onto the bed.

"I told you that I wouldn't and you still try, what the fuck is wrong with you?!" I shout, grabbing my stuff and leaving her there. I've had enough of this shit and I know it won't be long until I can finally leave her and then jail can have her.

I got a cab to the courts and my team slowly came in one after the other. We had about half an hour before our game started and then the women's team played in between each of our games. In total we had eight games today, nine tomorrow and eight again on Sunday so we will be fucked. Each game goes for forty-five minutes, they do this so that everyone has a chance to play and so we aren't too exhausted, so we play for six hours and tomorrow we play for six hours and forty-five minutes. There's a men's section and a women's section of teams, so the women's teams don't have to play the men's and vice versa.

The courts here are massive, each freshly done ready for today.

"Okay team come on, warm up!" I shouted, the boys all followed over and we started stretching and doing a few warmup drills. Sam was already sitting over on our side of the bench but as I looked over I noticed the women's team coming in. They didn't have to be here for at least another forty-five minutes but they obviously wanted to come watch the competition for who they would be versus down the line.

Scarlet saw me before I looked at her, her bright green eyes burning holes into mine as I gave her a small smile and she quickly looked away, turning back to Annie and Lauren as they were talking about something.

I need to focus, we are about to start and I need to focus on the game, not on anything else, right?

"Hey dude, can we chat for a sec?" Cal called over

and I nod, moving away from everyone else.

"What's up?" I run over, stretching as I go over to him,

"I know you've had a rough few weeks so I wanted to check that you're okay man." Cal tapped my shoulder and looked over at Sam, "is she giving you a hard time, I thought you loved Scarlet?" His eyebrows crease and my heart begins to break again as memories of what I did to Scarlet come back.

"Yeah I do, it's just.. it's complicated." I turn to look over at Sam, who's waving and smiling at me, I turn away from her. I do not want to talk to her, I can't even look at her right now.

"Well, if it helps. I think Scarlet will forgive you, it may not be easy but she will. You should think about her today, while we play, so you're not in your head about something else," he peeked over at Sam once more and a small smile crossed my face. Cal's been there for me through thick and thin and he knows when something is up.

"Thanks man, I'll think about it. Now you too have to stretch and warm up, go." I tapped his shoulder as he ran off, leaving me there to think about things. As I begin to walk over to the team my phone rings, Dad's name appears across the screen and my lips start to flick upwards.

"Hey, Dad, did you find something?" I questioned, trying not to look too serious or happy, do not need Sam knowing somethings up.

"Hey son, yeah I did. I have enough here to send Davis and Travis's dad to jail forever. For Travis and Sam," he sighs, he loved Sam, only because he was best friends with her dad but he knew I wasn't happy with her, "the police have already got Travis and are trying to delay his phone call because he will call Sam and warn her which won't help him but they are getting a warrant for her arrest to get her arrested in LA and bring her back to New York so she can be prosecuted. They both will be going to jail for multiple things and we can get restraining orders for you and anyone else needed once they get out if they do." He sighed again, "I just can't believe she did this,"

"I know, Dad, but I've been trying to tell you for years that she's a bit crazy." It's happening, they are going away. My insides start to dance as I push the feeling down, trying not to show too much.

"I know, I'm sorry for not listening to you, Miles, I'm here from now on, whenever you need." His voice is shaky, I can tell he is sad about not being around more but he's a busy man and I knew that.

"It's okay, I have to go. Thank you, Dad, you don't know how much this means to me."

"Good luck today son, I'm watching it live so I will see everything. You've got this." I smiled and hung up the phone, that's what I will think about, knowing that by the end of the day she will be arrested and gone, then I can go to Scarlet and beg for forgiveness. Explain what was happening, I dragged her into this even though she wanted to wait and now I'll do anything to get her back.

The buzzer went off for our five-minute warning before the match began and I ran over to put all my stuff into my bag. "Okay guys come in," I shout waving everyone over, "I just wanted to say how proud I am of all of you. We did this last year and won and I know we are stronger than we were. We've got this and we'll make it to the championships. I love you guys like brothers and no matter what happens you have all done so well." They all smiled as they pat each other on the back, clapping and cheering for one another. The buzzer goes off for a minute warning and runs onto the court, getting into our formation and I look around, Cal is in the middle ready to get the ball while half of the team's on our side and the other half's ready to cross the line when the buzzer goes off.

When that buzzer goes off I focus, only on my team, on the ball and on the game. Keeping a good breathing rhythm to keep up with the push I am demanding on my body and Cal gets the ball and the game begins.

We have two members hanging back in the other team's area, so we don't have to rush over unless we need to while most of us follow the ball, in case we need to pass off or take it from the other team.

The first half ends and I can see Scarlet's beautiful smile as her and her team stand on the benches cheering for us as we run off the court. The score's twenty-five to thirteen to us, the other team isn't as strong as we are and I knew this from the videos I studied. They usually try to play one half strong and the other weak, like we did in our last game but their strong half won't beat us. They are one of the weaker teams in the competition that are here and we're using it to our advantage. We tried to pick up which half they would push and which they wouldn't, we all knew the first half was their choice to hang back on. They don't have fantastic shooting skills but they were quick on the court and we will match that next half.

"Okay boys, what do we think?" I ask the team to see what they notice and what they want to plan for the next half.

"They definitely didn't push that half, it has to be this half that they will push so we need to keep up." Check, so they were paying attention.

"They are fast and smaller than us so we need to keep low and try to keep up, spread out as much as we can," check again, there's one more thing I'm looking for and Cal looked me in the eye and knew exactly what I was thinking,

"We can't stick to one person, pick an area and focus on the ball, not the person. They're too fast for us to only be on one of them so we need to make sure that we either have the ball or they don't get the ball into the hoop," god damn, this team is amazing.

"Well done, I couldn't have said it better myself, now let's get back out there and finish this!" We all cheer back onto the court and the women's team cheers behind us, shouting phrases of encouragement and I look over at Scarlet and she's smiling back at me, maybe I haven't lost everything.

We did exactly what the team said, we watched the ball making sure we had it or they didn't shoot. We were on fire but they were fast as shit, making the game a little close. We were all so tired but we pushed through it. Working our muscles and watching our breathing, and the final buzzer went off and we cheered along with the girls, we won, climbing our way to the championships. We knew it wouldn't be easy but after that first game the rest of the day will be rough. We shook hands with the other team and we ran over to grab our water and towels, they aren't finished for the day either. Everyone here plays for the full three days to try and get to the top, just a small mistake can take you from the top to the bottom. As I'm drinking my water, Sam runs over to me and hugged me from behind,

"Well done baby, you did so good. Oh, umm eww, you're all sweaty!" She walked back slowly and had her arms out in disgust.

"Well, no shit I just played for forty-five minutes, you think I don't sweat?" I huffed, wiping some of the sweat off of me before I saw the court doors swing open, blue and black uniforms officers walked in.

A smile threatened to cross my lips but I held it back, no matter how much I hate Sam I shouldn't smile about someone being taken away. Sam followed my sight and saw the police, her face went white and her body shakes, threatening to give out,

"What are they doing here?" She whispered, trying to not collapse at my feet,

"See, when you go around threatening people it'll bite you in the ass," I whispered in her ear, the smile slowly appearing on my lips, "and you should know better than to threaten me," I pulled myself away and waved over to the police.

"Samantha Rhodes?" The policeman came over and asked, looking her dead in the face, Sam couldn't move or say anything.

"Yes, this is her." I nod to Sam and she turns to look at me, her face is so white that it could blend in with paper.

"You did this?" She whimpered, her crocodile tears falling down her face,

"I told you that I'd never forgive you. Threatening me was probably the dumbest thing you've ever done." I stepped back and nodded to the police officer to take her away.

"Samantha Rhodes, you are under arrest for.." I walked away before I heard anything else. I didn't want to know what she was going away for, just that she would be going away for a while. She thrashed and kicked as they took her out, screaming for me to help her and I didn't feel any remorse whatsoever.

"What the fuck was that?" Cal ran over and put his hand on my shoulder, making sure I was okay.

"She threatened me and she's getting what she deserves, I can't really talk about it." He knew that Sam was awful for me and knew that I wouldn't do anything without a reason, so he nodded at me and went back over to the team when a policewoman walked back in.

"Are you Miles?" She asked, halting behind me. I turned to her and she put her hand out, trying to hand me something, "the girl said that this belongs to you and asked if I could hand it over to you," confused, I put my hand out and she placed the red stone ring in my hand. She knew it wasn't hers but displayed it like it was hers anyway. I smiled at the officer and she turned away to walk back out.

I put the ring back in the box I had with me, I carried it everywhere hoping I'd get the ring back from Sam and put it back in my bag.

The buzzer for the women's team went off and they all ran onto the courts, cheering themselves on, trying to boost their spirits. My team and I cheered them on as they played.

Their team was so good, they could be even better than ours. We watched and studied their strategies as they played hard. They were one on one in this game and I hadn't done much research on the women's teams but this team's tough especially being the first team that they have to play against. Each person on this team had their best spot and the girls had to buddy up so they could try and stop their team from doing their best. This is why Scarlet did that training, they swapped out when needed if they were tired or needed to be elsewhere and it wouldn't matter because each girl was good at everything.

The halftime buzzer went off and it was twenty-four to twenty-two to the other team and we cheered our girls on as they ran off and huddled up. I sat there and watched Scarlet in her element, her orange red hair braided back, exposing her soft skin, her bright green eyes moving over every team member as she spoke to all of them and her small yet firm hands moving as she spoke, explaining what's happening and how to do it. She's a great captain, a born leader and she is definitely doing her job well. These girls didn't make it to qualifiers last year because of Annie's leg but they were determined to get to the championships this year.

The warning buzzer went off and they went back onto the court, my team cheering phrase again just like they did to encourage us, the second half starts and they're on fire. They are pushing hard this half, trying to raise their score so they can be comfortable at the top without anyone threatening to take their spot and that's what they did. They were quick and agile the whole game while being defensive and aggressive when needed. By the time that buzzer went off their score rose above the other team by double, fifty-six to twenty-eight.

My team shot out of our seats, cheering and clapping so loudly that I think they could hear us back in New York and the girls shook the other team's hand and ran back over, cheering and clapping as well. My team got off the bench and went over to congratulate them before running onto the court to warm back up for our next game and I wait, to see if Scarlet would even give me a chance to explain.

Cal's over with Lauren and Scarlet and when he leaves, Lauren talks to Scarlet about something as Scarlet's green eyes look over at me. My heart skips a beat, this woman could drop me to my knees and she wouldn't even have to try. I look at Lauren as she pats Scarlet on the back and looks over at me and nods at me, giving me permission to go over to Scarlet so I nod back as she walks away. I get up from my seat and Scarlet turns to look at me, staring up at my eyes, her big green eyes already welling with tears.

"Hey, Ember, don't cry," I go to put my hand on her cheek and she steps back slightly.

"What happened, I need to know now!" She exclaimed, her hands starting to shake as a lone tear fell out of her eye.

"I can give you the short version now but I want to explain everything, please let me give you the full answer, I'm so sorry I hurt you, Ember." My voice shakes, god I hate this. I want to be able to hold her, to kiss her, to tell her that it will never happen again but I can't force it, I can't force her to love me again after everything that's happened.

"Okay," she sniffles, wiping the lone tear off her cheek.

"Dinner tonight, if you're up for it? I want to explain, earn your trust back. I will beg on my knees for you, Scarlet." I force myself to stay where I am, not to step any closer and kiss her soft lips forever.

"Dinner sounds good, umm you should probably go

warm up, your teams waiting." She steps back and turns away, walking over to Lauren and I can only pray that she'll understand what happened, why I was such an asshole, maybe there was a way I didn't have to completely humiliate her in front of everyone.

I need to focus, at least if I want to think about Scarlet it needs to be positive, ways that we could be together. I need to go and warm up though, so I walk over to the team as we ready ourselves for the second game.

We played like crazy all day, winning five out of six games and coming a close second in one of them. Still leaving us at the top but too close to the second and third placed teams. The women's team on the other hand smashed everyone they versed today, winning every single one of their games. Most of them scored quite high so their score on the board was way higher then second and third place but we still have two days of back-to-back games. I just hope that we can do as well as we did today every other day.

I'm so fucking nervous.

It's the first time in a while since I have even been able to have a conversation with Scarlet let alone actually being alone with her. I offered Lauren and Logan to come but Scarlet wanted to hear from me and me only and I wondered if Lauren and Logan have told her that they knew all along what was happening, trying to help her see her way through the dark.

I had a long shower and got ready. We're going to a nice place down the street but really every place in LA is fancy at least in my book so it was formal wear and I wasn't sure if I had anything let alone if Scarlet had anything. I did pack a suit for the presentation at the end of the three days of the competition but I can wear it now and take it to a dry cleaners tomorrow. I threw on the suit and added my favourite cologne, it smelt of vanilla and leather. I did my hair, not that I have much but curls take a bit more to get ready then straight hair and I went downstairs to the lobby, waiting for Scarlet to come down.

I waited five minutes and kept checking my phone, it felt like time was moving so slow and I was freaking out. What if she set me up to humiliate me? I deserve it honestly, I was a dick to her and I don't even deserve a second chance or to be able to explain my actions, but she wanted to talk so that's what I would do.

If time was going slowly when I turned to look at the elevator, time actually stopped. She's wearing the dress I bought her for her birthday party and she looked fucking beautiful in it. I dreamt of taking her back home and fucking her with the dress on and then again while slowly pulling it down her shoulders and hips until it fell on the ground and. No Miles, you cannot get hard right now man pull yourself together.

I realised my mouth was on the floor so I quickly picked it up and adjusted myself so no one would notice the big package I had in my tight ass suit pants. Her dress is all black with the top being all lace and solid fabric around her perfect breasts and it snatched in at her waist, flowing down from there. Her hair is half up half down, pinned back and curled just like at the party and my heart is going to break. Did she wear this to punish me, I deserve that too but fuck me she's gorgeous.

"Miles?" She whispered, moving herself in front of me so I could see her clearer, must have zoned out.

"Sorry, Ember, you look gorgeous, how are you feeling?" I asked, standing over her and her perfume overjoyed my senses, if we weren't in the lobby of a hotel I would bury my head in her neck and make her whimper.

"I'm okay, you deserve a second chance, Lauren spoke to me on my way out. Her and Logan knew right?" Her face was both sad and a little joy sparkled in her eye. She knew it was a setup, Lauren warned me that she was going to figure it out and I knew she was too smart not too.

"They did, but first before we get talking let's go to the restaurant. Don't want to be late." I held out my arm and looked over my shoulder. "Come on, Ember, the limo's waiting," she let out a small smile and my heart aches as she loops her arm in mine and we walk to the limo. I open the door for her and she smiles at me as she takes my hand to help her get in the car. I close the door behind her and my heart is singing a song of joy and love as I get around to the other side. I'm not sure if she will fully forgive me but even just being able to talk to her's enough for me right now.

CHAPTER 23 – SCARLET

Before Scarlet went into the elevator

"How do I look?" I opened my door and Lauren was waiting for me to come out on the other side. Her jaw hit the ground and her eyes couldn't seem to remove themselves from my body, "Umm you know you're engaged to my brother right?" I giggled and did a spin for her,

"I know that but girl, if I was attracted to women, I would be all over you because fucking hell!" She gestured to me, moving her hands up and down in front of me, "you look fucking drop dead gorgeous, Scar, I'm glad your giving him a chance, he still loves you." She helped me tie up the corset back, looping the tiny piece of string fabric through the loops.

"Does he?! That's not what it felt like when he broke me on the courts in front of everyone, or when he left me the night of the birthday party he planned for me." I was still fuming about everything but I knew it had something to do with Sam, she's fucking crazy, thankfully she was arrested today for assault and other things.

"He did do those things but you should listen to what he has to say, Sam's crazy and you knew Travis was behind something too, he was arrested yesterday, Mum called me. Both him and Dad, for similar charges." Lauren tied my strings and patted my shoulders, I turned and her face was full of sadness but she looked almost pissed too, "he never told me what they were doing and when he threatened you that night after your party I was so mad I could have killed him, doing Sam's dirty work." She paced around and then came to a halt, he did WHAT!

"I'm sorry, repeat that?" I stalked up to her and her face dropped to the floor.

"Shit, I wasn't supposed to say anything, he wanted to talk to you about it all." She sat on the bed and covered her face, sobbing into her hands,

"Hey, hey Lauren I'm sorry for getting mad, what's wrong, what happened? You can tell me we are going to talk about it anyway and I won't go until you stop crying, you'll make me miss my date." She lifted her head and laughed through her tears and snot, wiping it away with her sleeve.

"Dad was working with Davis, taking people's money. When Davis and Dad got caught we went bankrupt. Dad contacted Travis to talk to Davis and he promised him a good sum of money if he did something for him and he was told to get your money and he would get a piece of it. Obviously when he realised he wasn't getting close to you because of Miles, he teamed up with Sam as she promised him more money. So, they worked together. Sam got Miles, threatened him to not talk to you, he had to propose and to break your heart. Sam had Travis on standby if Miles broke the rules she set." Lauren finally took a breath and I could feel her heart breaking, the tears begging to fall back out.

"I'm so sorry I caused all this mess for you and your family. I didn't even know about the money, I'm assuming mum wanted to wait to tell me when I turned twenty-one. Is that why he did what he did, because of her?" It all makes sense, and I was so close to figuring it out when Lauren and Logan veered me into a different direction so I wouldn't get myself or Miles hurt. "Wow, this is so much to process, I- I need a minute." I sat on the bed next to Lauren, trying to put all the pieces together.

"I understand and I'm sorry for telling you, he wanted to tell you himself." She wiped her tears and went to leave the room,

"Hey Lauren," I called out to her, she slightly turned, "thank you for being here for me, for not letting me completely give up on Miles but keeping us both safe. You didn't have to do that so thank you." She gave me a weak smile and walked out, closing my door behind me.

What! The! Fuck!

Sam's fucking psycho and he was only trying to protect me. I am honestly glad Lauren told me and not Miles because I feel like I would've made a scene in the restaurant. It is so much to figure out and understand but still, he said the words that put a knife right through me, putting me in the hospital. Can I forgive him fully? Will we ever go back to what we were?

I took a deep breath and got up, checked my face in the mirror, making sure I didn't smudge my makeup and went to the elevator. I was so nervous for tonight, I do still love Miles with all my heart but my heart isn't full like it was, it's small and weak. I knew I would have to try and build it back up first.

The elevator opened and Miles was waiting in the lobby, checking his phone. I knew I was late but I needed time to think, to make sure that this is the right move. Mum would have loved Miles, he is sweet and kind but she would have also hated his guts for what he did to me, but mum was a firm believer in second chances.

I stepped out and he looked up from his phone, his jaw hanging almost to the floor, his deep blue eyes almost popping out of his head. I knew he loved this dress but we never got to do the things he promised to do to me last time I wore it so I thought I'd give him a hard time about it. I could see the dirty thoughts bouncing in his head as I walked closer to him,

"Miles?" I whispered, he's completely blocked out the world thinking about all the things he wished he could do to me and now I am wondering if holding out is a smart move or if I want him just as badly. He shook his head, coming back to the lobby and not the bedroom,

"Sorry, Ember, you look gorgeous, how are you feeling?" His face all flustered from the thoughts and I can see his slight boner in his tight pants as I stand in front of him.

"I'm okay. You deserve a second chance, Lauren spoke to me on my way out. Her and Logan knew right?" After Lauren explained what happened with her dad and Travis, I knew that her and Logan knew. They wanted to protect me and my heart, holding onto the little piece of hope that I would get Miles back was probably the only reason my heart didn't fail completely at the courts when he shattered it.

"They did, but first before we get talking let's go to the restaurant. Don't want to be late." Miles held out his arm to take mine, he was a gentleman and god I could use the help with walking, these heels are killing me already. "Come on, Ember, the limo's waiting."

I walked up to him and put my arm in his as we walked to the limo out the front, it reminds me of my birthday party, getting into the limo and partying with everyone but then the thoughts of Travis threatening me and Miles vanishing came back, my heart beating out of my chest and my vision starts going blank. I heard the door open and Miles put his hand out, grazing mine. It brought me back to reality, we aren't going to a party, he isn't going to vanish hopefully and Sam and Travis are in prison or at least arrested right now so we'll be okay. I smiled at Miles and took his hand to get in the limo and he made his way around to the other side of the car.

"So," I paused, thinking of the right words to say without exploding. "Can we start with why you humiliated me and shattered my heart, you know that it put me in the hospital, did Sam tell you?" I knew it was a hard and probably rude question to start with but I need to know why and if he really meant it.

"Oh okay, head first love it." He clears his throat and turns slightly to look at me, his eyes piercing mine as he begins to explain, "after everything that happened at your party, Sam wanted me to make it clear to you that you and I weren't ever a thing, to humiliate you in front of everyone so she knew I wouldn't go back to you when I really wanted to." He stopped, visions flash past his eyes and his breathing becomes shaky, I slide my hand in his and give him a smile.

"Hey, I asked. No matter how bad the answer is, I want to know." I needed to know, but I don't want him to panic about the truth. I can handle it, whenever I'm around Miles, I know that I can count on him, even after everything, there's a connection.

"Okay, she told me what to say and said if I didn't tell you that you meant nothing to me that she would get Travis to hurt you. I couldn't live with myself if you ever got hurt by him or anyone so I followed what she said, I broke you so she was satisfied and she wouldn't hurt you. I told her if I was to do this that she can't lay a finger on you and she agreed but I had to make it harsh. I'm so sorry, Sam told me you went to hospital and all I wanted to do was go see you and beg on my knees for forgiveness." Tears welled in Miles' ocean eye, he's telling the truth. Sam wanted him to fuck me up for her own evil joy, what a bitch.

"Miles, I'm sorry you had to do that but thank you for telling me. Honestly the way you said it was really believable, once you left I broke down. My body dropped to the floor and I couldn't feel, hear or see anything. Once I got to the hospital it was too much on my body and it shut down. I was asleep for a few hours and the doctor said it was a panic attack but it was a serious one." I played with my hands, not being able to look into his eyes. "Thank you for protecting me, it was shit but thank you," I breathed, fuck this is hard.

"I want your forgiveness, Ember. I want you back. I will beg on my knees for your forgiveness, in front of everyone if I have too. Please, just think about it." I squeezed his hand and gave him a tiny smile.

"I'll think about it but be warned I may ask you to kneel in front of everyone, you deserve to be humiliated a little for what you did." I giggled and his eyes lit up along with his face. I knew I would forgive him but I want to know everything that happened first before I tell him that.

We got to the restaurant and Miles, being Miles, opened my door and helped me inside. Taking us to our seats and holding out the chair for me, pushing me in as well. God this man's everything a woman wants and I see why Sam went psycho for him. We chatted about everything, what happened with Davis and how he found out about the money, Travis's dad and Davis working together, taking people's money and not telling them, Travis and Sam working together to get money and Miles back to Sam. Even about Sam wanting Miles to fuck her, he wasn't leaving any details out.

"You told her you wouldn't fuck her like the whore she was, really!?" I snorted and almost spat my wine everywhere, Miles' face went almost as red as my hair as he choked on air.

"Yeah I did, it's not what she wanted to hear, but I wouldn't lay a finger on her that way. I only wanted you, Ember and no matter how long it took I wasn't going to touch her." His face went serious, she pushed him too far that night and he drank himself sick because of it. Honestly it sounds awful but I wish this man would say hot shit like that to me because fuck man! I tried to adjust myself in my seat, trying to move the tight fabric off my clit but it didn't work that way at all.

"But all that time I just wanted to talk to you, Ember. Even to see you smile at me the way you used to before everything happened. She ruined that for me and I ruined it for you." He sighed and continued eating as did I.

We sat in silence for a minute and all I wanted to do was rip his freaking clothes off but obviously being in a restaurant with heaps of people in it, yeah no, I'm good.

"Well, change of topic. You guys did really well today, you should be proud." I smiled and swirled my wine in the glass.

"Yeah I am, they did great today but fuck me, Ember, your team is phenomenal. You guys are so high on the board that I don't think anyone will take your spot." His face lit back up and he was in his element again, basketball and me.

"Yeah, the team did amazing today. I couldn't be prouder. We've been better since Sam left so that's a bonus." We clinked our glasses to that and continued talking about Sam and her evil things she did to him, more basketball talk and him talking to Logan and Lauren about me, giving them updates on what was happening.

He really fought for me, even after what he did, he didn't mean it. He wanted me throughout everything and no matter what Sam did, he wasn't going to give her what she wanted.

We got dessert and we are just talking about basketball now.

"So, I have a question," I asked, twirling my finger around the rim of my glass.

"Of course, Ember. What is it?" He whispers, he thinks I'm playing a seduction game, well he's about to be kicked to the nuts.

"What's the plan for next year? For you?" He finishes college this year, then he can go and do whatever he wants. He could leave me again and move away.

"Well, once I'm done and have my lawyer degree, I will be working for my father as a lawyer with him. I plan on staying in New York, especially because there's something else I need that's there." His eyes go dark, going almost a blue-black colour and I can feel his erection from here.

"Oh really, and what's that, the thing you need so badly." I whisper, two can play at this game and no way was I letting him win.

"You, Ember. It's you. I need you, I want you." His foot sliding up slowly up my leg, lifting my dress under the table.

"Really, well if you want me so badly, I have one thing you need to do for me first, before you decide to get in my dress sir." I pull my leg away slowly and his puppy eyes beg me to bring it back. He craves my touch and I crave for his, but he'll need to humiliate himself first so that way we are fair and even.

"Okay, Ember, name your price. What do you need me to do?" He sits up and adjusts his seating. Poor guy probably has blue balls by now with how many times he's been hard since the lobby of the hotel.

"You said you'd beg on your knees for my forgiveness right?" A mischievous grin spreads across my face. Oh, this is going to be fun.

Going to sleep afterwards was hard, I tried to touch myself to relieve the ache of Miles but nothing helped, so I went for a freezing shower and went to work out. Last night was nice and I do forgive Miles but I just need him to fully be in it with me before I can trust him again and this will do that for me.

The girls started filing into the gym one by one and I saw Lauren come in with a massive smile as she ran straight over to me.

"Okay, details now please," she jumped over on the machine next to me and she's so excited that she was going a million miles per hour on it.

"Okay dude, slow down. You'll wear yourself out and we need to be on our A game today, we have seven games today and we were fucked after six so don't wear yourself out this morning girls, just enough to pump your body." Everyone agreed and started working out on different machines and stretched themselves out.

"Okay, now please. I'm dying to know what happened." Lauren was about to jump through the roof in excitement, god this girl's funny.

"Okay, okay, Christ. Well, he explained and we talked about everything all the way back to when I was still in Australia. When Davis found out about my money, how Sam got arrested and how long she will be away for." I paused, my cheeks flushed and I heard myself giggling.

"So, it went well then? Are you guys back together again?" She stopped her machine and her stare could burn holes into someone I swear to god.

"No, we're not." Lauren almost dropped dead, falling backwards on her machine, she's so dramatic. "But he's doing something today to make up for it." I laughed and Laurens eyebrows shot up in curiosity. I've never seen someone's facial expressions change so much or so fast!

"What's he doing! Come on, tell me!" She practically begged me to tell her, she even pulled the 'I will be your sister soon' card on me.

"You'll see when we get to the courts okay, Christ you need to chill out or give me some of that energy because I fucking need it."

"Rough night?" She pushed my shoulder and I almost trip on the machine,

"It was, and not what you think. We slept in our own rooms, you dirty girl." We laughed as we continued to work out. I can't wait for when we get there, he knew he'd have to do something but he didn't think I was serious when I told him what I needed him to do.

We got to the courts and I'm so excited to see how this would go and when I saw him his face already going bright fucking red, I knew this would be so good. Miles made his way over to us and he dropped to his knees in front of me. His hands and head are planted on the ground while he kneels,

"Oh, noble and beautiful goddess of grace and divine vengeance…" he paused, his ears are so red you could see them from outside the window, holy fuck this is going to be amazing.

"I come to you today a broken man. Nay. Not even a man. A worm. A fool. A walking, talking embarrassment wearing a shirt with your majestic face printed on it." He sits on his knees and pulls the bottom of the shirt out, showing it on display for everyone to see.

"Yes. Look upon it! Behold the shrine to her beauty plastered across my chest like the world's most desperate fan club merch. I wear it as a symbol of my shame," he pauses again and leans in to me a little so only I can hear him. "and also, because you made me, and I'm not in a position to refuse."

I giggled, trying to not let the loud, obnoxious laugh slip past my lips while he continued his embarrassing speech.

"I humiliated you. Publicly, Horribly. In a way that likely made people gasp, pause, and whisper, "Did he really just say that?" And for that, I deserve to be cast into the group chat as a cautionary tale. A meme. A man forever known as "her fucked up boyfriend who just broke her heart.""

Tears from hold my laugh back threaten to appear on my cheeks and I actually can't fucking breath.

"But YOU. You are grace, you are power, you are the main character. I, meanwhile, am the unpaid background actor who decided to humiliate you in front of all your friends and left you to fend for yourself. So, I beg and I throw myself at the mercy of your basketball shoes and ask you to forgive me. I promise to never again humiliate you or say another bad thing about you. I'll support your dreams and watch you play basketball like you're the god of the sport. I'll even wear the tiger onesie wherever you want me to and pretend that I am the baddest fucking tiger out there."

I could hear the laughs and giggles around me grow louder and I couldn't be prouder of his speech right now, considering he only had last night to prepare this.

"Let the shirt stay as my punishment. Let it be known far and wide that I messed up, and I am owned. I am yours, publicly and pathetically." He gets up and takes my hands in his, leaning over me and dropping to his knees again, dramatically.

"Please... forgive me. Or at least stop making me wear this shirt because we need to warm up and I don't want to ruin this masterpiece."

I pull myself together and help him up, staring into his big blue puppy dog eyes and smile, "yes Miles Grove, I forgive you." I pull him in for a hug and everyone cheers and laughs as we hug for a while, then he pulls himself away,

"I'll never let you go again, Ember, ever. You're mine, always." He reaches down and cups my face as I lean into him and a tear falls out of my eye. He chuckles as he pulls me in for a long, deep kiss while everyone cheers in the background. When he pulls away and kisses my forehead, I laugh at him and he goes over to change his shirt before warming up.

"Holy fuck man, you did good. That was humiliating as shit but it was so funny. I've never seen him like that, he must really love you if he agreed to do that." Lauren was pissing herself laughing as we walked over to the bench, ready to watch the boys play their game.

CHAPTER 24 – MILES

I don't think I have been so embarrassed in my entire life. I spent all night coming up with that speech and Scarlet just so happens to carry a shirt with her face on it, not saying it's a bad idea, I'll be wearing the hell out of that shirt but in front of everyone. I just hope it was enough.

The boys are now definitely in a good mood after my little humiliation act and should be as ready as ever to play hard today.

After everything that has happened I can now focus completely knowing that Scarlet has forgiven me and that I can play with my heart fully intact.

"Come on boys, let's go!" I shout as we run onto the court and everyone's still giggling like little school girls as they run onto the court, for fuck sake I am never going to hear the end of this shit.

The buzzer goes off and Cal smacks the ball in the air as the game begins. We're doing the one-on-one strategy for today, most of the teams that we are opposing have similar speed and build to each member of my team so we can work around it with our little advantages that we have on each team. One team we are faster than them, another we have strong defence, another we have to have good timing and so forth. This team was hard, they were just as good as us if not better so we had to be strong all game and push ourselves to win.

At half time we are close with twenty-two to twenty to them as we run off and huddle, trying to catch our breath. "Okay, well done boys it was a good half but we can do better. They're very similar to us so we need to try our hardest to stay on them and not miss our shots. I know this morning was funny but we need to be in the zone now." I huffed and the team hummed in agreement. "Now let's get back to it and win this thing." The boys shouted as we ran back to the court and when I turned to see Scarlet smiling at me, I blew her a kiss. She caught it and her face blushed as she pulled a loose strand of hair behind her ear shyly, god this woman's going to be the death of me.

We played hard and strong, the other team started to get dirty though, pushing and shoving my team, double dribbling to try and see if the referee would notice but by the end of the half we won, thirty-eight to twenty-nine. They went from being great to being in their heads, thinking they would lose.

"Oh my god you won, congratulations! You guys are getting further and further away from second and third place now." Scarlet jumped at me and wrapped her arms around me, I pulled her in tightly and spun her around.

"Thank you, Ember. I know I hope we can stay like that. The boys had a good time listening to me this morning so they're all happy," I chuckled and Scarlet's face lit up with amusement.

"Yeah well the girls loved it, Lauren practically peed herself laughing at you so I think they will all be in a good mood today, but I should let you know that uhh." She let go and took a step back, her face started going red and she's playing with her fingers.

"What, Ember? What's wrong, did something

happen?" I went to step closer to her and she pulled out her phone and turned it to face me, no. No, Fucking, Way!

"They-they," I stutter, for fuck sake. "They fucking filmed it!" I panic, now that's going to be everywhere, I guess I deserve that too to be fair.

"Yeah, I'm sorry I told them not to film it but it was too good and I can't confiscate everyone's phones, but good news is you're going viral," She giggled and showed me the video and literally everyone in the US has seen it by now.

I rolled my eyes and sighed, "Well, at least it's a reminder if I do something stupid." I pulled her in and kissed her, I can feel her lips spreading into a smile on mine.

"Well, I have to go warm up but I thought you should know from me before you see it." She pecked my cheek and ran onto the court.

I'm going to kill everyone. I swear I'll be grey by twenty-five.

The girls warmed up and I couldn't keep my eyes off of Scarlet. With every jump, run and squat, my eyes don't leave her at all. Her red hair bouncing around as she runs around with her team and her bright green eyes focused on the ball and the hoop.

The warning buzzer goes off and the girls slowly get into position, ready for the game to begin. Scarlet points at each person, making sure her team's ready and in position for Lauren to hit the ball to one of them if she gets the opportunity and the buzzer goes off, Lauren grabbing the ball and passing it off.

Scarlet did an immense amount of studying on the teams and she knew all their strengths, weaknesses and what the team did for their strategies. This is how they will win, Scarlet's mind is like nothing I have ever seen before. Her mind works in magical ways and she knew what she was doing when it came to figuring out what her team needed to do to win, combine that with her talents for the sport and a team that are just as good and you get this, a talented team that will top anyone they play no matter what happens.

At half time they were thirty to twenty-seven to them and by the end of the game the score was fifty to thirty. They worked so hard to not let them score in the second half and that's what they did. If they play like this all day they won't need to play the six games tomorrow because they'll be so high that no one will catch them in a day.

We went on after them and for the rest of the day we won every game we played along with the girls winning by miles in their games too. Making us both sit at the top spots for championships and I couldn't wait.

"Ember, can I talk to you?" I called out to Scarlet before she left. She turned, walking over to me as Lauren walked out and went outside without her. "I want to do this right this time and not mess things up. It's up to you how fast or slow we go this time, I don't want to force you into anything but I have a present for you. I wanted to give it to you tonight and was going to ask if you wanted to stay with me tonight?" I was blushing and my mouth went dry, I'm usually calm, cool and collective but with this girl, I was anything but that.

"Of course I will, you didn't have to get me anything to come to bed with you Miles, you know that right?" She giggled and grabbed my hand, walking us out of the courts and into a cab.

I went up to my room and cleaned it as it's a bit of a mess with all my basketball stuff lying around, it's been a mess the past two days with Sam and her shit being picked up and the tournament. The only thing that has made it all worth it was Scarlet.

About twenty minutes later someone knocked on my door and it was just room service bringing in the dinner

I had ordered for Scarlet and I. For the second time today, I was embarrassed as I had my tiger onesie on waiting for Scarlet and the poor service man had to see me in it, fantastic. I set up the food and put her onesie out on the bed for her and waited. Not long after another knock was on my door and I looked this time to check because no one else was seeing me in the onesie besides her and thank god. I swung the door open with so much confidence and it took her a minute to process what was happening before she started giggling.

"Nice outfit," she laughed as she walked in and then she went silent, stopping just inside the door.

"I got Logan to pack it for you, hoping I'd get to spend one night with you while we were here. I hope you don't mind," I stood behind her, letting her process what she needed to before she turned around with tears pouring down her face,

"You have my onesie for me?" She whimpered, god she's so cute.

"Yeah I do, I thought you would like to have a movie night with food and a comfortable outfit." I pulled her in and let her cry on my chest for a bit until it was all out of her system and she pulled away, sniffling back her tears and grabbed the onesie.

"Okay, can I get changed," I nod and point her to the bathroom and she closes the door to get changes. I don't expect sex or anything like that tonight, again it's all up to her.

She walks out and god she looks adorable in her onesie that matched mine. I beamed when she walked out and her face began to blush as she came into the bed with me and got comfortable.

"I got a bit of everything off the dinner menu. Steak, chips, salad, chicken and some pasta dishes." I pointed at everything as I explained it and her eyes couldn't keep up. "Want to watch a movie?" I put on the tv and we watched a few movies while we ate the truck load of food I ordered.

"So, you said you had a present for me?" Scarlet looked around, looking for the present I had.

"Oh, right, let me grab it." I went to my bag and searched for her present, hoping I didn't lose it. "Ahh, here it is. It's not really a present, more a return." I opened the box and showed her the ring I bought her for her twenty-first birthday. "I know it holds a lot of sad memories but I still want that promise to stand, I still want you and only you, Ember."

She looked at the ring and tears filled her eyes, her eyes can't focus on either the ring or me, going back and forth between us both.

"You kept it?" She sniffled, a single tear dripping out and down her cheek.

"Yeah, Sam thought it was rightfully hers after what happened but I got it back once she was arrested and wanted to give it back to the rightful owner." I pulled the ring out of the case and put my hand out, asking Scarlet for her hand. She hesitated and I hoped I hadn't already pushed too hard. "If you aren't ready for it, I can hold onto it." I squeezed her hand and she shook her head.

"No, I want it, I want you Miles. You're all I have wanted and I'm just happy that I have you back." She whispers, putting her hand in mine and I put the ring on her finger.

"I'm here, Ember. My heart only beats when you have it. I've seen you sweat your ass off on the court, I've seen you naked, I've seen you in this god damn onesie and I've seen you in so many clothes and no matter what, you're fucking gorgeous in everything and in nothing. I love you, Ember, always." I pull her in and kiss her, sparks ignite in my stomach and all I want to do is make this moment last forever. Scarlet's tongue sweeps over the seam of my lips and I open wide for her as her tongue finds every inch of my mouth as does mine. Our tongues twist and entangle with each other and I can feel my cock rising with anticipation. "I missed you, Ember." I pulled away and buried my head in her neck like I wanted to yesterday.

"I missed you too, my love," I paused, her body tenses and we both stared at each other for a moment, realising that we both wanted each other so badly and I had to ruin it. "Do you think that we could just eat and watch movies though, after today I am exhausted!" Scarlet hesitates, not wanting to upset me after being away from each other for so long.

"Of course, Ember, if that's what you want. Let's eat! The food will go cold otherwise." After a few movies and finishing all the food I ordered, I was stuffed but I realised I hadn't showered yet. "Shit, I need a shower. Would you like to join me in the bath, Ember? I have a spa bath in my room." I whisper in her ear, goosebumps appearing on her skin.

"A spa bath! Yes, please. My room doesn't have one, that's so unfair." She got up and slowly took her onesie off, revealing a matching sky-blue set of lingerie. Guess she isn't exhausted anymore. Scarlet turned and slowly made her way to the bathroom and started taking out her braid.

"You're going to drain me completely, Ember," I whimper. Staring at her long wavy hair as we sat in the hot water together with Scarlet sitting down in between my legs.

"Oh, we can't have that can we," she giggled, playing with the bubbles in front of us. "Can I ask you something, my love?" She whispered, moving her hair to her back instead of over her shoulder.

"Of course, Ember." I would do anything for her, especially since I have already begged on my knees for her in front of everyone, I don't think there's anything I wouldn't do.

"Can you help me wash my hair please, I need to wash it after today," Her ears went bright red, matching her hair colour almost to a tee.

"Ember, bend your head back a little." I grabbed the shampoo as she bent backwards, leaning against my chest, looking over her eyebrows with the biggest grin on her face. "I can't wash your hair if it's planted on my body," I chuckled and she giggled as she fixed herself up so I could wash her hair. "You know, Ember. I've never washed someone else's hair before."

"Really!?" She sounded shocked but I was an only child and I didn't love Sam for a while plus I never fucked her in the shower, hated it.

"Yeah, you're the first," I whispered as I washed out the shampoo in the water and grabbed the conditioner,

"Only add that to my ends please, my hair gets too oily if it's everywhere." She showed me where she wanted it and I followed her instructions.

This feels strange, helping someone else in such an intimate way. I haven't had to help anyone like this before and I know it's a simple thing to do for someone but I'll cherish this moment forever.

We hop out the bath and get into bed, entangle in one another cuddling as we fall asleep.

CHAPTER 25 – SCARLET

Last night was incredible and I hope to be like this always. I missed Miles and I was pissed at him for everything that happened but in reality, it wasn't his fault. Sam made him do all that and the only reason he did it was because if he didn't, I'd be hurt or killed. He still fought for me while with her, hoping there was something to help get me back to him and he showed me the proof just so I knew he wasn't lying.

I woke up and realised that Miles was still sleeping, one arm wrapped under the pillow and his other resting over my waist. His face is all squished on the pillow and his hair's hanging over his eyes. I watched him sleep for a moment before I tried to move, rolling over to look at the time on my phone, FUCK.

It's half past six. I woke up an hour late, I missed my workout and we play at half past seven. My team's probably about to leave to go to the courts.

"Miles, Miles!" I loudly whispered, poking his shoulder, trying to wake him up without scaring him,

"Hmm," he groaned, rolling around.

"Miles, it's six thirty, we need to get up and go. We'll be late!" I quietly shouted and jumped out of bed to get changed,

"What, it's fucking what!" Miles jumped up after me and got dressed as well, packing his sports bag.

"Six thirty, we're going to be late. I still have to go to my room and grab my shit!" I grabbed my phone and called Lauren praying she would answer me.

"Hey girl, where are you? We are in the cabs going over to the courts to warm up and I didn't see you." I can hear Tegan and May in the car as well.

"I was with Miles, I'm going to be late and I haven't even got my bag or anything packed for today!" I start panicking, my body begins to shake and my breathing becomes shallow.

"Don't panic, Scar, I have your bag." I stop panicking, Lauren has my bag, fuck she's amazing!

"What! How?!"

"I noticed you weren't at the gym and assumed you were with Miles last night, so I got the spare key from the front desk and packed your bag, I have your uniform and even a protein shake for you and Miles so hurry up and get here so we can play," Lauren giggled and I can't believe she did that, god what would I do without her.

"Lauren, you are fucking amazing, thank you. We'll see you soon," I look up to see Miles' brows furrowed and his head tilted to the side.

"I know, say hi to Miles for me, see you soon." She giggled again and hung up the phone,

"So, Lauren says hi and she has my packed bag and she has protein shakes for us both so pack your bag, I'm going to quickly do my hair and change so we can go,"

"Fuck she's good, okay quickly though. You can't be late."

We hurried to get ready and ran down the stairs instead of taking the elevator, no chance we're going on the elevator this morning and got a cab to the courts.

"Look who it is, have fun you two," Lauren laughed and handed Miles and I our drinks.

"Okay, one shut up, two thank you for these, you're

actually a life saver." I hugged her and she had such a shit stirring grin on her face.

"I know, now I need details." She whispered, trying to make sure Miles doesn't hear.

Miles just rolled his eyes as he gently grabbed my chin and kissed me, almost making me drop to my knees, "Good luck, Ember. Thank you for this, Lauren." He held up his cup and went over to the boys over on their bench, where they were all clapping and shouting.

"Drink up, I'll run warm up until you're ready, don't drink it too fast though, we don't need you throwing up everywhere." She runs over to the others as I sit down, slowly drinking my breakfast while I put my shoes on, watching Miles be bullied by his teammates for last night. I feel a little bad, we didn't even have sex and yet they're so sure we did, how?

I rolled my eyes and ran onto the court to stretch with the girls and Lauren inches over to me until she's right next to me,

"Can I help you?" I looked over and that shit stirring grin is still all over her face.

"At least tell me it was good, be disappointed if you wait weeks for him and the sex was underwhelming."

"We've had sex before last night, but we didn't last night." My cheeks feel so hot and Lauren's smile fades,

"WHAT! No sex! What did you do then." Her face is covered with confusion.

"We watched movies, ate a lot of food and had a bath together. He washed my hair." My face blushed at the memory of his soft touch on my scalp.

"Aww, that's adorable but Cal said he heard you so he just assumed," Oh for fuck sake Cal!

"You know he is probably going to be beaten for that right, I didn't even moan in bed, just when he washed my hair because it was so good," I whispered, Lauren and I giggled to each other as we stretched.

Afterwards we huddle and went over the plan for

today, we'll be so fucked today after two days of going hard. We need to maintain strength and wit today, we have six games today and each team was a little different but they're all shorter than us so we have a good advantage on defence with the height plus most of them aren't fantastic at defence themselves so long as we play to that and not burn yourselves out too fast, we can win by a long shot.

We're already close to the record for highest score in qualifiers and I want to pass it and with six games left, we can do it.

The warning buzzer goes off for a minute before the match starts, "Okay girls, come in." I shout and everyone runs over to grab a drink and huddled around me,

"We have a height advantage all day, most of us are taller than everyone on their teams but that doesn't mean that they can't defend. They're small but quick, they have bounce in their feet so keep an eye on them and their defence isn't the greatest but they could've improved since I last watched their videos. We are so far ahead that no matter what we have championships in the bag, we'll play our hardest and win these games. We've got this now, let's get out there and show them who we are!" All the girls jump and cheer as we run onto the court, everyone's pumped and ready for the day and honestly, all I'm focused on today is Miles. Having him back makes me feel full again, having him watch me play is everything to me as well as Logan and Mel being here watching, it reminds me of when mum and my siblings came to my games and watched me play, cheering me on until they had no voice left.

She'd be so proud of me and my siblings and I miss her every day, being away from her grave's heartbreaking but I can feel her here with me today, cheering me on in heaven above.

The buzzer goes off and Lauren grabs the ball and starts the match. We run up and down the court, this team's tough, they may be small but they are fast and tricky. They're also a little dirty, pushing us so we misstep, multiple fouls being called because they would do something wrong. I can hear Miles and Logan shout every time they do something wrong because the referee doesn't seem to see anything.

By half time we're twenty-two to twenty to us but a lot of those shots shouldn't have counted on their parts, they should have been fouled and most of their three-point shots weren't actually three pointers because they were over the line but apparently they still counted. It just means that the ref's biased and we just have to push harder to make sure we still come on top, I won't lose to cheaters.

"Okay girls come in," we need to figure this shit out because yes we are on top and we won't be knocked from first. Cheaters don't get to win, not against my team and I.

"Did anyone else notice what's happening out there, the ref is biased right?" Lauren squabbles as she takes a sip of water.

"Yeah I noticed it too, they are getting rough and their shots are being counted differently to what they actually are, we need to be careful." The team starts mumbling to one another, trying to figure out what we should do to help but all we can do is play the game and try our best to be safe. "We'll watch our backs, they are starting to push so we need to keep ourselves safe. If we lose that's fine we are still on top but I do not want to lose a player today, understand?" We all agreed and went back on the court, hoping that we will be fine for the rest of the match.

These girls are fucking crazy, they were the top team last year and obviously they didn't like us having their spot, but they're fourth on the board so no matter what they weren't getting first but we have been leading all season and that's pushing their buttons.

"Scar, watch out! Pass!" I heard May shout out as a

girl ran up to me at full speed like a bull running to a red cape. I passed the ball to her and sidestepped the girl, leaving her to run off the court from how fast she was running at me. The crowd all gasps and I could feel Miles' presence from here, he was going to murder someone and right now it's either that girl or the ref, either way I need to focus on the game, not on him and his deadly aura.

We have five minutes left and my team's hanging on by a thread. We pushed so hard to get our score up there so it won't matter if they score like crazy, we're at forty-five to twenty-nine to us and with five minutes left, it's impossible for them to beat that. We have been side stepping, ducking and weaving these girls all last half, they are throwing swings, jumping at us, running at us. We aren't safe. My heart begins to race, if someone gets hurt on this court.

No, don't think like that. Watch the team, shout if we see anything, that's what has kept us safe this half.

We've all shouted at each other with warning and have all successfully dodged anything that has come our way while still playing but with how tired we are, it may not last. I was watching Lauren dribble the ball up from the halfway line and as she's going in for the shot, three of their team members came up from either side and in front as she's sprinting to the hoop.

"Lauren, look out," *Thud!*

"Lauren!!!"

I ran over as the crowd screamed at the ref to call time out. He rolled his eyes as he blew the whistle and sent the girl off. Lauren's on the floor unconscious from the fall, she hit her head hard on the court floor.

"Someone call an ambulance!" I shouted and I heard running footsteps come up to my side, Logan. His eyes filled with worry and tears, breathing fast and heavy trying to not freak out, "Logan, breath, she's knocked out but still breathing, I need a towel and a bandage. She's bleeding a little, NOW!" I shouted behind me,

May and Tegan nodded and went to find the things I needed while Miles called for an ambulance.

"Is she going to be okay? Lauren, can you hear me?" He went to lift her head, trying to slide his hand under her head.

"No Logan don't touch her. Just in case of serious injury we can't move her neck or head." Miles grabbed his shoulders as he spoke to the operator, "an ambulance will be here in a minute, they're down the road." Logan sat in defeat, unable to help.

"It's okay, they will examine her and you can go with her, you're all she has left now." I pulled him in as he released his tears and cried into my arms,

"Thank you," he sniffled as May and Tegan came back with a towel. I poured water out of my bottle onto it and wiped her bleeding head gently and placed a bandage around the wound. The paramedics came in a few moments later and examined her, they were taking her to the hospital and Logan and Mel went with them.

"There's five minutes of the game left, you can either forfeit and lose or finish the match with the required numbers and win," the ref said with no sympathy in his voice. The other team's giggling to themselves with dark grins, for fuck sake. I should forfeit, our benched girls didn't come because they're busy with school and Annie hasn't been out of her moon boot for long and has only been cleared for a few weeks, what do I do?

"Put me in captain!" Annie walked over, putting her hands on my shoulders. "I'm cleared, I can play. I'm the reason we didn't make it to championships last year, let me help us get there. It's what Lauren would want." She exhaled, she's right. Lauren's dream is the same as all of ours, we want this more than anything and she'd want us to keep going.

"Okay, team, come in, now!" We huddled and I told them to play safe, they wouldn't be able to score enough to win the match so we need to hang back and be fucking careful. We ran back to the court and the ref blew the whistle to start us in again.

The other team went for shot after shot and we barely did anything to stop them. They knew they couldn't win but we did as much as we could to hold them back while keeping the team safe.

The final buzzer went off and we won at forty-five to thirty-eight, leaving the other team disappointed and disqualified. The ref was also let go for being biassed on the court, courtesy of Miles.

"Are you okay, Ember?" Miles pulled me in and spun me around, looking me up and down for injuries.

"I'll have a few bruises tomorrow, but I am fine. Have you heard about Lauren?" I can't believe what happened, it's all my fault. "I should've been watching more carefully, I didn't warn her in time and now she may miss out on her opportunity to compete, it's all..." Miles ripped me into his chest.

"Do not finish that sentence, what happened wasn't your fault, you didn't push her, you warned her. The team knew they weren't safe and continued to play anyway. You did everything you could and it still happened. You are an amazing captain, it's not your fault, Ember."

"Thank you, my love." All the sad feelings vanished for a moment, knowing he's here makes everything okay, like my world isn't crashing and burning to the ground.

"You're amazing and don't forget that." He squeezed me tightly and I pulled back and kissed him gently, then I walked back to my team as I pulled out my phone and Logan messaged me saying they just made it to the hospital and they were looking at her now, she became conscious in the ambulance, talking well and the paramedics couldn't find anything wrong with her neck and spine. Thank god.

I walked over and let the team know she's okay as the men's team went on to warm up, Miles didn't looking too pleased with what happened and with the fact that I kissed him and walked away as he adjusted his pants and walked weirdly over to the boys, I feel a little bad for him but I couldn't help but giggle.

"Thank you Annie, you didn't have to play. I just don't know what to do about the rest of the day," I knew Annie could play but I couldn't ask her to play unless she offered, she was injured and it was serious, it's her decision not mine.

"Scar, I'll play and you know it but thank you for letting me decide."

"Can you read my fucking mind or what?" I laughed and Annies smile grew bigger,

"No but I could see in your eyes how bad you felt about Lauren and then when I offered to help. I'm not injured anymore and if I can help I want to."

"Thank you, really you're a lifesaver." I pulled her in and we laughed as we all went and sat on the bench, we played as well as we could that game and now we're so fucking tired.

The rest of the day went smoothly, the men's team won all their games and by good amounts and we won all of ours. Annie absolutely killed it and we had the highest score in the history of the qualifiers, beating the previous record.

We went back to our rooms to get ready for the presentation tonight. I wore a red gown that was quite fitted but the bottom puffed out a little bit and put on matching red heels. I left my wavy auburn hair down, it hitting just above my waist, as I did my makeup there was a knock on my door. I went over and checked the little spyglass at the top and saw Miles.

"Hey, my love, don't you look dashing." I smiled as he walked in, not looking away from me once.

"Thank you, Ember. You look beautiful!" He breathed, his mouth hanging open as I did a spin for him.

"Thank you, are you ready to go?" Miles nodded at

me, not able to say anything and looped my arm over his as we made our way to the courts.

CHAPTER 26 – MILES

This woman's going to be the death of me, I swear. Wearing a dress like that and not having time to fully appreciate how she looked should be illegal.

"Just so you know, Ember, you're mine after this." I snarled at her as we saw the limo pull up. I helped Scarlet into the limo with her face red and flushed after my statement. She sat down and moved over for me to join her and she couldn't look me in the eye, she didn't even know what's coming. Annie has already opened the bottle of champagne that's in the limo and poured everyone a drink. Scarlet moved over to the girls and I stayed over by Cal and watched. She looks so happy with friends, her face is full and vibrant but later it will be flushed and making dirty noises for me.

"Hey man, uhh you okay?" Cal bumped my arm and I shook my head slightly, being me back to reality.

"Yeah man, sorry did you say something?" I could feel my cock rubbing on my pants again but I hid it well so no one would notice the massive boner I had right now.

"Yeah, I asked if you're ready for the award and if you have your speech prepared?" Fuck the speech!

"Ahh yeah, I do. It's in my head, I know what I'm

going to talk about, I just didn't write it down."

I wouldn't be here without my team, but this year the thing that really drove me was Scarlet. She's the reason I'm still here and how I got this far.

"So long as you're good dude, I just have to say, you've never been happier than right now, Miles."

"Thank man, you guys have always made me happy," I gave Cal a small smile, they've really pushed me to be better.

"We know that, but I'm talking about Scarlet," he nods over to her direction.

"I know, she has helped me through a lot." I stared back at her as she giggled with Annie and the rest of her team.

"Don't fuck it up again though, she may not be so forgiving the second time around." I rolled my eyes at him. I knew that she was upset but understanding about the Sam situation. But he's right, I'll never do anything to hurt her again.

We continued enjoying champagne and music until we got to the courts where they held the award night.

I got out first and put my hand out to help Scarlet but fucking Callum grabs my hand, a massive grin spreads over his face.

"Aww thanks, my love," he patted my shoulder and pissed himself laughing. I rolled my eyes and looked down at my hand, it was Scarlet this time.

"How nice of you, my love," she giggled. Oh, she wants to tease, well two can play this game. As she gets out of the car I pull her in and dip her down, kissing her deeply in front of everyone. Once I'm satisfied I pull her back up and her face is so red that it matches her dress.

"Scar, are you okay?" Annie jumped out of the limo giggling.

"Yeah, sorry I'm good." She side-eyed me and I smiled back at her all innocently. Her face is so flushed from the sudden gesture. "I want to go inside and see

Lauren. Logan drove her here." I grabbed her hand and walked her inside.

Lauren suffered from a hairline fracture in her arm and had a massive concussion from the fall but she's okay. She won't be able to play at the championships but Annie's stepping into her place, Lauren asked her too.

"Come on then, Ember, let's go find our seats." I couldn't hold my chuckle back as we walked in, she was trying so hard to not react to the kiss I gave her earlier but her face was still flushed.

We got inside and found Logan, Mel and Lauren sitting at our table, we sat down next to them as we all chatted and laughed at the jokes that Logan was cracking. He may be a shy kid but this dude's fucking amazing, Lauren's really lucky.

"Okay everyone, welcome to the award ceremony for this year's College Qualifiers." The host said into the microphone.

Everyone clapped and whistled as she finished the announcement.

"Now, the past three days have been tiring and I bet you're all exhausted so we will make this quick as most of you have to go home tomorrow." She turned as four people walked out, two each pushing stands covered by a red cape. "Now, you all did amazingly and should be so proud of even making it this far, so congratulations to you all." She clapped and everyone followed, "Now, to announce this year's top three teams from the male and female sides," she turns again and points her hand behind her as the people behind her unveiled the six trophies on the stands, "we will start with the gentlemen, in third place we have the LA team from Green's institution!" Everyone shouted and clapped as the captain walked up and accepted the award and read his speech. "In second place we have the Texas's team from Levi College." The team from Levi won last year and made it to the championships last year. We beat them this year though, taking first place but it was a massive achievement for me and the team to beat them.

"Thank you, I'll keep my speech short. Thank you to my team for their great efforts but I want to thank the team from Hudson College, they won this year and they did so well against us. You guys deserve it."

What the fuck! They played so dirty and he's thanking us, whatever.

"Thank you, and as he said in the first place we have the New York team from Hudson College." The team jumped out of their chairs and carried on like children and then the women followed right after. Scarlet and Cal being the loudest out of everyone, not surprising.

"Thank you, I ahh didn't write a speech down and had it in my head but it's gone." I chuckled and everyone in the crowd giggled with me. "Ahh I want to first thank my team, you guys are fucking amazing and I wouldn't be here without them." They screamed and whistled again.

"Second I want to thank my dad, he always supported me and has helped me through so many bumps in the road so thanks for that old man, and lastly I want to thank the one person who has helped me through so much more than she realises." I looked at Scarlet through the crowd, her big green eyes stand out with her wavy auburn hair and red dress. "You've been there for me through so much and you're the reason why I still played and had hope for everything even when shit went rock bottom. I love you and thank you for everything, Ember." The boys jumped up again, whistling and carrying on and pointed at her as she clapped, her face now red with embarrassment but she knew I loved her more than anything.

"That was a touching speech, thank you Miles." The host said as I walked back to my chair. "Now for the ladies, in third place," the host went through the third and second places from California and LA, their speeches going forever. "And last but not least, the team that has risen from the ground, smashing the competition and breaking the record for the highest points at the end of qualifiers," the crowd went crazy, as they should, these girls have put in crazy effort for this and they deserve all the recognition they're getting, "And also from New York, Hudson College!" The host shouted and the girls, the guys and I all stood and carried on. I help Scarlet up and kiss her hand as she walks up to the stage.

"Thank you everyone, I didn't realise we had to write a speech but ahh," she jumped a little, her little nervous hands shaking as she tried to read her speech from her phone but she took a deep breath and put it down. "This year's been crazy, I moved here at the start of the year and transferred from Australia, becoming vice captain straight off the bat as our vice captain had a broken leg but she has recovered well and save our asses today so thank you Annie and Lauren who's been there for my family and I since moving here even after the accident today, we all love you and will continue your dream by your side." Lauren whimpered, tears leaving her eyes. "And now I'm the captain and I couldn't be happier, so thank you to my team for putting me here and helping me in every way and to my love, thank you for everything, even when times were tough I knew you'd come back and we would lead our teams to victory, I love you too." I jumped up before anyone else and cheered and whistled so loud. Scarlet's smile makes me so happy and the way she walks down the stage makes me dick twitches as I watch her hips sway in that dress.

"Was that necessary, my love?" Scarlet has the biggest smile across her gorgeous face and I chuckle at her as I pull her in again, putting one hand on the small of her back and the other at the back of her neck. Our teams cheered as we kissed and when we pulled away Scarlet gently slapped my chest.

"Oh, Ember, yes it was, just wait until we get back to the hotel, you won't be able to sit on the flight tomorrow." I whispered in her ear and her eyebrows almost shot through the gym's roof.

We stayed for about an hour or so before we went back to the hotel.

Scarlet walked alongside the girls as we walked into the hotel, saying goodnight to everyone before we went into the elevator.

"That was a really beautiful speech, Ember." I grabbed her hand and kissed the back of her palm.

"Yours wasn't too shabby either, my love." She smiled, her face flushed from me teasing her all night. "So, there's been a lot of talk about what you're doing to me tonight. Are you going to follow through?" She whispers as she walks up to me from the other side of the elevator and stands right in front of me.

"When have I ever not followed through, Ember," my imagination flies wild as my cock twitches against my suit pants. "Maybe you shouldn't make me hard in the elevator though, Ember. The way you look right now and the teasing tone doesn't help." She giggled as she placed her hand on the top of my pants.

"Well, maybe I shouldn't touch it while we're in here then." Her eyes plastered on my lips as I reached down and moved the hair away from her neck, I leant down and nipped at her neck. She leaned into me, trying to get more than I am giving her. Not that she's going to get more, we are in an elevator and it's been so long, I'm not a fucking animal.

"No, Ember." I spun her, pinning her against the wall of the elevator, her hands above her head in one hand and my other cupping her jaw. "You will wait until we're in the room. I will not fuck you in an elevator for our first time in months." I demanded, this is going to be so fucking fun. We got off the elevator and led her to my room. I opened the door and let her walk in first, my eyes wandered all over her body and the dress as she walked in.

"I'm going to clean up first then I'm all yours, my

love." Scarlet sat down on the end of the bed to take her heels off, I slammed the door, startling her a little.

"I don't think so, leave the shoes on and pull up your dress." I demanded, her face shook but she obeyed. Her dress hiked up to her hips. "Spread your legs, Ember." I dropped to my knees in front of her as she spread her legs, her matching red panties drenched.

I leant down and ran my tongue from her knee to the middle of her inner thigh, tasting her arousal from tonight. "Wow, Ember. You taste so good." She giggles and I lift myself up, pinning Scarlet under me. "Now, you can get ready for a shower, I'll join you."

"Okay, my love, I love you," she giggled, her skin's flushed and her eyes are full of hunger.

"I love you too, Ember." I lent down and kissed her gently as I got up, holding out my hand. Scarlet sat up and I bent down in front of her, helping her take her heels off. "Once I'm done fucking the shit out of you, Ember, we can order snacks and I'll give you a massage because I couldn't imagine wearing these for more then five fucking minutes." Her feet are so red and angry, I picked her up and carried her to the bathroom, helping her take her dress off.

"Thank you, my love, you know I can do this myself." She lands on her feet and smirks at me.

"I know, but where's the fun in that," I slid the straps off her shoulders, her skin's so silky. I planted my lips on her shoulder, one by one, inching lower and lower. The dress slowly falls down with me as I lower myself.

"Miles!" Scarlet whimpered, her legs start shaking from all the excitement.

"I know, Ember, how about I run you a warm bath and I'll join you in a sec. I'll order food, how does that sound?" I lick down her stomach and her dress falls all the way to the floor, I can smell her arousal on her drenched panties.

"Yes please, my legs are so tired," she almost fell on the floor before I caught her, carrying her into the bathtub and turning on the warm water.

"Don't fall asleep, get refreshed because when I join you your legs are going to be more than tired." I slid her panties down and slid my fingers around her entrance, her back arching slightly in the water. "So wet, Ember," I leant down and kissed her, "I'll be right back," I closed the bathroom door behind me and ordered room service when I got a call from Dad. "Hey, Dad, what's up?"

"Miles, I wanted to call you and congratulate you and Scarlet on your big wins today. I am so proud of you two, I wanted to schedule a lunch with you two to celebrate." He sounded genuine, Dad has always been proud of me and I knew that but he was a busy man, putting bad people away.

"Thank you, Dad. Of course, I would love that. Let me talk to Scarlet and I'll let you know later if that's okay?"

"No worries, you guys have had a big few days, relax and have fun, have a safe flight back tomorrow morning, I will talk to you later, Miles."

"Thanks, Dad, we will. I will message you when we land tomorrow, love you, Dad." We never really exchanged I love yous but I wanted a better relationship with him. Ever since mum passed away, he's been diving into work to distract himself and I don't blame him for that, but sometimes that leaves me out of the picture too.

"Love you too, Miles, I'll wait for your message." He hung up the phone as the food arrived in the room, I walked it into the bathroom and Scarlet had her hair out, wet.

OH. MY. FUCKING. GOD.

"You okay, my love?" Scarlet's leaning against the side of the tub, her eyes filled with worry, "Who was on the phone, I heard you talking to someone?"

"Yeah, it was Dad. He was congratulating us on our big wins today and asked to have lunch with us when we get home, nothing to worry about, Ember." I sat the food on the tray beside the bathtub and got undressed. Scarlet eyes are searing my skin, watching me get undressed until her eyes fall onto my hard cock. Her face lights up a little and her stare becomes hungrier. "What are you looking at, Ember?"

She sucks in her bottom lip, biting down on it gently and she moves her hair to one side of her face.

"Just how good you look right now, my love." Damn, this woman has me in a choke hold.

I stalked towards the bathtub, slowly getting in. Scarlet leant back into the corner and watched me get in, taking in the view. I got closer to her and pinned her against the wall of the tub.

"How are you feeling, Ember? Are you refreshed or do you need something to eat first?" I knew she was exhausted, but after this long and waiting months to be able to touch each other, we needed this.

Scarlet leant forward a little, her lips gently grazing my jaw, "Will you feed me, my love, then I may be refreshed enough," her lips leaving its mark on my neck. She pulls her face back until she's inches from mine, our lips almost touching. I nod and reach over for a spoon and feed her some of the food I ordered.

I put the spoon full of soup up to her lips as she stares into my eyes with those piercing green eyes and wraps her lips around the end of the spoon. God, I can imagine the spoon being my cock and her lips wrapped around it, it twitches in the water and her eyes drop down to the moving water as she pulls her lips away with a smirk, "If it's too much, my love, I can feed myself," she giggles, she knew what I was thinking but I enjoyed the view way too much.

"Did I say it was too much, Ember?" I can't handle the sarcasm right now, "if you keep teasing me, I'll bend you over this tub and fuck you until you can't handle it anymore." I seethed, she knew what she was doing but I have so much tension from the past few months that I don't think I could handle any more pushing.

"Well, sounds to me like you're all talk, my love, I'm waiting," she reaches for my hair and pulls me closer.

Oh, well I fucking see then.

I reached for her wet, wavy hair, pulling her into me, fisting it and pulling her head back gently as I buried my face into her neck. Planting a line of kisses and nips around her neck, her little whimpering breathes rings in my head. She smells strongly of caramel and flowers and her hair is so soft in my fingers, I pull her face into mine, smashing our lips together. Scarlet leans in and wraps her legs around my waist, trying to deepen the kiss. I feel her naked skin on mine and my cock twitches, trying to find the sweet spot.

I trace my hand down Scarlet's body, her breath shakes and her back arches with my touch. "I love those little sounds you make, Ember." I find the apex in between her thighs and I rub her clit with my thumb while kissing her. Our tongues clashing with each other, our teeth hitting one another and I suck in her bottom lip, pulling on it with my teeth.

"Miles please!" Scarlet cries, begging for more.

"Please what, Ember, tell me what you want." My voice drops, demanding for her to tell me what she needs. I put more pressure on her clit, speeding up the motion with my thumb and she moans quickly, her head flying back to the edge of the tub. I move forward, grabbing her breast with my other hand, licking and sucking her nipple.

"Miles, I need you," she whispered, her body moving in rhythm with my thumb. I move my hand down, tracing her entrance with my fingers.

"What's the magic word, Ember," I push two fingers into her pussy, slowly pulling in and out.

"Please, Miles, I need you." she cries out, trying to get herself off on my hand.

I speed up my hand, letting her push herself over the

edge. Her body quakes and stutters, as she cums I pull my fingers out and slide the tip of my cock into her entrance. She gasped as I thrust straight into her, leaving no time to process what's happening.

She moans loudly as I continue with the long and hard thrusts, getting her close but leaving enough time in between that she can't cum yet.

I lean back into her and place my mouth on hers, Cal's room is right there next to mine and I got enough shit about it last time, even though we didn't have sex, I don't want to hear Cal's opinion on the flight home tomorrow. I speed up, thrusting fast and hard. Scarlet's moans are captured in my mouth as she tightens around my cock, leaving it slick from her cum.

"You're so loud, Ember, look at you." I whispered, spinning her around, bending her over the edge of the tub.

"I can be quiet," she demands, turning and looking me up and down, her face almost going sad and worry raises in her eyes.

"No, you can't, Ember, and you won't. I love the noises you make." I chuckle and slam back into her, she lets out a loud moan again and I lean over, placing my hand over her mouth. I can feel her groan of disapproval in my hand but I don't want to hear Cal's opinions on my sex life.

I pump into her, pulling in and out slowly, teasing her after she said she could be quiet but obviously she can't.

Scarlet bit the inside of my hand, wanting more so I thrust harder and faster, bending her over more so I could hit the sweet spot. She moans quietly into my hand as I can feel her tighten around my cock again. She bites my palm as she releases, her legs becoming wet from the water and her cum as it drips down her legs. I pull out slowly and place her back in the water, her face is flaming red and her wet hair is messy and stuck to her face.

"Clean yourself up, Ember, I'm going to be waiting for you on the bed, don't get dressed." She smirked and pulled me into her, my lips pounding hers.

"Okay, my love, I won't be long," she nipped at my bottom lip as I got up.

I grabbed a towel and wrapped it around my waist, sitting on the bed waiting for Scarlet to come out.

She stayed in the bath for a while, soaking her aching body and then joined me on the bed. We spent hours over the night with each other and fucking each other on every surface possible in the hotel room.

"Wow, that was insane!" Scarlet huffed, lying down next to me on the bed as she tried to catch her breath.

"Definitely needed that. You okay, Ember?" I rolled over and pulled her into me, cuddling her so she felt warm as we laid naked on top of the bed.

"Yeah, my love, I'm okay. That was incredible but fuck I'm tired." She yawned, covering her mouth with her hand as she snuggled into my chest.

"Me too, I can't move so I guess we're sleeping naked," I chuckled and Scarlet giggled at my comment.

"Guess so, my love, good night." She looked up at me and kissed me gently as she laid back down, her naked body basically on top of mine as she moved around to get comfortable.

"Good night, Ember."

CHAPTER 27 – SCARLET

God what a night! The presentation was beautiful and spending the night with Miles made me feel so tired but relaxed, knowing that he was mine again.

I wake up hearing Miles yelling at someone on the phone, he sounds stressed and scared. I turn to look at my phone and it's five in the morning, I slowly get up and sit on the side of the bed. What's making Miles so worried this early in the morning?

I go to get up and Miles opens the bathroom door, his face filled with sadness and anxiety.

"What's wrong, my love?" I jump out of bed and reach for him, he grabs my arms and holds them in front of us, not letting me touch him.

"That was Dad, something's happened to him, he's in the hospital and they don't know what's going on." his voice cracks as he stands in the bathroom door, tears well in his eyes.

I haven't met his dad yet, but Miles loves him. Even though they don't see each other often, he always knew his dad loved him and that he was proud of Miles.

"Is there anything I can do to help, my love?" I squeeze his hands, his face staring at the floor. I pull my hands from his and touch his face, bringing it to look at mine, "he's strong, what can I do to help you?" Miles breathing quickens, his heart is pounding out of his chest, he's having a panic attack.

I jump into action, leading Miles to the edge of the bed, sitting him down and grabbing a cold wet cloth to put on the back of his neck. I kneel down in front of him and put the cloth on the back of his neck, his eyes lock onto mine and the panicked look in his eyes makes me want to panic, but I know that won't help. He needs me. I take some deep, slow breaths and bring him in for a hug, still taking deep breaths, trying to get him to take them too. After about a minute, his heart slows and his breath is steady. I pull myself away and wipe his tears from his cheeks. "Hey, my love, you okay?"

"What was that? I couldn't breathe." Miles' face made me want to cry, he hasn't cried in front of me before and it's not an easy thing for some to do.

"It was a panic attack, I'm so sorry about your dad but we aren't home. We need to focus on getting home and then we can go see him right away, okay?" Miles nods and I pull him in for another hug, his arm wraps around my back this time, squeezing me tightly into him.

Miles lets me go, we grab our things out of our rooms and walk to the elevator. I moved our flights forward and messaged Logan to let him know that Miles and I are going early because he has a family emergency. The team's flight isn't until lunch time but it was six and our flight leaves at seven, so we need to go now.

We get to the airport, go through security and by the time all that is finished we have a spare fifteen minutes to kill.

"Do you remember when we first met?" Miles whispered, looking around the airport.

"At school?"

"No, Ember, in the airport in Australia, last year." He chuckled, taking my hand in his.

Wow it's almost been a year since we moved to America, this year has gone by so fast and with all the drama that has happened I completely forgot.

"I do actually, you stole my necklace," I giggled and Miles dropped his stare to my necklace.

"I didn't steal it, it fell off and I held onto it just in case I met that beautiful red head again and I did," his fingers run through my hair and cups my face, "thank you for everything, Ember, I love you."

"I love you too, my love," he pulled me in for a sweet kiss and the announcer called our flight. We walked over and got on the plane, taking off just before seven.

Our flight was long and tiring but the moment we landed we got into Miles' car and drove over to the hospital. He's been on the phone since we landed and the doctors wanted to talk to Miles about his dad. I knew that meant it was something serious, it's what they did with my mum.

"Are you going to be okay, Ember, I can take you home first so you don't have to be at the hospital." I turn and look at him confused, does he not want me there for him? "You know, because we are going to the hospital, I don't want to upset you, with my dad being in hospital. I don't want it to bring up anything about your mum and make you upset."

"No, I'll be fine. I'm not going anywhere, I can handle it." Could I? I haven't been in the hospital since I did my injury earlier in the year and the panic attack but that was different. This sounds serious, I can't let my personal feelings overcome me when Miles needs me.

"If it gets too much please tell me, Ember," he grabs my hand and I nod, he kisses the back of my palm and we pull into the hospital car park. We went up to the VIP floor, Miles' dad was a well-known lawyer here in New York, he's rich too so he obviously got whatever he needed to be comfortable.

"Mr Grove, thank you for coming so quickly, I know you just got back. Congratulations on your win sir, you played well." The doctor shook Miles's hand and turned to me. "Miss Bowen, wow huge fan!"

"Hey doc, thank you but we're here for my dad, what's wrong with him?" Miles's voice was strong but I could hear the worry in his voice as he spoke.

"Right sorry, he fainted in his office this morning, his assistant found him and called us. We ran a bunch of tests and it looks like he had a heart attack from all the stress of work." Miles' face went white and he wobbled a little. I caught him from behind and helped him to the chair behind us so he could sit down.

"A heart attack? Besides stress, was there anything else?" Miles' voice is now full of worry, no hiding it.

"Just stress, he needs to reduce his work load and his stress, change his diet up a little and do some exercise, that's all we can really do. He needs to be careful Miles," Miles looks up at me and I squeeze his hand, he gives me a weak smile and turns back to the doctor.

"Thank you doc, I'll talk to him," the doctor nods and walks to the bench, sitting the charts on it. "You ready to meet my dad for the first time, sorry it's under such bad circumstances, Ember."

"Hey, no. It's fine, my love, don't apologise. I'm ready, are you?" I'm worried Miles will flip out or break down, seeing a family member in a hospital bed brings out all the emotions.

"Yeah I am, let's go," he let out a deep breath and stood. Leading me to his dad's room. Miles knocks on the door and a nurse opens it, smiling at Miles and I and walking out.

"Miles," his dad calls out, coughing a little as we walk in.

"Hey, Dad, how are you feeling?" Miles walks into the room first, straight to his dad's side. Looking him up and down for any other injuries.

"I am fine, I keep telling the nurses I'm fine, but they want to keep me overnight." His dad rolls his eyes at the answer and Miles chuckles.

"You had a heart attack old man, you need to stay so

someone can keep an eye on you," Miles' dad looks past Miles and sees me in the doorway.

"Miles, how could you be so rude and not introduce me to this beautiful lady," Miles' dad waves over to me and I shyly smile as I walk over to see him.

"Dad!" Miles quietly shouts, his face a little red with embarrassment as he stands up next to me, putting his hand around my back. "Dad, this is Scarlet. Scarlet, this is my dad, James."

James smiles and holds out his arms as I walk up to him. He pulls me in for a hug and pushes away from me gently, looking at my face and features, taking in the view I guess.

"Wow Miles, you did really well with this one, I see why you like her more than Samantha, she was never right for you." James said gently, Miles definitely got his strong features from his dad but his eyes are different from his dads, softer.

"Nice to meet you, James, your son's amazing." I say, turning to look at Miles who is watching his dad and I with a big smile on his face,

"That's good to hear, I would hope he is." James starts coughing and Miles rushes over, handing James some water. "Thank you son, now I have something to ask you." James looked at Miles, he put the water down and took Miles's hand. "The doc told me I need to reduce my workload and my assistants are fucking useless, I need someone who knows what they are doing working with me, to help me."

"You want me to work for you? Dad, I'm not finished school yet."

"You have what a few weeks left," Miles' gaze sets on me and I smile at him, it's nice that his dad wants him to work for him.

"I have three weeks left and then a week of tests and exams, then I'm away for a week and a bit for championships, then I'm all yours." Miles' dad's face lit up with joy and I couldn't help but smile at Miles.

He's wanted this since I knew him and definitely before that. He's been studying to be a lawyer for four years and all he has left is to take the bar and finish his exams, then he can work for his dad.

"That's perfect, that gives me enough time to rearrange my staff and divide everything fairly among them. You will work right under me, taking my case and I will overlook you, that will take a lot of stress off of me. Scarlet, I have a favour to ask you now."

Miles face turned from joyful to confusion. "Dad, you just met her! You can't ask her for a favour."

"No, please, Mr Grove," I shot a stern look at Miles before I turned back to his dad.

"Please, call me James," James cut me off and shook his head, I giggled at his response.

"Okay, James, please what's the favour?" There's no way I would say no, that would be so cruel and it's Miles' dad, he's family to me now.

"The doc said I need to start doing more exercise, Miles tells me that you plan on either coaching or opening up your own basketball fitness centre, correct?"

"Oh, umm yeah that's right." I look at Miles confused and his smile tells me that he has spoken in detail about me to his dad, which is super cute.

"Would you be able to help me with exercising, I have never been good with fitting it in my busy schedule but with a little help, I may be able to actually look after myself, only if you can of course. No stress if you can't."

"Of course I can, once we are back from championships I can start helping."

James smiled at me, "Thank you and of course I will pay for your time."

"No sir, I won't accept that. So long as you show up and do the work, I'll be happy," I smile back at him and he laughs. His laugh is very much the same as Miles' and I can really see Miles in James, they are both grumpy around everyone but the ones they love and both are super hard working.

"Sounds like a deal, now please I would like to sleep a little before the nurse comes back in to poke me some more."

Miles and I say our goodbyes and go back down to the car, "I'm so sorry about him, you don't have to do that for him," Miles grabs my waist, pulling me into him suddenly.

"It's fine, I'd love to help your dad. I never got to do this with my family so if I can help your Miles, it's no stress at all." I stand on my toes and kiss him.

"Okay, so long as you're fine with it, Ember."

We drive back to my house and unpack our bags. I jump on my computer and I log in to my school portal to see what tests I have left. These are our last weeks of the semester and it's warmed up outside now, not as hot as Australia gets but it's definitely warm.

"How many tests do you have, Ember?" Miles leans over behind me and kisses my jaw.

"One tomorrow and one Friday. How many do you have?" I turn to look at Miles, his lips crashing on mine.

"Just one, the rest are in my last week and then the bar so I need to study for that." His mouth lands back on mine, the kiss is sloppy and needy. His tongue slipped into my mouth, claiming every inch. I melt in my chair as his hand gently stretches across my neck and the other hand reaches for my inner thigh,

"Miles," I whimper as his lips move down my jaw and sinks his teeth into my neck. My body goes limp and his tongue runs over the mark, "I'm sorry, my love, I am so tired. I don't think I can right now." I whimpered, tears filling my eyes, I don't want to make him feel bad,

"Hey, hey why are you crying," Miles' brows pull together, "I'm not mad, it's okay. Here, let's go to bed and cuddle. It's getting late and your siblings won't be home until even later so we may as well get a good night's sleep for school tomorrow." I nod and Miles picks me up and carries me to bed, laying me down gently as he cuddles beside me and we both fall asleep.

CHAPTER 28 – MILES

Finally, the last week of college. I'm so happy to be this close to being done but these last few days were rough. Scarlet and I had our exams at different times throughout Tuesday and Wednesday, not seeing each other until practice and even then we're so busy trying to prepare our teams for championships that we didn't get to actually talk to each other until after we got home.

Championships work a little differently to the qualifiers, they have a single-elimination system also called knockouts that they use to eliminate teams to get their ultimate winning teams.

We will be playing other countries, thirty-two to be exact, it leaves sixteen teams to play against each other until there is one winner for both male and female teams.

Today's Thursday and I got up early to get ready. I left a cup of coffee on the nightstand on the mug warmer next to Scarlet and went over to Dad's office. I wanted to stop by and have a look at what I'll be doing for him when I come back and start in just over two weeks.

"Mr Grove, good morning. We didn't expect you in

for another two weeks." The girl at the receptionist was a year older than me and had also wanted to date me for the longest time, but with Sam and her insecurities, she learnt the hard way that I wasn't interested.

"Morning, Jane, just here to see Dad and to have a look around, it's been a while." I gave her a smile as I walked towards Dad's office. The overall office was simple with glass walled offices and minimal decor.

I walked over to Dad's office and checked in with his secretary. "Morning, Cheryl, does Dad have a moment?"

"Oh, Miles, good morning. He does actually, since reducing his work load he has quite a bit of time."

"Thank you, Cheryl," I gave her a nod and walked past her desk.

Cheryl was like a second mum to me really. She hasn't ever been romantically involved with my dad but she was always around, helping him with everything, she was there for me quite a bit too. I knocked on Dad's door and he turned and waved me in, he was on the phone to someone, no surprise there.

"Thanks, Ron, keep me posted," he hung up the phone and walked over to me, pulling me in for a hug, "Morning son, I didn't expect you. I would have cleared my morning otherwise."

"No need, Dad, I just wanted to come check out the office, it's been a while. You have had renovations since I was last here. The place looks so much bigger." The office used to have a bunch of yellow and white walls, making the inside look really old and small.

"We are doing well for ourselves here, but I'm currently getting your office set up, it's next door. They are putting in a connection door to mine so you can come in if you ever need me." He was a sweet man, and I knew I would succeed working hard under him.

"Thanks, Dad, but there's another reason for me coming here. We are going to France on Saturday for the championships and I needed to ask you something."

L.M London

Dad's brows creased together and he sat down at his desk, "Of course, Miles, what is it?"

I squirmed in my chair, taking a deep breath and looking Dad straight in the face, "I want to ask you for mum's engagement ring please." My hands are clammy against each other, fuck I'm so nervous.

Dad's face immediately lit up and he jumped out of his chair, almost climbing over the desk, "Oh, Miles, congratulations! You think Scarlet's the one?"

I smiled, I was worried about Dad's response as he really wanted Sam to have it but I knew she wasn't the one, she wasn't worthy to wear my mother's ring. Scarlet is.

"Yes, Dad, I know she is. I'm going to propose hopefully after the championships if we win. If we don't then I'll plan a date somewhere and do it then but I have hope that at least her team will win." Dad picked me up and spun me around, just like when I was little. "Dad, you're going to throw your back out, put me down." I laughed and Dad chuckled as well, walking around to his chair side of the desk, opening a drawer.

"Here Miles, I like her and I know it's old school and I know you can't ask her dad because well.." He paused, obviously because her real dad was a stupid dick who left her mum and Davis was in jail, hopefully forever. "But is there someone you can ask permission for her hand?" I took a deep breath, neither of them deserve to know about her, but there was someone I was planning on asking tonight.

"Yeah, her brother, I plan on asking him tonight, I just wanted the ring to show him, ask if she will like it." The ring's beautiful and I always loved the ring mum had on her hand. It was a two carat diamond stone, oval cut with little red stones around it with the metal shaped into vines around the big stone.

"Well, let me know what he says and I've booked my flight to come watch you play over the two days. If you need any help preparing for whatever you want for your proposal, let me know, I will pay for anything." Dad pulled me in for a hug, his eyes going glassy.

"Dad don't cry please," I won't cry with him but he doesn't cry often. He refused to cry in front of me when mum passed but I did catch him once or twice.

"I am just so proud of you Miles, I couldn't be happier with the son that I have."

Shit don't cry. Don't fucking cry.

"Thanks, Dad," we let go of each other and he showed me around. Introducing me to the staff and showing me around every office and room we could get into.

I got back in the car and drove over to Scarlet's house. She had strategic and scenario training with her team today. She wanted to go through everything that they knew about other countries. My team had that tomorrow, some of the men on my team had exam's all day today so I wanted to give some of them a break before we had to train and then fly over to France and practice there.

When I got home, Logan and Lauren were at the door. Lauren had a doctor's appointment for her fracture, which unfortunately isn't going to be healed until after championships but she's still coming with the team. She's going to be like a coach, watching over the team and telling them what they need to improve on.

"Oh hey, Miles, no tests today?" Lauren turned and smiled as she walked inside while Logan waited at the door for me,

"Nah none today, how was the appointment?" Lauren's face was full of sadness but she was trying to push past it as she cleared her throat.

"It was good, it's healing just slowly so no championships for me for sure. I'm going to go upstairs, I'm tired." Logan kisses her forehead as she makes her way upstairs,

"While I have you Logan can I talk to you please?" I walked to the kitchen while Logan followed and poured us both a cup of coffee,

"Yeah dude what's up?" He sat at the island as I handed him the cup, a pit at the bottom of my stomach started to form, fuck why am I nervous again.

"I need to ask you something serious," I take a deep breath and look Logan dead in the face,

"Okay, you're worrying me dude, did something happen between you and Scarlet?" His face went pale, thinking something bad happened to Scarlet and I.

"Oh, no dude. Sorry I'm just fucking nervous, okay," I took another deep breath, "I want to propose to your sister in France when we're all there for championships. You all will be there, my dad's coming and her team is like her second family, it's the perfect spot to do it." I pulled my phone out of my pocket and opened a picture of the ring, Logan's eyes filled with excitement.

"Dude, one you don't need my permission but you have it and two that ring's fucking beautiful, I hope it wasn't too much?" His questioning tone turned into a stare,

"No, it wasn't, it was my mother's ring. She passed away when I was twelve in a car accident. Dad never thought it was an accident but he always spoke so highly of her and he knows that Scarlet deserves this," I finally relaxed, I have his permission, I can finally start planning.

"I do have a question first." Oh shit, the nerves came back fast, almost knocking me on my ass.

"Of course, what is it?" The air went thick and suddenly it was hard to breathe, the tension in the air was strong.

"You graduate in a week, your ceremony happens in just over two weeks, Scarlet still has two more years after this year. What are the plans for you? Are you staying here, can she finish school?" The questions were needed, I knew what I wanted and so did she.

"I will never be in the way of her dreams, I'll be working at my father's firm once I graduate. I took the bar exam yesterday so I have to wait to hear about the results. She can continue school how she is and where she wants to go or whatever she wants to do, I'll follow. I can be a lawyer anywhere."

Logan's face went from serious to a happy smirk, he held out his hand over the island counter.

"Well then, welcome to our family, brother." I smiled back at him and shook his hand, it's so nice hearing that word.

"Brother, I like that." We both laugh and I hear Lauren standing at the door, her face is about to explode with happiness.

"Holy shit, you're proposing in France, Miles!" Lauren runs around the counter and gently jumps in my arms, hugging me with tears in her eyes.

"Careful of your arm babe," Logan jumped up and Lauren stared at him all serious as he sat back down, she turned back to me and she got all excited again,

"Congratulations, show me the ring, please Miles." I of course showed her the ring, she is Scarlet's best friend and Logan's fiancée so I couldn't not show her.

"It's like the ring she already has," Lauren's head tilted to the side, confused.

"Similar yeah, I designed hers based off of this. Her ring has a red stone in the middle and little diamonds just wrapping around the red stone, this has the diamond in the middle while the red stones look like vines around the stone, they should stack together when she wears them." I made sure they did, I knew I wanted to marry her before we were together, I knew she was mine.

"Aww Miles, see you put up this tough and serious wall in front of everyone but you're actually a big softie for her." I smiled and put my phone away in my pocket.

"Only for her,"

Lauren smiled and rolled her eyes, "Of course, well I need to get to training, can you take me please babe?"

"I'll take you, some of the men have a training session

for an hour soon, if that's okay" I look at Logan and he nods. Logan says his goodbyes and calls Melaine, their younger sister to tell her what's happening so she's aware of the proposal. She's at school right now and then has work later so I won't see her probably until France.

"Thank you for taking me Miles, I just wanted to say that I'm so happy for you guys but if you hurt her again, I will find you and bury you with my bare hands,"

Jesus fucking Christ.

"I won't hurt her again, I will bury myself if I hurt her again." Lauren laughs and I smile as we get out of the car and walk into the gym.

CHAPTER 29 – SCARLET

God, thank fuck school's done. I don't think I could handle school and training for the championships at the same time. Trying to study other teams from different countries is hard and what's harder is that I will be competing against my old Australian team at some point if they win.

The knockout timesheet has been put out and we will see them in the final round if we both make it. I know that some of the girls were happy for me but others weren't, they may be a little salty that I'm here and not there.

"Hey girls, how's the strategy training going?" Lauren walked in and behind her was Miles, my heart started beating fast, he looked so tired but so good at the same time. You know when a guy looks sleepy and worn out but they make it look hot as fuck, yeah that's Miles right now.

"It's exhausting, these countries are crazy," Tegan shouts out and we all walk over to where Lauren was sitting.

As Lauren talks to the girls about how she is and what will be happening with her because of her injury, I went over to Miles, who was carrying Lauren's bag for her, cute.

"Hey, Ember, how are you? You look tired." His voice sounds troubled, he's really worried about if I'm tired, he needs to look in a mirror.

"My love, you're worried about me but you look like a zombie, a hot one but still. You look exhausted, do you have training today?" He hasn't had much time to rest, he was studying most nights. I finally got to see him and didn't come to bed until late and then woke up before me to study more.

"Yeah, they should be here in about fifteen minutes. We won't be in the way will we?"

"Nope, I'm about to send the girls to warm up and actually train now, these other countries are really skilled. I'm worried we won't make it past the first round." These teams are crazy but only one had me worried.

"You guys are amazing, you will make it past. Oh wait, you should see your old team right? I heard they made it to the championships, that's amazing." He puts down the bags and I pass the ball to him as we walk onto the court. His lips slightly tip up in a tired smirk, god that's so hot.

"Yeah they did. I'm more worried about it than happy but I know they are super proud of themselves and I am too."

"Why are you worried, Ember? That was your team, your family. Surely they should be happy to see you make it that far, right?" His voice changes from tired to concerned. I'm not even sure what to think about them, they are my family, well they were my family and I left them, not by choice but I still left them.

"Some of them weren't happy about me leaving, they said I was never good enough to make it to qualifiers let alone championships, it's why I wasn't there last year when they made it. I got them there but I was too young and not experienced enough according to the captain and her friends so I didn't go to the game, I watched but wasn't allowed to play."

Miles face went tense, I could feel his anger and frustration radiating off of him. "They what!?"

"My love, it's okay. We are all different now and," before I could finish the rest of the men's team walked in and Miles looked like he was going to literally blow.

"We will finish this conversation later, Ember, but I want to let you know that you're way better than their whole team and most of the teams that went last year. You and the girls are phenomenal and will win, we all know it." He cups the side of my face and kiss my forehead gently.

"Thanks, my love, I better go. Don't want your friends to see that you can be soft," I giggled and turned away towards the girls.

As I walked over I could hear Cal making fun of Miles about kissing me in front of everyone when Miles just called them all over, ignoring what he said. Imagine, people knowing that he can be soft every once and a while.

We spend about thirty minutes going over drills and stretches, finishing training. I told the girls to have tomorrow off so they can pack and sort anything out that they need to before we leave. I plan on spending it with Miles, as we haven't had any time for ourselves this past week and it's getting a little lonely. I sat on the bench on the other side of the court, waiting for Miles and the boys to finish up their training so Miles could take me home.

The boys are in the middle of a four versus four match and I miss watching Miles play with his team, the way he communicates with them, the skill, the way his body moves, god I need to get laid. The sound of squeaky shoes on the court and the ball bouncing just feels like home, watching their team play and watching Miles be with his family makes me happy for him.

After the men finish training, Miles is still trying to shoot and practice even after his team leaves, something's obviously on his mind.

"Hey, my love, what's wrong?" I walk over to him and he continues bouncing the ball until he lets out a deep sign and grabs the ball.

"I just keep thinking about what you said, about the Aussie team, I can't believe they thought that about you. We all watched your videos when the head master told us you were moving here and joining the women's team and you're phenomenal. Not just your freshman year either, your audition tryouts for the team there and throughout high school. You're a natural, Ember and they said that to you!" He seethed through his teeth, shooting the ball and missing. "Fuck," he muttered under his breath, walking over to the bouncing ball.

"You all watched my videos, why did you guys watch it? I wasn't joining your team."

"Oh, uhh, well, Sam wouldn't shut up about how a new girl was joining and how the girls were saying she was amazing but Sam was jealous and was acting like you weren't good at all." His expression went from nervous to grossed out when he talked of Sam, it was kind of funny. "So, I watched some of the video's from your freshman year, mainly the last one, getting your team into qualifiers and it was a joke they didn't let you play but I may or may not have watched all your videos." His face goes red in embarrassment, he turns away from me slightly.

He did what?!

"My love, did you stalk me?" I giggled as I put my hand on his shoulder to turn him around, his mouth was shaped in an awkward smile as his head turned around.

"What, I would never," I folded my arms and raised my eyebrows, he stalked me. "Okay, fine. Maybe I looked at a few more videos but you were so good and you were so pretty, I couldn't keep my eyes off of you."

"I *was* pretty, am I not now?" My expression changed to annoyed and poor Miles's face went to panic mode.

"No, Ember. That's-that's not what I meant, you're gorgeous, beautiful," I burst out laughing and try to cover my mouth.

"My love, I was joking, thank you for the compliments though."

Miles was not happy, he fully faced me and the embarrassment vanished, frustration rushed over his face and he grabbed me around my waist and flung me over his shoulder.

"My love!" I shouted, kicking and punching around, "Miles! Put me down now!" I screeched, trying to escape his grip that was on the back of my thighs.

"No, you want to shit stir, Ember, now you will suffer the consequences. First one, you will be carried to the car like this and the second one I can't do here because I will not let anyone else see you naked! You're mine!" He spat, gripping the back of my thighs harder as he grabbed our bags.

"My love, please put me down. I will behave I promise." I begged, trying to get his massive hands off my thighs. The heat of his hands running up my thighs and into my core, fuck I really need to be laid if I get turned on by his hand on my thighs.

"No, Ember, it's too late for that. We are going home right now."

"Everyone is home right now, my love, we can't be loud!" I shouted as he gently threw me in the car, putting my seatbelt on for me.

"I texted Logan on the way out, they are going on a date in twenty minutes and Melaine's at work for hours, so we have the house to ourselves." He closed my door as I crossed my arms over my chest and crossed my legs over each other, pushing up against the door in a tantrum. "Come on, Ember, once we get home you won't be sooky anymore, you will be begging for me to touch you." The way he said that sounds so hot but I'm so angry right now that I move even closer to the door as he tries to reach for my thigh. Miles sighed and took his seatbelt off, leaning over towards me. His hand reaches around the back of my neck and I completely shatter, way to stay strong Scarlet.

His hand finds its spot on the back of my neck and his other hand reaches for my face, pulling me in close to him. "What you're going to do is not be in a cranky mood for being punished after what you pulled," his lips graze mine as his hand on the back of my neck reaches up to my hair and he gently fists his hand full of my hair, "now, come to me, Ember so I can at least get ahead start on making you feel better," he pulls me even closer, his warm lips dragging on my neck, my body shakes with anticipation, wanting more. Traitor!

"This will not help," I said stubbornly, knowing full well that it probably will, considering it's been over a week since we've even kissed. His teeth sinking into my neck gently and kissing the sensitive spots as he reaches back up to my lips.

"Are you sure about that, Ember?" His teasing smirk reaches to my frown and opens my lips with his tongue, pulling me into him so he can find every inch of my mouth, claiming what's his. My body goes limp with his touch as it plants itself on my skin.

"Ahh yeah, I'm sure," no I wasn't but it will take more than neck kisses and his tongue in my mouth to make me feel better after the humiliation he just put me through.

"Mmm okay, Ember, let's get home, but first take your panties off." He sits back in his seat, putting his seatbelt back on and puts the car in drive. "Now!" The demanding tone sent shivers down my spine. The temptation to not listen to him is bouncing through my head but I know better than to not listen.

I shimmied my pants off first and then my panties, lucky my singlet jersey almost goes to my knees so no one will see anything if they look in the window. I cross my feet, his air-conditioning is making everything turn into fucking icicles. Miles's face goes from a smirk to an almost smile as he places his warm hand on my freezing, naked leg.

"Spread them and lean back, Ember, let me warm you up," I froze. Is he going to touch me all the way home! What if someone sees us? I hesitantly spread my legs and sat back, I already didn't do what Miles said once and look where that has me.

"Good girl, Ember, now relax. No one will see you, I need to get you warmed up for when we get home. You won't be able to move after I am done with you."

I laid back, my core already tightened, waiting in anticipation. Miles starts moving the car as his hand slowly makes it way up my inner thigh, goosebumps crawl all over me and shivers run up and down my body as he reaches the top. "Wow, Ember. Someone's excited." His hand reaches for my clit and his thumb gently rolls over it, applying the most minimal pressure.

This teasing asshole.

I try to lean into his hand more, trying to get more pressure on my clit. Miles pulls the car over and puts his hand on the top of my inner thigh, "Do not move, Ember. I told you to spread your legs and sit back. This is your punishment. You better listen, Ember." He seethed, someone isn't pleased about my tantrum and I knew that I won't be pleased if I don't fucking listen. I need this, I need him, on me, in me, fucking hell.

I nod and spread my legs wider and lean back, trying hard not to move into his motions. His hand raises slightly as he gets back onto the road, placing it on top of my clit again and my whole body locks. Don't move, don't move, don't fucking move.

His fingers teasing my folds as his thumb returns to my clit and he applies just enough pressure to feel good but not enough to do anything. I let out a frustrated sigh, Miles's eyes snap onto me and he lets out a quiet chuckle and shoves a finger inside me. Fuck, I leant back and arched my back, wasn't not expecting that so quickly. His finger was set on a slow but hard pace, my body was quaking with the touch and feeling of Miles. I looked over at Miles, who was watching the road, but I could see the tempting smile on his lips. I knew he loved teasing me but this is so annoying, I wanted more, I needed more.

"Miles, please." I begged, I needed more than a finger and his thumb on me, I won't finish with just this and I didn't want to finish with his fingers, I wanted to watch him shatter with me.

"Seeming as you begged so politely, Ember." Miles added another finger, slowly stretching me out and setting a rhythm that made my eyes roll to the back of my head. My body went flying and I couldn't hear anything, all my senses vanished with the pace he set. I didn't even realise we were home until Miles's other hand grazed my jaw and pulled me in for a deep kiss. The need for the kiss was wild, he obviously missed me too. "Come on, Ember, let's go inside." He gets out of the car and comes around to open my car door, as always.

"Thank you, my love," I go to step out of the car but Miles has different plans.

"No, Ember." He picks me up, baby style and closes the door, "I won't let you waste your energy walking." Well shit, okay then.

Miles walked us up to the door and turned off the security system and took us up to the bedroom, locking the door behind us, "Just in case. Now take your shirt off and sit on the edge of the bed," Miles demanded and I did just as he said but I wanted to tease a little too. I slowly took my top off, revealing my bra underneath. I knew he wanted it off too but he didn't say so I left it on and slowly walked over to the bed, his face going hard and frustrated.

I sat down and I crossed my legs leaning forward, waiting for Miles's next move. He stood and watched, taking in every inch of my skin. "Take it off, Ember," his eyes were on my bra. I reach around my front and pull it over my head, my breasts bouncing on my chest after being released from their prison. Miles' eyes go dark and I can see his cock twitch with the movement, he tilts his head to the side and a smirk washes over his face. "So she can listen," he walked towards me and cupped my face with his hand, "Now, I want to punish you, Ember and it's been over a week since we have spent any time together, but I want to make sure you're not too tired for this." His tone became sympathetic and a little sad. We're both exhausted, you could see the purple bruises under his eyes but I wanted this just as much as he did. I placed my hand on his, sliding my hand up his arm and pulling him into me.

"I want this, I want you, my love." My nipples are so hard they could literally cut paper and my core is so hot and tense that I am going to explode. "I need you, Miles, now."

Without a second thought a quick, sexy smirk flew over Miles's lips before he leans down and his face slams into mine. Teeth clashing, spit flying and our tongues going wild, nothing was stopping this moment. It wasn't a loving or sweet kiss, this was a feral and needing kiss, we both had waited and needed this more than anything. Miles' lips left mine and made their way down my cold, bare body, leaving a line of saliva down my skin as he ran his tongue down. His hands grip tightly on my knees, pushing my legs apart and sliding them to my inner thighs and squeezing, almost kneading my thighs. He crouches down onto his knees and he settles his hot mouth and tongue on my clit, working in circles around the swollen area. My head throws itself back in pleasure and I go to lie back but hands reach around my ass and squeeze them tightly.

"I said sit, not lay down, Ember," he purrs into me, the vibrations of his voice rattling through me, pushing me close to the edge already. "Not yet, Ember. Can't have you looking this good straight off the bat, I cannot finish in my pants." He chuckled and I sat back up, giving him a frustrated look. I'm so close and this man won't let me cross over the edge, two can play this game.

He thrusts his fingers in me and his tongue matches the rhythm of his fingers, my hips join in. My hand runs through his hair and my other hand digs into his muscular shoulders, leaving nail marks in them.

"My love, please." I begged, my legs shaking from being forced to wait, my core's aching so bad that it may explode.

"You're so pretty when you beg, Ember." Miles makes his way up on his feet, running his hands over my curves until he reaches my face and pushes me onto the bed backwards. Falling backwards, laying naked, looking up at him as he takes in the view like it's his last breath. "I take that back, you look fucking stunning, Ember."

He crawls on top of me and slides one of his hands in my hair as he kisses me and the other returns to my clit, slowly circling. I moan into his mouth and I can feel his lips turning into a smile as he deepens our kiss. This kiss was loving and sweet, savouring every moment we have missed over the week.

Miles rolls over and brings me with him, putting me on top of him and I lift my head up, "Let me, my love," I reach down to his button on his pants and slide his pants down slowly, teasing him as much as he did with me. A deadly look crosses his eyes as I pull his boxers down, his cock flicking up in front of me. I place one hand on the bottom and spit on the top, moving my hand slowly up and down. Giving him a taste of what's to come. Miles groans and sits up on his elbows.

"Did I say you could do that, Ember?" I shake my head in response and slowly plant my lips on the crown of his cock. Miles's eyes widen and his head leans to one side as I slowly lower my mouth down his length. I look down as I lift myself slowly up, placing my tongue on his vein as I come up,

"Eyes up here," he demanded, putting two fingers under my chin to lift my eyes, they snap straight onto his as I sped my motion up. Miles's head goes back slightly, letting out a deep breath as he looks back at me and he slowly thrusts as I go back down. "Hang on, Ember," his hand fists my hair and I raise back up. He sets the rhythm with his hand in my hair, thrusting long and hard to the back of my throat. Tears shed down my face and moans escape my mouth onto his cock as it twitches with each sound. "Fuck," he howls as he floods my mouth with his cum, his hand slowly releases my hair and pushes back the strands out of my face so he could get a front row seat, "Make sure you swallow all of it, Ember."

I continue the motion gently as I swallow every drop, Miles' thumb wiping over the corner of my mouth as I release his cock from my mouth. His hands immediately pull me up to him, placing me straight onto his cock, thrusting in hard and slow.

I let out a moan of pleasure as he does it a second time, and a third. "Miles," I whimper, pleasure washing over me as I shatter almost immediately from the motion.

"I know, Ember, come here." He whispers, gently bringing my head down to his as he kisses me passionately. His tongue sweeps around inside my mouth, tasting himself on my tongue. He quickens the pace and I can feel myself building back up inside, Miles' hand finds my swollen clit again and places enough pressure to help me go over the edge a second time.

Miles moans crash against mine as he explodes inside me. I lay on top of him, sweat dripping off us both as we try to catch our breath.

"Fuck, Ember, you'll be the death of me." Miles whispers in my ear and kisses my forehead as he rolls over to me and spins me. My back is against his chiselled abs and my ass is against his cock, which somehow is still hard. I giggle as he nuzzles his face into the nape of my neck, "You know, I have one final punishment for you, Ember." His hot breath caresses against my neck, sending goosebumps across my body.

"Really, do I deserve all these punishments, my love." I whimper, my legs still shaking, trying to recover from my last punishment might take a minute.

"Are you saying you didn't like the punishment?" His tone makes me freak out inside, fuck, did I just offend him!

"No, of course not, my love. It was a fantastic punishment," my voice cracks, way to not sound nervous Scarlet.

"Well, the thing with punishments, Ember," he pauses, moving himself behind me. His body vanishes for a moment before his hand quickly lifts my leg and his cock returns but...

"Miles!" I shout, my body in shock as he thrusts his cock into me and places my leg pack down, positioning himself back into a cuddle. Wait, that isn't his dick in me!

"You're not supposed to enjoy them, Ember, well these types of punishments are for enjoyment but you need to be taught who's in charge and listen when you're spoken to." He lays behind me but I can feel the smugness from here, I don't need to see him to know he's happy with himself.

"What are you doing, my love?" I try to rock my hips, trying to figure out what's in me and then I feel it move, forcing a moan to slip out.

"You will lie here and go to sleep with this vibrator inside of you, Ember. This will teach you to listen the first time, not throwing a tantrum." He chuckles as he gets himself comfortable, clicking the vibration up.

Ex-fucking-cuse me!

I flip around to face him and he holds up the remote with the biggest grin on his face. "Go to sleep, Ember, you will need your strength tomorrow. We need to get organised for France." He places a gentle kiss on my neck and I finish over the feeling and vibrations. As my body calms down, thanks to Miles turnings the vibrator down low, I look at him and his eyes are fucking closed and he's twitching!

Why do guys do that, close their eyes for five fucking seconds and then they twitch like they are having a seizure as they fall asleep!

"My love?" I whisper, but nothing except a quiet snore answers me. I let out a heavy sigh and lay there, looking at my wall for what feels like forever before falling asleep. The vibrations remain low all night, making me toss and turn, my body begging for more but Miles hid the remote and I would be in trouble if I removed it, so I laid there, trying to go to sleep.

CHAPTER 30 – MILES

All I could feel when I woke up was Scarlet trying to move herself around, trying to get some sort of friction while I was asleep with the vibrator I bought as a 'just in case' item.

"Morning, Ember, what are you doing?" I grab the remote and turn it up slightly, a small moan comes from her swollen lips.

She froze, holding her breath from shock. "Morning, my love, uhh, nothing, nothing at all." Her breathing starts again, shaking with every word that leaves her lips as I turn it up again.

"Would you like some help with that?" My lips graze her neck, making her back arch.

"Yes p-please." I leaned into her and my lips caressed her neck as she let out breathless moans, her hips matching the rhythm I've set for the vibrator. I finally pull it out of her as she cums and I move on top of her, looking into her stunning green eyes and her auburn red hair.

"What is it, my love?" Scarlet wipes her face, trying to see if drool or something was on her face.

"Nothing, Ember, you are just so beautiful. I can't believe you're finally mine." I drop down and my lips settle onto hers, our tongues making knots with each other and our teeth clashing against one another. The head of my cock sits at her entrance, waiting for her to let me into heaven. Her hips rolled under me, pushing me inside her. Moans and groans come from both of us as we match pace and I drag my mouth down to her nipple, taking the whole thing in my mouth, suckling and nipping my way through both sides.

Fuck I'm getting close and Scarlet hasn't even finished from me yet. I slide my thumb up her thigh as I thrust into her, reaching her clit and forcing enough pressure and movement to push her over.

"Miles," she whimpers, back arching as I wrap one arm around her back, sinking deeper into her,

"I know, Ember, cum for me." Her breath starts shaking and her pussy tightens around my cock as she cums around me. The pressure of her tightening around me sent me flying, I fell gently on top of Scarlet as I cum inside her.

"Did you have to leave that inside me all night with barely any vibration on, my love?" Scarlet said, trying to catch her breath.

"A punishment is a punishment, Ember. Don't throw tantrums and you can have as much as you want." I wink at her and she rolls her eyes as I gently fall beside her, taking her into my chest. "We need to get up, Ember. One last day before France, maybe I should help you pack?" I need her to wear something stunning one night so I can propose, I have it all planned in my head on how I want it to go. We are playing in the championships in Paris and I want to do it on the courts after she wins but if she doesn't win, I have a backup plan to do it on the Eiffel Tower.

"Help me pack? Don't you need to pack?" She pushes gently away from me, her eyebrows furrowed as she looks at me.

"I packed yesterday but we're there for a week and only playing for a few days so we should have outfits packed for going out, it's supposed to be beautiful while we're there." I kiss her forehead and get up, putting my clothes on and helping her to the bathroom. "Get ready and I'll help you pack while you shower." Scarlet nods and I turn to her closet and start packing things I know she'll need or want. Underwear, bras, sports clothing and I spent ten minutes looking for the perfect dress for her to wear on the night I plan on proposing for the backup plan. She walks out of the bathroom, her hair's wet against her skin that shows through her singlet and her legs are on full display in denim shorts, I swear this woman's trying to make me cum in my shorts.

"What's that for?" She walks over and picks up the dress she wore on our last date,

"I plan on taking you on a date at least once while we are in Paris, Ember, and you look beautiful now but I know you will hate me if I don't tell you to bring something nice to wear for a date." I can feel my hands going clammy and sweaty with each word leaving my mouth, my voice forcing itself not to crack as I stand there looking at her, hoping she fell for the words I said.

"Mmm, alright then, my love. Let's grab a few options then, just in case." As she walks away I let out a massive sigh of relief and follow her.

The next morning, I roll over in bed and notice Scarlet's missing, naturally I start freaking out! I ran out of our bedroom and straight down the stairs, hearing laughter coming from the kitchen. I bolt to the doorway and Scarlet's and Lauren's head fly in my direction as I realise that she's okay.

Thank fuck for that.

"My love," Scarlet giggles as she covers her face, Lauren quickly turns back to look at Scarlet and I can feel the tension in the air, "Please go upstairs and put some pants on."

Fuck my life.

I look down and realise that I am only wearing jocks, oh but the worst part is that I have the biggest boner right now and Lauren got a full site of my cock through them. I instantly turn and quickly walk up the stairs as I hear laughter from the kitchen behind me, I'm never going to hear the end of that.

I get dressed and go back downstairs, instantly going for the coffee while the two girls sit at the dining table, giggling to themselves like they are twelve.

"Morning, Lauren, are you all packed for today?" I manage to get the words past my teeth as I sip my coffee, not being able to look either of them in the face.

"Yep, we packed yesterday so we were ready for today. I'm so excited, I have never been to Paris before so I can't wait!" She said, practically jumping out of her chair in excitement. "You looked all packed this morning, Miles." Scarlet snorts and coffee splashes out of her mouth as Lauren and her piss themselves laughing over the dick joke.

"You need to calm down, it's too early for this much excitement babe," Logan walks around the bench to grab the coffee too and stands beside me. "Are you guys ready to go? We have to leave for the airport soon." Logan sounds like he could fall asleep standing right now, I don't think he sleeps at all now that he's working for a big development company.

"Yeah we are ready, just having breakfast," Scarlet snickers and Lauren starts giggling again,

"Yeah breakfast with a view," Lauren cracks up and Scarlet's trying so hard not to burst out laughing, smacking Lauren's arm as she walks over to me and kisses my cheek.

"What?" Logan's eyebrows shot up to the roof as he looked over us all.

"I got worried something happened to Scarlet this morning because she wasn't in bed but I didn't have pants on so when I came running downstairs and these two were here, your fiancée got a front row seat to my morning wood." I stare into my cup, wishing that I could literally drop dead right now. Logan looks at me like he's seen a ghost while the girls are pissing themselves laughing.

"It was a good view, my love." Scarlet adds as she sits her plate in the sink and walks out of the kitchen with Lauren.

"Tell me you had boxers on?" Logan whispers, also not able to look at me in the face,

"I had jocks on, tight jocks on. Your fiancée saw everything." We stood there in silence for a minute, processing what happened before Logan took a deep breath and turned to me.

"I need to ask, how much did she see?"

"The whole eight inches man, I didn't realise she was here and I thought something happened to your sister." I can feel the panic boiling over the embarrassment that's already out for display.

"Damn, well at least you were wearing something, it may not have been much but still." He sits his empty mug in the sink. "At least my sister's lucky," he chuckles as he follows the girls upstairs. I'm so glad everyone can joke about my morning wood.

We all get to the airport and we check in and wait for our flight to Paris. The whole flight Scarlet and I planned for our practices and games as we have to book in advance like qualifiers so everyone has a chance to train before the games. Scarlet left it a little late and had the late night training slots for her team, which almost made her have a panic attack. I really need to know what to do when they happen. The late night sessions are seven to nine so they will need to train, go back to the hotel and sleep almost immediately to keep on schedule and to have enough sleep if they have an early game, which we don't find out until tomorrow.

"What if we don't make it past the first round? This will all be for nothing!" The panic starts to spread across Scarlet's face as she rubs her face with both hands.

"You'll make it and if for some reason you don't, you made it to the championships! All those teams at qualifiers didn't, even the teams that didn't make it that far didn't. You made it, Ember. You will go further, I believe in you." I kiss her forehead and continue to help her with strategies and teams.

Once we land, we meet our teams at the hotel the Basketball Association picked out for the championships and we make our way to our rooms.

"Did you want to have separate rooms, Ember?" I whisper to her, I'm practically holding her up. She's exhausted after the plane trip, the panic must have knocked her out.

"No, please. Stay with me," she demanded quietly, barely able to speak but I could hear the panic as the words left her mouth.

"Okay, okay, Ember. I'll stay with you," I picked her up and walked her to our room.

"Aww how sweet Miles, aren't you just a gentleman." Cal laughs behind me, I turn to look at him with a cold stare. He immediately shuts up and clears his throat.

"I will see you tomorrow Cal," I called back as I walked into the room. It's a nice room, a big king bed with closet spaces, a massive bathroom with a big bathtub and a double shower. A massive TV with all streaming platforms and free room service provided by the association.

I place Scarlet down on the bed, taking her clothes off her body and changing her into her PJs so she can sleep in peace.

"Thank you, my love," she whispers, as she snuggles herself into the thick blanket that covers the bed.

"No worries, Ember, I'll unpack and join you in a sec." I kiss her forehead gently and sweep my hand over her hair, looking at her features as she sleeps. God, she is everything to me.

I go over and unpack everything into the closet and

get dressed for bed, curling up into Scarlet as I fall asleep.

CHAPTER 31 – SCARLET

I can't believe I left the session scheduling to the last minute, leaving us to the last spot in the evening which fucking sucks!

I roll over as I wake up from the shittest night sleep I think I have had in a long time to see Miles already awake, sitting on the balcony we have in the hotel room with two mugs on the table with him.

"Morning, my love, did you sleep well?" I yawned as I walked outside to sit next to him.

"Good morning, Ember, I slept for a few hours. Being away from home makes it hard for me to sleep." He smiled up at me and held out his hand as I placed mine in his, he pulled it to his lips and gently kissed the back, "that cup's yours, Ember, just the way you like it and breakfast should be here soon." I sat next to him and took a sip of the coffee next to me, fuck this is good.

"Thank you, when do you guys train today?" I asked, I knew it was in the afternoon but I didn't know when exactly.

"Five to seven this afternoon, we got a good time, just like training at home," he chuckles as he takes a sip from his mug,

"You guys finish up when we arrive, that's kind of

annoying means we won't see each other at night then."
Miles talked about date nights while we were here
which would have been amazing because Paris is
beautiful. Filled with lights and love, the streets look
like something out of a movie.

"Yeah, I realised that on the plane, I just didn't want
to stress you out more yesterday," his face fills with
worry as he takes my hand back in his.

"I'm okay now, my love, thank you for yesterday.
You really helped, I haven't been like that in a while."
I haven't had a real panic attack since Miles has been
back.

Miles smiled at me and we turned to look at the view
and thoughts of what happened a few months ago came
rushing back. Right now, is not the time for this shit. I
wrapped my arms around my waist and squeezed,
trying to remove the memories from my head. "Come
on, Ember, let's go see everyone else before we have
training." Miles reaches for my hand and leads me out
of the hotel room and down to the lobby where both
teams are chatting to each other.

"Scar, this place is beautiful! Cal was just saying that
they train before us so we can use half the court while
they train and vice versa if you guys are okay with
that?" Lauren runs over to us and her face is full of awe
as she looks around the lobby. The hotel is beautiful,
it's filled with fresh flowers every day and the decor
reminds me of all the hotels we see in movies.

"I don't have a problem with it. It gives both teams
more time to practice." Miles says, turning to me to see
what I think.

"Yeah, fine by me," Lauren's face is taken over by a
big grin as she runs back over to the teams to let them
know what's happening.

"You okay, Ember?" Miles turns to me fully, his big
blue eyes staring into mine.

"Yeah, I just have a weird feeling. I don't know how
to describe it." I did though, I just don't want to think

about how Miles left me on the court or never visited me in hospital after what he said. I knew it wasn't his fault but those words still left his mouth.

"Maybe you're just home sick, let's go join the team and get some food, I'm starving."

We walk out and go find a cafe for lunch, looking around as we all walk through the streets of Paris. It was stunning, I couldn't believe what my eyes were seeing.

"Hey, Scar." Logan and Melaine come up from behind me. Miles moves and goes to walk with Cal and Lauren as they come up beside me.

"You okay? You look down." Mel grabs my hand in hers, she always knew when I was down, she's like a psychic.

"Yeah, just thinking is all." I look down at the ground, 'deep breathes Scarlet' playing in my head just the way mum would say it.

"About what? You look like you might have another panic attack, did Miles do something?!" Logan's voice went deeper, knowing what happened and having to pick up my pieces after what Miles did, he would never forgive him again if Miles did something.

"No, he hasn't done anything but be there for me since then. I just can't stop worrying that it may happen again, or something else." My voice shakes as tears well in my eyes.

Do not cry Scarlet, not right now.

"Scar," Mel stops me and pulls me aside, "Miles loves you, if you think something will happen or you're worried about something you need to tell him. Don't bottle it up, that will only make it worse." She pulls me in tightly, the tears in my eyes threaten to come out as she hugs me. "He's here for you, we're all here for you but I think it's something else." She pulls away from me, hands on my shoulders, tilting her head slightly as if she is trying to figure out what's going on in my head.

I took a deep breath, "The Australian team's here, I

don't want them to be like well, themselves. Most of them are fine but the captain is like Sam and Miles is amazing. What if she tries something like she has." A single tear finally escapes my eyes, dripping down my cheek.

"Miles won't do that again and if he does, I know how to kill someone and make it look like an accident," Mel smiles and wipes my tears from my cheek.

"Well, that's a little scary you know that but it's convenient just in case," we giggle as we make our way back to everyone else.

Time goes by so fast here, or maybe it's just the view of the whole city. As we go through the streets and visit the attraction the city has to offer we realise that it's almost time for the men's team to go practice.

We make it to the courts for the championships and they are remarkable. The floors have just had fresh paint and polish, the hoops and backboards look brand new and they have redone the rows and rows of chair stands for the crowds in the next few days. My heart almost skipped a beat looking at the amazing gym, I've wanted to be here ever since I could remember and it's only just clicked that my dreams are coming true.

"Wow, these courts are extraordinary, I wish ours looked like this or even got looked after a little bit." Tegan expressed as she picked her jaw up off the floor and followed everyone to the benches beside the courts.

"Which side do you want, Ember?" Miles bumped into me, bringing me back to reality.

"Oh, either side is fine. Let the teams pick, they're all super excited about it," I smiled, trying to hide all the anxiety and panic I have building in the pit of my stomach.

"Are you sure you're okay, Ember? Did you want to talk to me about it?" His eyes soften and his look makes me want to spill everything to him until I can't breathe anymore but we have training and the team and championships are my number one priority.

"Later, I'm fine right now just can't believe I'm here is all." I smile up at him and reach up to his face, planting a kiss on his soft lips and walk over to my team, who has picked their side already. "Alright ladies," I shouted, walking over to my team, who are all bouncing with excitement, "Let's put some of that energy to work hey." Everyone shouted and nodded in agreement and we went to work. We did some stretching warm ups and started with our specialised training focusing on our weakness, just like we did before qualifiers. Making sure that everyone is amazing all over the court is what our team really needs to push through to the end of championships.

We continued on with our normal training regime for the next three hours, trying to perfect as much as we could without injuring ourselves or getting over tired. "That's a wrap, girls, well done." I shouted from the side lines. For the last half an hour of training, I have been working on feedback sheets for each girl to let them know what their strengths are and what needs to be worked on a little more. Everyone always will have strengths and weaknesses no matter what but we have been refining our training and everyone's as good as they need to be. I couldn't be prouder of my team, they have been putting in so much effort and energy into training and helping me where they can to get us to this spot and I'm so thankful for them all.

"Please line up and I'll give you your sheets as you leave." Each one lined up and I handed them their sheets, explaining what was on there. Everyone understood and was more than happy to continue to work on it when we come in tomorrow.

"You ready, Ember?" My soul almost leaving my body as Miles' voice rings through my body,

"Christ, you scared the shit out of me." My heart is beating out of my chest as I try to calm my breathing down.

"Sorry, are you okay? Are you ready to talk about it

yet?" His head tilts to the side as he looks me up and down.

"Well, I uhh," as I try to find the words to explain what the hell was going on in my head, the doors to the gym swing open, slamming against the walls. "Oh no," I whisper as a group of women walk into the gym wearing matching gym wear.

"Oh hello, I didn't realise anyone would still be here." A tall, tanned woman spoke. Her luminous blue eyes peeking through her deep, black hair as she walks over to us, she's like a copy and paste of Miles' hair and eye colour. There's no fucking way she didn't realise someone was here, she planned this as soon as she saw my name on the schedule. "Wallaby, how wonderful to see you here. We're so proud of you." She said, trying to cover her sarcasm with her fake cheery voice.

"Hello Eva," I hissed. No one has called me that since mum passed, and Davis said it when he wanted something but I hated it being on her lips.

"Come on now, is that how you greet your old captain?" Her hideous smile covering her lips as she stops right in front of me, Miles still towering behind me, watching confused.

"You're lucky I even said hello, we'll be leaving now." I looked behind me and my team was already reading the room, walking out the door behind the Australian team as they stepped aside.

"Now now, no need to be so rude." Eva chuckled, her eyes snapping from mine to the tower behind me, "and who's this," she walks beside me with more sway in her hips then she already exaggerates, "Eva, and you are?" She holds out her hand to Miles, trying to get into his pants no doubt.

My heart races again, threatening to come up my throat and onto the floor, this is what I was afraid of, I knew this would happen. Miles was out of my league and I knew that but I also knew he loved me and he already made one mistake and swore he would never do anything to hurt me again but why do I feel like this.

Miles looks at Eva's hand and moves around the other side of me, "Miles, Scarlet's boyfriend." He snaps, keeping distance from her so her grubby paws don't touch him.

Eva's body language changes from hot and cool to rigid and angry. "Ha, right," she chuckles, turning to face me again with a hint of determination in her eyes. "I guess we'll see you later wallaby, careful not to jump too fast." She says as she walks away from us, with the sway back in her hips, god if she swayed anymore she may fall over.

Miles opens his mouth to say something but I storm off, I can feel my face going red with anger and embarrassment as I walk past my old team mates. It would be so nice to catch up with them but I know better with Eva, she would have told them to ignore me or something worse just to throw me off my game but I won't have it! I will play against them and show them what they are missing out on.

"Ember, slow down!" Miles shouts, speed walking to catch me, "what was that? Is that what's wrong, her?" He grabs my hand to stop me in my tracks and points back over to the gym.

"She took everything from me! My ex, she could offer more than I was ready for. My mum, she made me stay at practice longer than anyone else to 'improve' my skills and make me miss visiting hours at the hospital. My games, she made me put in all this extra effort to only give me a max of fifteen minutes of play time if I was lucky." Tears streaming down my face, sizzling as they touch my angry skin. "She took everything from me and I just got you back, I made captain and I've worked my ass off for this and she's going to try to destroy that, no matter what!" I sit on the metal seat on the sidewalk, unable to stand as my body shakes with the frustration and anger that was building inside me.

"Eva? She is the reason you have been like this since the plane." Miles crouches down in front of me, his warm hands resting on my shivering knees.

"Yes, that's all she does. She took this away from me last year and that was the last thing she could take from me. Now she's here and I have so much to lose." The thoughts of her saying 'Sorry wallaby,' or 'You just aren't ready yet,' haunting my head.

"Ember, you are here. She didn't take that from you, I'm here and I will always be here. I will not leave you again, not ever, no matter what happens. You have an amazing and supportive team that you brought here, Sam was never going to get them here but you did." He lifts my chin with his fingers, wiping my frustrated tears off my cheeks. "We all love you unconditionally, Ember, all here for you. Now, I personally cannot wait until you kick her ass! The look on her face will be amazing." Miles chuckles and that sound, right there, made all my frustrations and worries vanish.

"It will be pretty funny won't it." I giggled, well kind of more like a muffled giggled with sniffles and tears.

Miles stood up and held out his hand from me. I looked up into his eyes and all I could see was an ocean of love. I placed my hand in his and we walked to the edge of the road to call a cab and went back to the hotel room.

CHAPTER 32 – MILES

My phone starts buzzing as I jump onto the exercise bike for my morning workout, 'Ember' showing up on my screen. "Morning, Ember, you okay?"

"Hey, my love, where are you? I woke up and you were gone." Scarlet whispered, panic flowing through her voice.

I immediately stop the bike and start walking out of the gym. "Sorry, Ember. I'm at the gym downstairs but I'm coming back up right now." I barged through the gym door, going straight for the elevator.

"Oh okay, no that's okay. I was just worried you went somewhere and there's no message or note."

Fuck, good one you dumbass.

"I will get dressed and come down, I need to workout anyway. See you in five, my love."

"Are you sure, Ember? Okay I will see you soon, message me if you need me though, I love you always." I wanted to throw my phone at the wall, why the fuck did I not message her at least letting her know where I was. I knew she wasn't having a good time after last night and I just made that worse, fuck.

"Yes, my love, I'm fine. I love you too." I could feel her smile through the phone and my heart fluttered as she hung up the phone. I took a deep breath to calm myself down before I got a boner in the middle of the lobby and made my way back to the gym.

About five minutes later, Scarlet walks through the door of the gym. Her wavy hair tied up in a messy bun, which I fucking love. Wearing a matching sky blue workout bra and legging set that fits her body so well, fitting in all the right spots.

"Hey, my love," she walks over to the machine I'm on, "need a spot?" She giggled, knowing full well that she wouldn't be able to help me much if something happened.

"I'd love one, Ember, especially if it's you." I winked at her as I placed the barbell back on the rack, wiping the sweat off my forehead. "How are you this morning, are you okay? I'm sorry I didn't even leave a note to say where I was going, I should know better." I move closer to her, inches apart but her forehead comes up to my chest.

"I'm okay, my love, I promise. I was just worried because what if something happened to you and I had no idea where you went." She pulls me in for a hug, even though I am covered head to toe in sweat, she doesn't care.

"I know and I'm sorry. I will message you next time." I pulled her in tighter, releasing all the stress and anxiety that I know she will have after that stupid move I pulled.

"Well, I should go workout, the girls will be down soon anyway. I can't believe that the championships start tomorrow. Have you seen the board?" Scarlet pulls out her phone to show me the women's championship knock out board. "We won't have to face the Australian team unless we both make it to the finals. So, either we won't make it or they won't." She exclaimed, not being too happy with that answer.

"Or you both make it to the final and you have a chance to redeem yourself not just to them but to yourself, because you'll make it that far, Ember." I pulled her in for a kiss as I heard the gym door open,

"Oh shit." Lauren whispered. I pulled away gently from Scarlets sweet caramel scent and turned slowly to Scarlets and my team who had to just walk in at this fucking second.

"Uhh morning captains, ready for the final day of relaxing before we fuck up everyone," Lauren screeched. I need whatever she's on because she has way too much energy for it being six in the morning.

"Morning Lauren, alright team stop dawdling, let's work out so we are ready for our last day for training." Scarlet shouted out and everyone walked over to their warm up machines of choice and started. God, I love when she's demanding like this, it's hot.

"What are you looking at, my love?" Scarlet turns back to me, a sexy smirk filling her perfect lips.

"Nothing, Ember, just how hot you are when you're bossy." I chuckled and kissed her again.

We spent about an hour in the gym working out, getting ready for a day of stamina training before we have our time in the court gym today. Most of us have high stamina but even then having to spend the full time on the court due to the rules stating we can only have one extra in case of injuries but other than that we all have to be on the court for the whole game.

We picked out a park that was long enough for us to do our training with both teams. There weren't a lot of people here which was good because having twelve people doing stamina training wasn't a small thing.

"Okay everyone," I shouted, getting everyone's attention as the conversations went quiet. "Both, Scarlet and I have quickly explained what today's about." Scarlet's head whips to mine and I could hear the team quietly freaking out.

"I am sorry, my love, who explained today?" One of her eyebrows raised as her head tilted to the side.

Oh shit.

My face goes hot, no doubt red as well as I remembered when she said my name and I punished her. I cleared my throat and turned back to the teams, who were all waiting for Scarlet to freak out on me.

"Sorry, Ember, let me repeat myself. Both of us have explained."

"No, my love, repeat what you said the first time properly," she moved closer to me and whispered in my ear, "or do I need to give you a worse punishment than you gave me?" Her voice teasing my head as I can feel my cock slowly rise, clearing my throat again to calm myself before everyone here sees the show.

"Apologies, both Ember and I have quickly explained what today's about." I turned to Scarlet who's standing beside me, all proud with a massive cheeky grin spread across her face and the teams were all covering their mouths or looking away from us, trying not to burst out laughing.

"Cut it out," I demanded. Everyone immediately stopped laughing and stood up straight looking at me with nervous faces. "Now, we will warm up by running around the park." Everyone groaned, the park wasn't massive but to run around it wasn't an easy task, "now, and if I see anyone walking or jogging you will do it again."

Everyone went off running at a good pace, trying not to disappoint me.

"Was that necessary, my love," Scarlet's voice was menacing, she knew she hit a spot on me.

"You just wait until you find out what's waiting for you tonight after training," I bend down closer to her ear, almost touching it with my lips, "better save some energy for it."

Scarlet's face goes red with heat as I pull myself away. "Now, Ember." I stand beside her and gently smack her ass to get her moving, "this warm up is for us too, come on. Need to lead by example." I run off as I turn and see Scarlet not far behind, following me in my tracks with a grin on her face.

I pass by most of the women's team as I catch up with Cal, out in the front trying to show off.

"Morning Cal, hope you're ready to have your ass kicked today," I tease as I run past him.

Cal and I have always been competitive with each other when it comes to training and games, trying to see who can out do who. Which works out for me because it means he's motivated.

"Come back here Miles! I will beat you!" He shouts as I lose him in my dust. No, he isn't.

I make it back to the starting point and grab my water as Cal makes it to the start, "you started after me and still beat me. You're insane." He huffed as he bent down putting his hands on his knees, trying to catch his breath.

"Keep practicing bud. You were closer this time though, you will get there one day. You still have all next year to kick my ass," I chuckle as I watch Scarlet come through next.

"Damn, my love, you're so fast!" Scarlet was the fastest on her team because she has crazy stamina and I didn't find that out on the court.

"Practice, Ember, plus I'm fucking tired just after that. You look like you walked that." She turned to look at our teams slowly trickling in after one another.

"Well, I have insane stamina, as I have been told," she smirks and walks over to her water, leaving Cal and I where we stand.

"That is something I did not need to hear by the way," Cal's face is all scrunched up in disgust. I burst out laughing as the last ones made their way to the starting point.

"Poor, Cal. You'll be fine bro." I tapped his shoulder as he walked over to the rest of the team and Scarlet walked back over, giggling to herself. She fucking knew what she was doing, of course she did.

"Okay everyone, take five to grab some water and

stretch your legs then we will start training." She shouts across to everyone and they all sit, drinking their water.

For the stamina training, we created a circuit training workout so the teams will be split into groups of three and go through four different exercises for about five minutes each. Since stamina's something we rely heavily on, we need to make sure we can last long enough on the court without feeling like we need to cough up a lung. The exercises we have are jump rope, burpees, a mini running course from tree to tree and stair climbing.

"Okay everyone, break over." Scarlet shouts and everyone stands up, watching her and waiting to hear what she has to say. She thinks that she isn't a good captain, only if she could see herself right now. Everyone immediately listens to her, knowing what she is doing, how to control her team but is kind and sweet to them. The perfect combination and she doesn't know it. "We have set up the exercise for the circuit. Split into groups of three and you need to mix them, not three men and three women, there needs to be a mix." She points to both teams as they split into their groups. Scarlet turns to me, guess it's my turn now.

"Okay everyone, we have jump rope, burpees, stair climbing and lastly a running exercise to go from tree to tree." Everyone looks over to each exercise as I point out, "You will be at each for five minutes at a time with a minute cool down period and we'll be doing this for about an hour, so you will do each exercise three times before being done here." I could hear everyone groan and moan about the time we need to train for this.

"Hey!" Scarlet roared, everyone stopped their sounds and looked at her. "If you don't want to do it we could've stayed home but we are here and we need to build on this so you don't feel like you're dying on the court. You can all do this, it's just like normal training without basketballs. Now stop complaining so we can do our stretching before we start." Everyone nods and spreads out to do the stretches that Scarlet does. See, good captain material right here. We spend about an hour and a half doing the training before we call it for the day before we do our training later today.

It's about nine in the morning now that we have finished our training and everyone's exhausted while Scarlet is literally sitting on the bench, looking like she hasn't moved an inch in the whole hour and a half of training. Fucking Jesus, if I had her stamina we would be screwed.

"Alright guys, who's ready to go find something for breakfast," Scarlet jumped up, walking over to our teams as everyone mumbles to themselves as they stand. I hold back a chuckle as Scarlet walks over to me, "what's so funny, my love?" She folds her arms over her chest and pops a hip out, waiting for my answer.

"You seem like you did nothing yet we all look like we just did a marathon." I push my hair out of my eyes and grab my phone out of my pocket, searching up breakfast places in the area when Dad calls me. "Hang on, Ember, it's Dad." I point to my phone and she nods as she walks back over to everyone, getting them ready to go like they are her kids. "Hey, Dad, how was your flight?"

"Hello, this is Dr Brown from the New York Hospital. Is this Mr Grove's son, Miles?" A voice from the other line says I stop in my tracks, I can feel the life draining from my face as I stand, watching the trees blow in the wind.

"Yes, this is him, is my dad okay?" I whispered. Feelings whirling in my head as I try to not to jump to conclusion of what the fuck happened to make my dad end up in hospital for the second time in less than six months.

"Mr Grove suffered from some serious trauma to his abdomen and head and was found in an alley near the airport. We are calling to inform you that he needs immediate surgery on his abdomen as there is free fluid in his stomach and may need brain surgery. We are monitoring his brain closely but it is a high possibility." The doctor continued talking about what injuries Dad suffered from but I couldn't hear anything he was saying. Dad got jumped at the airport, he didn't even make his fucking flight.

I drop to the ground, crashing down on my knees as I listen back to the doctor, "Do we have your permission to do the surgery?"

Surgery! Dad needs surgery to survive and I know he would want every measure to stay alive.

"Yes, do the surgery." I demanded as I heard footsteps come up behind me and a hand resting on my shoulder. I turn and see Scarlet's worried face looking down at me, I place my other hand over hers as the doctor starts talking again.

"Are you able to come in and sign some forms as we may need your consent for other things. As this is immediate surgery and is necessary we don't need it for this but we may if complications come up."

Holy shit, I am an eight hour flight away from home and there is a big storm in New York right now, so there is no way I would be able to get home to sign anything.

"I'm in Paris for a basketball tournament, my dad was coming over today that's why he was near the airport. I can't get home, not with the storm over New York. Are you able to send them to me via email and I can sign them where I need to?" My voice shaking with worry, who the fuck would do this. Dad has many enemies from putting people away but hasn't had anything like this done before. I'll fucking find out who did this and kill them with my own hands.

"Normally we wouldn't, but under the circumstances that's fine. The police will call you soon for your statement, just to see if you may know who did it or anything that may help them find the person. If you have any questions or concerns please call my personal number. I will be staying with your dad until he is cleared."

"Thank you, please keep me updated on his progress." I feel the colour from my face drain completely as a wave of nausea hits me hard.

"Of course, sir, bye now." The doctor hung up and I stared at my phone, hoping that I would get another call to stay that it wasn't him or it was a false alarm.

"My love, what's wrong? Are you okay?" Scarlet bends down in front of me, her face is full of anxiety and she looks scared. Fuck, I try to pull myself together but the thought of my dad in hospital in a critical condition while I am here for a stupid competition makes me sick. "Miles, talk to me." Scarlet pulls my face up to hers and pulls me in for a kiss, knocking out my threatening thoughts and helping me breathe again. She pulls away, her eyes worried as she looks over my face. "What's wrong?"

"It's Dad. Someone jumped him at the airport and they found him in an alley near the airport. He's in critical condition and is going for abdominal surgery, there is free fluid in it and they are monitoring his brain but it's a high possibility he may need brain surgery too." My voice cracks and tears roll down my cheeks as I fall into Scarlet's shoulder. Her hands wrap around the back of my head and back as she pulls me closer, letting me sob into her chest.

I could hear talking as I continued to let out my tears on Scarlet but I couldn't make out what they were saying, the thoughts blurring my senses. Scarlet gently pulled away from me and cupped my face in her warm hands, "Come on, my love, let's go to the hotel and cuddle in bed with some food. We can find these people together." She wipes my tears with her hand and softly kisses me as I sniffle my snot back in. I nod and she helps me up, as we turn I notice that everyone else is probably gone to get breakfast. Which I was fine with,

I would prefer them not to be around while I broke down, I don't like people seeing me weak but I feel safe with Scarlet and our teams but still, if I can help it, only Scarlet can see me like this.

CHAPTER 33 – SCARLET

The whole cab ride to the hotel Miles looked down at his blank phone, hoping someone would call him with good news on his dad, or the police call saying they caught the fucked up person or people who did this to his dad.

We get up to the hotel room and Miles gets a call from the police and I go into the bathroom to change to give him some privacy. I couldn't imagine what was going through his head. I remember the call I got about Mum being permanently admitted to the hospital because her cancer got so bad but cancer was something that we tried to fight for a while before it was too late. Miles started his day in the best mood and then got the phone call that his dad is on a thin line of life or death.

I got dressed in my PJs, Miles wanted to watch TV and eat food so I thought I would get comfortable for the next few hours before we went to go to training, which I said we could cancel but Miles wants to take his mind off of what happened before he goes and actually kills someone. I walk out as Miles hangs the phone up, his face still pale, no good news then.

"Do they have any leads yet?" I whisper as I crawl onto the bed next to him, pulling him into my side.

"They said they have a few leads and suspects but just wanted to confirm some names and if I had any others they may have missed." Miles pauses and pulls himself away from me, turning himself towards me. There's pain in his eyes as he opens and closes his mouth, trying to get words out.

"You don't have to tell me if you don't want, my love, so long as you are okay, but I'm here for you, always." Miles's face doesn't change, his eyes still drooping with worry as he shakes his head.

"No, it's not that I don't want to tell you, it's just how to tell you, Ember," he whispers, running his hands over his face. How to tell me? What the fuck?

"What is it?" I squeeze his hand, trying to not freak out before I even know what's going on.

Miles clears his throat as he opens his mouth, "The police brought up Davis," he paused as I let go of his hand.

Davis! There's no fucking way he did this. He's in prison, in a max fucking security prison, with minimal visitation. He couldn't have, right?

"They think," the words vanish to ash in my mouth as I can feel my stomach churn. "They think he did this?" My stomach stirs again and I get up and run to the bathroom, throwing my head into the toilet as vomit explodes out of my mouth.

Miles rushes over from the bed and lands on his knees next to me, pulling my hair back out of my face as I vomit more into the bowl. "Let it out, Ember." Miles' hand rubbing circles around my back as I lean on the edge of the bowl with my arm.

"He is supposed to be in prison, with minimal visitation. He couldn't have done this." I whimpered, my stomach churning again as I rushed back into the bowl.

"They are investigating it, Ember, he's just a suspect because Dad put him in jail, same as Sam and Travis, but they were working with him so they aren't high on the list."

He already tried to get people to do his dirty work for him once, why wouldn't he do it again. He was a powerful CEO and before the promotion he was well known and powerful anyway. He could have connections to literally anyone.

"He's doing it because of me," I whisper, he wants my money. Mum left me money knowing he wouldn't be around to help once she passed and now that he failed twice he's going for a third time but targeting the people I love.

"We don't know that, Ember. He could have done it because Dad put him away." Miles starts gently stroking my hair, his hand still rubbing circles on my back as I slowly get up. He grabs my waist, holding me up while I walk to the sink to wash my mouth out.

Wait, targeting people I love.

"Lauren," I whisper. Lauren got hurt at qualifiers, he knew I wanted to go to the championships and he surely knew Lauren and I were close and maybe that Logan's engaged to her. He could've gotten the team to hurt her at qualifiers through connections, but what connections did he have with that team?

"What about her? She's fine, she was watching us train this morning."

"No, not right now. At qualifiers, when she got hurt. Davis did that, he knew we were close. I just don't know how he got to the team to do that." Thoughts running wild in my head as I try to figure out what the hell was happening.

"That team always plays dirty, maybe they were just playing like they always do and she was just in the firing range." Miles helps me over to the bed and sits me down on the edge as I wiggled my way into the blanket.

"It didn't seem like an accident and I didn't think much of what actually happened. Just that she needed help and to go to the hospital." I opened my phone and started searching up the team that was versed that day and went through everything with Miles. He decided to help, at least it helps us both get some closure on if it was an accident or if it was intentional. It could also help us get closer to knowing if Davis did it or not.

We went through family trees, work connections and more when there was a knock on my door. Both mine and Miles's head whip into the direction before Miles slowly goes to get up. I grab his hand and panic begins to run through my veins.

"Check first, be careful," I whispered, Miles nods and grabs a knife from the food cart, just in case. He looks in the peep hole and turns to look back at me, rolling his eyes. He puts the knife down on the cupboard beside the door and opens it wide.

"Hey guys, sorry did I interrupt something?" Laurens face was instantly filled with worry when she saw my face. "What is going on?" She walked in and Miles closed the door behind her. "Why do you look like you saw a ghost or are sick?" She checks my face for any signs of illness or injuries.

"Just looking into some stuff for Miles' dad, the police have some leads so we are just looking into it." I say, trying to not worry her with the Davis and Travis stuff. I know what we all went through was traumatising so the less we can speak about it the better. Lauren's face loses colour slightly as she clears her throat.

"Okay, so long as you are okay for tomorrow. I was just checking on you because it's half past two and you weren't downstairs ready to go to training." Lauren turns and looks at Miles as he checks his phone and swears under his breath, rushing to the closet to get changed and quickly slamming the bathroom door behind him.

"Shit, I didn't realise the time, thank you. You all go ahead and we will meet you there." Lauren smiles and closes the door behind her as she leaves. I jump out of bed to quickly get changed and tie my hair up as Miles walks out, ready to go.

Was Laruens face worried? She almost looked sick when I mentioned Davis, maybe because he got her brother thrown in prison.

"Ready, Ember?" He pulls me close, he doesn't mean am I ready to go either.

"Yeah, I will be okay. Let's go train and take our minds off of this stuff and focus. For your dad, you know he would want you to try your hardest and win, so let's do this for him." I reach up on my toes and gently kiss Miles as his face softens and he pulls me in tightly.

"For Dad." He quietly says as he leads us down the road and into a cab to the courts. We are about halfway to the courts when I get a message from Lauren.

'Pre warning, the Aus team's here. Apparently they have the training spot before the men's team.'

Fucking of course they have that slot now. They originally had the nine to eleven slot but they must have swapped with another team so Eva could see Miles or me, who knows.

"What is it?" I show Miles my phone and he looks up at me after reading the text, "did they really swap just to piss you off?" He rolled his eyes, handing me back my phone, as we walked outside, waiting for a cab.

"Most likely, she's trying to get to you. She always wanted what was mine." Miles looked back at me, softly placing his hand over my knee as we sat in the car.

"She can't have me. I'm all yours, Ember, always." He leans in to kiss me when my phone starts buzzing again, way to cock block Lauren,

"Hey, Lauren, what's up," I answer, Miles is officially fed up with the interruptions.

"You read my message right?" She whispered, obviously trying to not let the AUS team hear her.

"Yeah, we were just talking about it." Miles rolls his

eyes at me and looks out the window.

"Well, umm, it gets worse." Umm, what?

"What do you mean it gets worse?" Fucking Eva, always finding ways to fuck with me, even now. Miles snaps his head back towards me with a scary look on his face.

"Well, Eva's asking Cal if they can share the court until we are supposed to start because they started late and well, Cal said she has to ask Miles."

I wanted to throw my phone so far out the window, no one would ever see it again. I turn to Miles who looks as pissed as I feel and he grabs my phone from my hands, "we'll be there in a sec. Do not let Cal tell her yes!" He hung up and lent forward to the cab driver. "We'll get out here, thank you." Miles hands the cab driver more than enough money to cover our trip as we get out and sprint to the courts. We were stuck in traffic but the courts were only a few blocks away so we knew we could run it faster than the cab could get us there, plus that could be our warm up.

We get to the courts and Miles swings open the doors, slamming them hard against the walls, almost pushing them off the hinges. Everyone turns around to see us walking in, I can see Cal and Lauren's face's freaking out but Eva just has a sexy yet evil smirk across her face. She really thinks she can take Miles, yeah right, good luck with that one.

"Miles, thank god you're here." Cal exclaims as he walks over to us. "Did Lauren tell you?"

Miles nods at Cal and walks past both of us as I stand next to Cal. "He's pissed isn't he?" He asked, wincing as the words left his mouth.

"Yep, definitely pissed. We didn't have a good past few hours so he has built up anger and stress to release."

Cal gulped loudly and a massive grin swept across my face, she's about to get the word beat down she needed a long time ago.

I make my way over to Eva and Miles as she's asking him ever so nicely to let them train on the other side for an hour as they were late, but you know making it a big sob story.

"So do you mind if we just use this end of a little while longer," Eva lifts her hand to touch Miles' shoulder but before I could even move to intercept, Miles smacks her hand out of the way. Eva gasps dramatically like someone just punched her in the face, which she deserves.

"I do mind, so no. Your time is up, you need to get off now." Miles demanded as he turned to place his bag down on the bench. Eva's face is mortified, she can't believe she was turned down. "Did you not hear me or do I need to call the association to explain to them that a team isn't following the guidelines?" Miles turned back to Eva who's stunned in place, she snaps back into reality and crosses her arms across her chest.

"Fine, we'll leave, but this isn't over." She turned to me as she said the last part of her sentence, hoping to hit a nerve. I just rolled my eyes and walked past her, bumping my shoulder on hers as I went past. Eva gasped again before huffing away in a fit, calling her team off the court as they walked out the door. My old friends were hanging back, wanting to talk but Eva turned and yelled at them so they left with the team and closed the doors behind them.

"Well, isn't she just lovely," Cal said, walking up behind us.

"Yeah, she's a joy to have around." I chuckled and turned to my team. "Okay girls, go stretch and warm up for five while I get sorted." They nod and jog over to start warming up, Miles's team follows after them.

"Are you okay, Ember?" I nod, sitting down on the bench when my phone goes off again.

'Watch your back.' Fucking Eva, lovely little threats like always.

"Is it her?" He peers over at my phone.

"I think so, it's not from her normal number so I'm not sure." I put my phone down and change my shoes.

"What, my love?" I can see the cogs working in Miles' head turning as he stares at my phone.

"What if it isn't her?" He whispers, trying to figure out what's happening.

"What, Davis?" I feel sick again, my stomach swirls around as bile rises to my throat.

"Maybe, it's a possibility. We need to take it seriously though, with everything happening I will not lose you and Dad." Miles's eyes are glassy as they fill with tears.

"Hey, your dad is fighting right now, he's fine. The surgery went well and his brain's looking good. He will be okay and I have you here with me, I'm not worried, my love." I kiss his cheek as I get up and walk over to my team.

"Hey, are you okay?" Annie stands up and comes over to me. Concern written all over her face,

"Yeah, just a few things going on right now but I am here to focus on basketball and this team." I place my hand on her shoulder as I walk over to the team. "Okay ladies, let's start." Everyone jumps up, ready to train, "in two hours we are having a mock game against the men. We are better than them," the girls giggle as I turn to the men's team and Miles has his arm crossed staring at me. I smile back and blow him a kiss, his straight face breaks slightly with the edges of his mouth rising.

"So, we have two hours to train and then put our skills to the test against the top qualifying men's team, so let's get to work." The girls cheer and we start our training.

CHAPTER 34 – MILES

We get ready for the mock game, setting up like usual with Lauren and our spare refereeing the game for us. Lauren blows her whistle and we start, the girls get the ball first and Scarlet almost immediately gets a three point shot, fuck she's so good. Fucking Eva has no clue what she's up against if she wasn't good enough last year she definitely is now.

We go back and forth for the full game time and by the end whistle the women's team wins, thirty-nine to thirty-five. Fuck these girls are amazing and Scarlet made them this good.

"You should be proud, Ember," I went to shake her hand and she already had the biggest grin on her face.

"I am, the girls are doing great and I think we have a solid chance at winning."

"I'm glad that kicking my team's ass has boosted your confidence." I smile at her and pull her in for a kiss.

"Hey, you're supposed to shake hands, not make out on the court," Cal shouts from the sidelines, everyone starts laughing and cheering as I give them the finger while kissing Scarlet.

"Get a room," Lauren giggles out as I hear the door to the courts open, Eva.

"What she said, Christ." Eva's face crutches in disgust as she walks over to us. "I need to talk to Scarlet." Eva stands in front of us, looking Scarlet up and down like she is nothing to her.

"Okay, speak then?" I stated, pulling Scarlet closer to me.

"What, you can't talk to anyone without your guard dog around." Eva snickers in Scarlet's face, pointing at me.

"Isn't that what a guard dog is for? What do you want?" Scarlet scoffed. Yes Ember, fight back.

"I'm here to warn you, calm down." I'm fucking sorry, what? Scarlets' eyebrows furrow and her head tilts.

"Warn me? What about?" I can hear the strain in her voice trying not to break but her legs are already going weak as she leans against me. Panic fills the room as Eva looks Scarlet dead in the face.

"Davis messaged me, he's after you. He wanted me to take Miles from you, same as his ex did. I don't know it's just what he said, but obviously that won't work a second time. Plus, I am here to win fairly not by fucking around so, as your former captain I thought it was the right thing to do." She crossed her arms as she turned and walked out.

Scarlet holds herself up until Eva's completely out of view before falling down on the ground. Her breathing becomes shallow and quick. "Ember, hey breathe. It's okay." I sit next to her, pulling her into my chest, taking deep breaths while her head is on my chest, helping her breathe. Everyone runs over and I hold my hand up and they all stop, standing inches away waiting for Scarlet to be okay. "Hey, Ember, like you said I'm here. Nothing will happen while I'm here." Scarlet nods against my chest as she tries to take some deep breaths and eventually slows her breathing and is able to move.

"Thank you, my love, oh." She turns and everyone's faces look like they just saw someone die, which isn't far off of how I feel when she panics, I don't want her to end up in hospital again because of her attacks.

"I tried to send them back but that's as far as they would go," I whispered to her and everyone nodded almost in sync.

"Ahh, I'm okay. Thanks guys," everyone moves towards the bags and I notice Lauren's face as she turns, almost looking pissed but I turn back to Scarlet, she needs me and I need to focus.

"You sure, Ember? I will grab your water okay?" She smiles up at me, sitting up a little as I race over to grab her bottle and I see Lauren outside on the phone, almost looking frustrated. Are her and Logan going through something, surely we would know. Get your head in the game Miles, I turn back to Scarlet and hand her the bottle so she can have water.

"Hey, do you know if Logan and Lauren are going through something?" I ask Scarlet, probably not the best time to ask but still.

"No, not that I know of, why?" She sips on more water as she takes in a deep breath.

"Lauren just seems a little frustrated earlier and now she's on the phone and looks like she's pissed."

"Mmm, I'll ask Logan when we get back to the hotel. Mel, Logan and I are having dinner together tonight so I'll ask him tonight." I smile at her as I help her up and grab her bag, walking out to the road and calling a cab.

We get to the hotel room and Scarlet's getting ready for dinner with Mel and Logan. I can't stop thinking about how Lauren acted today, it wasn't like her to be like this, hopefully there is a simple explanation for it. "Okay, what do you think, my love?" Scarlet walks out of the bathroom, doing a spin in the doorway. I looked her up and down and again as I took in the sight of her. Dark denim jeans with a cropped white shirt and glossy black heeled boots, I noticed she was wearing my ring I gave her before the stuff with Sam and Davis.

"You're wearing my ring?" I looked at her as she

lifted her hand and smiled at it.

"Yeah I thought it was time I should start wearing it again. I forgave you a long time ago but I wasn't ready to wear it but now I am." She walked over to the duchess with our wallets and room keys on it. "Oh, Logan texted me asking if Lauren could come because she's been a little down lately and asked if you wanted to come too, seeming as if it's not just the siblings anymore." She sat on the bed next to me and leant down to kiss me,

"Of course I'll join you, Ember, just let me get dressed." I leant forward and gently kissed her as I got up to get dressed. I wore a simple black top with black dress pants, to make it look a little presentable.

I walked out of the bathroom and my phone started to ring, the hospital. I rushed over and my hands were shaking as I swiped to pick up the call, "Hello."

"Mr Grove, it's your dad's doctor." His voice is unreadable, serious sounding but nothing to go off of if there is good or bad news.

"Is my dad okay?" My voice trembled as I stared down at the bed, begging God or Jesus or anyone who would listen that my dad is okay.

"That is why I'm calling, he woke up for a brief minute and wanted to see you. All his tests have come back clear, he will be okay, just needs to be in hospital for a while to recover."

I felt my soul leave my body and come back with those words, he'll be okay.

"Miles?" Scarlet sitting in front of me, waiting to hear what's happening.

"He's okay," I whisper, barely able to breathe let alone say anything right now.

"Yes, he is okay. When he wakes up again I will get him to call you."

"Please let him sleep tonight, but if he wakes up tomorrow I will be playing sports all day. If I send you a link for the live broadcast, can you let him watch it?"

He was trying to make it to the games and I knew he would want to watch.

"I can do that, send it through and we will set up a TV in here for him so he can watch, have a good night, Mr Grove."

"Thank you, you too doc." As I hung up the phone, I took a deep breath. It felt like the first real breath I have been able to take since I knew Dad was in hospital.

"Hey, he's okay. Is he cleared?" Scarlet stands and pulls me into her, her heartbeat racing against me.

"Yeah they cleared him, the surgery went well, he just has to recover now. They are going to let him watch us tomorrow when he wakes up." My voice breaks and I could feel my tears slowly dropping out of my eyes.

"That's great, my love, he'd want that. Now, are you okay to still go to dinner? I understand if you aren't okay." Scarlet's soft hands slowly wipe away the water on my cheek.

"No, I'll come. I'm good, let's go." I clear my throat and take another deep breath as we walk out of the hotel room.

CHAPTER 35 – SCARLET

While in the cab going to dinner all I could think about was what Eva said to me earlier.

Davis is after you, he messaged me.

How was he able to message her? Did he message her or was it a third party that actually messaged her? How did he even know Eva?

He was never around when I talked about basketball last year so he shouldn't have any recognition of her or very minimal at least. I knew that he might try to come for me again but all he wanted was the money, right? If he just asked for some I could have given him some but he didn't just want the money, he wanted me dead too and he never really said why.

"What are you thinking about, Ember?" Miles' voice cuts my thoughts in half.

"Just, I don't know how Davis had access to Eva, he didn't even know about her. It just doesn't make any sense." Then it clicked, he could literally just search up the Ryder University women's basketball team and he would see Eva as the captain. "Never mind, it's literally all over the internet, but still doesn't explain how he could message her and how he knew she would agree to help him."

"Did Davis think of you as his, Ember? Or did he just see you as your mothers and once she was gone, maybe he didn't want you around." I turned to Miles as my eyes stung as tears pooled, Miles' face filled with panic. "Which is stupid because he obviously doesn't know how amazing you are." Miles rips me into a hug and kisses my forehead, trying to comfort me.

"Nice save, my love." I giggled and kissed his cheek as I moved back into my seat. I could hear Miles taking a deep breath of relief after I spoke. He has gone through so much the past twenty-four hours, I don't need to be one of them.

As we walk into the restaurant I notice Mel at the counter and Logan and Lauren at the table. As I look over at the couple I can feel the tension in the air, something's going on with them.

"Hey guys, have you ordered already?" I walk around the table and hug both Logan and Lauren, trying to ease the tension.

"No, we were waiting until you guys got here, Mel's just getting drinks for us," I turn and see Miles helping Melaine with the drinks she ordered. I take a seat next to Lauren and Miles sits beside Mel and me. Lauren looks a little stressed tonight, same as what Miles was talking about earlier today.

"So are you all ready for tomorrow, the championships start and I'm so excited to watch you all play!" Mel gushed, her face about to explode with joy and excitement.

"I think us girls are ready, we kicked the men's teams ass today in a mock game so I think we can handle the women's teams." I bumped Miles's shoulder and he rolls his eyes at me as a massive grin sweeps my face.

"They didn't kick our ass, they won by a few points, but my team's pumped after that game, knowing the women can beat them. They can't wait to take that tension out on the court." Miles looks at me and I just smile at him. Sure, we only won by a few points but we still won.

"I think you all have got this," Lauren looks down at her phone, "excuse me." She pushes her chair out and walks outside.

"Logan, I need you to be honest with me right now mister, what the fuck's going on between you two?" I turned to Logan and demanded that he tells me right now before shit gets real.

"Okay, one calm down," he lowers his voice, taking a breath in. "Her mum was diagnosed with cancer a few months ago and it's aggressive. She got a job to try and help cover the bills since her dad and Travis went to jail, they don't have much money left." Logan's eyes soften as he continues to explain that Lauren's job has been harassing her to come do more hours and not taking no for an answer, they fired her and now she's stressing out about money.

"Why didn't anyone say anything to me, did you know?" I turned to Melaine who looked away from me, not being able to look me in the face.

"We knew how hard it is to go through the same thing, but you struggled more than we did when mum got diagnosed and when she passed. We didn't want to bring it up for you." Mel muttered as she slowly looked at me.

"You could have told me, I know what she's going through," I uttered, rage fuming off my skin.

"So do we!" Logan shouted, people looking over from other tables. "We know what she is going through as well, but it's not just that. She's been visiting Travis in prison, confiding in him which has me stressing out because who knows what he is saying to her."

She's seeing Travis in prison. Miles' hand slides onto my inner thigh, circling the area with his thumb like he used to. I look up at him and he gestures to breathe. I take some deep breaths in and out, trying to calm my thoughts down.

"I know you guys went through that, I'm sorry but she

is seeing Travis. Does she say what they talk about?"

"It's okay," Logan takes another deep breath, "no, she doesn't and now that she's lost her job she's been seeing him more and talking to him everyday on the phone, it's worrying."

I can't believe it, she knew what Travis and Sam did. She helped me through all of it and yet she's going back to him when things are hard.

"She knows if she asks, I can help her with her mum's treatment right?" I pull out my phone to look at my account.

"I know, I have told her that and she refuses. I have even offered her money to help considering we are getting married eventually I thought I should help but she refused that too. I don't know how to help, so I thought a night out would be good to clear her head but it's not going well." Logan's face dropped as he looked past me and I turned as Lauren walked back into the restaurant and her eyes were red and her face was puffy.

"Hey, you okay?" I whisper as Lauren sits back down,

"Yeah, fine." She stated, not even looking me in the face as she stared at the menu.

"Okay, well are we ready to order? I'll pay," Miles gets up and waits for everyone to tell him what they want before going up to the counter and ordering our food.

The four of us sat and talked most of the night while Lauren stayed pretty quiet, just listening to the conversations. No matter what we said or asked her, she never really said much.

We were getting ready to go when Lauren's hand sat on my shoulder, "Hey, can I talk to you please?"

"Yeah, of course." I turned to Miles and kissed him, telling him to go with Logan and Mel and we won't be long. He said goodbye as he left with my siblings. "What's up?" I turned back and Lauren's face completely changed from the sweet best friend I knew to the devil himself,

"I'm so sorry, but not really," her grin spread wider across her face as everything went black.

CHAPTER 36 – MILES

I wait in the hotel room for about half an hour before something starts to feel off. Scarlet isn't answering her phone, which she always does and her location isn't at the restaurant or here at the hotel. I call Logan, hoping that Lauren has told him that they were going somewhere for a while,

"Hey, Miles, what's up? Logan casually says.

"Have you heard from Lauren or Scarlet?" The words leaving my mouth so fast they barely sound like words.

"Umm, no actually I haven't. I have been working so I didn't realise what time it was. I'm sure they are fine," I could hear the clicking of his mouse and keyboard. I put Logan on speaker while I check Scarlet's location again. Panic and sweat builds on my skin as I zoom in on the location, an alley?!

"Scarlet's phone is saying they are in an alley," I look for the restaurant to see where they are and it's streets away! "That's no where fucking near the restaurant, are you sure Lauren never said anything about why she has been talking to Travis."

My first and only thought when Logan said she has been visiting Travis was that something is up and all day she has been acting weird with Scarlet, like letting a mask slip.

"No, she just said she needed to speak to someone who knew their mum well and that was Travis, why?" Logan's voice becomes confused, the clicking sounds stop as I hear a chair being pushed back.

"Why the fuck would she talk to Travis, Logan. He was a dick to her and we all know it, what was Travis doing before he went to prison?" I jumped up and threw my shoes on and grabbed my phone, wallet and my gun as I walked out of the room, straight to the elevator.

"No, she wouldn't. She couldn't." His voice quietens as the realisation comes to him. "Where are you, I'm coming too." I hear clothes ruffle and his door open and close through the phone.

"I'm in the elevator, I'll meet you downstairs." Lauren was sweet and so kind that you wouldn't think she would do something like this, but who knows what Travis has put into her head while Davis is whispering in his ear.

I get downstairs, already calling a cab when I see Logan come out of the elevator, "You don't have to come," I state, seeing his sister and fiancée in a situation like this will not be easy.

"I'm coming, I care about Lauren but Scarlet's my sister, my second mother. If something happens to her and Lauren does it, I'll never forgive myself now let's fucking go before something does happen!" He walks out the doors fast and we get into the cab, going to the alley where Scarlet's phone is.

About twenty minutes later we made it to the location of the phone. "It's supposed to be here, she's supposed to be right here!" I shout, looking at my phone with her location on it.

I turn to Logan as he bends down and picks something up, Scarlet's phone. What the fuck's going on!

"Well, either they drove past here or she's here somewhere and they dropped it by accident." Logan starts to look around, seeing if he can find something to tell us where she is. We look around the alley, there was rubbish, doors to the back of buildings and some homeless people.

"Excuse me, sir." I walked up to one of the men sitting in the alley with an old looking tent and a dog beside him. "Have you seen this girl with anyone around here?" I pull out my phone, showing him a photo of Scarlet, hoping to god that he has seen something.

"Oh, yeah. I saw someone with orange hair being carried into that old warehouse there." He pointed to the old building at the end of the alley, "but the people carrying her were big men, there were two of them and a girl was with them too. She had a crazy look in her eye when she looked at me." His voice trembles with fear as he pulls his dog closer, Lauren.

"Thank you, sir, here," I pulled my wallet out and handed him a few hundred dollars of French currency. "Please take it, as a thank you." The man grabs the money and my hand.

"Thank you, sir," his old skin stretching into a smile across his face.

I smile gently back at him before turning back to Logan, "Let's go."

I grab out the gun that I had sitting behind my back as we walked to the door, "You have a fucking gun!" Logan quietly exclaimed.

"Don't you?" I turn to him and he has nothing in his hand. "Do you want to die? You have no weapon, Logan, call the police. I'm going in to get your sister before something happens." Logan pulls out his phone and immediately calls the police as I gently open the door, trying not to creak it as it opens.

The warehouse was almost pitch black with the streetlights peeking in through the cracks of the curtains. I stepped into the cold building, scanning for anything moving or something that may come out at me while walking through. Years of gun training with Dad may actually pay off, not that I will tell him that unless I have too.

The warehouse was quite big, every room looking the same as I walked through. There were at least three stories to this building and I had to try and move fast but quietly through here to find Scarlet before it was too late. The tension around me started to build as the thoughts built. What if I'm too late? What if she is hurt and I couldn't protect her.

'Isn't that what a guard dog is for?'

The thought of her snapping at Eva warning us about Davis jams its head into mine. You're supposed to be her guard dog and now it could be too late.

I searched the whole bottom floor in less than five minutes, no sign of people or Scarlet around. As I make my way up the stairs to the second level of the building I hear a bang, not of a gun but of something heavy hitting the floor above me. I rush up the stairs, trying not to trip or make any sound as I try to follow the sounds. I hear a bang from above me again, the third floor, the fucking top floor. I race up the stairs and hold my pistol up in front of me, looking in each door to see if anyone's in there.

I get to the end of the hallway, the last door, they have to be here. I stood in place for a moment, frozen, trying to prepare myself for what I am about to see. Scarlet could be injured, bleeding, dead.

Fuck Miles move!

My feet slowly move in front of the of as I peek in the crack of the door and I see the back of a blonde haired woman, Lauren. "See all you had to do was give him the money and all this wouldn't be happening," Lauren shouted, raising her hand and slapping someone in front of her. Lauren paces past the person in the chair, her orange hair covering her face as she is leant down to the side from the impact of the slap, Scarlet.

"Why do people not know how to use their words, you know if anyone had just asked I would have given them however much they wanted!" Scarlet spat back at Lauren, who turned around with a disgusted face before gesturing to one of the men in the room, coming over and punching Scarlet in the side. My body went to move forward without thinking but as I started moving I could see Scarlet's eyes through the crack, she wasn't giving up, not yet anyway. I stood there looking at her until her eyes looked up in between the men that were at the door and saw something, she saw my eyes.

Her face lit up a little, not too much though, she knew I would come and had been waiting. She spat blood out to the side as Lauren walked back in front of her, this time holding a blade.

"See, then it would have been fine but Davis just wants you dead now." She fiddles with the blade in her hand a little as she walks back and forth in front of Scarlet. "Once you're dead, the account would go to him but because he's in prison it would go to his kids, which I'm engaged to one while the other adores me like another older sister and after we kill you, these guys are going to make it look like they took us both but leave me alive so I can take the money." She stopped in front of Scarlet, lifting the blade a little to her side as she swipes it across Scarlet's face.

Oh, fuck this!

I pulled the door open slightly as I poked my head in and while Lauren was turned to Scarlet, holding my gun in front of me as I aimed for one bodyguard's face and shot. The sound of the gun going off and the guard dropping to the floor startled Lauren as I heard her scream but I wasn't paying attention to her because I knew Scarlet could handle it if something happened. I quickly spin to the other guard but as I turn, my gun's knocked out of my hand and his fist lands on my cheek. My head slams into the floor, my vision going blurry for a second before I see the guards foot coming down onto my head. I roll away as he stomps the floor, putting a hole in the old wooden slates, getting his foot stuck.

"So, you are big and stupid, great aspects for a bodyguard," I slid for my gun and shot him in the face as well, leaving his body to fall on the wood.

"If you move she dies!" I turn slowly, facing Lauren and Scarlet. Lauren has Scarlet in a headlock with a gun pointed to her forehead, tears falling down Scarlet's face.

"Lauren, put the gun down," I held my gun out, not willing to move it just in case this goes south.

"No, I need this!" She shouts, shoving the gun further into Scarlet's head, "I need this money, Mum will die without it!"

"Lauren, put the gun down and we can just discuss this. We can help you," I whisper, trying not to trigger anything to her. If she shoots it won't only be my world that will vanish, there's Logan and Melaine and the rest of Scarlet's team, I can't let her do it.

"No!" She shakes, putting her finger on the trigger, "if I don't do this, he won't give me the money to save Mum. Even if you gave me the money, he said he'll kill her himself if I don't kill her!" Her body slowly started to shake with adrenaline.

"We can help, my dad can help you with Davis and we can help you pay for treatment, you should've come to us." I step closer, trying to minimise the distance between us so I can grab the gun or pull Scarlet away.

"Travis said you guys wouldn't do that because you hate my family! That's why you put Travis in prison!" Tears fall down her cheeks as she tightens her grip on Scarlet's neck, making it almost impossible for Scarlet to breathe. Her face is going red slowly from lack of oxygen.

"I didn't like Travis, but I wouldn't put someone away for no reason, he threatened to kill Scarlet for Davis, just as you are doing. Sam controlled him but it was all for Davis. Lauren, please," I begged, stepping closer again, her grip slowly unclenching from

Scarlet's neck. A loud sigh comes from Scarlet's mouth as the colour returns to her face, thank god. "Lauren, I'm begging you, please put the gun down and we can figure this out." I'm inches from the woman as she slowly lowers the gun from Scarlet's head. Scarlet's eyes watch the gun lower before she turns and pushes Lauren into the wall, knocking the gun out of Lauren's hand as she hits the wall.

Scarlet run's to my side, hiding behind my back as she catches her breath, "Thank you, my love," she whimpers as she catches her breath. I smile at her quickly before walking over and grabbing Lauren's gun, unloading the weapon and placing it on the table beside the chair.

"You could've just spoken to me, Lauren, I would've helped!" Scarlet exclaimed, moving to my side while holding the side of her face. Shit, she is bleeding badly.

"Here, put this on the cut. Can you make it down two flights of stairs?" My eyes never leave Lauren as I hear Scarlet whimper a response and slowly turn, "Logan's down there calling the police, get him to call for an ambulance for you and send the police up." Scarlet stops in her tracks.

"No, I don't want to press charges!" She shouted, limping back over to me before she tried to push past me.

"I don't fucking think so, you're not going near her right now. She just tried to kill you, that's attempted murder, Ember. You don't have a choice right now! You need to see a doctor for all the trauma your body has had." I could see her green eyes filling with tears as she turns away and hobbles away from the room,

"Now, you will stay right there until the police come and tell me everything that happened between you, Travis and Davis right fucking now." I demanded, sitting down on the chair Scarlet was just on as Lauren sat up onto the floor and wiped away her tears.

"Okay, I never spoke to Davis, only Travis," she

moaned as she adjusted herself from the pain of the fall. "Mum got diagnosed with aggressive cancer before Travis went to prison, he wanted the money for his own reasons but I went to see him to tell him that mum was worse and that I had to start juggling work and school. He's my brother, my family, Miles, he deserved to know about Mum. So, he told me that there was a way to get so much money that it could pay for all of mum's treatment and then some," Her voice starts trembling as she tries to remember the conversations between her and Travis.

"Surely you knew that it was coming from Davis though, you're not stupid, Lauren," I stared at her, my heart shattering for her a little, knowing what it's like to have parents in the hospital.

"Travis told me if I killed Scarlet that the money would go to Logan and Mel because Davis is in jail and because I'm engaged to Logan, I would be able to access the money with his permission but I would only have to wait a few months before I could steal as much as I wanted and run away." Water continues to fall down her cheeks as I hear footsteps coming up the other end of the hallway. "Miles, I need to ask you two favours please," Lauren sniffles, taking a deep breath as she watches the police walk in. I hold my hand up, making them wait while I listen,

"What!" I seethed, I can't believe I'm listening to this shit after what she just fucking pulled.

"Please look after my mum, she'll be all alone and I wouldn't be able to live with myself if she died while I was in prison." She slowly stood up, limping as she got up,

"And two?" Scarlet wouldn't let Lauren's mum die because her kids are stupid. She went through this before and I know she thinks Lauren is her best friend but after this,

"Look after Logan for me," she smiles, the tears falling into the creases of her lips as the police put cuffs on her wrists behind her back. I nod as they walk away, staying behind before walking downstairs to where Logan and Scarlet are sitting together, Scarlet's arms wrapped around Logan as he cries into her shoulder.

"Hey, my love, thank you for saving me!" Scarlet smiles up at me as Logan turns to me, trying to wipe his tears and snot away quickly before clearing his throat.

"That's okay, Ember," She stood up and I pulled her in so fast that she couldn't find her feet, "I'm just happy you're okay, I don't know what I would've done if I was too late." My voice goes raspy as I squeeze her tightly, trying not to let my walls completely shatter in front of them. I have to stay strong for them.

"Ouch, my love please I'm injured," Scarlet cries as I loosen my grip and look her up and down. Fucking idiot, she was just beaten to death and you squeezed her, for fuck sake.

"We need to get you to a hospital."

"An ambulance is coming," Logan stands up, joining our little circle, "She's gone, isn't she?" Logan's voice cracks as he tries to look past me to the police car with Lauren in it.

"Yes, Logan, she's going away with her brother and Dad," I move in front of him. No one needs to see someone they love be taken away, doesn't matter if they did something wrong or not.

"I'm so sorry, Logan." Scarlet pulls Logan into her, his head resting on her shoulder as he whimpers into her shoulder again.

"You go with her to the hospital, I'll go get Melaine." I pulled Scarlet and Logan in for a brief hug,

"Oh shit, I haven't even called her, she has no idea what's going on!" Logan frantically pulls his phone out of his pocket, dropping it on the gravel.

"It's okay, I'll call her and explain to her when I get her. Just worry about her for now while I can't." Logan nods and I gently peck Scarlet on the forehead as I get into my car and go back to the hotel.

CHAPTER 37 – SCARLET

When we get to the hospital the doctors and nurses rush to get me situated, putting in an IV and checking me for spine and head injuries. I know I was hit a few times in the head and in the sides but my face felt fine beside the cut on my cheekbone. Logan's standing outside the bay, pacing back and forth, looking in at me, making sure I'm okay.

Not long after I'm set, Miles and Melaine come into the bay, Mel's crying and running straight to my side. "Scar, oh my god! Are you okay?" Her tears leaving streaks down her face and her eyes puffy, she must have cried the whole way over.

"I'm okay Mel, did Miles fill you in?" I groaned as I sat up in bed.

"Yes, please don't move if you can't." She stepped back, looking at me like I was going to break if she even breathed on me.

"I'm not broken Mel, it's okay, just a little sore." I turn to Miles, who looks like he's about to murder someone. "No broken bones or fractures, just a few bruises and a cut. They want me to stay overnight and they said I can still play tomorrow, I may just be a little sore so plenty of ice." Miles's face relaxed a little as I spoke and Mel started crying again, cuddling into my side.

"I left you there with her, I should have stayed."

"We all left her, it's my fault." Logan walks in, he hasn't been able to step into the bay since we got here, I knew he felt like this was his fault, "I proposed to her, I made her a part of our lives, it's all my fault she did this to you." His voice cracks as he makes his way to my other side and crawls into the other side of me.

"Hey, I'm a big girl, I can handle myself plus I have a pretty good guard dog." I smiled up at Miles and his face softened, revealing a small smile behind that murderous glare. "Plus, it's no one's fault, we know why she did it and who was actually behind it. None of us are to blame," I pulled my siblings closer, telling them that they are forgiven and that I am safe.

As I turn back to Miles I see a head poke into the curtain behind him, Miles turns and looks back at me with a smile as he steps aside, "Annie!?"

"Hey, Scar, umm I hope you don't mind," she pulls open the curtain and all the girls are standing behind her.

"Aww guys, what are you doing here," Logan and Mel move themselves over to Miles as the girls walk in and hug my sides, "You didn't need to come, I'll see you all tomorrow." I couldn't hold back the tears that were forming in my eyes, they came for me, they were worried about me.

"I saw Annie in the hallway when I was trying to talk to Mel and she butted her way into the conversation and rushed everyone out of bed and brought them here." Miles crossed his arms over his chest with a smirk spreading across his face.

"I'm sorry, but we are family. When I heard you were hurt I rushed everyone here, what happened?" Annie looked around at the four of us. I looked at Logan who looked like he was going to drop dead.

"Miles, can you take Logan and Mel to get something

to eat please?" Logan instantly walked out of the bay and Miles wrapped his arm around Mel's shoulder, walking her out away from the bay.

"What is it? Also, where's Lauren? I tried her and Logan's room but it was empty." Confusion rises to May's face as she watches Logan walk out.

"Lauren was working with my stepdad to kill me for my money, she needed it to pay for her mum's treatment after she lost her job. I felt bad but after what she did to me, there's no way around jail for her." My voice cracking as I hold back tears, trying to explain what happened to my team as they all listen.

"Holy shit, she was working with him all along?" Tegan sat on the end of my bed, zoning out a little trying to understand what happened.

"From what I understand, at least after Travis went to jail, she was talking to him about their mum when he brought the idea up," the whole team stared at me with wide eyes, their brains working overtime trying to understand how she could do it.

"I'm so sorry, we should have noticed something," Annie pulled me into her gently.

"Hey, no." I demanded, "none of you will blame yourselves, this isn't on anyone but her okay. We are a team and she broke that, that is on her. I'm okay, and we will play tomorrow and the next day with all we have and kick ass." I shouted quietly, trying not to make too much noise as we are in a hospital. Everyone nodded and hummed in agreement as Miles, Logan and Mel walked back in with food and coffee.

"Okay ladies, maybe we should all go back to the hotel and get some sleep, we have a big day tomorrow." Annie herded everyone out as they all said their byes, leaving the four of us in our little bay.

"Here, Ember, we got you some food and tea because we didn't want the caffeine to keep you up." Miles hands me the tea and places the food down on the trolly tray next to me, kissing my forehead gently,

"Thank you, my love," I turn to Mel who's still crying, "hey, what's wrong?" I reach to wipe her tears away when she moves away from me.

"We should have told you about her mum, maybe this could've all been avoided if we were just honest with you," she raises her hands, covering her face as she sobs into them.

I reach over and pull her into me, "Melaine Bowen, do not blame yourself. You too, Logan, I do not blame you two okay, you guys are amazing and I wouldn't be here without you guys so no matter what, know that this wasn't your fault and that I love you guys." Mel sobs get louder as she tucks into my arm gently, Logan is at the end of the bed with his arms folded, trying not to look me in the face, "Logan, if you do not get your ass over here," I opened my other arm as he looked over, waving him to come here with a stern face.

"Okay, thank you, Scar. Really, I'm sorry, I can't believe she did this." He sits inside my arm as Mel cuddles me,

"I know bud, me neither," I rub his arm as he places his head on my shoulder. Miles standing at the end of the bed, watching me like a hawk.

"No one's trying to hurt me here, my love, you can relax." I giggle as Miles' face tightens and his posture tenses more.

"I let my guard down once, it's not happening again, not while he's still breathing."

Davis.

I smile at him and a hint of a smile falls past his defences before he fixes his face again.

About thirty minutes go past, us sitting and me reassuring everyone I'm fine and it's not their fault before Miles takes them back to the hotel and I go to sleep.

The next morning, I rolled over to see Miles asleep in the chair beside my bed, with his hand placed over mine. Definitely not letting his guard down now. "Morning, my love, when did you get here?" I squeeze my hand over his and his eyes fly open, sitting up quickly in his chair.

"About an hour ago, I had to almost barge through security to come see you because it's not visiting hours yet, but I have my ways."

"I'm sure you do," I laughed as the doctor walked in with his clipboard in front of him.

"Morning, Scarlet, how are you feeling?" He looks up and examines my eyes for any head damage and my hands and toes for spine damage.

"I feel pretty good for someone who was almost beaten to death doc." The doctor smiled up at me as he wrote down his notes on the board.

"Well, I think you are fine to go. I know I said you can play basketball today but if you are in pain you need to sit out," his voice demanded as he put the clipboard at the end of the bed.

"Not an option, our spare isn't available anymore so I have to tough it out." The doctor's eyes almost popped out of his head as I spoke.

"I will make sure she's fine doc," Miles stands and shakes the doctor's hand, "thank you for all your help."

"No worries, and please come back if anything happens. Ask for me and let them know your name and I will be here." I nod to the doctor as Miles thanks him.

"Okay, ready, Ember?" Miles grabs my jumper he bought with him and holds out his hand to give me some support.

"Yes, so ready!" I grabbed his hand and we walked out of the hospital into the car, "do we have time to go to the hotel so I can shower, I don't smell great." I actually smell horrendous, I haven't showered since after training yesterday and after the beating I took, my body sweated like crazy!

"Yes, Ember, plenty of time. My game doesn't start until ten and yours isn't until eleven,"

"We get to watch each other play today!" I almost jumped out of my seat, I haven't seen the timeslots for the games, just who was versus who.

"Yep, we should be able to watch each other both days." Miles' hand slides up my inner thigh, rubbing circular motions on my skin.

"That's amazing, my love, I am actually excited for today. I'm not worried." Lies. I'm a little especially after last night but Miles wasn't going anywhere and I can handle myself, prove that much last night.

"I know, Ember. No one can put you out." His hand squeezed my leg lightly as we pulled up to the hotel.

Miles helped me to the elevator, eyes staring at us from left and right. My skin covered in bruises and the cut on my cheek probably doesn't help but Miles didn't do it and people can just keep their thoughts to themselves. Miles opened the door to the room and I almost dropped to the ground, tears well in my eyes as I looked around the hotel room. The team had decorated my room as if they were welcoming me home, there were flowers of so many varieties everywhere and a big sign written with our team colours was, 'Welcome back, Scarlet! Let's kick ass today!' in big capital writing.

"Did you know about this?" I turned to Miles and he was just as shocked as I was. He shook his head as we walked in and looked at the flower filled room. There were presents on the end of the bed with candles, sweets and stuff that will help me recover like a rub to put on when I'm sore and a heat pack.

"This is going to be a mess to clean up," Miles looked around, trying to get to our closet to grab our clothes for today. "Oh, hang on, the team and I put in some money for these." Miles went over to the bathroom, bending down to the cupboard under the sink. Pulling out a gorgeous blue and purple jersey with our school name on the top and my favourite number on the back with *'Captain'* written in fancy letters at the bottom.

They got new jerseys for the championships, "How did this happen!" The words barely left my mouth as it hung open when Miles handed it to me.

"They have been planning it since after qualifiers but wanted to surprise you with it, say cheese." Miles was holding his phone up and I held up my jersey and smiled so wide that I could see Miles grinning from left to right past the camera. "For someone who was beaten, Ember, you are still fucking gorgeous." He gently placed one hand on my lower back and the other cupping my cheek as he pulled me in for a deep kiss, I almost melted in his arms. His tongue sweeps over the crease of my lips, wanting to have what's his.

"Sorry, my love, but we will be late if we don't hurry up and I really need a shower but I'll need help?" I slowly walked past him as he watched me walk past, his eyes not leaving mine. "Coming?" I turned to the bathroom and I heard Miles rush behind me so fast that he tripped on multiple sets of flowers. I lifted my shirt and dropped it on the floor, spinning to look at Miles, his eyes filled with worry and his face drained of colour.

"What is it, my love?" I looked in the mirror and I almost passed out, my skin's blue and brown with bruises and my face is still a little swollen from the hit's I took. Tears started to roll down my face as I quickly turned away, trying to cover my skin with my hands.

"Hey, it's okay, Ember." Miles took my hands and gently removed them from my skin. The expression on his face isn't shocking anymore, it's confidence, almost hot. "You are a fighter, Ember, those are your battle wounds. You fought hard to keep yourself alive and awake while you waited for help. Do not be ashamed of them, they show how strong you are. No matter who tries to blow you out, Ember, you still burn strong!" He runs his thumb over the cut on my face, "and honestly it looks fucking badass and hot. I'm in love with a badass." He mutters to himself.

345

A small giggle erupts through my throat as he plants his lips on mine gently, "Now, you're right. You do need a shower, come on I'll help you." He chuckled as he got undressed and joined me in the shower.

Usually in the shower together means hot sex with Miles, but this wasn't like that, it was intimate and caring. He helped me wash myself because I couldn't quite move around like normal, he washed my hair and helped me dry myself. He blow dried my hair for the first time and I threw it up in a messy bun, knowing it will be taken out and put back up multiple times today anyway. I got dressed in the new jersey with some workout leggings and basketball shorts over the top and stood in front of the full-length mirror we had against the wall.

"Your mum would be so proud of you, Ember. I bet she's just as excited as I am to see you win today!" Miles placed his arms around my middle as he stood behind me and kissed the top of my head, staring at me in the mirror as I looked at myself more.

"She would be furious at Davis," I sniffled, my throat aching as I held back my tears, "but she would be so excited today, she would have a banner and have face paint on, the whole works," I laughed, imagining how she use to be when we were at games, she was always my biggest cheerleader.

"Well, maybe you will like the next surprise then," Miles kissed my head again as I turned to him in confusion. He smiled at me and reached for the door handle and swung the door wide open.

"Morning, Scar, ready to kick some fucking ass!" Logan and Mel are standing in the hallway, wearing the same jerseys with my number on it and the writing 'No. 1 Fans' on the back where 'Captain' is written on mine. Their faces covered in blue and purple face paint with a massive banner, written in blue writing saying, 'From dreams to reality, welcome to the championships sis! We knew you could do it!'

I covered my mouth with my hands, trying hard not to ball my eyes out as I pulled Logan and Mel into me, "You guys are so cute, I love you." The tears finally fell and Mel and Logan wrapped themselves around me, gently squeezing me. "You guys look like mum," I pulled back giggling as I wiped my tears away, assessing what was in front of me. They were literally copy and paste of mum at my first game, she had the same design of face paint on her face with one side yellow and one side red and a massive banner with *'From dreams to reality, finally on the court! I knew you could do it!'* and a handmade jersey with my name on the back and 'No. 1 Fan' on the back.

"We found the photo of you and Mum at your first game and we used it for inspiration. We thought we all could use some of mum's support today." Logan's voice is quiet as he gives me a weak smile.

"We definitely do, now," I sniffled again, cleaning my face with my hand, "let's go, we have a big couple days of ass kicking to do!" I shout and Logan, Mel and Miles all cheer as we walk to the elevator.

CHAPTER 38 – MILES/SCARLET

Miles

Running off of no sleep and four coffees is definitely not the way I wanted to start my first day at the championships but all I can think is how lucky Scarlet is and how if I would have been too late, would I have even come to the games? Seeing Scarlet this morning with all the bruises on her body and the gash that is sitting on her cheekbone made me want to burn the whole world down for being able to do this to her but I knew she was strong, that she would hold her own until she was found.

I look at Scarlet and her siblings in the back of the cab as I get into the front seat, seeing her here with her siblings, I knew she was fighting for them, for us. Scarlet looks at me, her green eyes glistening with excitement as we get to the courts and I smile back at her as I get out and open the door for everyone.

"Thank you, my love, you ready?" Scarlet stands in front of me as I turn and look up at the gym. This is my second year for championships but my team has a title to uphold. I knew that no matter what, I was happy to be here after everything that's happened and with

Scarlet by my side, I knew we could do anything.

"Yeah, Ember, let's become champions." I hold her hand as we step through the doors of the gym, the stands filled with basketball fans, scouts from famous teams and other teams, waiting to watch the biggest event of our lives. The lights blaring down onto the courts as the first round of teams are slowly finishing up.

"Hey guys, you made it!" Cal pulled Scarlet in for a hug and turned to me, taking a step back as he looked me in the face. "Calm down, Miles, I wasn't going to hurt her," I glare at him as we all walk over to where our teams are sitting in the stands. Everyone gets up out of their chairs, clapping and cheering as Scarlet and I walk over.

"Guys, cut it out." Scarlet muttered, waving to everyone to sit down, her face going red with embarrassment.

"They won't stop, Ember, something traumatic happened to you, these guys are family. They will cheer and clap louder if you tell them to stop," I chuckled as everyone cheered louder. Scarlet covered her face, trying to hide her massive grin and rolled her eyes at me, taking a bow in front of the teams. Everyone cheered as they got down and surrounded her and hugged her, "If any of you hurt her, I will hurt you more." I shouted as they all slowly and carefully hugged her, my eyes darting to each member, making sure Scarlet doesn't so much as twitch when they touch her. The buzzer sounded behind me, ending the games going on and calling the next round of teams to warm up. "Right guys, wrap it up and move your asses onto the courts now!" I turned back and most of the men were already hauling ass to the court and the last few were slowly cheering Scarlet as they made it to the court. The women's team split as Scarlet walked over to me.

"Good luck, my love, kick ass," she reached up on her

tippy toes, our lips drawn to each other like electricity as we kissed for a long moment.

"Okay lovebirds, split it up. Miles needs to warm up!" Cal shouted from the court and the women giggled as Scarlet and I split from each other.

"Want me to split you, Cal?" I turned to him and my team, all of them pointing straight at him as if I couldn't tell who was who. "Guess I better go, Ember." I kissed her forehead and walked over to my team. "Let's get started then."

Scarlet

My stomach was filled with butterflies as I sat down on the stands, watching the men's team start their game. I'm really here, I made it.

The buzzer goes off and the match starts, Cal slaps the ball hard straight to his team as they play back and forth with the other team. Shooting a three pointer within the first thirty seconds.

My team stands up and we go wild, cheering them on as Miles looks up at me in the stand and points to me as he runs back to his side. My face starts blushing as I see Mel and Logan come back with coffee and food. "Here, Scar, Miles said you didn't eat so I got you some coffee and a bacon and egg roll from the canteen." Mel handed me my coffee and roll with the biggest smile on her face.

"Thank you, Mel, I needed this!" The coffee scent immediately hit my senses, nothing is quite like this. Watching the man you love play his ass off for the championship title for two years in a row and to be here to compete for your first ever title, with my family all here supporting me, well my true family. "How are you guys holding up?" I bent down, mostly talking to Logan. He was heartbroken when Lauren was taken away last night and I tried everything to stop her from being sent to jail but she went too far, there wasn't anything I could do besides pay for her mum's treatment, which I was going to do no matter what the results were.

"I'm fine, my heart's shattered and it may never heal but I'm here and you two are okay. That's all that matters to me," Logan takes a sip of his coffee and looks at me with a small smile while Mel leans against his shoulder.

"We are here for you, no matter what, Logan," Mel snuggled into him, tired from being up late last night. Logan said neither of them got a lot of sleep last night after being worried about me, not surprising.

I smile back at him and open my food as I look back at the game, watching Miles and his team absolutely dominating the other team. Every time they got points, we jumped out of chairs and cheered the loudest. I could see all of the men's team grinning when we would shout and cheer their name.

They played hard all game, defending shots, grabbing the ball from the air and shooting when they could. They had a pattern down that the other team couldn't keep up with, ending the game with a score of thirty-nine to twenty-five.

The teams shake each other's hands as they walk off the field while we walk on. I wrapped my abdomen and my wrists before getting up and joining my team to warm up. "Go get 'em, Ember!" Miles shouts from the stands and I turn and wink at him as I make my way to the hoop.

"Okay, ready girls. We have a plan, stick to it, if it's not working communicate it. We go this, even being injured I know that we have this in the bag, we will win." I chant as my team starts clapping and cheering, the men's team following from the stands with the cheering.

"For Scarlet!" Annie shouts, clapping loudly as my team shouts in sync, "For Scarlet!" I stood there, looking over everyone, I couldn't have a better team, a better family than this.

The buzzer sets the minute warning before the game starts and we all move into position. Annie's in the centre, ready to hit the ball to whoever she can get it too, Tegan and May are on the middle line, ready to rush over when the buzzer goes off just in case Annie hits it that way and Jamie and I are behind her at our end in case she hits it back or the other team hits it this way.

The buzzer goes off and the game starts, Annie hitting it towards Tegan as she dribbles the ball past two of the other team members and passes it to May as she runs into the inner circle, going for a layup as the ball bounces off the backboard into the hoop, scoring us two points off the bat. Our team goes wild as May and Tegan run back to their positions and the men's team go wild in the stands while Logan and Mel join in.

I stay down the defending end where we hope not a lot will go on so I can rest my body a little before we get into the intense games between winning teams, but as the game goes on the other team slowly starts catching up to our score while I try to defend but I can only do so much with my body right now, leaving the score at half time fourteen to nineteen to them.

"Fuck, I'm letting us down, I'm so sorry guys," I pant as I splash water on my face, I need to push through.

"Do not even start!" Annie demands, passing me a towel to wipe my face, "You could never let us down, not after everything you have done for us! You're injured, we knew that you would be limited and yet you still played while knowing you can't do as much as normal." Annies words hit me hard as I drink the water Miles hands me.

"Okay, here's what we will do." I waved to everyone to huddle in so we could come up with a new strategy, one where I can be more helpful. "I'm a shooter and we all know this, so I will hang on the three point line and stay there unless I really need to move. I can shoot and be useful while the rest of you do what you do best." Everyone nods and hums at me as the buzzer goes off, we run back to the court, getting into our new positions.

Miles and the men's team screaming and chanting from the stands with Logan and Mel holding my banner up high and proud above their heads. God, I love these people.

The game starts and our plan falls into place, the girls handling almost everything on the court while I worry about making sure the ball goes into the hoop with some of the girls being down here to help just in case it doesn't make it in. The game grows in intensity as we have five minutes left and we are only ahead by one point while they shoot and get a three point shot in the hoop.

Fuck, we need to move this along, push through Scarlet, for you and for your family!

Annie throws the ball in and Tegan and May run down the court, passing the ball back and forth as needed as they come down to Jamie and I, waiting for the ball so we can shoot. Tegan goes to pass to Jamie but a woman stands in front of her as Tegan goes to pass, the ball leaving her hands. I quickly run over and intercept the ball from the other women and turn around fast, gaining my feet right before the three point line and take a second to stand my ground, focussing on the hoop as my feet leave the floor and the ball flies in the air, hitting the backboard and the rim. My body is screaming at me for moving so much. *Go in, go in!* The words chant in my head as the ball rolls on the rim, leaning into the hoop and giving us our advantage back. Everyone's cheering loudly on the stand and calling my name over and over again, but I don't lose focus, I'm in the zone now and we only have three minutes to get a bit more of an advantage on the team.

The other team throws the ball in and as one of their team members grabs the ball and turns, I'm already in her face, not giving her an option to move. As she goes to pass, I snatch the ball from the air and bounce it once before passing it to Jamie, who's in the circle, waiting for me to pass to her. The ball lands perfectly in her hands as she jumps and throws the ball into the hoop, earning us another two points on the board.

Fuck yes!

Our team cheers with the crowd as the final buzzer screams, ending the game at thirty-three to thirty to us. We turn and everyone's running at Jamie and I, huddling around us, being careful not to hurt my almost broken body. We all cheer and cry for a minute before shaking the other team's hand, thanking them for an amazing game.

We walk off the court and Miles runs at me, gently picking me off the ground and spinning me around. "Well done, Ember, you did it! One game down, only four more to go!" He places me down, my feet hitting the floor as he shoves his face into mine. My body slowly melts from under me as our kiss ignites me from the inside out. Everyone cheers and whistles as he deepens the kiss, as we part Miles rolls his eyes and helps me over to the stand, placing a few ice packs on the sorest parts of my body.

"We have about an hour break now before we have to go back on so do you need anything, Ember?" Miles rubs my shoulders gently, relieving the tension in them.

"Another coffee maybe, my love, I'm so tired." I whispered, trying not to moan in front of literally everyone. His hands feel like heaven as he slowly adds more pressure, careful not to hurt me while trying to help.

Logan gets up and walks over to the canteen, he still isn't himself but he will take a while to get back to himself.

"Hey Mel, can you go with him? Just keep him company today please?" I turned to Mel who looked like she was thinking the same as me. She nods and walks over to Logan's side, chatting to him about something.

"He'll be fine, Ember, he just has to figure it out on his own, don't push too hard." Miles leant down and his lips caressed my cheek, leaving an imprint on my skin.

"I know, I'm just worried." He loved her and she needed help, he could've helped but there wasn't anything he could do.

The rest of the day went by so fast, sitting and watching Miles and his team devour everyone in their path to victory as they won their second game, to the quarterfinals. Our second game went mostly smoothly with one girl bumping into me, making me land on my side where I got punched hard. That was painful but lucky it was at the end of the second half and I had about a two hours break before the next game. Miles rushed over to me at the end of the game, picking me up off my feet and his murderous aura was bouncing off the wall. No matter how many times I told him it was an accident, he said that it didn't look like it and stared at the women with a furious look.

CHAPTER 39 – MILES

The first day of games was complete, both Scarlet's and my team making it to the quarter-final, with eight teams remaining on each side.

I wasn't letting Scarlet go with anyone else without me this time so she and I waited for the last cab before heading to the hotel and ordering dinner.

"Are you okay, my love? You were a bit tense earlier and it's growing on your face." Scarlet's soft hand reaches to my leg, her warmth snapping me out of my thoughts of seeing her tied up to a chair with Lauren holding a blade around like it was a fucking toy.

"Yeah, sorry. I'm okay, promise." I put her hand in mine and kissed the back of her palm, placing our hands on my leg. "What do you want to eat? I'll order it before we get back so it's ready when we get to the room." Scarlet and I decide on dinner as we make it to the hotel and when we get to the room most of the flowers have been taken out and the room's spotless with a few flowers in vases on each bench, "At least it's cleaner in here." I chuckled as Scarlet headed straight for the bathroom.

"Can you run me a hot bath please, my love? I need to soak." Already taking her jersey off, leaving her bruised skin exposed.

"Of course, Ember," I went to the tub and put some soaking salts in as well as some petals from some of the flowers that were still lying on the floor. I hear Scarlet groans as I spin to see her struggling with her leggings, "Need some help?" Scarlet's face is full of defeat as she nods slightly at me, "it's okay, Ember, let me take care of you." I bend down in front of her, slowly pulling her leggings down her legs. Her breath shaky as she lifts her feet out of the holes. I pick her naked body up and walk her over to the warm bath, lowering her in the water and crouching down at the side.

"This feels so good," Scarlet moans as she lowers herself in more, "can you wash my hair again please, my love, it's so gross from today?" She turns her face to me with big green puppy dog eyes, pleading for me to help her out.

"No need to beg, Ember, lean back." I wet her hair with the tap and lather shampoo on her gorgeous wavy, auburn hair.

"I got the hair from my mum, apparently my dad had jet black hair so it wasn't likely that I'd get mum's ginger hair. She named me after it when I was born." Her voice staggering as I massage her head.

"It's beautiful, Ember, it's how I noticed you at the first meeting, after the airport." I washed the shampoo out and added conditioner to her hair before rinsing it out.

"I'm glad you like it. Is that where Ember came from?" She turned slightly, looking at my eyes as she brought her hand to my hair, running her nails on my scalp.

"Partly, but you're also the most powerful player and person I've ever seen, plus no matter how many times you get knocked down or blown out, you still shine and have a little fire left to burn." The words made me blush as they left my mouth, making Scarlet blush harder.

"That's so sweet, my love. I didn't realise you were

so soft." She giggled, gently pulling my hair towards her as she leaned back, placing her lips on mine.

"Oh, Ember, be careful what you say. I'm anything but soft," I whisper against her mouth, her lips smirking against mine.

"Prove it," she moans into my mouth. Hunger fills my senses and my cock straining against my pants. I immediately stand and lift Scarlet out of the bath, placing her on the bed. Her body covered head to toe in bruises, I tower over her as I stare, hesitating to touch her without hurting her.

"Don't tell me you're scared of some bruises, my love," She sat up on her elbows, heat filling her eyes.

"Not some bruises, you're covered in them. I don't want to cause you pain." I pleaded, looking at her bruises moving as she sat up.

"It looks worse than it feels, I promise, I'm not in any pain, my love." She places her hand over my jaw, pulling me into her. Our mouths open and our tongues clash, hungry for the taste of each other as they sweep across our mouths. I fall with her onto the bed, catching myself so I don't land on her and place one hand on her breast, flicking and pinching her nipple. Scarlet moans against my lips and I roll her nipple in between my fingers,

"If you hurt, stop me," I demanded against her lips. Scarlet nods and I burrow myself into her neck, my teeth scraping her skin as I kiss her breast. Relieving the pain of my fingers on her nipples with my tongue as I lick over it and suck it gently into my mouth. Scarlet's back arches into me as I make my way slowly down her stomach to her swollen clit. My hands on both her breasts, kneading them as I scrap her clit softly with my teeth and swirl my tongue on the bundle of nerves.

"Miles!" Scarlet moans as she shoves her hand into my hair, pushing me into her, needing more. My hand slowly makes its way up her inner thigh, tracing her soft skin as it makes it way up. Scarlet's body shakes as I plunge a finger into her entrance, pacing it with the rhythm of my tongue. I push another finger in as I move my tongue around her, licking every inch of her.

"Please, Miles please!" Scarlet's voice trembles as she begs to be pushed over the edge. I speed up my rhythm and move my tongue and teeth around her clit. Scarlet's body quacking as she finishes over my hand. I crawl up her body, placing her legs over mine as I drive my cock into her, leaving her breathless as I move deep and fast.

"God, you are going to burn me, Ember." I bend down and run my mouth down the nape of her neck as I thrust in and out of her. Her moans flow through my head like a sweet song as I scrape her skin and follow her jaw line to her mouth. "Come on, Ember, finish for me." I place my thumb over her clit, playing with the nerves as she cums around me, putting pressure on my cock as my vision is filled with colours, shattering inside her and gently laying on top of her until I'm done.

"See, told you. No pain." Scarlet pants as she kisses me gently on the top of my forehead while I try to catch my breath.

"I'm glad you're not hurt, Ember." I kiss her soft lips and roll off the bed, pulling my pants back over myself and heading to the bathroom to clean myself up. "Here, let me help you first before I go clean up." I grabbed a towel and ran it over Scarlet's limp body and tucked her in bed while I cleaned up.

Right as I close the bathroom door a knock is left on our door, I look out and our food's ready. I open the door and the kitchen staff places the food on the end of the bed for us and leaves us to eat.

"Wow, my love, how much did you order?" Scarlet's eyes almost popping out of her head as she looks at the big spread of food across the bed.

"Well, we played all day and just had sex so I thought we would need enough fuel to help you heal and recover for tomorrow," Scarlet giggled and stuck into the food as we watch Tv and went to sleep.

I rolled over to see Scarlet still sleeping, curled up into my side with her red hair out and flowing on the side of her face. Jesus she's so fucking adorable.

I kissed her forehead and tucked the blanket into her as I got up and went to the bathroom. I closed the door gently behind me, careful not to wake her up as I opened my bag and pulled out the ring my dad gave me, inspecting it making sure it was exactly what I wanted to do. Today's the day, the final day at the championships and then we head home tomorrow. Scarlet and I are leaving early with Logan and Melaine so I can see Dad and so she can bring Logan home and go through Lauren's things.

Why was I so nervous? My hands shook as I closed the box and sat it on the bench while I got ready. She's the one, she's who I want to be with, who I want by my side no matter what. Always with me as I am always with her.

"Are you in the bathroom, my love?" Scarlet knocks on the door, scaring the shit out of me that I almost drop the ring box into the toilet next to the sink.

"Yes, Ember, I'm in here. I'll be out in a second." I panted, taking a deep breath and putting the ring in my pocket and opening the door, "Sorry, Ember, you were asleep like two minutes ago." I pulled her into my chest, running my hand over her hair.

"I was, but I heard the door close and woke up properly." She nuzzled into me, fuck I thought I was quiet.

"Shit sorry, I tried to be quiet."

"It's okay, let me get ready and we can go get breakfast. Today's the big day!" She smiled and closed the door behind her. Today is the big day, but she doesn't realise that it will be bigger than she expects.

I waited about five minutes while Scarlet got dressed and we went downstairs and out to a local cafe that was beside the hotel where Mel and Logan were already waiting for us. "Morning guys, ready for the big day!" Mel jumped from her seat and hugged me and then Scarlet.

"So excited," Scarlet expressed as she squeezed her siblings, "Have you guys ordered?"

"We ordered the drinks but not the food, we were waiting for you to come downstairs." Logan said, as he looked down at his phone, turning it off as Scarlet sat down.

"Logan, want to come with me to order the food?" I asked Logan, two lines appeared between his brows and I raised my eyebrows at him.

"Uhh, sure," Logan pushed out his chair and walked around the table, following me to the line in front of the register. "Surely you don't need me to help you order the food," his tone was a little more light hearted then it was yesterday, hopefully some good news will help him.

"No, I don't but I wanted your help with this," I pulled out the ring box and opened it, showing him the shiny ring that's the opposite to the one Scarlet's wearing now.

"Is that the engagement ring?!" Logan put his hands out, asking for a closer look. I hand him the box and he turns his back fully to Scarlet and Mel as he pulls the box closer to his face, "It's gorgeous Miles, did you design this one or the one she's wearing?"

"I designed the one she's wearing to match this one. This was my mother's ring, and Dad gave it to me before we came here." Logan handed me the box back, patting my shoulder.

"Well, welcome to our crazy family, Miles. Congrats man, is today the day?" We get to the counter and order the food everyone wants and wait until it's ready.

"Yes, I'm praying to anyone that listens that her team wins and I want to do it once they win on the court with everyone there." I couldn't help but smile, imagining getting down on one knee in front of the whole gym after she achieves her dream.

"That's romantic. See and here I thought you were a hard ass." Logan chuckled as we grabbed our food and headed back to the table.

"Finally, I'm starving." Mel whined as we sat down, putting the food down on the table.

After about an hour of talking and enjoying our breakfast we head over to the gym for the final day of the championships.

CHAPTER 40 – SCARLET

The last day of the championships and there are only eight women's teams and eight men's teams left to play today, one of them being the women's Australian team. We haven't crossed paths with them but I have also been avoiding that possibility as much as possible, knowing that they have a high possibility to be in the finals makes my stomach turn, Eva will pull anything to win.

The bruises have eased today and I have no pain anymore. Even if I touch my side there's minimal pain which allows me to play at my full pace again. "Morning captain, are you ready for today?" Annie walks over as we make our way into the gym, the rest of my team stretching as we have to play the first game today.

"Yep, no pain so I'm ready to go full on," I turned to Miles and handed him my bag as he kissed my forehead, walking over to the stands with Mel and Logan. Logan looks extra happy today, he smiled at me as he walked up to the stand and sat next to Miles, both of them looking off. Logan's got a grin on his face and Miles looks warm and approachable, maybe that's a good sign that today will be a good day?

My team and I stretched as the minute warning buzzer blasts through the gym, my team goes to their positions for the game. It's similar to yesterday with Annie in the middle, but May and Jamie are in the back ready to defend and Tegan and I are waiting to cross the line, ready to shoot at any moment. As the game starts the other team smacks the ball to Tegan by accident and she dribbles the ball and passes to me once I'm at the line. I turn and side step my opponent who swears under her breath as I jump and shoot, getting three points almost immediately. The crowd goes wild as the ball bounces on the floor and the other team gets ready to throw in. Today we are versing the best of the best colleges and we need to be on our A game.

They throw the ball in and they make their way to their end, Annie tries to intercept but gets pushed out of the way, making it a foul play. The crowd boos and gasps as Annie gets up, "I'm okay!" She shouts to me, the ref awards Annie with two free throws as it was a personal and illegal foul. We line up around the key, Annie at the top while I'm on one side with an opponent and Tegan on the other with someone else. Annie shoots, getting the first shot in and as she goes through the second one someone shouts from the stands. Even with the shouting Annie gets the second one in and the association removes the person from the courts, Jesus people are fucking stupid.

We play back and forth and at half-time we are twenty-eight to twenty-one to us, playing strong and hard we continue like this all game and by full-time we win, making the score thirty-six to twenty-five.

As we walk off, Miles' team is already stretching and jogging onto the court. "Well done, Ember, way to fuck them up." Miles kisses me quickly as he continues to jog onto the court. I hopped up on the stand, sitting next to Mel and Logan as the men's team warms up.

"So you look really happy today, any reason why?" I nudged Logan with my elbow, he turns to me with his brows furrowed and a confused grin on his face.

"Does there have to be a reason for me to be happy? I'm simply happy with how far you have come." Logan swung his arm around me, bringing me into his shoulder.

"Aww Logan, thanks." I moved closer to him, getting more comfortable as Mel turned to look at us,

"Let me in on this cuddling action please," she begged, Logan and I looked at each other and laughed, opening my arm up so Mel could be in the hug too.

The buzzer goes off for the warning as they get ready to play against a team that I have had my eyes on since qualifiers. They are a dedicated team with amazing dynamic and synergy. Miles' team has excellent communication and works amazingly together but it will be a tough game as the teams play style and dynamics are so similar.

The buzzer goes off again and the game starts off well with Miles and Cal scoring a few times in the first few minutes, but as the game continues they slowly get drowned out. The halftime buzzer goes off and I can see the frustration on Miles' face. I hopped off the stand chairs and went up to Miles, handing him his water. "Hey, you guys still have this. You are sixteen to twenty-one, you need to shoot at least twice and then stand guard the rest of the game, you can do this, my love." His eyes soften and the anger and frustration slowly floats away as a smirk appears on his lips.

"Your right, Ember, we've got this. Thank you." He pulls me in for a quick hug and turns to his team, hyping them up for the next half and as the warning buzzer goes off they cheer and pump each other up as they run back onto the court.

The game starts and they are starting on defence, trying to make sure they don't let the other team get any shots in while they try to drag the team down their hoop to open up a chance for Miles or Cal to shoot while having no one on them. Smart.

Brenndon intercepts the ball from the other team and dribbles it past the opposite team, most of them being on the opponent's side and passing it to Miles, who shoots for a three pointer.

Thanks to me, he can shoot those shots fucking great now.

"Yes!" I shout as others jump up and cheer and whistle after Miles gets the shot. Turning to me and blowing me a kiss, he's gone really fuzzy today.

The final buzzer's about to go off as our men's team gets the ball to Miles, the ball leaving his hands for a three pointer as the buzzer goes off, hitting the rim and going in before the buzzer finishes, leaving them on a score of twenty-two to twenty. We all jump out of chairs and onto the floor as they shake the other team's hand and run over to us. Miles running straight into my arms, spinning me around in circles,

"We did it, we made it to the semis!" He shouts, planting a kiss hard onto my lips.

"You did it! Congratulations, my love!" I pulled him closer to me as I placed my head on his sweaty chest. Everyone cheering for them as the next round of teams go on. We get an hour break now for food, well two hours but we wanted to watch the game and didn't want to miss anything while waiting for food.

After our lunch break the girls and I stretch but I notice Miles looking nervous. "My love!" I shout, waving him over to me.

"Hey, Ember. What's wrong, are you in pain?!" He scans me head to toe, checking me like he can see pain.

"No, but you look really nervous so I wanted to check on you before we go on." I kissed his cheek quickly and cupped his face with my hands, "What's wrong?"

"I'm just nervous about the next round of games, the team we're against is really strong. We beat them in the final last year and they were hard to beat then, but now they have stronger players." He looks over at the men's team that they play after we're done, they look strong.

They're more muscular and bulkier but they are also taller than most of Miles' team.

"Damn, it's okay, don't stress. You could still beat them, you have agility and your skills are amazing, they are just big." Miles laughed behind me and kissed my hands,

"You're right, well get out there and show them how you burn, Ember." He pulls me in again but the kiss is gentler and sweet, not greedy and hungry like he always is. I nod and run over to my team as the warning buzzer goes off.

"Okay girls, we're almost here. We can do it, just two more games and we'll be champions!" I shout and the girls cheer, throwing their hands above their heads as we position ourselves but this time I stay in defending and May moves up to the shooting side. Jamie's our best defender and she prefers to stay down this end and Annie's fast and has the most experience out of all of us so she gets the centre spot as she wanted. Tegan and I are our best shooters and May's versatile. She's great across the court and she likes to swap it up unless we need me up at the shooting end if we are falling behind. The game starts with the buzzer and we play hard going back and forth, the score being kept closer with us being on top the whole time. By half-time we are twenty-three to nineteen and by the final buzzer we win at twenty-nine to twenty-five. The crowd goes crazy as we shake the other team's hand, their faces down but happy for us to continue on to the finals.

I turn and see Miles, Logan and Mel shouting and cheering as we walk off, flapping the banner from yesterday above their heads.

"You guys are ridiculous looking," I giggle as they make their way down the stand.

"You love it, Ember," Miles handed me my water and their buzzer called them onto the court, "Well, wish me luck." He walks up to me, embracing me with a kiss as he winks at me and runs off after his team.

"He's in a good mood today," Mel sounded perplexed, I turned to her and her brows creased.

"I know right? I asked him why he looked like that and he said it was just nerves for the game," I shrugged and took a sip out of my water as we sat on the bench. The buzzer starts their game and the other team begins the game by shooting and scoring three points partially from the get-go.

"Holy shit," Logan breathed, shocked from what we just witnessed. Do they even have a chance against these guys?

Miles and his team pushed through and get a few points but the other team started pummelling them and by half time the score was ten to twenty-one. The men's team running off the court looking pissed off with the first half, I need to do something and now!

"Okay guys, come here now!" I demanded, the men all looked at me with confusion filling their faces while Miles let a smirk slip and walked over to me, the rest of the team followed. "The first half was rough, but you guys are fighters. You need to get your head in the game and play like it's the last chance you will get. These guys are huge and have a massive advantage but with size there's weakness, so find it and give it your all!" I shout and the men's team nod and shout in agreement, they start pumping themselves up again, bringing the energy and excitement back to their faces.

"Wow, way to hype my team up, Ember. See, you burn brighter than you think." Miles cups my cheek and rubs it with his thumb, I gently lean into his hand.

"You looked like you needed it, maybe this will help too." I reached up to him and we shared a tender kiss. Everything goes quiet around us as I zone everyone out, while Miles pulls my lower back closer to him, deepening our kiss.

"I definitely needed that," Miles mutters against my lips with his, I smile and lightly kiss him again.

"Glad to help, now go kick ass, my love." I push him

back and he walks backwards, starstruck looking me in the eyes as he winks a final time and runs onto the court.

The second half begins and the men's team push hard and work together to try and beat the other team but it wasn't quite enough to win as the final buzzer goes off and the final score is twenty-five to thirty. As we all cheer and clap for them, their face's slightly drop, knowing that this is as far as they go in the championships. Miles is shaking their captains hand, moving off to the side and chatting to him as if they have known each other forever. Even though his team just lost their chance to hold the title two years in a row, he looks happy and is okay with coming this far.

"You guys did great in the second half, you should all be so proud of yourselves," I say as they all walk over with their heads down. "Hey, don't be sad by this, you have made it this far while others didn't make it here or even to the qualifiers. You did, you will come back stronger next year." The men raise their heads and shake my hand as they walk past, some thanking me for supporting them all. I look over to where Miles was but he isn't standing there,

"Did you like being touched by multiple men, Ember?" Miles breathe running down my neck, sending shiver through my body,

"I'm sorry? Are you talking about the handshakes I got for supporting your team, my love?" I turn and cross my arms over my chest, leaning into one hip and tilting my head, "That's a gross way to put it."

"What's gross was seeing my team put their hands on you." He pulled me in fast and hard, his lips caressing my ear. "Your mine, Ember. My light, my fire, my Ember." He grates his teeth gently on my earlobe, "Understand?"

My body goes limp, heat builds up in my stomach as he pulls his face away from my neck, "Mhmm," managing to even make a sound of acknowledgment is crazy to me.

"God, could you two get a fucking room, some of us still have a title to win and would like not to throw up before playing." A familiar voice cuts into our sweet moment, pulling away I see raven hair and piercing blue eyes standing in front of me, Eva.

"You know, you could just not look or better yet just leave." I pointed to the door, knowing she won't leave without a fight.

"Mmm, no thanks. I'm here to win and I can't wait to wipe you across the floor, Wallaby." Eva walks away giggling with her minions while the friends I did have on the team slowly move behind her, their eyes looking at the floor as they go past.

"I forgot you had to verse them, it's okay. Just breathe and show them how bright you burn, Ember." Miles presses a kiss against my forehead as I turn and walk onto the court, my team already warming up.

"Are you ready for this, Scar?" Annie asks as she passes the ball to Tegan and moves to my side, watching the Australian team warm up. "I can trip her and make it look like an accident just say the word," I snapped my gaze to Annie who had a serious expression on her face as she stared at Eva. "I'm serious."

"I know you are, and that's what scares me a little," I awkwardly laugh as Annie and I turn to warm up with the team.

The minute warning plays and my team and I huddle quickly, "Okay girls, this is it. Go big or go home right, we've got this. Don't listen to them, they will try to play mind games and fuck with your head so just focus and communicate with the team only." Everyone nods and splits to their positions with me at the line ready to go to the shooting side and May with Jamie in the defending ring.

This is it, I'm ready!

CHAPTER 41 – SCARLET/MILES

Scarlet

This is it. The buzzer rings and Annie smack the ball to Tegan as she dribbles it and passes it back to Annie, not able to get the ball to me while Eva's on my ass and weaving her way through the Aussie team and shooting, the ball bouncing off the backboard into the hoop, two points yes!

"Mm, maybe it's not you I need to worry about, then again it was never you I had to watch." Eva glanced at me through the sides of her eyes as one of her girls threw the ball to her. Right before the ball reaches her hands I sprint in front of her, snatching the ball before she could touch it and shooting from where I was standing which wasn't right at the three point line but a little further back.

"Mm, maybe it is me you should watch instead of talking shit." I snapped back, Eva's mouth is stuck to the floor as the ball lands in the hoop and I position myself back to where I need to be and the game continues. The Aussie team gets past us a few times but with May and Jamie down there and us waiting for them to throw the ball in our direction when they get the rebound, we are smashing them. Eva's strategy with shooting is to try and get the bigger shots in and have one or two of the team members in the inner circle to catch the rebound which happened most of the time and my team was catching all the rebounds.

"You know, maybe you should do something. Letting your team do all the work isn't very captain-like of you." Eva barked at me as she missed yet another three point shot.

"Maybe if you utilise your team to their strengths and not try to be the whole team you might have some points on the board." The buzzer for halftime goes off as I finish my sentence, leaving the score at twelve to twenty-five to us. Everyone on our stand's screaming so loudly that I couldn't hear my team run over to the bench for water.

"You're crushing them, Scar, what the hell is Eva doing?" Logan shouts, trying to talk over the crowd,

"She's trying to play on her own, not trusting some of the girls to play well against me and it's turning them against her. Plus she keeps trying to get in my head but I've been snapping back, it feels so good. It's like I have a whole new bout of confidence." I opened the bottle and took some mouthfuls of water as Logan laughed and Miles made his way to my side.

"You're doing so well, really burning them out there, Ember," Miles runs his hand over my hair and cups my face. "I am so proud of you," his eyes go soft and loving as he brings his lips closer to mine, almost asking permission for a kiss.

"I'm not done yet, my love, still have thirty minutes," I giggled as I leant forward, my lips sealing over his as Logan joking gagged beside us.

"You two really do need a room." Miles and I laughed and I turned to my team who were all drinking and wiping their faces with towels.

"Okay team, come here." I demand, everyone moves closer to me so they can hear over the screaming crowd.

"There's thirty minutes left, Eva may use her team now that she can't carry them against us so be ready for anything. Let's make these last minutes count!" The girls jump up and down in excitement, surrounding me and swinging their arms around me and each other in a group hug.

The minute alarm sounds and we split and run back to the court, ready then ever to become champions.

Miles

This is it, she will become a champion and my fiancée all in the span of like five minutes and I'm shitting my pants. I spoke to the association members to let me announce the proposal over the speaker with the mic once the game's closing to an end. Losing for Scarlet isn't an option and I know she will fight and burn like crazy to get there.

The buzzer starts the game and Eva's stuck to Scarlet like glue, not leaving her side for one second making it hard for Scarlet to shoot. Lucky, her whole team can shoot well unlike Eva's team, they have their strengths and have to play to that and Eva's weakness, well it's Scarlet's sassy mouth burning her and her defence. Scarlet may have a bad smell following her around the court but Scarlet's fast and skilled, something Eva didn't think she was or could ever be.

As Scarlet goes to shoot at the three point line, Eva 'trips' on her shoelace and falls over on top of Scarlet. The crowd gasps and I'm already up and moving down the stand quickly, she may not look like she is in pain but she is still bruised and if she lands wrong, it could be game over.

"Ember, hey talk to me. Where does it hurt?" Scarlet groans while gripping her side, the side where the men with Lauren punched her hard. "Okay, okay it's okay. Time out!" I shout, the ref blows the whistle, sending everyone off for fifteen minutes to give Scarlet something to recover as they don't have a spare anymore, courtesy of Lauren.

I lifted her off the ground into my arms and walked over to the bench with all their shit on it, "Move the shit off now!" I shout, the girls moving their stuff off the bench as I lay her on the bench, putting her bag under her head. "I'm going to lift your shirt, okay, Ember, hold on." I whisper, planting a kiss on her hand as I lift the side of her shirt up. Scarlet winces as I barely touch her skin lifting her shirt.

Holy Fuck.

Her skin's angry, tender to the touch and her bruises are more vibrant than they were this morning. Eva definitely didn't do this by accident, she knew about what happened surely. "I need an ice pack and a first aid kit, now!" I demanded, my voice carrying itself throughout the whole gym. I didn't care who grabbed it, I just knew that I needed to be here and something needed to calm her skin down.

"Here!" Annie shouts, passing me an ice pack and Logan runs over with the first aid kit.

"I'm so sorry but this is going to hurt for a minute, Ember, you have to burn bright for me okay?" Scarlet moans while slowly nodding her head as I place the ice pack on her side. Scarlet's screams filled the gym, making the other teams that were playing stop.

"Shh, hey. Hey, Scar. It's okay, just breathe okay, breathe with me," Logan cups his hands over her face and takes some deep breaths, Scarlet slowly trying to copy but whines every time.

"I think her ribs are broken or fractured, she needs to go to the hospital." I whisper to Logan, Scarlet's head flicks up from the bag, their eyes red and puffy from crying.

"No, I won't go!" She cries, slowly trying to get up, "we have five minutes left and I didn't hear it crack or snap. I just fell on it, it's not broken. I won't leave, not until the game's done at least, promise me you won't take me away, Miles." Her eyes look broken, knowing that she may have to forfeit and lose this opportunity isn't an option to her.

"Okay, Ember, I promise. So long as you know it's not broken but I'm wrapping your abdomen with some of the rub on it to help your bruise and skin to calm down." I stood up, grabbing the bandages in the kit and wrapping her abdomen as she tried hard not to react. "Okay, all done." I put my hands out to help her up as she smacks them out the way.

"I got it, my love," she slowly stands, straightening her back and taking some deep breaths in and out, assessing her rib. "See, not broken, just heavily bruised," she kissed my cheek as she walked over to the court.

I turn to Eva, her face astonished as Scarlet walks onto the court and tells the ref she's good to go. By accident my fucking ass.

The ref nods at Scarlet and blows her whistle. "Before we continue, number thirty-two, you're disqualified, do you have a spare to go on for you?" The ref stares at Eva as she drops to the ground, covering her face as she cries. Their spare walks over and tries to rub Eva's back but she smacks their hand and runs off the court and out the doors, that's what you deserve.

"Okay teams, return to the court for the last five minutes." The ref shouts and everyone gets in position, Scarlet standing at their shooting end. I keep my eyes on her the rest of the game, making sure she doesn't wince or drop in pain. I want to propose after the game if they still win but she needs a doctor.

I turn to Logan as I watch Scarlet play, "maybe I shouldn't worry about proposing, she needs a doctor." My heart slowly breaks, she is in so much pain and trying to fight it, now isn't the time.

"Dude, she will kick your ass if you take her to the hospital right afterwards if she's determined to stay for

the award ceremony, you need to do it after the game."
Logan demands quietly, leaning back in his seat.

He's right, she will literally burn me if I take her away
before she wants to go. As I get up to get the mic setup,
Scarlet shoots a three pointer without wincing or
reacting to raising her hands, she doesn't want to show
weakness and she is doing a damn good job. This
woman's so strong, so powerful, ready to burn down
anyone and anything for what she loves and that's why
I love her. Knowing that she will make me lose control
if someone even breathes the same air as her is
something I didn't think I was capable of. I never felt
like this with Sam and she always wanted that. The
protective and possessive boyfriend that would burn
everything for her, but I didn't love her like I do with
Scarlet.

I walk over to the stand with the mics as the buzzer
goes off and the crowd goes wild. "The champion team
of this year's College Basketball Championships goes
to Hudson College women's team!" A voice shouting
over the mic as everyone goes nuts. As I walked over
to the court standing behind where Scarlet and her team
were shaking the Aussie team's hand, I got down on one
knee, waiting for Scarlet to turn around. The voice over
the speaker started talking right before she turned. "It
looks like we have one more surprise for you here today
folks!" They shouted and Scarlet turned to face me, her
eyes looking me up and down, trying to understand
what was happening. Her team's pooling behind her
with their phones out, recording this so she can see it
later.

"Miles? What are you doing, my love?" Her voice
trembles with nerves as she slowly steps up to me.

"Scarlet Bowen, when I bumped into you at the
airport in Australia and saw your necklace on the floor,
I prayed everyday that I'd see you again and then one
day you showed up. You started at my school and
played the same sport as me, I was stunned, it was like

our paths were meant to cross." Scarlet started to quietly sob as the crowd awed to my words, "Now, I'm not good at lovey dovey speeches but you mean everything to me, Ember. I love you always, I'll be here for you, always and I'll stand by your side, always." Scarlet laughed through her sobs, bouncing up and down slightly with excitement. "Will you make me the happiest man alive and marry me, Ember?" The crowd goes silent, holding in suspense for her answer. I open the ring box and the diamond on the ring sparkles in the light from the gym and the red stones bleed into the light as Scarlet gasps at the sight of the ring. Tears falling down her chin as she looked up at me, her mouth slightly opened with shock. "What do you say, Ember?" Sweat pooling on my forehead, please say yes, please fucking say yes!

"Yes, of course I'll marry you, my love!" The biggest smile overtook my face as I stood up, pulling the ring out of the box and placing it on top of the promise ring I got her months ago, fitting perfectly with one another. "It's gorgeous and you got it to match, thank you." Scarlet jumped in my arms, crying into my neck as I buried my face in hers. Both of us laugh as we pull apart and I cup her face and pull her into me, kissing her deeply and passionately as everyone cheers and goes crazy over the newly engaged couple. I zone everyone out as I kiss her, only she matters to me, she's all I have wanted for months and now she's mine.

"Congratulations!" Mel shouts as she runs over and joins in for a hug as Scarlet and I split our lips apart, her face filled with joy.

"Way to go man," Logan patted my shoulder as he joined in the hug. I smiled at him as we all laughed.

Scarlet pulls away from me and turns to her team, everyone standing in anticipation to see the ring, "Look who's engaged!" Scarlet sang as she showed her hand to her team and everyone one of the awed and stared at the ring.

My team comes running at me, "Congrats bro!" Cal shouts as they all crash into me, almost knocking me off my feet.

"Jesus Christ, you guys almost fucked me up," I chuckled as they all wrap their arms around me.

"Don't be a drama queen, we didn't think this day would come!" Cal grinned, knowing that it wasn't going to happen with Sam.

"Me neither."

CHAPTER 42 – MILES

The award ceremony finished as Scarlet got her trophy and all her team got a medal for their championship title. Scarlet's face is beaming, she's so happy as she shows her team the trophy and I know she's where she needs to be.

I step up to her team, clearing my throat, "I'm sorry ladies, but I need to take someone to see a doctor." They all sighed and begged me not to take her. "Nope, no excuses. She's had more than enough time here and I would like to see her be my wife so if you will excuse us." They all smiled and blushed as Scarlet said bye to them all.

"Your wife, mmm, that has a good ring to it," Scarlet giggled, staring at her new ring on her finger.

"Well, she does have a good ring on, but I prefer Ember." I chuckled as she slapped my chest for my smart ass comment. I opened the car door and helped her in the car and went to the hospital.

The doctor came straight away and did an Xray and Scarlet was right, no broken bones and no fracture but the bruising was intense so she needed to rest which wasn't going to be hard considering we were flying home tomorrow for the whole day.

"Keep ice on it and do not lay on that side, let it rest."
The doctor closed the clipboard up and I thanked him
for everything as we went on our way.

Our final night in Paris was just staying in our room
while I packed and Scarlet watched TV with a tub of
ice cream. She deserved the treat after what she went
through, plus no one says no to a champion, is what I
was told. The next day we got on our flight with Logan
and Mel, who wanted to come home early and when we
got home, we immediately ordered dinner and went
straight to bed.

The next morning I got up early and cooked everyone
breakfast, trying to calm myself down about today.
"Wow, I'm getting my husband treatment already, do
I?" Scarlet walks into the kitchen, rubbing her eyes and
stretching her body gently as she sits at the bench,

"I've cooked for you before. Plus I wanted to ask you
if you could come to the hospital with me to see Dad."
I placed the plate of food and a mug of coffee in front
of Scarlet as she stared at my face.

"Of course, my love, whatever you need." She kisses
my cheek and takes a sip of coffee. I turn back to the
rest of the food and I hear both Logan and Melaine walk
down the stairs, yawning and stretching as they sit
down at the table.

"Oh, thank you Miles," Mel hooked in and Logan
inhaled his coffee before getting up for some more.

Scarlet and I looked at each other, trying not to laugh
out loud as I shook my head and tidied up.

We got ready and hopped into the car to go see Dad.
Once we walk up to the reception desk, I see Dad's
doctor comes around the bench. "You must be Miles,"
he held out his hand, I placed mine in his as I shook his
hand firmly.

"Yes, that's me, how's my dad?" The doctor
explained that he's okay, he's healed well and there
haven't been any complications and he will be out of
here in no time. They just wanted to watch his abdomen

a little longer as he had extensive surgery. "This is his room, I'll let you go in, I have other patients' to see first but I will be back, if you need me let the nurses know." I nod at him as he turns and walks down the hallway.

I reach for the door handle and freeze, my body unable to move. He is okay Miles, he's fine.

"Here, let me, my love." Scarlet pushes beside me as I gulp and step back. I take a deep breath in and out as she swings the door open. "Hello, Mr Grove," Scarlet whispers as she walks in first and I follow after her.

"Ahh, Scarlet, hello. How are you, darling?" Scarlet goes closer to Dad as he kisses her cheek. "Congratulations on the championship title and on the engagement, do you like the ring?" Dad points to her finger, Scarlet looks down at them and smiles wide.

"I love them, they are beautiful, thank you, Mr Grove."

"Oh please, call me James." Dad turns to me and his eyes soften slightly and he holds out his hand, "Come here, son." I move closer, placing my hands over his.

"I'm so sorry, Dad, I wanted to come back but there was a storm and I didn't think they would target you otherwise I would have arranged security or something." Dad holds his hand up in my face, stopping me from talking.

"Do not apologise for anything! I locked him up so he was bound to go after me, I just can't believe Lauren did that to you, Scarlet, I'm so sorry. How is your brother, they were engaged right?" He places his hand over hers, her eyes filling with tears as she gently sits on the edge of the bed.

"They were, he's okay now. Miles cheered him up from what I hear so he'll be okay." She sniffles, wiping the tear that fell out of her eye. Dad rubs his thumb over the back of her hand, trying to comfort her.

"Well, I'm glad you could help son and you have picked a beautiful bride." Scarlet giggled and I softly laughed under my breath as Dad pulled out his phone.

"Now, I have some ideas for the wedding." Scarlet sits closer to him as they go through photos and ideas for the wedding. I stare at them both, being here together, alive and well.

This is it, this is what I want, this is what I needed.

ACKNOWLEDGEMENTS

So, this has taken me the longest to write so bear with me for a moment while I have my little spiel!

Firstly, I would like to thank you, my readers! You guys have helped me achieve my goal and being able to put out my books and have someone other than myself read them is still really scary for me to think about but it's happening, and I just want to let you know that you are amazing! So, thank you so much for reading and I hope you enjoyed it as much as I did write it!

Secondly, I would like to thank all my family and friends that supported me through my journey publishing this book! I didn't tell a lot of people about it, including a lot of family, because I wanted to surprise everyone with it. So, thank you to my gorgeous friends as well, you guys know exactly who you are and I wouldn't be here without any of you. You guys are amazing, and I couldn't have done this without you all.

Thank you to my Nan, who pushed me to do it, even though I wasn't sure if I should, but she said to me, 'You should write it, I think writing a whole book is amazing and I wish I could write a whole book.' We would talk about bits and pieces of my book when we were together looking at all the quilts she made for my family and even that was enough to help me get through the rough patches throughout writing, so thanks Nan.

Thirdly, to my amazing boyfriend. We have been

through so much together, so many different things and through everything you continue to support me.

When I wanted to put my stories on paper, he was so excited for me and pushed me to write it, even when I wanted to give up. Whether I wrote chapters or only a few words, you would always congratulate me on them and share your happiness and excitement with me which really helped me to finish this book. I don't think I could have done this without you here so thank you baby.

Lastly, I want to thank everyone who has supported me throughout my whole journey. So, everyone on my social media, TikTok and Instagram. Everyone who does know about it now so my parents, some of my partners' family and friends. The people who helped me with the beta and alpha phases of my book, thank you so much for helping me get my book to where it is, I literally couldn't have done it without your input and help. Finally, I want to thank my readers one last time. It's crazy to think that people are actually reading the book I came up with in the car one day coming home and didn't think I would ever put it into actual words, let alone a full book for others to see.

This whole journey has been an amazing experience and without all of the people I mentioned, I wouldn't be here right now, finishing the final touches to Love in the Paint and continuing the series for Logan and Mel, (characters in the book), so truly from the bottom of my heart, thank you everyone.

I hope you all enjoyed the book and the journey it took to get here. I look forward to seeing you all again in Book 2: Love in the Web!! Yesss! Book 2 name drop!! Thank you again and see you all later!!